MW01675527

AOS Publishing, 2025

ISBN: 978-1-83432-031-1

Cover Design: Meredith Lindsay

Visit AOS Publishing's website:
www.aospublishing.com

Enjoy the journey!

DAHLIA

A Novel

Christian Laurian

For Taryn.

Don ' t bother me.
I ' ve just
been born.
Mary Oliver - Dream Work

A person does not belong to a place
until there is someone dead under the ground.
Gabriel García Márquez - One Hundred Years of Solitude

Because she was going to take them with her,
and there was going to be a great burning,
until the land was full of its stink.
Stephen King – Carrie

I yearn and I seek.
Sappho

PRELUDE

The world begins with watching.

Not with seeing, as that would imply knowing. Only watching. From the outside in, face pressed against the glass. Inside the house, outside the frame. Watching, watching, watching.

There is sound. It passes through like liquid. In the absence of wind, only howling. Laughter. Screaming. Songbirds. Clash of metal. Birth of the machine. And through it all, the infernal watching. Bearing witness to the best, the worst. Forget. Repeat.

Remember.

The trouble starts, as always, with desire. Or maybe it's less than that. An awareness of desire. An understanding of 'want'. A hole that cannot be filled, for the hole was never meant to be made.

A flatfish will spend its whole life content in the mud. Buried in sand, shit and shadow, it will live out its days without thought of its misery, as it has always been what it is. One day, however, something shifts. Unease grows its first leaf. The flatfish swallows its meal of the day—tiger shrimp 3 days dead—and doesn't feel full. Something is off.

The flatfish stays put, doing what it has always done. Sand, shit, and shadow rain down. But it is already too late. The end has already begun.

Dissatisfied no longer, the flatfish has an idea. It will move somewhere else. It has occupied the same stretch of ocean floor since forever. Watching. Waiting. No more.

It beats its muscular body and lifts upwards. A warm current supports its ascent. As it rises, there is a glimmering overhead that grows brighter. The flatfish is intrigued. With greater vigour, it pumps and writhes, drawing closer and closer to the glimmering. The light grows, stretches far and wide, until it is all the flatfish can see. It eclipses everything. Even instinct.

The flatfish swims faster and faster towards the glimmering light. It has no idea of the border the light represents. When it arrives at the surface, there is no admission to be had. Surface tension pushes back. Gravity does its job. The flatfish struggles against the waves to no avail. It can taste the air, taste the freedom. It senses that something beautiful lies just beyond reach. But no matter how hard it beats against the border, the flatfish cannot pass.

All it can do, pressed up beneath the world above, is watch.

Part One

Serenata

CHAPTER ONE

My name is Jack.

I am 34 years old, and I live on the west coast of Canada with my wife, Dahlia. I love my wife. She is a wonderful, wonderful woman, and I am lucky to have her. I tell everyone this, this irrefutable fact: that my wife is a wonderful, wonderful woman. My seven-word mantra of devotion. But most importantly, I tell myself

(*my wife is a wonderful, wonderful woman!*)

when I feel myself believing it isn't true.

They say that opposites attract. That is a half-truth. Everything opposite attracts in some way or another, but so does everything similar. It is a confusing set of rules we have here on planet Earth. You know what I think? I think the similar parts seek each other out, but the opposite parts convince you to stay. Call it curiosity. Call it inquiry. Call it love.

And love I do. I love my wife. She's beautiful and clever, and an overall extraordinary creature. I find myself enchanted in the way a hermit, holed up in a forgotten stone cave, might feel upon seeing the sun for the very first time. In a word, Dahlia is my sun.

Which would make me the moon in this celestial casting. Inert, cold, and worthy only of reflecting the sun's best parts. Except that is another half-truth. I love my wife not just because of who she is. I love her because of who she has made me become.

Like now. I am spilling fresh blood and whistling. "Michelle", by The Beatles. My father was a fanatic, collecting Lennon memorabilia like a rat hoarding tinsel. My childhood was permanently soundtracked by those four pasty Brits, warbling away about submarines and LSD. I despised them. Did you know that Lennon was a wife-beater? Yup. I know. He told *Playboy* magazine he would knock "any woman" around, as if they were goddamn Bobo dolls. *Playboy*, of all places. People can be so phony.

Still. The point stands. A few years earlier and I would've treated any inkling of Britain's golden boys as a chance to get the fuck out of dodge. I was like a live wire in a rainstorm. Anything could set me off, crackling and spitting. Helplessly exposed to the world and its infinite torments.

Dahlia changed that. She changed everything. The trouble is, I can't decide if it was for better or worse. I think the former. I believe the former.

I have to.

"Honey?" I call, putting the knife down to soak in the sink. My voice echoes in a house so empty. "Where are you?"

~ ~ ~

We met on campus while I was studying engineering—or rather, struggling to keep my head afloat in a program I had no interest in. My father'd insisted. He was the one funding my education, after all, so he wielded a significant amount of power over my destiny. In the beginning, that is. In the beginning.

Dahlia wasn't even taking classes there. This was at UBC: a monstrous, sprawling jungle infested with rich kids and brainiacs. It sat on the end of a forested peninsula, cut off from the world in a bubble of obscene wealth and ingenuity. I had slipped through the cracks by the grace of god; although which one, I couldn't imagine. My grades were modest but not dazzling, while my submission letter was a solid representation of "Meh". But alas, spring came, and with it, a creamy letter of approval for one Jack Anthony Donner. Come ride this ticket to the magical world of electrical engineering. Ooo la la.

I could picture a blue-skinned Kali or bearded Zeus, pointing down and laughing at my illogical twist of fate. I had applied to numerous universities, all within the tight perimeters of **ENGINEERING**, but nonetheless scattered across the continent. Shitty little institutions that would take in hobos from the street just to fill a lecture hall. My only hope was to be transplanted somewhere, anywhere, away from my father.

But no. The mailbox spat out a single acceptance letter: one measly letter for the only university I had no interest or expectation of going to. And that was that.

For 3 long years, I kept my head afloat. I drove an hour and a half through thick wads of traffic. Filled my brain with algorithms and numbers. Sat dutifully through one boring lecture after the other. My days chugged by with the thrilling monotony of a man's fifth wedding: all routine and no passion. And achingly, obviously hopeless from the jump.

In those same 3 years, I'd amassed a grand total of two friends. It was as if my other peers could smell my shortcomings before even speaking to me. At the time, Dad and I were averagely wealthy. We shopped at Walmart. My sweaters were cotton, not cashmere. We were comfortably uncomfortable, but far, far from poor.

Still, that wasn't enough. Strolling around the manicured gardens of campus gave me the sensation that I was surrounded by Rockefellers and Waltons. I was destitute, viewed from the tip of upturned, privileged noses. And I certainly wasn't a genius. The nerds were just as prejudiced as the rich. It was awful.

Allan was a shrivelled white boy who revered Old Spice as sacrament and only wore chinos, while Li was a business major who practically swore as she slept (Fuck Youuuuu, Fuck Youuuuu). Li's great annoyance in life was that her Vietnamese mother, in an act of blistering unoriginality, had given her daughter the same first name as her last. Li. Li Li. This, I think, was the source of her volcanic rage and filthy mouth.

I, meanwhile, was Jack: engineering dupe from Saskatchewan, that mythic land of wheat, tundra, and meth. Needless to say, we did not fit in. We stuck out like sore thumbs in fingerless gloves. By a hitchhiker. In the dead of winter.

~ ~ ~

"This party is fucking dead. We should go," said Li, tonguing a Corona. That night, she had dressed in corduroy overalls and a mint beret, the trio of us huddled in the kitchen of a stranger's apartment. Li lived in a dorm, so she'd tip us off about potential parties, which we would crash, uninvited.

"We literally just got here. I told you that 9 o'clock was too early."

Allan's bespectacled eyes swept the apartment, before zeroing in on a musty-looking man by the window. He nudged me.

"Do you think I could score something off that guy?"

Back then, that's all we ever seemed to be doing: looking for ways to get high. Secretly, of course, as it wasn't a good look to be a junkie at one of the most prestigious universities in the country. But it was a fact, like gravity. Everyone was. Eternally on the hunt, pupils dilated, lips drawn, cash folded.

The musty-looking man was definitely in business. He was sporting a crop of shoulder-length dreads that looked like they still smelled like August, despite it being the middle of January. Li and I pooled our fives together, and Allan whisked them away in a cloud of Old Spice anticipation. Minutes later, he returned, a bag of green richer.

It is at this point that I should mention my height. At 24 years old, I stood at a gawking six foot seven. It was a source of great discomfort for me, being trapped in a hulking, giant body. Nothing ever fit right. Beds, pants, showers, you name it. Always too large in a world too small. Let me tell you: the world is a lot dustier from above. And that bald patch *is* growing.

When I was in university, I was still fighting my nature. I hunched and cocked my neck, anything to appear more approachable. It was useless. No amount of stooping and arm-crossing could hide me. I was here for the world's taking. Feast your eyes upon the soft-hearted, lumbering freak.

All of my dissatisfaction had rendered me toothless. Weak. I was moving through life without purpose or direction. Like a ship at sea being battered from wave to wav—

You get the idea.

The issue was this: I didn't have a fucking clue what I wanted. Nor who I wanted to be, what I wanted to do, nothing. This, my friends, is a very dangerous place to be. It may be the most dangerous place of all.

~ ~ ~

Allan had cleared a spot on the counter to start grinding and rolling. Meanwhile, Li, who had polished off her second beer in 15 minutes, was starting to loosen up a little. She eyed the busying apartment with the early signs of a smile before turning to look up at me.

"You seeing anyone these days, Jack?" she asked. I shook my head.

"No, not really. I was hanging out with that girl, but…"

"The vegan? With all the ugly tattoos?" Allan interrupted, jerking his head around. There was a fleck of spit that had found its way onto the outside of his glasses. It clung there, a bead of wet light.

"What? No, I've never dated a vegan. I was kinda seeing this girl named Megan."

Allan scrunched up his face. "Megan? No, I could've sworn…weren't you complaining about those flavourless salads? Quinoa? You definitely were. I remember it." He looked at Li and me defensively.

Li put her hand on her hip. "That was me, dumbass. I have that new roommate, the fucking health nut who just transferred from McGill? And you have *spit* on your glasses. Again."

Allan blushed scarlet but said nothing. He turned around and went back to rolling without wiping off his glasses. Probably as a sign of silent protest.Li cleared her throat. "Anyways. Megan? She's done? What happened there?"

"Nothing, it just…you know. Fizzled out, I guess. Wasn't meant to be. Nothing crazy." I sipped my drink, a cheap apple cider, with a shrug. It was a tired story. I was sick of telling it, and Li was sick of hearing it. She frowned.

"I just don't understand. What are you doing to these girls, Jack? I swear, none of them seem to last more than a fucking month. I mean, you're…" She gestured to my stature and face, implying that that was enough.

Li had a hard enough time biting down F-bombs as she did giving compliments. The closest thing to one I had heard was when we'd been at the beach during the summer. Li took one look at my naked torso and gave a curt, "Looks good."

Besides that, zippo. Another trickledown behaviour from her parents, the infamous Lambasting Lis. They could find fault in a cloudless sky or Betty White. It was impressive.

Li looked at me expectantly for an answer. I shrugged again.

"I don't know what to tell you, Li," I lied. "Just didn't work out. Can we talk about something else? How's your new roommate?"

Li's eyes narrowed like whenever she could smell bullshit, but she let it drop.

"Ugh, she's fine. Besides the vegan thing. The fridge is overrun with chia cups and kale, and she makes smoothies non-fucking-stop. Day in and day out, all I hear are fruits being pulverized. She puts the weirdest things in too, like carrots? Peanut butter? Who the hell wants to have peanut butter and carrot puree for lunch? It's disgusting."

Allan turned at the comment, his tongue swiping a second joint sealed. "My mom puts peanut butter in her smoothies. But not with carrots. She uses whey protein." He smiled at this, like it was a culinary secret.

"Well, thank you, Mr. Ramsey. Anything else I should know?" Li said, dripping with sarcasm.

"No, I think that's it. Just peanut butter and whey. And milk, of course. It's pretty good, like a peanut butter shake. You should give it a try." With this, he turned back and began sweeping weed crumbs back into his grinder. Li looked at me in disbelief.

"Idiot," she mouthed silently.

This was our dynamic: Li pummelling Allan, cat-like, while I stood around as witness. Even in the company of outcasts, I felt on the fringe.

Li probably had the potential to roll with a more sought-after crowd—a cruel streak is often desirable amongst the popular—but I suspected she was a little too raw for their taste. Most people who act mean do it for fun, out of boredom or lack of empathy. But equally so, from a place of power.

Li lacked that final ingredient. She came from a dysfunctional, low-income family who was scrimping desperately to put her through university. Her compulsion (if you could call it that) to poke and mock was a defence mechanism from years of being treated the same. It came from an authentic well of pain.

"Are you done yet? I feel like we've been waiting forever. I would've helped roll if I knew you'd be so slow." Li threw her third beer into the garbage bag slumped against the wall. She started to saunter over to the fridge for a fourth when a voice came from behind us.

"Hey, do I know you guys?"

It was our party host, presumably. He was a preppy-looking guy with Scandinavian cheekbones and watery eyes. He wore a white collared shirt underneath a sweater-vest, rendering him both pubescent and middle-aged in the way that maddening clothing combination only can.

The thought of him shrunken down to a little boy, snapping open a briefcase to begin work as a professor, flashed in my mind. I could picture him, apple in hand, horn-rimmed glasses pushed high, asking the lecture hall in a pitched, childish voice: "So what *do* we interpret Socrates to have meant when he said, 'What you think you become'?"

I coughed out a laugh before I could stop myself. The host gave me a glare.

"Something funny?" he asked, a tad hostile. He leaned against the doorway, arms crossed. I cleared my throat.

"No, sorry I…ahem. I was thinking of something funny right before you spoke. Sorry." In my mind's eye, the child professor was rubbing his apple (a juicy Red Delicious) on his pants bottom, much to the uproarious laughter of the class.

Shut up, shut up, shut up, I told my brain, fighting back another laugh.

Thankfully, Li stepped in. "Yeah, don't mind him." She shot me a look. "He's cool, don't worry. I heard there'd be a party here tonight from Melissa, she's in my statistics class. Is she here?" She finished this in a buttery-smooth tone, one reserved exclusively for winning people over. Which was a rare and beautiful thing to witness.

"Uh, no, I haven't seen her yet," the host said, looking over his shoulder. "But usually I prefer when—"

"Do you smoke man?" Now it was Allan's turn to shine. This was their strategy, distract and entice. I had seen this dance performed many a time, with varying results. Tonight, however, seemed like a success. You could practically see the host's ears perk up at the words. Allan displayed one of his freshly-rolled joints in an open palm. It glistened, fat and wet with saliva.

"This is some premium kush, my guy. Blue Dream. Ever had it?" The host shook his head. Allan grinned like a madman.

"Oh boy, then you're in for a treat. Some top-notch shit right here. Here, take it! My gift from me to you for having us. But you save that for yourself, lots of people looking to score around here. Don't let it go to waste."

"Well, thanks, I…"

"Don't worry 'bout it," said Li, patting him on the shoulder and slipping past him into the living room. "And thanks for having us. We were just going to step outside for a quick smoke, but we'll be back. Say hi to Melissa for me."

She cocked at us with her finger to follow, her sweetly smiling face dropping like a mask behind his back. Allan followed in suit, with me in tow.

The host stepped, bewildered, out of the doorway to let us pass.

"Thanks, man! Great party!"

"Yeah, thanks," I echoed, towering over him, before disappearing into the crowded living room. The music had been cranked up high, and it piled upon me along with the babble of drunken voices.

"Excuse me, sorry. Excuse me," I said, weaving my way through the bodies. No one seemed to break conversation for less than a second to let me pass, hardly glancing to see what massive person was trying to make their way to the door.

As we slipped on our boots, the sound of our host's voice cut across the talking heads. "What was your guys' names, though?"

None of us turned at the sound. We cracked open the front door and disappeared into the hall, before heading out into the damp freezer of the outside world.

~ ~ ~

"I think that went well," remarked Li, the three of us huddled beneath a nearby eaves. She blew out a cloud of vapour. "And I'm glad Melissa hadn't shown up yet. We don't actually talk to each other. She seems like a stuck-up twat."

There were fat, lazy flakes of snow parading down from the heavens. Under the blonde glow of the streetlamps and the light pouring from the buildings, everything felt obscenely calm. I closed my eyes and breathed in the smell of winter, relishing the silence after the cacophony of the party. My reverie was rudely snuffed out by the sound of Allan hacking away as he took his first inhale of cannabis.

"Goddamn!" he whooped, waving his hand in front of his face. "This shit is strooong!" Allan broke back into a series of coughs before eventually subsiding into gentle huffs.

He offered the smoldering joint to us both. "Want some?"

Li and I looked at each other reluctantly. Li extended her hand first, gloved in black and speckled with stars. She sucked down a hit before erupting into loud coughs herself. The joint nearly went sailing into a snowdrift by the force of her reaction.

"What...*cough*...the...*ackugh*...FUCK is that?" she bellowed, eyes bulging. Her whole face had flushed dark in the shadow of the eaves. She whipped her head at Allan once she had caught her breath, who peered back at her from behind his foggy glasses like a white-eyed mystic. Although I couldn't see his pupils, I knew that they had widened in fear.

"Allan," Li said threateningly. "What did you just fucking give me?"

Another cough bubbled up from inside her, forcing Li to turn and hack some more, her mint beret tumbling off her head in the process. Suddenly she dropped down to her knees and began violently digging through her enormous bag. Her lungs refused to back down in their assault, heaving and contracting repeatedly. Allan flicked his foggy gaze from me to Li in panic.

"God, Li, I...are you okay? Are you having an allergic reaction? I swear that guy said this was primo shit, that it was Blue Dream, and I..."

Li stopped digging to lift a single gloved finger in Allan's direction, silencing him. With her other hand, she fished out her prize: a three-quarter-full mickey of cinnamon whiskey.

"Shut up," she snapped, before taking a swig of whiskey. It swished around in her throat before descending with a heavy swallow. The silence of the night returned, albeit far more ominously. Allan and I stood, uneasy, the joint smoking away on the ground between us. The snow fell on.

At long last, Li rose to her feet and plucked her beret up from the ground, dusting it off with a grunt. Allan opened his mouth to speak, and then wisely closed it. What wasn't wise was what happened next. A sort of veil seemed to pass over him, causing his features to ripple and relax. A dopey smile spread over the canvas of his face and transformed him into a beaming caricature. He giggled.

"Allan," I began, "this isn't the time..." but Li had already seen. She turned to face her friend, tittering away in the presence of her suffering.

At the sight of her, Allan broke into higher, more intense giggles. I cringed at the sight, fearing the worst. A vision of Li leaning over and popping Allan's head clean off like a Lego block came to mind. I had to stop the carnage before it began.

"Hey, Allan, knock it off! Are you alright, Li? Whatever that was, it seems like it..."

"Jack!" she gasped, spinning around to face me. Her eyes had ballooned to two black disks. "Jack, Jack, you *have* to try this shit. Oh my fucking god, I feel, like...electric. Like all tingling and shit. Allan, what the hell? What did we just smoke?" And now Li had dissolved into a geyser of giggles, her face transfigured from stone to sunshine. I had never seen her act like this before. It frightened me. But I also couldn't help but nervously grin back, their laughter rolling in thunderous, infectious waves.

Allan snatched up the joint and held it between his eyes. The heat of it melted a portion of his fogged lens away, and I could see the same dark disks in place of pupils underneath. "What *are* you?" Allan whispered, and then took a huge hit before I could intervene to stop him. The flame changed from murky crimson to an enraged hornet as he inhaled.

"Wait, wait, Allan! We don't know what the hell is in that thing. Maybe we should go talk to that guy you bought from."

Li laughed at my concerned tone and put her hands on my arms. She was still smiling.

"Relax, Jack! We're fine." She had to pause as Allan began coughing. "Maybe there's a little something spicy mixed in that Blue Dream. But whatever it is, it's *marvellous.*"

"It gets easier the second time around, Li," said Allan, washing down his hit with a sip of whiskey. He passed the joint to her, who pressed it to her lips and drew in. I took a step back, my stomach turning over in discomfort. A cold wind tousled the falling flakes as the two of them cackled hysterically, chattering away like finches.

Sensing my retreat, Allan stepped forward, emboldened into action. He held the joint—halfway scorched into oblivion—aloft for me to take. Li grinned in shadow, gently swaying from side to side with ecstasy. The joint glowed.

"Trust me, man, you don't want to miss this. Shit is *magical.* I'm telling you, whatever Tarzan sprinkled on here, it's..." He puckered his lips and drew his fingers together in union, before letting them explode into a five-nail firework. Chef's kiss.

I had missed when he'd nicknamed the dreadlocked dealer Tarzan, but it made me laugh. Allan took this as a good sign in convincing me. He thrust the joint into my hand.

"Yeah, that's right, Jackie! Let's get this show on the road. Come join us on cloud nine." He stepped back as if to admire his handiwork, nearly tripping over Li, who had crouched down to play with the snow. Her starry gloves were nowhere in sight.

I stood still, staring at the burning joint between my fingers. I knew what I was going to do before I did it.

"Fine," I said, more to myself than anyone. I brought the joint to my lips and drew in smoke. The tip crackled orange, and Li clapped excitedly from the ground at the sight.

It took less than a moment. My lungs, drunk on the virgin clean air of the coast, were accosted by fumes. They responded with absolute vengeance: my chest cavity contracted with enough force to collapse my ribs upon themselves. I doubled over, in pain, in shock, blasting the ground with my cursed breath. Allan and Li cheered.

"You've got this, Jackie! You'll be good, big breaths, now. Biiiiig breaths," Allan called out. My vision swam spotty, then greyish, then white. I let my body wring itself weak with coughing. My eyes filled with tears. I hacked my soul away.

Eventually, the misery subsided. I felt my brain turn to slush inside my skull, then reformulate into something sparkling, crisp, and pulsing. Li was right. I did feel electric.

I stood up to my full height again and experienced a rush of pinpricks cascading down my body. Blinking away tears, I looked around at the world, which had become vibrantly bright, almost uncomfortably so. The snow, which before had shimmered absently, now practically scintillated. The streetlights shone like suns, the night alive with colour and shades in unspeakable ways.

"Guys?" I asked, my mouth curling upwards in a shit-eating grin. "You weren't kidding when you said—"

My sentence was cut short by something dangerous and life-threatening. It cut through the air and into my brain, shattering it slowly. My heart tripped over itself, then wondered why it did.

The words sang into my being as gospel, as truth. *Something was about to change.* My body was alive with energy, my vision overrun with light. I closed my eyes for a moment, savouring in the sensation like a good last meal.

Something was about to change. Slowly, I turned and faced my future.

"Hello? Sorry, but are these yours?" the voice had asked, cutting me short. Words like water, like glass. Crystalline balloons that floated and popped for my ears and my ears alone.

So it felt. So it seemed. And the speaker? She stood, draped in glittering snow that enveloped her figure as if it belonged to her. As if she was made of it, ruler of it: the season, sprung from the pit of her soul. An aura of light clung to her, and when I blinked, it did not depart. It seemed to have grown.

She held in her hands a pair of starry gloves. Li's, who must have tossed them in her delirium. She held them up beside her bright face and waggled them cheekily. Her eyes met mine.

"I think these might be too small for you, handsome," she said. Glass words. Water words. *Pop pop pop.* I felt my innards slither with desire. With hunger. Or maybe fear. I wasn't sure. All I could do was stare and smile.

This was how I first met my wife.

CHAPTER TWO

"Walk me through it one more time, Miss. From the beginning."

The man stands with his tie loosened, hair mussed. His shirttail has sprouted from the back of his pants and is growing longer by the minute. It's Wednesday, and very hot. Hot enough that your body is slathered in sweat, as if you are melting right out of your skin. Ditching this human form and becoming elemental again. Wouldn't that be nice?

"Okay," I say calmly. My fingers are arched on the counter, primed for prayer. I have been ready for some time now, yet my brain is short-circuiting in the stuffy airless space.

I try again.

"I need three racks of lamb, twenty-four of the Mediterranean breasts, nineteen of the Cajun Alabamans, five full salmons, four dozen of the Wagyu skewers, and one serving of steak tartare. Oh, and a large charcuterie platter of…" I wave my hand at the circular rinds of meat. "Whatever's best."

The butcher scribbles this down, beads of sweat crawling out from beneath his paper hat. He finishes and reads it back to me. I nod.

"Yes, perfect. And I need everything delivered by tomorrow, before 11." I slide a piece of paper with my address across the counter, which he grabs with a frown. A drop of red juice transfers from his hands to the page, soaking through to become a miniature, bloody firework.

"That's a big order for such short notice. Our turnaround is usually 48 hours, especially with a custom charcuterie." He mispronounces this final word, coming out as 'shark-cutie-airy'. I laugh and he immediately blushes red. Simple men, simple solutions.

"Yes, I realize that. And I'm so sorry for the inconvenience. I'm willing to pay for transportation and preparation costs with a forty percent gratuity. And I'll put in a good word for your store with all my guests. Is that alright?" I know his answer before he can open his mouth.

We settle out a few final details, during which I make him blush twice more for fun. It gives me a rush to see how people respond so malleably. I do have a bit of an advantage, of course, but no one ever said life was fair, did they?

Another party. Another trip around the sun. Another clustering of friends and loved ones to celebrate the fact that I haven't died yet. Dahlia lives on! I step out of the butcher shop and into the thick oven of July. God, how I love being a summer baby. Everyone is in such good spirits, and the air seems charged with a heady sensualism. It makes me wet just breathing in the season. I feel like nothing bad can ever happen again.

~ ~ ~

Mom had always allowed me to do my own planning, as soon as I was old enough to. She relished having the day to herself, the reprieve from responsibility. I was turning 13 when she first offered me the job, a Platinum AmEx card clutched against the stem of her cosmopolitan. I was in the yard—or 'the grounds', as she called them—playing tug-of-war with Mango.

Mango was our enormous, gleeful golden retriever, with what Mom suspected to be a touch of Down's syndrome. As we played, Mango couldn't decide if the point of tug-of-war was to pull back or advance forward. Still, she clutched the rope between her teeth, her eyes rolling in her skull rapturously.

"Daaahlia! Baby, put down the toy for a second. Mommy has something she wants to ask you." My mother's voice was already creaking under the weight of her fourth cocktail. The day had barely cracked noon.

I let the rope go slack, causing Mango to face-plant into the grass.

"Oh, Mango! I'm sorry!" I said. Mango righted herself immediately like a cork, flashing me a dirt-smeared smile. I smiled back.

"Honey! Mommy wants to take a lie-down, so hurry up. I have an important question for you. It's about your birthday." My ears perked up at the word, and I skipped across the lawn to where she stood. She was wearing a fuchsia kaftan with sunglasses, as was customary.

Despite sporting a walk-in closet that was bigger than some people's apartment, I only remember seeing my mother in three kinds of clothing: formal (four floral dresses on rotation, one pantsuit), athe-leisure wear, and kaftans. The latter was for day-drinking, so this was what I saw her in mostly. Billowy and boozy. This was Mom.

"Sweetie, remember not to play too rough with Mango. She's not the brightest bitch of the litter. And…oh! You've got dirt all on your knees. Wipe that off before you come inside."

She was right. My knees were filthy. I liked to drop down onto all fours when playing with Mango. Towering over her on my bipedal legs felt wrong and unbalanced. It only seemed fair to even the odds. Height-wise, at least.

"Yes, Mom, I will." Right then, it was me who was being dwarfed. Mom stood on the end of the raised, wooden deck; a spectre in rippling pink. I had to peer up at her, a good five feet from eye-level.

"Okay, baby. I trust you. Now, Dahlia dear, I know it's your big day coming up but—" She swatted the air at invisible gnats. "You know Mommy is no good at planning parties! I don't have the knack for these things. But I do it for you, honeybun, because I love you. Unless, of course…"

She paused to drink from her blush-tinted elixir. I waited on bated breath for her to swallow. I had never seen my mom drink quickly. She sipped luxuriously, each mouthful treated with utmost dignity. So classy, was this act, that I didn't even realize my mother was an alcoholic until years after she was dead. At the time, I felt like I was witnessing a healthy, passionate affair between a woman and the bottle.

"Unless, honey, you'd like to plan things yourself? I'll handle the guest list, obviously, but I could leave you in charge of refreshments, entertainment, theme. That sort of thing."

She was red-faced and grinning under her Versace shades: chunky frames that would leave dents on the bridge of her nose. She then floated down to my vicinity, cosmo held aloft, and extended her Platinum card with gusto. I snatched it from her hand without a moment's hesitation and clambered onto the deck to give her a hug. Mom received me warmly, her laughter sparkling like the sun through her drink.

"Oh my god, yes! I would love that so much. Thank you, Mom!" I said, earnestly. This was me, playing perfect daughter. I had gotten so good at it that it hardly felt like an act anymore. I *was* perfect daughter, to a tee.

Mom took another sip above my head.

~ ~ ~

Now, handing a credit card with an upwards limit of one hundred thousand dollars to a 12-year-old might seem like a foolish thing for a parent to do. And it is, objectively. But between the two of us, I was by far the more responsible one. My father had vanished into a cloud of shame and young mistress pussy when I was 6 years old: young enough for minimal psychological damage, but old enough for me to hate him. To this day, the scent of Dolce and Gabbana cologne and patchy goatees makes my blood boil.

It really wasn't so bad, growing up with a single mom. Especially one as lax and self-oriented as Sharon Voronin, née Trevi. I say self-oriented and not selfish, because there's a difference. Sharon was a loving, generous mother, but she couldn't help but put herself first. The world revolved around her, and frankly, I was fine with that. Let her live out her days in a drunken bubble, driving to luncheons and club dinners with friends who hated her guts.

And of course they would've hated her! To this day, I've yet to meet a person more untouched by the realities of life than my mother was. She was born wealthy and pretty and white. Triple whammy of privilege. Her worst health scare was a broken toe in grade six (rogue bocce ball) and contacting mono at age 16 (from too much kissing). Her parents were attentive but not domineering, and had retired early to Costa Rica. She had never had a job. She could tan without getting sunburnt, and seemed immune to hangovers and acne. She had travelled the best parts of Asia and Europe (extensively), met a "nice" man with an even nicer tax bracket, gave birth in under 2 hours, and had natural curls. It was absurd.

My mom was extremely proud of what an easy baby I had been. Her genius. Her angel. She would rave to complete strangers about how little she had had to do as a new mother.

"I've taken shits that were more work than you, honey," she'd confessed to me one day, floating by in a duck-shaped pool inflatable. Three sheets to the wind; strike that, four. And why shouldn't she be? What did she have to worry about? Nothing, it seemed like. She had been born without karmic debt. Given free rein to rack up as much earthly pleasure as she desired. Even her husband leaving her was a gift.

"Now that you're older, dear, I might as well tell you the truth. Your father was a terrible lover. So inattentive and just...just awful."

This was at Thanksgiving dinner when I was freshly 11. Apparently that was old enough to hear how much my father had sucked in the sack. She'd polished off her apple toddy and went on.

"I mean, really, what kind of man doesn't know how to French kiss? He was half Greek, for god's sake! And...oh, I really shouldn't be saying this, but what the hell...I have *never* encountered someone more ill-suited for cunnilingus. Like some brain-damaged wolf eel, I tell you. Just flapping aimlessly about...say, have you ever seen a wolf eel, pumpkin? On one of your animal shows?"

I had not. But as soon as dinner was over, I'd rushed to investigate on our old desktop computer that shrieked whenever it was turned on. Mom didn't believe in technology, and neither did I, but for different reasons. Still, the horror of seeing a gap-mouthed wolf eel slowly buffer onto the screen was never forgotten. I had a hell of a time equating this slimy demon from the deep with my own father, and I'd promptly went to get my mom to find out more. She'd screamed upon seeing the pixilated wolf eel, punching the OFF button with a closed fist.

"Jesus H. Christ, Dahlia! Are you trying to give me a heart-attack?" she'd slurred angrily. Apparently she had forgotten her nonsensical metaphor from the dinner table. When I'd tried to defend myself, I was sent off to my room to "read my comic books, or whatever". Like I said, self-oriented. She didn't even know what I did most of the time. The woman was out of touch with reality. Regardless, no talk of wolf eels ever graced our house again.

~ ~ ~

Nobody likes a person with a happy childhood. I understand that. On paper, I can barely stomach my own upbringing. Let's do a visualization exercise, shall we? Picture a Tudor-style mansion on steroids, nestled in the bosom of a temperate rainforest. Add lots of dark wood and glass to the renovation. Throw in a pool, sprawling lawn, garden, tree-fort (decrepit but still accessible). Make that house a 20-minute walk from a semi-private beach. Subtract one father and substitute your remaining guardian with a juiced-up ditz whose primary concern is staying up to date with men's pro-league tennis. And *voilà.*

You have ground zero for my life at large.

But enough about all that. Birthday, birthday, birthday. My 13th, to be specific. It's so easy to become distracted, to bounce from thought to thought like a stone skipping water. Surface and no depth. I swear I'm getting better at all that. Staying grounded in one place for longer than an instant. But still. Be patient with little old me.

At 13, Sharon's Platinum AmEx card was a gateway drug. *The* gateway drug, if we're being honest. You see, up until that point, I had been satisfied with very little. You may not believe that, based on the lavish surroundings I grew up with, but it's true. I was enchanted by vanilla ice cream and the smell of fresh laundry. My favourite time of year was whatever it was *right now.* I loved every song I heard—passionately—even though I rarely understood what they were saying. Food...forget about it. I'd devour anything you put in front of me.

Which was a blessing, because my mother was an appalling cook. She believed mayo and tomatoes constituted a reasonable sandwich filling. A plate of pickles was sometimes lunch. And dinner. Even Mango ate better than we did at home. Her kibble was chock-full of nutrients that kept her body bodacious and her coat glossy. Did I mention she also had different coloured eyes? And two full sets of teeth?

~ ~ ~

After my mother had sashayed back into the house, off to shake up a new drink, I'd stood on the deck and savoured my new treasure. I held within my hands great power, more power than I really understood at the time. But I could feel it, reeling off the plastic like radioactivity. I'd seen my mother wield this tiny rectangle like a battle-axe. It granted wishes. It bought favours. It caused people to speak or be silenced. And now, for a moment in time, it was mine.

Honestly, I was surprised my mom had brought up resuscitating my birthday party at all. The previous 2 years had devolved into having her own friends over for cocktails and (maybe) cupcakes. When Mom had asked if I wanted to invite any of my school friends, I'd declined. She didn't ask why. Nor did I offer any explanations. It really was none of her business.

Again, none of this had ever really bothered me. I knew how to please myself, and on birthdays, I was happy with whatever I got. Chiefly, my great joy was that I was still here. Still alive to see another year. Only now, things had changed. Now I had a say in how I wanted to commemorate my anniversary of arrival.

I followed my mom's footsteps into the house and went straight to the computer. It awoke with a scream that set my back teeth on edge. I waited patiently for it to turn on, riffling through the desk drawers heaping with investment and financial papers in the meantime. Zeros, zeros, and more zeros.

Finally, after several minutes of loading, I was able to surf the web. Glacially. I typed '13-year-old girl birthday party' and started scrolling.

Most search results highlighted that a 13-year-old was a tricky customer, because they were just on the cusp of teen-dom. What was cool and hip, but also not too adult? Mom Blogs debated this point to death, but generally agreed on letting your child take the reins a bit. Because, after all, they were at the age where they were "finding their voice".

"Most 13-year-old girls are looking to their peers on what's appropriate. They want to feel grown-up and fit-in, but they also have that glimmer of innocence left! PARENTS, if your child still wants to have a princess or Disney party at this age, LET THEM!!! This may be your LAST chance to experience those final fleeting moments of childhood before they become GRUMPY, HORMONAL TEENAGERS!"

This was from an impassioned blogger named Darla, who wrote exclusively about parenting tips and exotic cheeses. Her next posting was for a pungent French cheese called Epoisses de Bourgogne. Darla had reviewed:

"Musky, creamy flavour with a nutty tang; well-worth the overpowering stench! This was a favourite of Napoleon and Robespierre, but it is certainly an acquired taste. WARNING: when it starts to smell like ammonia, TOSS IT! 4 out of 5 stars."

I clicked off her page in disgust. Then clarified my search to be for 'all-ages party ideas' and away from the ramblings of parents bemoaning the fact their children were (gasp!) growing up.

Now the screen was spotted with photos of masquerade parties, pink parties, scavenger hunt parties, and an ominously titled 'silent disco party'. I clicked through half a dozen options before landing on a winner. A Hawaiian Luau party. It showed a group of people adorned in wildflowers while dancing; long strips of brown paper hung from their waist. In the background was a display table covered in shells, pineapples and...flamingos? The description tagline read as such:

"Bring a slice of tropical paradise to your next birthday with this exotic party idea! In lieu of boring birthday cake, enjoy delicious Hawaiian cuisine, try the limbo, wear grass skirts, and play beachball! A Hawaiian Luau party is the perfect party for all ages, with unique decorations and plenty of inspiration to choose from. Trust us, you don't need fire breathers and a pig roast to have a good time!"

All of that sounded interesting, but what really caught my eye was the final sentence. Fire breathers? Pig roast? What kind of party called for something like that? I did some more digging and discovered what a traditional Luau truly was: a celebratory feast for the birth of a child, bountiful harvest, or to honour the gods. It was a joyous yet consequential affair, a far cry from the watered-down parody of today, plastic shells and tiki torches be damned. And they didn't even have flamingos in Hawaii!

Someone needed to show people how it was done. I had been to other kids' birthday parties and they all sucked ass. Mostly. Ashley Bannon's sailboat party had been fun, but that's because I loved being on the water. And they had served ice cream cake.

Otherwise I was bored out of my gourd. I rarely went, even though I was invited often. Everyone wanted me there, which was nobody's fault, but my cross to bear. At 12 years of age, I hadn't learned to navigate my social magnetism. I felt swarmed by my peers and their strange ways. How foolish of me to think that things would be any different as an adult.

I jotted down a list of ideas, supplies I'd need to throw the absolute best party any 13-year-old had ever thrown. By the time I picked up the phone to make some calls, I had filled two pages with my chicken-scratch. At the sound of the dial tone, I cleared my throat, prepared to deepen it to my mother's raspy tenor. Let the festivities begin, I thought idly.

~ ~ ~

Jack is waiting for me in the car with the roof up. The convertible was a peace offering, if not a pricey one. It's a Porsche 911 Carrera, with a red leather interior and body the colour of a freshly-shucked pearl. From it spills the Beach Boys, trilling atop a lush bed of strings and harp on low volume. I smile as I slide into the driver's seat and kiss my husband's cheek.

"Sorry I took so long. The guy inside was new." I pull my seatbelt on and start the car. The seat is scorching to the touch, practically burning a hole right through my skirt. Jack rests his hand on my thigh, before removing it on second thought. I frown at this, but don't make a comment.

"How could you tell?" he asks.

"Tell what?"

"That he was new. The butcher."

I turn and give him a look before backing out. "The better question, hon, would be how could I *not* tell. It's always so obvious when someone's new at their job. They stick out."

"Is that right? I didn't think so. Maybe sometimes, but..."

"Of course it is. They're nervous, and can't meet your eye for too long. They ask too many questions. Or not the right ones. And they're so *painfully* helpful. It's pretty obvious." I have my eyes glued to the road, but I can feel Jack staring at me.

"Or," he says slowly, "maybe they're just that kind of personality. Nervous, or extra friendly. I feel like it's jumping to conclusions to assume otherwise."

What to say? Jack's right, even though he's wrong. My reasoning would sound silly if I were to externalize it. Instead, I reach over and pat his hand, resting on his leg like a hairy, tanned tarantula. Keep smiling.

"I suppose you're right. Maybe I'm too quick to judge. Either way, I'm glad to have that done. Food was the last thing on my list, so now everything should be fine for tomorrow."

I say this breezily, as if I hadn't a care in the world. The light in front of the car turns red, and I pull to a stop.

"Good, I'm glad to hear. Is there anything else you need help with?"

"No, no, I've got it covered."

"You sure?"

"Yeah, of course. You just relax."

"Okay. Just let me know."

The light flashes green and I turn onto the highway. As I accelerate I take my husband's hand into mine and raise it to my lips. I plant a kiss on his skin, then return his left hand to my thigh. Where it belongs. I hold him there gently, so he can't move it away. With my free hand, I weave the car through the river of traffic. The hot air beyond the closed roof roars, as the convertible hurtles towards the opalescent gates of Heaven, waiting for us to return.

CHAPTER THREE

The first thing that hits me when I wake is the smell. Vomit. It's followed by a lightning-strike right to the brain; a low, thunderous headache in pursuit. I groan and roll away from the stench to face the wall, but it's everywhere. The air is ripe with it. Someone has to clean up the mess.

I ease myself into sitting and survey the room. Dim yellow light pushes its way through the curtains and illuminates my bedroom. There is a pile of clothes on the floor, caked in sick. Dishes piled on the desk, along with papers, books, empty water bottles. Some filled with piss. On the wall, the black Kit-Cat Klock my mother gave me hangs noisily.

Tick-tock-tick-tock, it says, eyes and tail swishing in sync. *Tick-tock-Jack-fucked-up.*

The smell is making my stomach turn, threatening to keel over. I stagger to my feet and cross the carpeted floor. Pull open the curtains and sliding window. Freezing air pours in. Outside, the skies have turned from wet snow to rain. In a few hours, all the white will be erased from existence. The world will fall back into grey.

As if to mimic the heavens, my vision swims hazy, nearing black. My knees buckle and I come down—*fee-fi-fo-fum*—

with a crash to the floor. I miss catching myself with my hands and instead slam the ground with my full weight.

"What's going on up there? You tryna fall through my goddamn ceiling?"

Through the floor, walls, door: my father's voice. Booming. I opened my mouth to speak, to call back and assure him that I'm fine. No need to come up. Everything's fine. Jack's All Right.

Instead, what erupts but…oh joy, more vomit. Vile, brown, and nasty. It scalds my nose, makes my eyes water, and soaks into the filthy carpet. My body feels like it has just swum a hundred miles of open ocean. It is gummy and weak, full of liquids that have no business being inside me. I surrender to the waves of purging, bobbing in and out of consciousness.

It takes me over half an hour to get up again. Gravity seems to have tripled in strength, become a personal enemy. But finally, I conquer.

I crawl, stumble out of my bedroom to the shower, peel off my boxers, and then climb inside. I sit on the tub floor, legs pressed against my chest, and let the water stream down on top of me. It is only after a few minutes of sitting, trying not to puke again, that I notice the thick black numbers slowly melting off my forearm. I grasp for the handle, managing to turn off the shower before they become too indecipherable to read.

Soaking wet, I stagger back to my room, retching at the scent. I find a blank scrap of paper, and transcribe it best I can. There is a seven, which might also be a one, but the rest is all legible. My memory of last night is a void. These numbers are all I have left.

~ ~ ~

Now, I come from a long line of male extremists. My grandpa was a chain-smoker who needed to have a hole drilled into his throat just so he could breathe. Even then, he hadn't quit. He'd died before hitting 50, when I was only 3 months old.

His father before him, my great-grandfather, had been a man-whore. He, Lewis Donner, drove all across the continent as a trucker pumping unsuspecting women with his seed, staying for the first months of pregnancy when he could "watch them grow", before jumping ship, state, or county. To our knowledge, there were thirteen Donner half-breeds reared from the same twisted root.

He'd confessed—or rather, boasted—in his senility that he'd done it for one reason and one reason only. He found pregnant women sexy. He was turned on by their bodies, the way they swelled up and changed. Not to mention, he was enthralled by the fact that a part of *him* was growing inside of them, contorting their wombs and worlds beyond recognition. Hence why he would always leave right before they gave birth. He couldn't care less about the product, and only about the packaging.

"Besides," Lewis had grinned, according to my father's account. "By that point, none of'em skanks would even want to screw no more."

When he finally died, my dad took his ashes and scattered them atop the manure pile of our neighbour's pig farm. I'd argue that was the last truly decent thing he did.

My dad had gone the classic route. He chose the bottle. Or maybe the bottle chose him. His drinking began not long after his chimneystack of a parent died. When Momma'd told me this, I'd imagined a smelly black vapour oozing out of my grandpa's corpse and slipping into my father's body. The demon of addiction, changing hosts.

Clearly my father had been possessed by the very thing that had killed Grandpa. He needed to be helped, before it killed him and then came for me. Momma had laughed humourlessly at this. And said:

"Listen, Jacky, you're safe from being an addict as long as you know you aren't one. Whatever shit makes your father the way he is, that's on him. Your grandpa isn't to blame. There ain't no demon inside your dad. Just his own foolishness and blindness to it."

As a boy, this had initially comforted me. But eventually, I began to see the holes in Momma's logic. A person doesn't exist in a vacuum, and the failings of fathers affect their sons, no matter how you spin it. The issue wasn't just my dad's issue with temperance. It stemmed much farther back, a circular trail of griefs that extended as far as lineage could allow. What my mother was right about, however, was blindness. If you cannot see what you have been burdened with, you cannot know how to free yourself from it.

Of course, these days, my dad was estranged from the drink. He had been for years. But what had replaced his drunken stupor was arguably worse. Rage. Lots and lots of rage.

~ ~ ~

A terrific pounding comes from the door. This jolts me, causing my legs to shoot out and kick the walls of the tub. I'd drifted back to sleep sitting in the shower. Lukewarm water pours down, with interludes of freezing spurts.

"Jack! What the hell are you doing in there?"

I grip the sides of the tub, blinking—*open, close, open*—disoriented. What am I doing in here? With my foot, I push the faucet off, letting the flow of water fizzle out and die.

"I'm fine, Dad. Just…showering." Jesus. My voice is a ruin. It sounds waterlogged and lonely. I lean my head back against the tiles and brace myself.

"For 40 fucking minutes? Where do you think you are, Buckingham Palace? First you come home at the crack of dawn, stomping around and waking *me* up. Do you know how hard I work, Jack? How many hours I put in to pay for *your* food, for *your* education? You think acting like a degenerate's gonna help your future?"

There's a pause, in which the only sound is water dripping. I clear my throat, all my energy put into enunciation. "No, Dad. Of course not. I'm sorry I woke you up."

"Goddamn right you are. I get two fucking nights a week where I don't have to wake up early to go work. To feed *your* lazy ass. To pay for the water you waste without a thought. Well, I'm sick of it. Something's got to change around here. And by something, I mean *you.*"

Dad works as a mail carrier, and has ever since we'd moved out west. His job fits his restless nature and aptitude for solitude. What it means for me, however, is that he is always home in the evening. Waiting to spar.

"I know, Dad, I'm sorry. I can look at getting a second job. Maybe when this semester ends, I…yeah, I can do something then. Right now, I'm going to be so busy with classes. And the shop isn't giving out many shifts 'cause it's the slow season, but I can always ask. I'm sorry I woke you up. I'm sorry." My apologies hang in the air but there is no response.

I pull the curtain back and stick my head out slightly, listening. Silence. My father has left mid-conversation. He does this sometimes, in the heat of an argument. Just stands up and leaves when the other person—me—is speaking. He's had his fill of fighting. The boil's been lanced.

As if to confirm this, I hear the sound of his stereo being cranked up downstairs. John Lennon starts yowling about Old Flattop. *Abbey Road* will continue to blare for the next few hours. I climb unsteadily out of the tub and towel off, humming a single, tuneless note to drown out the music.

When I come back to my room, I take my vomit-soaked clothes and stuff them into my overflowing garbage. Then I tie the garbage bag closed and throw it out the window, where it falls in the space between the duplex next to ours. Tomorrow's problem, I think, as I fall back asleep with my head sandwiched between two pillows.

~ ~ ~

It's Sunday when I come to again. A patch of sun is stamped on the wall, a rarity this time of year. I've learned since moving here that the sun can vanish for vast stretches of time, leaving the city in a state of darkness for weeks.

In the prairies, such a thing is unheard of. Sure, it may get cold enough to kill you, if you stay out long enough. But the sun isn't something that abandons you entirely. You can rely on it for comfort. For certainty.

On the west coast, however, you trade in sunlight for lushness. Something is always in season, even in February. Greenery in winter. In exchange, much of the year is defined by liminal, grey darkness. The cloud cover sits so low you can practically hit your head on it. The sea turns the colour of porridge, of dead fish. It becomes suffocating, like being inside of a shoebox. You'd feel stifled to even step outside.

A sunny day like today, then, can't be wasted. The rancid reek of my own stomach has dissipated, and the unmistakable call of starlings has replaced the morning air. With any luck,

Dad will be gone running errands, like he sometimes does on Sundays.

I clamber out of bed, stretch, and set about righting the wrongs of the past. To begin with, I needed to clean my fucking room. Then I could go out for a drive, maybe walk by the sea. Something outdoorsy to cleanse the palate. Wipe the sludge from the brain.

As I begin to tidy up, a memory from Friday night comes back to me in gauzy form. In it, I am talking with someone—or something—enormous. Their face is obscured, their voice: muffled. What I remember instead is the feelings they left me with.

Excitement. Entrancement. And a touch, invaded. I push this aside and remind myself to collect the vomit bag outside before Dad finds it.

The last thing I need is another reason for him to hate me.

CHAPTER FOUR

It takes nearly 2 weeks for him to reach out. Okay, maybe closer to 8 days. But still. Too long. By that point I'd almost (not even slightly) forgotten about him. Maybe I'd been mistaken in my intuition, I thought. Or perhaps he'd been scared off. It certainly wouldn't have been the first time.

The call comes through on a Saturday. I'd spent the morning down at Whytecliff park, a skip and a hop from home. One of my favourite things about winter has always been the silence. Everyone's retreated: back to their homes, their cars, their underground malls and high-rises. Suddenly the beaches and trails are deserted. All that fills my company on the rocky shores are the rains. Whom I worship. Whom I adore.

I liked to take off my boots and sample the various terrains with my bare feet. The rough etchings of gravel, frigid tidal pools. Velvet moss beds, inviting me into themselves. Exposed roots. Mud. Polished shore stones. I'd plod along in giddy silence, becoming drenched. Only after I'd lost all pedial feeling, when my toes had shrunken down to ten bloodless raisins, would I reluctantly start the trek back to the house.

When the call comes, I am sitting on the edge of the bathtub, breathing life into my legs with hot water. I'd put a jazz record one—Nina Simone's *Wild is the Wind*—and the house is tranquil, still. Until the landline begins ringing.

If I had known what the call represented, the future it held, I would have ripped the phone from the wall and thrown it into the Pacific Ocean. I would have closed the blinds, turned the music up, and danced till my back was sweaty and I couldn't stand anymore. I would have lived on as I had: relishing the world in its natural splendour, until I was an old, crumbling relic of a woman. And I would have died with grace. And most certainly honour. If I chose to keep living, that is.

Of course, I am, and was, a humble slave to the present. Blind and all. The phone rings and my heart sings. I know before I cross the foyer and into the kitchen, trailing a string of suds and footprints behind me, that it is him. The man. The one.

I pause, pressing my palm against the ringing receiver. Vibrations of uncertainty travel across miles of wire, or perhaps through the air like magic. Upon arrival, they shake the phone in its holster, penetrating the pores of my skin. I lift the receiver and speak in.

"Hello?"

A beat. Then:

"Hey." It's him, all right. "I, um, had your number written down. But I forgot to call."

His voice sounds shy, almost guilty. A far cry from the self-assured man I had met. Yet it is unmistakably him. There is a huskiness to his tone, a power, even if it is currently buried in diffidence. I have seen what lies beneath.

"That's alright," I say. "I know things happen." There's more silence. Just dead air and the whine of electrical currents.

"My name's Jack." This makes me laugh.

"I know, you've told me."

"Yeah, well I…"

"And I'm Dahlia. Since we're doing introductions again." I slide down to the floor, my back pressed against the wall. The tiles feel cold against my bare skin. This was not how I imagined this conversation going.

"Cool, cool. Nice to meet you, Dahlia."

"Nice to meet you again too. Jack."

"Yeah, you too. So I…um."

I wait for him to continue, but there is only more silence. Nina's final song of the record, "Either Way I Lose", comes to its natural end.

What was this conversation, fourth grade? Why was this so awkward? Surely I couldn't have felt what I felt that night, only for *this* to be the culmination. Some stammering, limp-dicked salutation 2 weeks too late. No sir. Not today. Not me.

He clears his throat, a rough *ack-hem* that assaults my ear.

"I'm sorry, but…god, this sounds so shitty. I swear I'm not a bad guy. Honest to god. But I…I don't remember meeting you. Like, at all." Now it's my turn to be speechless.

What the fuck?

"Hello?" he asks, after a few moments. "You still there?"

"Did you hear the dial tone?"

"No."

"Then obviously I'm still here."

"Okay, well—"

"What do you mean you don't remember meeting?"

"I mean…I don't remember anything. It's completely blacked out. I just had your number written on my arm the next day."

"So you don't remember…anything?"

"Uh, yeah. Mostly. I remember being inside at the party and then—"

"Henry's?"

"Who?"

"Henry," I say slowly. "The guy who was hosting the party? The one who got taken away in an ambulance after having a seizure?"

"Jesus Christ, what? Is he okay?"

"I don't know. Probably. I don't keep up with everyone."

"You don't keep up with your friend to see if they're alive or not?"

"Excuse me?"

"I dunno, that just...seems kinda weird to me. If he's your friend, you should probably check up on him. See if he's okay or not."

Then: "That's what I'd do."

"You didn't even know this happened until a minute ago!" I exclaim. "Now suddenly I'm the bad friend because I didn't go visit him at the hospital? I'm not Mother Theresa, okay?"

I couldn't believe what was happening. Were we...arguing*?* I'd spent weeks fantasizing about this moment. Now, instead of anything resembling the disarming spark of our first meeting, we were squabbling. Like seniors.

"Listen, I'm sorry. I didn't mean to upset you."

"You're right. You should be sorry." Here came the hurt, disguised as anger. "You know, *Jack,* it's pretty rare for me to open up the way I did that night. Especially to a stranger, and I've been racking my brains on why I even did. So to hear that you don't even remember me *at all,* it's, well. It's upsetting."

There is a sigh on the line. "Yeah, yeah, I know. I feel like shit about it. My friends gave me something...I actually don't know what it was. But it totally fucked with my head. All I know was I was at...Henry's place, and the next thing I remember is waking up in my bed. Feeling like a semi had just driven over my head."

This gives me pause. I remembered his demeanour from that night. He'd been giddy, gregarious, almost vaudevillian. It'd taken me off-guard. We'd started talking right away, just the two of us outside for nearly half an hour. There was this magnetism about him, a gravitational pull that felt easy, much too easy. I kept catching myself, a moment too late after a snatch of sentence had left my mouth, wondering 'why am I saying this?' And through it all, this feeling of being sedated by his presence. This stranger who felt like home.

Now I could trust none of that. I'd been duped into believing an illusion. And it wasn't even his fault. Not entirely.

"Look, Jack. I'm sorry that happened to you. I should have picked up on something not being quite right with you that night. Honestly, I've never met a guy who was so open. It was refreshing. And nice." All I want to do is hang up the line and be done with it. Men. What fucking idiots.

There is more silence, during which I replay more snapshots of the night. Gloves. The hysterical laughing of his two friends, before going back inside. Black lambent eyes. Snow. Fascination. The two of us dancing. Alcohol. A scream ripping through the room. Henry's squirming body. A black felt marker in hand, writing on skin. The stampede of students fleeing ship. His final look of abhorrence at the flashing sirens, before running away too. Me. Venturing into the storm. Into the lightless, surrounding woods. Silence. Crashing waves. Finding my own way home. End.

"Well, I'm sorry it happened too. You sound like a nice girl, and I didn't mean…yeah. I just feel bad this happened. Maybe we could meet up sometime, though? Like for coffee or something. I'd like to make it up to you."

I do not waste time with my reply.

"No. I'm sorry. I just don't think that'd be a good idea." I rub my forehead with my fingers. My legs have curled up to my chest, protectively.

"Oh, okay. Yeah, I understand." He sounds genuinely dejected, which stokes the anger inside me. What does he have to be upset about? He doesn't even remember me.

"So you really can't remember me, like at all? Not even what I look like?" At this point, I'm just rubbing salt in my own wound. But I want to hear him say it.

There is a long pause, in which I can hear shuffling. He must be pacing on the other end. I try to picture where he's calling from and come up with nothing. Just a black void and Jack. Handsome Jack. No. *No.* Just Jack. *Just fucking idiot Jack.*

"No. I don't. I'm sorry. I wish I had a different answer."

He begins to say something more, but by then I've already slipped the phone back into its cradle. There is a click as the call ends. The rain outside has stopped its faithful drizzle, leaving the roof untapped. I'd long pulled the batteries out of the clocks, so there isn't even a tick to be heard. In the silence that swallows me, I feel, for the first time in forever, utterly and profoundly alone.

~ ~ ~

I am not one for pity. I've found it to be a useless emotion, along with jealousy, shame, and regret. There is nothing to be gained from feeling sorry for oneself; much less, another. That's the role of compassion: the space where action takes foot. Pity is just spinning your wheels in the mud, while feeling sad that there's mud in the first place.

So when the call ends, and I am met with this black mountain of emptiness, I refuse to let it sour my mood. I switch the record from Nina to Jimi, trading in luscious piano riffs for taunt rock that raises the hairs on the back of my neck. "Purple Haze" snarls through the tall speakers, and I begin to dance.

I take the party of one into the living room, which has vaulted ceilings that connect to the second-floor landing. Out of the nine-foot-tall windows, hemlock and maple trees jive in sync with the wind, which has picked up significantly.

"Let it gooooooo!" I wail theatrically, hips and limbs flailing about. Dancing has never been a strong suit of mine, the coordination never quite making sense. At least in the way most people would categorize dancing. Of course I knew how to move. But I preferred to be possessed by the music, let it express itself more organically.

Unfortunately, this made for some rather unorthodox movements, or as my girlfriends called it, "weird-as-fuck dancing". At the club, I was strictly limited to a simple step-touch combo with a bumping head. Anything more robust would've resulted in accidentally giving someone a black eye. Again.

It's why I preferred my own company. Freedom from everything. Freedom of self. When I was alone, I could unfold myself, allow all parts of me to stretch and hang out. I could act, talk, think, look, be any way I wanted. No hesitation. No seconding-guessing or conforming or judgement. I couldn't understand why people were so afraid of themselves.

For me, being alone was a guaranteed riot.

But now, *now*, this pit has formed inside me. Some niggling sapling of discontent. I knew who the culprit is, who is to blame for resuscitating dead hope, only to kill it all over again. Jack. I conjure his image and bury him beneath a mental rockslide.

There. Be gone.

After 30 minutes of furious dancing, I collapse on the couch, gasping. I press my hand to my heart, eyes closed, taking in the frenetic expressions of my central organ. It's hard to believe such a little thing can be responsible for running the whole show. Ceaselessly pumping behind the scenes. Without reprieve. Or applause.

"Thank you, heart," I whisper. It's not often that my body goes a day without thanks. How ironic, that the thing I once loved had to be hated in order to be loved again. Life is so full of circles it makes my head spin.

I lay there, dizzy and panting, until the record needle slides to a stop. But by then I am not afraid of silence, or what it might bring. I embrace the emptiness, from which I came, with open arms.

Outside, the wind begins to bray.

CHAPTER FIVE

"So? What else did she say?" Li asked, her mouth full of mustard.

We were sitting in the campus dining hall, surrounded by mobs of hungry students and their disgruntled professors. Li was polishing off her second hot dog, a banned item in her household. I'd had my doubts that she even liked them, that she ate them purely out of spite. The last of the mustard-drenched bun disappeared with a plop, washed down with a hefty chug of Gatorade. My turn at bat.

"She said she doesn't want to meet with me."

I pushed my food around—spaghetti bolognese—with a pang of disgust. I'd heard some girl in front of me order it, and when it'd come to be my turn, I'd ordered the same. It hadn't hit me until Li and I were sitting down at our table that I didn't even *like* bolognese. Still. Ten bucks was ten bucks. I slurped down some noodles and grimaced.

"Well, why not? If she went through all the trouble to write her number on your fucking arm, why doesn't she want to see you again?"

"Because I told her. That I didn't remember her."

Li let out a huge sigh and rolled her eyes.

"Jesus, Jack, I *told* you: deny, deny, deny. This girl could be your soulmate for all we know, or at least, a really good lay. She went through the trouble of giving you her number, even with your cell being dead. And a guy having a fucking seizure on the floor. I just don't understand why she had to write so goddamn big on your arm."

It was true. The ghost of permanent marker was still there, enormous and dark, almost 3 weeks later. No amount of scrubbing could erase it entirely.

"Li, I couldn't just lie about that. I didn't know anything about her, how the hell was I going to fake that?"

"You can fake anything if you believe hard enough," she sniffed.

"Okay, well, I doubt that. You're telling me you could perform open-heart surgery just because you *believed* you could? What about speaking Portuguese, or professional mud wrestling? Could you believe your way into doing those?"

"Seu palhaço fedorento," Li hissed. "I spent a semester abroad in Brazil, remember? Some friend you are."

"I thought they spoke Spanish there."

"ENH," she said, mimicking a buzzer. "Wrong. Portuguese if you please."

"Okay, well..."

"And you're right, that's not what I meant. Of course you can't believe your way into being a surgeon. I'm not a fucking idiot. But I do know you, and you give up before even trying. I'm sure you blew your chances before even telling her about...the mistake."

"The mistake?"

"Yes, the mistake! The fucking laced weed that made us black out and almost killed a guy!" A couple of girls passing by turned to look at the sound of Li's impassioned voice. She casually flipped them the bird and carried on.

"So yeah, maybe you couldn't have faked remembering her name or what she looked like, or whatever the fuck you two were talking about for so long outside. But you could've tried to at least…I don't know. Not be such a defeatist. Fight for something for once, Jack."

I opened my mouth to argue but stopped. I looked back down at the plate of spaghetti, thinking about Li's words. She had a point, which I hated to admit. Nor would I. I refused to give her the satisfaction of my abdication.

I cleared my throat and changed gears. "I thought you didn't believe in soulmates."

"What?"

"Just now. You said she could be my soulmate. I thought you didn't believe in all that."

"I don't. At least, not for me. I believe I'm destined to have many sordid love affairs that leave one of us, or others, heartbroken. I believe that one day, I'll be widowed, and most certainly pregnant, because that'd be just my luck. And I'll have to choose between being a single mother, giving it up for adoption, or having a late-stage abortion. I believe 9/11 was an inside job, chemtrails are real, and the moon landing was not. But no, I don't believe in soulmates. For me. You on the other hand…"

"What about me?" I asked, choosing to ignore the rest of Li's insane spiel.

"You…you just strike me as the kind of guy who's got someone waiting for them. Like you fit that stereotype. The romantic searching for his other half."

I laughed at this. "Really? That's what you think of me?"

"Well, yeah, okay, fuck you. I'm trying to be nice here. Nevermind." Li crumpled up her hotdog wrappers, soaked with condiments. She began to wipe her hands clean, irritated.

"Hey, Li, I'm just asking. I didn't mean to piss you off. What about me makes you think that?"

Li looked up from her hands and stared me square in the face. I waited for a moment as she seemed to scan me over. When she was done, she shrugged.

"I don't know. You just do. That's why I'm always fucking asking if you've met a girl yet. Something tells me you've got a person out there. Waiting. Seeking you as you seek them, or however that stupid saying goes." She paused, and then said, "When I look at you, I see someone who isn't entirely whole on their own. Like there's a piece of something missing. So maybe that missing piece is a person. I think some people are just built like that."

The two of us stared at each other for a moment. This was the second time I'd seen her since the incident, and the first since we'd both discovered Henry's fate: her through the gossip grapevine, and me from my phone call with Dahlia. Both times I'd seen Li, however, I was unsettled by the fact that she seemed different. Not in an entirely bad way, but most definitely, *different.* Allan too. There was a shift in…openness. A willingness to express without the usual hang-ups. I'd been so fixated on my problems that I hadn't had time to notice: had something changed in me too?

"What do you think was in that joint, Li?" I asked, the thought bubbling up once again.

She blew out a chestful of air in response, clearly disappointed that I'd chosen not to engage with her comments.

"I don't know, Jack, and honestly, I don't really fucking care. I'm just glad we're okay, and we didn't wind up like Henry. I heard he's all screwy now in the head. Thinks there's invisible people trying to get inside him. He'll probably be fucked up for good now. Because of *us.*"

"No," I said, quietly. "'Cause of that dealer. He's the one who gave us laced shit. Allan was just trying to be nice by giving him some. We didn't know."

Li stood to her feet and picked up her tray. “Yeah, but we’re still the ones who gave it to him. Allan feels fucking sick about it, and honestly, I kind of do too. You’re the only one who doesn’t seem to care much.” She let out another sigh and shook her head. “I’ve gotta go to my next class, Jack.”

“Wait, Li, I do…” I started to defend, but Li had already turned to leave, vanishing into the thinning hoard of students. I sat for a few minutes by myself, thoughts racing, before standing up to throw my near-full plate of spaghetti in the trash. It landed with a mingled splatter amongst other paper plates of the same.

~ ~ ~

My last class of the day was Ancient History. I had shot myself in the foot with my schedule, never stopping for help at the guidance counsellor regarding which courses to take, which not. Now I was in my third year with a mishmash of semi-failed classes at my back and a littering of academic impasses on the horizon. If I wanted to take the required Course 202, I needed to take 101 first, but of course I hadn’t, because I’d been a stubborn idiot who didn’t ask for directions.

Prerequisites were demanding their pound of flesh and I had nothing to give. So now, in order to advance forward in my degree—*good old electrical engineering, zap-zap!*—I’d need to work backwards first. Play catch-up with elective courses I had skipped.

In truth, I believed most of paid higher education to be a grand scheme straight from hell. People spent years getting degrees they had no passion for, while digging themselves into a canyon of debt that would take even more time to escape from. Or they learned bits of useless information and—having no use for it—charged other people exorbitant amounts of money to learn it from them. Until they grew up and realized they had no actual use for it either. Rinse, repeat.

Of course, this didn't mean that I didn't believe in learning. I was an avid reader, was painfully curious, and stood by the idea that people were meant to evolve and grow. Until they died. A lifelong student at the university of life. But what I didn't buy into was the subtle scam of post-secondary. Education came in many forms, not just in the shape of a three-hundred-dollar textbook. And a decade of debt and regret.

Ancient History fit the hole of my missing 'Social Science 100'. It was only week 4, and I was already fantasizing about nooses. If I'd had the money to bribe my way into one of the more desirable—and therefore overpopulated—classes, I would've been happier. But instead, I got the scraps. With a groan, I found a spot to sit in the lecture hall and waited.

Almost 16 minutes after we were supposed to begin, Professor Klein walked in. A new record. She briskly made her way to the front of the hall, where she deposited her overcoat and briefcase.

On the first day, one of the students in the front row had complimented her bag, asking if her "daughter or niece had done the beading". A valid question. The bag was an eyesore from the back row: an incongruent spectacle of yellow, pickle green, and brown beading that looked ready to come undone at any given moment. It was presumably of childish craftsmanship with sentimental value, as no one in their right mind would carry around a bag that hideous if their own kin hadn't made it.

But we were wrong. Professor Klein had been deeply miffed by the comment, and retorted that it was a 'prized family heirloom made by her great-grandmother'. Allegedly, the bag had been passed down through the family after barely escaping Europe after the Second World War.

"But wouldn't you mean before or during the war? Why would your family need to escape afterwards?" Another student had asked, to which Professor Klein's high, pale cheekbones had flushed red, a stormy expression enveloping her face.

"Enough questions! Let us begin!" she'd barked, a damning trace of German accent slipping through. From that day on, much of the class had taken to calling her Professor Braun behind her back. Being an engineering major in an androgynous harem of historians, the dig went completely over my head for the first few classes. Today I decided to get to the bottom of it.

"Why do you guys call her Professor Braun?" I whispered to a cluster of history buffs. They gave me a look, an "I can't believe the types of people they let in here these days" kind of look, before one of them hissed back:

"Hitler's mistress, Eva Braun. You've never heard of her?" I shook my head. "Should I have?" A ripple of sniggers passed through the pack, attracting Professor Braun—pardon, Klein's—attention.

"Vat is going on up there? Am I not speaking clear enough when I ask you to listen quietly? I came here to be an instructor, not a babysitter." This sent a fresh wave of laughter through the group, causing Klein to scowl.

"A generation of inbreds and buffoons…" she trailed off, before pointing up to the whiteboard.

"Vas exactly vhat you have vith the Habsburg Family in the 17th century. By this point in their history, members of the family vere plagued vit issues such as enormous tongues, gastrointestinal malfunctions, diabetes, schizophrenia, epilepsy, blindness, and of course, the infamous Habsburg jaw. If you vill all turn to page one hundred and fifty-seven in your textbooks, you vill find the photo of King Charles II of Spain, largely considered the vorst example of the Habsburg's inbreeding over the centuries."

There was a mass shuffling noise, followed by a cacophony of gasps and ewws as the lecture hall all landed upon the photo of the king.

The painting was cartoonish in its grotesqueness. Charles sat in front of a black background, a pillowy cloud of grey wig hair framing his ghastly face. His lips and jaw protruded twice their normal length, his nose a misshapen hunk of pancake batter. One of his enlarged eyes veered sideways, breaking free from focus. His skin seemed to be melting right off his face. The king, for better lack of words, looked absolutely awful.

"Settle down, everyone!" Professor Klein waved, as the class erupted into a mixture of jeers and excited murmuring. "May I remind you all that royal portraits vere painted to be as *flattering as possible,* meaning Charles vas likely much vorse for vear than he is depicted here. To elaborate, might I have a volunteer to read the coronary insert at the bottom of the page?"

A few moments went by before a girl in the third row tentatively put up her hand. Klein gestured for her to begin.

"His body…ahem, sorry, his body…"

"Speak up, Joanna! Ve cannot hear you!" Klein boomed.

"His body did not contain a single drop of blood and his heart was the size of a peppercorn," projected Joanna, clearly regretting her volunteering choice. "His lungs were corroded, his intestines rotten and gangrenous. He had only a single…um, testicle, black as coal, and his head was full of water."

More excited mummers swept over the class once she had finished speaking. Professor Klein held up her hand for silence.

"Thank you, Joanna. Now, as ve vell know by now, ve cannot take everything ve read to be fact from such sources.

History is riddled vith extremists and exaggerators, as humans have always loved a good tall tale. But ve also know there is some truth to the coroner's autopsy of Charles. How can ve come to such conclusions?"

"Because there are other primary sources that verify his physical abnormalities? The coroner's autopsy is clearly heightened, but there are several other accounts describing Charles medical challenges from the same time period. They also come from people who were in close proximity to Charles in life, such as family and members of the court."

This came from one of the history buffs I'd spoken to earlier, who wore a red cashmere sweater so vivid it hurt my eyes. His hair looked like it demanded a full bottle of pomade. Maybe two. He caught me staring at him and gave me the stink eye.

"Yes, precisely, Leroy." Leroy? I thought they'd let that name die out in the 80s. My mistake. "Ve can logically assume that the coroner vas vying for some extra attention vith such a sensationalist report. And it vorked! Here ve are, reading his vords 300 years later. Isn't life funny like that."

Professor Klein paused and walked over to stand behind her desk again. She took a drink from her thermos and looked out steely into the hall.

"So. In the end, the very thing the Habsburgs had done, to keep their family in power for *centuries*, vas the crux of their downfall. Ve historians estimate around seventy to eighty percent of all marriages vere inbred. Nor vere they the only ones. This vas the norm across royal families, all across Europe, for hundreds and hundreds of years."

She paused again, letting the feel of a few seconds pass by. Imagine that multiplied to minutes, hours, days. Months. Years. Decades. Rinse, repeat. Rinse, repeat. Rinse…

"Vat the Habsburgs vanted, like most people then and now, vas power. They took it, by any means necessary. Even if it meant marrying uncle to niece, cousin to cousin, brother to sister. For hundreds of years, Habsburgs, and most other royal families, kept relationships almost entirely consanguineous. Until it eventually came to be their ruin. Now vhat do you make of this class?" Her question hung barbed and waiting in the air, like a scorpion's tail.

"That it's fucking gross," someone in the group near me muttered.

Fair. More than fair.

The lecture hall sat in suspended silence. No one knew what to make of something like that, besides it being unfathomably nasty. Someone coughed. A cellphone buzzed.

Professor Klein looked over the room, hands planted on her desk, before letting her head hang slightly. Suddenly she didn't seem so imposing and tight-assed, not the strict history professor who students had quick-labelled to be the descendant of a Nazi because of an ugly briefcase. Now Professor Klein looked tired.

I imagined being her, looking into the annals of history for a living, seeing all that we could in glaring retrospective clarity. All the wars, betrayals, rapes, struggles, rises and falls of kings, queens, ideas, movements, nations. All the suffering that brought our species to where it was today. And yes, too, the inbreeding, like a shit-stain on a map. What to make of it all?

"I think," she began finally, "that it proves one thing and one thing only. Vhen it comes to getting vhat ve vant, human beings are villing to do some horrible, unspeakable things. Perhaps ve can *never* stop doing those things. Vhy? Because there vill always be something else that ve vant. Something ve vill do whatever it takes to have. Always."

CHAPTER SIX

By March, the bowels of the earth had begun to move, extricating all that needed to go in order to make room for new life. All my girlfriends were going through a mass exodus of breakups, largely by their own hand. It was as if their own biological clocks were in sync with grander, cosmic cycles: discarding their winter suitors in favour of more promising springtime mates. It was a funny thought, if wholly inaccurate. But then again. Who's to say for sure?

"I really thought he might be the one. Y'know? I just really, really, *reallllly* wanted a win," Stephanie was snivelling, the six of us crammed into a booth. She was the lone lioness out, the only dumped in a gang of recent dumpers.

We were at Naranja's, a favourite haunt of the girls with—you guessed it—an orange theme. Each tiny booth was illuminated by an orange wheel that looked more like a UFO underbelly than sliced citrus. Or perhaps an egg yolk. Organic. Regardless, the atmosphere was quiet, the lighting dark, and the drinks, drinkable. It was our go-to place to gossip and complain about men. Coincidentally, it was also the place where I contemplated suicide the most.

"We know, sweetie, but you have to..." Yvonne mimicked a Pentecostal priest ringing two bells with the upside of her hands. "Let that that man *go!* I mean, remind me *how* long Brandon was staying at your place for, paying no rent?" We all leaned in for Steph's answer.

"4...months," she blubbered, a balloon of snot inflating from her nose. Joanna flagged down our server, a skin-and-bones gay man doing way more than what his job description called for. He sashayed over with a suspicious glint in his eyes.

"Something else I can get you ladies?" he lisped, casting a disapproving glance at the heap of used napkins. Stephanie blew heartily into the last clean one before throwing it onto the pile.

"Hi, yeah, sorry to bother you, but do you think we could get a few more napkins? Maybe a tissue box? Our friend here—" Joanna shot a look of pity Steph's way. "Is having a rough go. Bad breakup. You know how it is."

"Uh-huh. So I see."

"Yes, and could you possibly clear away these used napkins?" Genevieve added. "Our drinks should *hopefully* be out soon and there's barely any room on these tables as it is..."

In truth, the table was large enough to accommodate a full-grown Malamute and her nursing pups, but most of the empty space was claimed by elbows, purses, and Stephanie's napkin mountain. The server gave a nod, really just an irritated twitch, and left. Minutes later, he was sweeping teary napkins onto an empty tray. He wore huge, yellow cleaning gloves to do the job, with a mask of revolt to boot. As he worked, Stephanie swept a fresh napkin under her eyes to erase black tracks of mascara, utterly oblivious.

"I mean, look, I *know* what you all thought of him, but I'm telling you...Brandon was a super sweet guy! Yes, he didn't like the whole 'boyfriend/girlfriend' label or whatever, and his personal hygiene wasn't *great,* and he had a bit of a coke habit, and..."

"How could he even afford that without a job?" Anita whispered to me. I just shrugged.

"And, you're right ,Yvonne, he was too controlling about not letting me go out with you guys, but that's just because he was protective! He wanted me to be safe, which is more than I can say about..."

"Steph, I love you, but I'm going to stop you right there," Yvonne interrupted. "You're telling me you think Brandon was being protective over you, in a *healthy* way, because he would barely let you see your friends? Including brunch or movie night?"

"Well...yes," Steph replied tentatively.

"Girl, how can you say that? That man was a piece of shit, and I'm glad—"

"Wait, wait, one second, Jo. Stephanie, babe, do you really, honestly believe that? He got mad at you for coming to my birthday party. At my own apartment, for god's sake. There's nothing protective or noble about that. That's being a control freak," Yvonne said.

"Yeah, but there were other guys there, and Brandon was worried..."

"Who fucking cares? That's life. There are going to be other people, and yes, *other men,* when you go places! You should never let some guy dictate who and where you go, babe. Like, ever. This is not the Middle Ages."

"Here, here," roused Anita, toasting an ice water to the air. Our drinks were nowhere in sight, despite it being a near-empty restaurant.

"He wasn't...controlling me, or whatever," Steph defended. "He just didn't like when I'd be out late, or if he didn't know the people, or he'd get grumpy if he'd had a bad day..."

The table let out a collective groan.

"Stephanie! Do you hear yourself? This man was manipulating you! And telling you where and when you could go places! That is the *definition* of controlling," Yvonne said, exasperated. She went on.

"Not to mention, he moved into your apartment, where he didn't pay rent, didn't help with cleaning, ate up *your* food, and then left you for some random bartender chick? Like, I'm sorry. The audacity of this motherfucker. I have to agree with Jo here and say...that man was a piece of shit. And I say *was* because we're leaving his ass in the past."

"Amen to that," Joanna seconded. Stephanie just looked off, glum but silent.

"Oh yay, I see salvation!" Genevieve cried. And here came our waiter, arms trembling under the weight of six cocktails and a pitcher of blood orange sangria. He steadied himself at our table and began unloading his cargo, which was greedily snatched up.

"I have an old fashioned with a twist, a cosmo with a twist, one double strawberry daiquiri with a twist, a Long Island iced tea with a twist, a mojito with a twist, and finally...an orange thunder."

None of us—excluding Stephanie—refused to cave to Naranja's draconian drink menu, featuring exclusively orange-centric cocktails. We each insisted on ordering our own bar standards, which in turn came with a subtle "fuck you" from the bartender. An orange rind twist.

"Bon appétit, ladies," our server said, with as much sarcasm as he could muster. Nobody seemed to notice. They'd already taken their respective drinks and were gearing up for a toast. I grabbed my cosmo glass and held it aloft.

"Cheers to no more stupid men! And good skin."

A totally vapid declaration. Most of these girls—bless their hearts—would be back to their boy problems in no time. And alcohol was not the thing to be drinking in the name of good skin. Still, I put on a smile and clinked glasses with my friends.

"Cheers!"

~ ~ ~

I'd been a part of this clique for about 14 months. Yvonne and I had first met while Christmas shopping, right when I'd been growing tired of my previous friend group. It was divine timing. I'd been in this vintage boutique, shopping for a silk scarf, when Yvonne had approached me.

"I just have to say…I absolutely *love* your hair. I've never seen black hair like yours, it's so…" She'd grasped at the air, as if trying to pull a word out of it. "Luminous."

"Why, thank you," I'd replied. "You look rather luminous yourself."

That was an understatement. The woman standing in front of me was transcendently gorgeous. Knock-your-teeth-out pretty. She wore a sapphire-blue overcoat with a red lip, and dangly earrings that resembled golden waterfalls. Her gaze was sharp, piercing. Upon closer inspection, her brown eyes held gold flecks within them, two honey-soaked galaxies. It was as if a young Naomi Campbell had been anointed by Aphrodite herself, then plopped into an overpriced boutique on Main Street. And now was speaking to me.

"You're sweet," Yvonne said. "Who are you shopping for?"

"Oh, just a friend. She's obsessed with *Thelma and Louise*, so I thought I'd get her one of these silk scarves. So she can recreate that iconic look." I grabbed one from the table and showed it to her. "I've already bought her the glasses."

Yvonne had tipped her head slightly. "Prescription?"

"What? No, sunglasses. Louise doesn't wear glasses."

"I thought Velma was the one with glasses."

"Velma? Like from Scooby-Doo?"

"That's the only Velma I know," Yvonne replied, a touch haughtily. "Why does your friend want to look like her?"

I'd paused, baffled by the miscommunication. "I think we're talking about different people. My friend is obsessed with *Thelma and Louise,* like, the female Bonny and Clyde movie? You're thinking of Velma and Daphne. From the cartoon."

Yvonne snapped her fingers. "That's her name! Daphne! I knew Louise didn't sound right."

This made me laugh. I was usually in the other position, not knowing pop culture references. Now the tables had turned, if just for a moment. It felt good to be the one holding the cards.

"What's so funny?" she asked.

"I just can't believe you don't know who Thelma and Louise are. They're iconic. And Louise wears her scarf like this." I'd draped it over my head to demonstrate. "Not around the neck, like Daphne. And she's got big, cat-eye sunglasses. It's like...the look."

"Never heard of them in my life." There wasn't a drop of irony in her voice.

"Wow. Usually I'm the one who's in the dark about this kind of stuff."

Yvonne had smiled. "Well, I find that hard to believe. You've got a look to you."

"Do I? What kind of look?"

"It's your eyes. They're very intense. You've definitely seen some shit, which means you know some shit, too. I can always tell about these things." Yvonne had then quieted, suddenly serious. "You know, I'm actually a bit psychic. It runs on my father's side."

I'd smiled back, thinking nice thoughts, aggressively.

"Oh yeah? That's cool. I can definitely see that for you. Are you and your dad pretty close?" Yvonne readjusted her purse on her shoulder.

"Well, we were. When I was a kid I was like his shadow, always close by. He definitely spoiled me a bit too, compared to my sisters. They're both older and…" She caught herself mid-sentence and blinked forcefully, giving her head a little shake. "I'm sorry, I don't know why I'm telling you this. I don't even know your name—"

"Dahlia," I said, extending a red-gloved hand. "And don't you worry. I'm the one who asked."

She'd smiled again, guiltily. As if she'd been caught doing something she wasn't supposed to. "I'm Yvonne. It's very nice to meet you." She looked over my shoulder, eyebrows raised. "And where do I pay for my therapy session, Dr. Dahlia?"

She laughed, a little too heavily, at her own joke. I joined in.

"Oh, you can settle up with my receptionist Beth-Ann over there." I'd pointed to the grizzled woman running the cash register. She looked like she belonged in hospice, not in retail.

Yvonne had kept chuckling. "Beth-Ann…god, what a stupid name for a receptionist. I like you, Dahlia, you're fun. Do you live around here on Main, or…"

"No, no. I live over on the North Shore. Gleneagles? It's close to Horseshoe Bay." Yvonne's eyes had widened.

"Oh, damn, you're out in the boujee area. Alright. I see you."

"What can I say? Those therapist checks pack a punch."

"Ha ha, I bet they do. Say, would you like to grab a coffee sometime? It's so hard to meet good people in this city. New ones, at least. I've got a solid friend group but they're mostly girls I've known since school. I'm trying to branch out, network and all that shit."

"I know what you mean. People here can be strange."

"Right? I don't get it. Like would it kill you to say hi or smile or something? It's weird."

I actually had no clue what she had meant. My experience with people could not have been more different. But I'd nodded in agreement.

"You're so right, Yvonne. It really is weird."

We had exchanged numbers, or rather, I'd put my digits into her cell. When she asked why I didn't have a mobile phone, I'd lied and told her I'd forgotten it at home.

"The battery..." I'd trailed off. She held up her hand in solidarity.

"Ugh, I feel you. This stupid thing is always dying on me. I need to get a new one pretty soon, maybe one of those touchscreen styles? They look pretty cool." She looked at her watch and cursed. "Fuck, I need to get going. I'm meeting someone for drinks later and I need time to freshen up beforehand."

Yvonne looked ready to walk New York Fashion Week, or maybe win *Project Runway*. I couldn't have imagined what more she could do to look any better.

"Better hop to it, then," I'd said, at a loss. "Give me a call sometime and we can hang out. Good luck with your first date." I'd given her a small wave, and went back to my scarf-shopping. She was almost out the door when she'd stopped and turned.

"Hey, Dahlia. How'd you know it was a first date?" she'd asked. I'd flashed my teeth.

"Lucky guess," I said. "Or maybe I'm a little psychic, too."

She'd let out a final laugh, and disappeared onto the busy street. 2 months later, she was introducing me to all her friends as her *"new* best friend". I'd quickly assimilated into their group. Around the same time, I had cut all contact with the clique of friends I'd been hanging out with for the previous year. Nothing personal. I just couldn't stand being bored.

~ ~ ~

Now, as I sat in the booth at Naranja's, listening to the girls spill about their recent breakups, I could feel the old feeling creeping back. The boredom. It was a routine that was wearing out its welcome. Part of the reason I was so attracted to Yvonne and her clique was that they all seemed like man-eaters. They stalked, scored, and skedaddled, man after man after man. They weren't ashamed. They ordered first and finished last. Except for Stephanie, the sole weak link, they always came out on top, no matter how messy the entanglement got.

It had been thrilling to gather with them, at Naranja's, Venables, or one of the girl's apartments; listening to them spin a fresh tale of melodrama that was dating in this age. We'd laugh and mock the appropriate targets—the ex-man, cheating side piece, the domineering parent, irritating house pet—before moving on to the next story. Then we'd get wasted, and go find some new meat. It was a blast. At first.

While Genevieve droned on and on about Jason and his erectile dysfunctions (who knew you could have more than one?) I could feel myself nodding off. Like all new things, the shine had dulled. The novelty of this social circle was undeniably waning. Pretty soon, I would need to move on. I picked up my third cosmo and drained it dry.

"Dahlia? What about you?" Joanna asked expectingly. Genevieve had finished dishing about Jason, who was officially old news. My turn.

"Oh, nothing. I've been in a bit of a dry patch recently," I confessed. It was true. All my motivation for casual flings had evaporated, as quickly as it had come on. The fever's been cured, doctor! I sucked on my orange twist and thought about silence.

"Really? Nothing at all? You were on a roll for a while there—"

"Well, now I'm not," I replied, a bit stronger than I intended. I cleared my throat. "I don't know, I just feel like maybe...like maybe that time is wrapping up. I'd like something more long-term. Concrete. Everything has its season, right?" I reached for my glass, immediately regretting that I'd finished it off. Where was that grouchy server?

The girls looked at me like I'd just endorsed bestiality.

"Babe, you can't be serious," Genevieve said. "You're what, 24? You're young, you've got your own place, all the time in the world..."

"And you're gorgeous," Stephanie chimed in.

"Well yeah, obviously, but what I'm saying is...you've got everything going for you right now, Dahlia. This is the time to enjoy that, live it up! Not get hitched by some man who won't appreciate you—"

"They never do!" Anita chirped.

"—or try to put you under his thumb or whatever. Absolutely not. We're not going to let you bow out now." Genevieve was finishing her degree in political science. I guffawed at the idea of her in government if that was the best argument she could muster.

"Listen," I began, "I hear you, and I appreciate you, all of you, but I—"

"You know what we need?" Yvonne said, cutting me off. She gave me a wicked look. "I think we need to change the vibe. Enough of this talk about relationships and have-nots. We need..." She paused for dramatic effect. I rolled my eyes, internally. "Fresh blood."

The girls cackled and squealed with delight. In a flurry, they were collectively flagging down our waiter. Skinny Gay begrudgingly went to print off the bills before it was one last trip to the bathroom, coats, and then out into the streets. 10-minute turnaround.

As I stood with Anita and Yvonne outside, waiting for the rest of the group to come out from the bathroom, Yvonne turned to me and pulled at the front of my jacket.

"You doing okay, honey? You seem kinda off today." Her breath smelled like fresh lime and old mint.

"Yeah, of course. I'm good."

"You sure? What was up with that comment back there, then?"

"What comment?" I asked, playing dumb. She steeled her gaze.

"You know which one. Seriously. Did something happen recently, or—"

"No, no, nothing like that. I just…"

I blew out air.

"I've been feeling a bit…a bit…"

"A bit what? Spit it out."

"A bit bored," I said, defeated. Normally I didn't like sharing my true feelings. I kept those tight to my chest. Out of instinct. Out of necessity. I regretted my lenience for secrecy the moment I saw Yvonne's face.

"Bored? How the hell could you be bored? You have, like…everything." She sounded genuinely hurt.

"Yeah, if I had as much money and freedom as you do, I don't think I'd ever be sad again," Anita said, standing off to the side with a cigarette. She took a drag, looking precarious with her puffer jacket and high heels. I gave her a look.

"It's not as simple as that," I said plainly.

"Isn't it? What more could you want? Like, actually…"

"Well, for one thing, a family would be nice. Someone to share life with. A career," I retorted. The sting of three cosmos had sharpened my tongue.

"You do have a family, D! You've got us. And you'll find a…a partner or husband or whatever, but you've got lots of time. What's with the rush all of a sudden?" Yvonne said.

"Yeah, and fuck a career. You never need to work in your life if you don't want to. You can do anything! Go traveling! Who cares!" Anita took another huff, her words steadily becoming more slurred by the minute. "Do you know what I'd do to have that? What most people would do for freedom like that?"

"Okay, okay, I get it! I'm sorry I said anything." I rubbed the centre of my forehead, feeling irritated. At this point, I was ready to just go home.

"Babe, you don't have to be sorry for anything! We just care about you and…well, we want you to recognize what you have. You've got the world, baby girl," Yvonne said, giving my shoulders a squeeze. A creeping of a smile betrayed my mouth.

"Exactly! That's why you don't need some man coming along and fucking things up," Anita said from behind her.

"Ugh, yes, you guys are right," I said, in a tone almost akin to surrender. "Sorry for being such a suck."

"Enough! You are nothing of the sort," Yvonne said, decidedly. She had a way of speaking in which every word sounded like absolute truth. It was one of my favourite things about her. Besides her magical, golden-flecked eyes.

"What are you three hussies doing out here?" Genevieve interrupted, Stephanie and Joanna hot on her tail. "You talking shit?"

"Oh, yes," Yvonne said. "We were just saying that you should get your lips redone. They're looking a little skimpy."

Genevieve slapped her shoulder with her clutch.

"Bitch." She smirked.

"Okay, ladies, what's the move? Should we head down to Gastown or hit Granville?"

"Well, it's Thursday, so Granville would probably be busier. We could try The Pearl?

"Ugh, gross. Some rando grabbed my ass there a couple weeks ago," Joanna said, crinkling her nose. "And the music there sucks."

"Okay, how about Odyssey? They've got good music?" Yvonne countered.

"I'm good with that."

"Yeah, same here. And it's close enough to walk to."

"True. Thank God—"

"And Mary and Joseph."

"—it's not raining."

"Amen, mamacitas!" Genevieve shrieked.

And with that, we were off.

~ ~ ~

The Odyssey was just warming up for the night. A tinge of pink and teal light leaked out of the stained-glass windows, paned to look like different figures. There was a Cyclops, Scylla, Siren, et. cetera, each representing different characters from the actual story. Of course, there wasn't much of a budget for these things, so the windows were pretty crude. The Cyclops looked more like a bulldog, while the Siren just looked like Pamela Anderson wearing a toga after a long weekend bender. None of it really screamed Ancient Greece.

Still, "*it's thought that counts*" and all that. Whatever you silly people say.

"There's no line. I can't tell if that's a good thing or a bad thing."

Yvonne checked her watch. "It's past 10, so we should be fine. If it's not picked up in half an hour, we can leave." The joys of having a confident leader.

We did not need to have our IDs checked, or pay cover. One of the girls (definitely Genevieve) had slept with the bouncer: a swollen, butt-chinned jock with long eyelashes and an even longer penis. Allegedly. Genevieve was known for her poor spatial estimates and love of hyperbole, so I took this with a grain of salt. Besides, not my type. He looked like he would fuck like a Chihuahua humping a jackhammer. Gross.

"How're you ladies doing tonight? Y'all looking fine as hell," he marvelled, pursing his lips. One by one, the girls filed past him and into the club. I brought myself to full attention and held my head up. When it was my turn to pass, his eyes widened ever so slightly. I noticed they were both different colours, and immediately I felt a pang for Mango.

"Woah," he muttered, inaudibly to everyone but me.

"Hi there," I smiled. "Have a good rest of the night."

"Uh, yeah, you too," he practically stuttered. And I was in, walking to coat check. Anita came up from behind me, grabbing my hand and laughing.

"Jesus, Dahlia, at least wait until we get inside before you start flirting with people," she said teasingly. I laughed back.

"I wasn't! It's called being nice. You should try it sometime."

"Mhm. Sure."

"Ladies! Pass me your jackets. I've already got all our coat check tickets with me. Then only one of us has to worry about them," Yvonne announced, her voice crisp and bright as clean air. "I have to pee, so hurry up!"

"That's why you should have gone at the restaurant!" I told you—"

"Yes, yes, and I'll be sure to listen next time. Just hurry up. I want to get us a spot in the corner."

"Yes, I know, we're hurrying."

From the inside, the club was decorated with faux marble pillars and a ceiling of fake ferns. All the servers wore white cloth of various wraps and fashions, clinging scantily to their naked bodies. The building heat was permanently turned up, so everyone inside—whether they were dancing or stationary—was anointed with a veneer of sweat. Every 15 minutes, six automatic sprayers issued a puff of "Mediterranean Jasmine" over the sticky bodies, masking the scent. I knew what it was called because I'd found the exact smell at a homeware store, sold in a metal can and advertised for *Bathroom Use Only.* The club owners must have needed to dump a new can into their misting machines at the end of each night, judging by how often those things went off. On the plus side though, it made the lights look cool. Jasmine fog and lasers.

"You grab us a spot. I need to find a bathroom, stat." Yvonne waved a hand over her face and coughed. "Ack, I forgot it takes a sec to adjust to the smell. Lord, that is powerful."

"Fucking noxious."

"Do you want us to order you a drink?" Joanna asked.

"Yes, please. Tequila sunrise. Double. Dahlia, come with me?" Yvonne extended a hand.

I took it, giving it a squeeze. "Of course." I turned back to the girls. "We'll be back in just a moment. Order me a cosmo, and if they're out, get me a dark and stormy."

"You got it. We'll be just over there. See you soon, loves." Genevieve blew us a kiss and we all parted ways: me with Yvonne and the rest to the table. Yvonne led the way, expertly parting the way through the crowd. Overhead, the music was pounding, heavy and black like molasses. The air was thick with humidity and toilet spray. And the subjacent sweat. Couldn't forget the sweat.

The girls bathrooms were at the back of the club and down a flight of stairs. Each step had been individually lit up, alternating between blue, white, and amber. Cut into the wall of the stairs, three different inserts of a papier-mâché statuette were displayed, each of the statue of David.

"Do you think they know that he's Italian, not Greek?" Yvonne asked, looking back at me with a smile. She had finally let go of my hand, now that we were descending the steep stairs. Not that I would've minded holding on to her.

"Definitely not. I don't think they even know he's David."

Yvonne laughed.

"I can't believe they put the men's bathroom on the main floor, and the women's in the basement. It's barbaric. Men's world 'til the end," she grumbled, reaching the bottom stair after sidestepping the whole way down. She turned and helped me down the last two steps.

"Love that dress on you. Where'd you get it?"

"Oh. It was my mom's."

"Oh, I see. Well, it's beautiful. She had great taste." Yvonne's face was serene, sincere. It was just the two of us in the basement hallway. We stepped into the bathroom—semi-private—and I locked the door behind us.

~ ~ ~

"Do you miss her?" Yvonne asks gently, hiking up her skirt to sit down on the toilet seat. A second later, a formidable stream blasts the bowl. "Fuck, I really had to go. Too much of that nasty sangria."

"Right? Like how do you screw up wine and juice."

"Seriously. It's child play." She sighs deeply, relaxing her body into a slouch. "Anyways. Back to you. Can I ask how you like…feel about all that? I couldn't even—"

"Yvonne, babe, I love you but…I'm really not in the mood to talk about that right now." I gesture to the darkened bathroom, my body, anything. A magician waving his hand over reality before performing a trick. Nothing to see, nothing to see…

"Right. Yeah, sorry, sweets. My bad. Let's talk about something else."

She stands and flushes, strides over to the water basin. I walk over and stand beside her, leaning against the paper towel dispenser. She stares deeply into the mirror, a silver circle encircled with golden Grecian tile. Fluffs her hair and tips her head back.

"Am I starting to get a bit of a double chin?" she asks.

"What? Are you kidding? You?"

"Yes me, Dahlia. Who else is here?"

"Of course not," I say. "You're perfect. You look beautiful."

Yvonne smiles. "Well, you look beautiful too. As always."

We lock eyes. Rushing tap water fills the room.

~ ~ ~

20 minutes later, we were both braving the climb back up the stairs. We wove our way through the increasingly busy club, fingers interlocked. As promised, the girls were waiting at a high-top table in the far corner. No one commented on the length of time we were gone.

"Hey, babes! So Nico over there…" Genevieve waved at a 50-something-year-old man at a nearby high-top. "Bought us a free bottle of bubbly, isn't that sweet? They're just grabbing some glasses at the back."

"It's not free if someone had to pay money for it, Genevieve," Yvonne shouted back, grinning. She plopped down on a free seat, her shoulders loose and low. I squeezed in to sit beside her.

"Oh, you know what I mean. These are your bevvies, by the way. Dahlia, I'm sorry, but they don't make cosmos here. So I got you a dark and stormy. Double."

"Thanks, love." I picked up my copper cup and surveyed the room.

There were far more people than an average Thursday. Tourists? No, that couldn't be right. No one foreign showed up until spring. Otherwise there was nothing to see but grey skies and black water.

"For you, ladies!" A bartender materialized by the table, carrying six champagne flutes in one hand and a bottle of Dom Pérignon in the other. He scattered the glasses around the table, and twisted off the cork of the bottle. Disappointingly, only a faint hiss and poof of foam occurred; no canonic cork bang, shooting haphazardly into the club and blinding a dancer or two. What a shame.

"Oh, I'll take a bit more than that, please," I spoke-yelled into his ear when he stopped pouring a quarter way of my glass. The music made it hard to talk and even harder to hear.

"Oh, but Pérignon likes a little breathing room, and—"

"She said she'll take some more!" Yvonne trumpeted, pushing the butt of the bottle up with her finger. Another two quarters of champagne tumbled out the spout.

The bartender looked startled but said no more, begrudgingly filling the other five glasses with generous pours. He bowed his head slightly, cradling the empty bottle, and vanished.

"Weirdo," Yvonne mouthed, squeezing my leg.

"Cheeeeers, bitches!" Genevieve sang out. Six flutes of crystal—definitely not for normal patron use—clinked together to produce a disjointed, resonant sound.

"To us!"

"To us!" we echoed vainly, and took a swig.

I'd blame the cosmos, since they couldn't fight back. They had to accept the blame without argument. Those pink devils had tampered with my motor skills and rendered me sloppy. See, this was why I didn't drink. I only needed to remember the slapstick theatrics of my dead mother to have more than enough reason not to. She, at least, had the charm and good graces to pull off the whole clown bit. I couldn't afford such slovenliness. I was better than that.

Regardless. With the arm power of a recent orgasm and three sturdy cosmopolitans, I brought the champagne flute to my lips with twice-needed vigour. There was a crack as it whacked against my front teeth—thankfully not splintering them—and poured much of the two-hundred-and-fifty-dollar mixture down the front of my chest. My sea foam green dress was doused. Despite feeling a cold wetness creep across my body, I still kept on drinking.

"Oh my god, D! Your dress!"

I polished off the rest of my glass and looked down. Yup, there was the rest of it. It looked like a bird had shit yellow liquid all over my chest. Very unattractive. I laughed.

"Oops," I said coolly. I really couldn't care less. I grabbed a flimsy bar napkin from the table and started dabbing half-heartedly. I already knew what was to come.

"Oh no, babe!"

"Honey!"

"Dahlia, what happened!"

"Napkins! We need napkins!"

"Really, everyone, it's fine," I said, loud enough to breach the music. "It's just champagne."

“We need to get you some water. We should go back to the bathroom, try to wash it out. Otherwise it’ll leave a stain,” Yvonne said, concern in her eyes. I shook my head.

“Oh, baby! Are you feeling alright?” Stephanie cooed, her own woes momentarily forgotten.

I was feeling fine. Great, actually. I had reached a point in the night where my senses, normally so fine-tuned they sometimes terrorized me, had become pleasantly dulled. I was starting to feel nice and stupid. Suddenly, everything seemed so much easier. I definitely wasn’t thinking about killing myself now.

“It’s. Fine. I’ve got a million more dresses at home.” I waved to no one in particular. The same bartender reappeared beside me, this time bearing a stack of bar napkins and looking triumphant. I grabbed his arm gently and leaned over close to his ear.

“If I was a different girl, I’d tell you to wipe that smirk off your fucking face.” I leaned back and plucked the napkins out of his hands.

The bartender looked positively stunned. I beamed.

“Thank you so much!” I tittered, as Yvonne started to aggressively blot at my dress with napkins. “I’m so sorry for being so clumsy…I should’ve listened to you with the whole ‘breathing room’ thing. I’ll know for next time, right?” A big saucy wink, flicked his way.

“Um, yeah. Sure,” he muttered, before turning tail and disappearing into the crowd. He never came to our table again.

“I really need some water here…it would make this a lot easier,” Yvonne huffed.

“Yvonne, you’re making this a bigger deal than it is. Relax. It’s just champagne.”

“But your mother’s dress—”

“I said relax.”

She reluctantly conceded.

I let out a sigh and rolled my shoulders. I was letting my guard down a bit too much. Aggression was not a good look, not for this version of Dahlia. These girls knew me as a very particular kind of person. Sweet, agreeable, insatiable. Only one of these things was actually true.

"Sorry everyone. I didn't mean to change the vibe," I said loudly, infusing my words with subduing power. They took effect almost immediately.

"It's fine!"

"Yes, you're good!"

"Don't you worry, D, you didn't do anything wrong."

"Yeah, I'm just sorry 'bout your dress."

Even Yvonne had given up dabbing me with those paltry little napkins. I turned my attention back to my dark and stormy, burying my gaze into the depths of the cup.

"Should we go dancing?" Anita suggested.

"Yes, hold on a sec. Let me just finish my drink."

"Okay, well, chug it! I wanna move."

"Wait a minute. I think I know him."

"What? Who?"

"Him. From my history course."

"Where?"

"Over there. The tall one."

"Oh, shit."

"Jesus."

"I know, right? It's unsettling. Like what were his parents feeding him…"

The girl's comments float past me, unnoticed, until the last few. The ice at the bottom of my drink seemed to have transported into the pits of my stomach. I put the copper cup down and turned around to where they were looking.

The Odyssey had filled itself up with drunken bodies and bad decisions. The coloured light display of lasers and strobes were whirling to attention, puncturing the jasmine haze that hung above everybody's heads. Except one. There, standing by the entranceway in the sole pocket of normal light, was Jack.

CHAPTER SEVEN

A prickling. A scorch of blue burning traversing my skin. I jerked my head up from where I'd been looking—the floor, sticky with spillage—and looked around. Nothing but poor dancers and plastic plants. I shook my head, unsettled, and turned to where my friends should've been.

Li's friends, I should specify. No, almost. Li's *brother's* friends. Two zit-riddled nerds fresh out of grade school. One of them, Danny, had the biggest overbite I'd ever seen. Or perhaps the smallest underbite. I guess it depended on how you looked at it.

At the moment, Li was haggling with the bouncers outside. Her voice, stridently demanding a long-dead "birthday discount", carried all the way up the stairs and through the entranceway. Not even Justin Timberlake's "SexyBack", remixed beyond recognition, could drown her out.

"I'm telling you! I've been coming here for years, and they always honour a two-for-one on birthdays!"

"And I'm telling *you* that The Odyssey hasn't had any sort of birthday promo in over a decade," the bouncer insisted.

"For fuck's sake, that is simply not true. I celebrate all my birthdays here, and my friends' birthdays, and..." All of this was a load of hogwash. Li despised going out clubbing and had only been persuaded by her brother to come out tonight because it was his 19th birthday. His first-time drinking. And also that she would get free booze if she came.

"Lady, if you're going to use that kind of language, I'm going to have to ask you to go."

"What! Are you fu—"

"Hey, hey, no we're cool, we're cool! Li, *please* just give the guy the ten bucks. We want to go here, it looks so dope!" This came from Li's brother, Dung. His name meant "brave and heroic" in the Vietnamese tongue, a fine combo. The problem was that neither Li nor her family spoke Vietnamese. They'd all grown up here in Canada, speaking English. Her parents just didn't know how to name their kids, or perhaps they didn't care. Probably the latter. Li Li and Dung Li. And the recently christened Gladys Li, their baby sister. It was a fucking mess.

There was a kerfuffling sound as Li obliged with the ten-dollar cover. Next thing I knew, the four of them were tromping up the four stairs and through the entranceway. Li looked spitting mad, the three boys: euphoric.

"Fucking scammers. All of them," she huffed on her way to the coat check.

"Li, dude, he was just doing his job…" I began.

"Holy shit! This place is crazy!" Danny exclaimed.

"Damn, look at all the lights! And those columns. So sick!"

"Do you think we'll meet some hot chicks here?" Noah asked, his voice pitching and rolling like a whiny schooner. He began digging through his front pocket, before slapping all over his pants.

"The fuck you doing, Noah? You got ants in your pants?" Dung asked.

“I’m looking for my chapstick. In case I kiss someone. Do you guys have one?”

“Why bother? I’ve got something you can kiss right here,” Dung said, grabbing his crotch and splitting into hysterics with Danny. Teen boys and their love for cheap humour. You could put a top-hat on a turd and they would die from laughter.

“Christ, you guys. You’re technically adults now, so fucking act like it,” Li snapped. It was clear that letting her pregame a whole six-pack of seltzers had been a mistake. I’d forgotten how quick her fuse became after drinking gin.

“Oh, relax, Li. We’re just having fun.”

“Yeah, chill out.”

Noah stayed silent.

After a lengthy coat check, we all made our way to the bar. What I hated most about clubs was the crowd. The sensation of greasy strangers pressed up against me made my skin crawl. To make matters worse, everyone was also prone to staring at me. In such heightened, tight proximity, I felt more alienated than ever. The gyrating hips, beady eyes, bursts of laughter. Close-knit friend groups. Couples. All happening at shoulder height. Everyone looked so small and seemed so happy.

“This place smells weird,” Li announced, leaning against the bar-wood. The bartender could clearly see us—or at least, see me—but made no effort to come our way. He was busy making eyes with a pair of blondes on the far end as he polished glasses.

“Hey, buddy! You going to do your job or what?” Li shouted. The music had switched to Destiny’s Child, mounted over a jungle-like beat. My head ached.

“Li, please, you’re going to get us kicked out,” Dung begged.

"I am not. You've never even *been* to a club. You have to be assertive. Otherwise these assholes will walk all over you."

"Whatever you say," was Dung's response. Li narrowed her eyes and then went back to harassing the bartender.

At long last, the bartender moseyed over, white toga swaying.

"Whadayawant," he asked. He clearly was a fitness freak, by the way he filled out his costume. Two angry nipples protruded through the cloth like accusations.

"*Finally.* I'll take a tall gin and tonic, double, and Jack here will take a Corona. Right, Jack?" She whipped her head back. I just shrugged.

"Uh, sure." Alcohol was alcohol.

"What do you three want?" she said, turning her attention to the boys.

"Um, I guess...gee, I don't know. Maybe a tequila shot? Or wait, maybe later, how 'bout..."

"Are you going to order or not? Holy fuck." Li was practically foaming at the mouth with irritation by now. It'd been a steady crescendo since I'd met the four of them at Li's place for pre-drinks and cabbed here. I hadn't seen her anger reach such a pitch. But then again, I hadn't ever seen her with her own blood family. Only stories. The whole situation was making me nauseous.

"Fine, jeez. I'll just get...a gin and tonic."

"Me two."

"Me three."

"Sheep," Li said cuttingly, before stepping aside to let Dung pay for his own birthday drinks. I scanned the room, looking for a way out. A faint, smelly haze was suspended about people's heads, which meant I was directly thrust inside it. I coughed. It smelled like boiled flower heads.

"We should go dancing," Danny proclaimed, once all of us had a drink in hand. The three of them sipped their gin and tonics slowly, trying desperately not to make a face.

Li rolled her eyes and pointed to the far corner by the stained-glass windows. A string of high-top tables, all occupied by jocular, handsome faces, passed by as we walked over. Several people gave a look of disapproval at the rag-tag crew I'd aligned myself with. It was obvious we did not belong here.

"What is it, Li?" Dung asked, once we were squeezed off to the side like castaways. The music was marginally quieter here, really just a heavy rumbling.

"Nothing. I just wanted to be somewhere we can drink without getting trampled. Is that okay?" she stung.

"Yeah, of course. Obvi," Dung said. He looked down into his glass wistfully.

"Hey, we forgot to cheers," I said, trying to lighten the mood. I extended my beer. "Happy Birthday, Dung. Congrats on being a full-blown adult."

"Yeah, cheers, Dung. Happy birthday." We bumped glasses.

Dung smiled up at me. "Thanks, man. I'm glad Li asked you to come."

"Yeah," I lied. "Me too."

The past month or so, I'd been filling in for Allan as Li's placeholder friend. After learning what had happened to Henry after the party, Allan had slowly dwindled into obscurity. He had always been prone to guilt-fits, and this was easily the worst of them. Evidently, the kicker had come from a visit to Henry's home, where Allan had lied and told the mourning family they'd been friends. I don't know how the hell he found them, but I do know what it did to Allan. On the last time the three of us hung out, he'd told us what he'd seen. Henry was confined to the four walls of his house, where he was being taken care of by his mother. She'd quit her job to look after him.

"You should have seen his face," Allan told us, his own expression haggard and limp. "His eyes were all bugged out and darting around. And he could only speak in a sort of gibberish. Like all grunts and moans and stuff. The whole time I was there, he kept swatting at nothing, like there were fucking bugs flying around him. His mom said the doctors think it's schizo. Apparently some drugs can trigger it to happen and it never goes away. Ever."

3 weeks after he told us, Allan withdrew from all his courses at UBC. Neither Li nor I ever saw him again. The university put out flyers warning illicit drug use. Life went on.

As a result, I had taken Allan's place as Li's primary friend. And chew toy. Her aimless aggression found a home in me, as well as demands to go to different parties or events with her. I quickly learned that despite her prickly exterior, Li had a crippling fear: being alone.

~ ~ ~

"So…are we just going to stand here all night or can we go dancing?" Noah asked, emboldened by the liquor in his veins. The three of them had been sucking at empty glasses—second round—for a few minutes, not saying much. Li seemed to hold power over what everyone did and didn't do. Including me, I shamefully realized.

"Ugh, fine. Yes. Let's go dance," she grumbled, depositing her empty glass on the floor. Dung, Danny and Noah followed suit, not knowing better.

With much awkwardness, the five of us squeezed our way to the dance floor, which was already colonized to the limit. The overwhelming aroma of body odour and artificial floras became stronger the closer we got, as did the music. Whoever was DJ'ing had switched to their own mix: a disharmonious concoction of squealing horns, metal whines, and ear-shredding bass. It felt like a sonic stake being driven right through the skull.

I, however, seemed to be the only one bothered. People were shaking and moving, spilling drinks, making out. The three boys whooped with overstimulated pleasure. Even Li was drunkenly bobbing her head, eyes closed.

For me: near-paralysis. I felt ridiculous—practically stone-sober—trying to move with the crowd. Every movement of my body seemed artificial, every attempt at enjoyment a failure. The nausea had leaked into my bloodstream and was spreading rapidly.

"Fucking move, dumbass, or get off the floor," someone beside me yelled, after bumping into my static body for the second time. A couple people looked over (and up) to give me a look of repulsion. A six-foot-seven pariah on the dance floor.

"I need some air!" I shouted to my group. Nobody heard or reacted. I tapped Li's shoulder, whose eyes flew open.

"I'm going outside for some air!" I repeated, gesturing to the club's entranceway.

"Whatever! I'm not your mother, Jack! Go ahead!" she yelled back dismissively. I slunk off by myself, hitting my head on a low-hanging fern on the way out.

"You can't take that outside with you," said the bouncer, seeing my half-empty Corona as I descended the stairs. I brought the neck to my lips and chugged it away, then threw it in a garbage can by the base of the stairs. When I walked past him, he muttered:

"Glass goes in the recycling, bigfoot."

He was looking the other way by the time I turned at his comment.

~ ~ ~

The city air had never tasted so sweet. It had begun to drizzle rain, and the streets were congested with taxis and anxious drivers. Swarms of people passed by, most of them dressed decadently for their night out, their laughter sharp and frequent.

The rest were wrapped in tattered clothing. There was an enormous population of street people in the downtown area, from backbreaking rent prices and drug addiction. It was a rarity to not see someone tweaking on crystal meth, or slumped cold in a doorway from opiates. Most of the street people were harmless. Cursed by misfortune. All of them were suffering.

It was the main reason I found it hard to come downtown. It made me sick to see the division of wealth so brutally at play. Some of the richest individuals on the planet lived in this city, shitting in their seventeen-bathroom homes with six vehicles and an underground pool. Turning a blind eye to the mess they refused to fix, despite having the power to do so.

You could always spot the type right away. They barely looked at you, wore clothes that weren't flashy but retailed at five hundred dollars a shirt. They laughed only amongst each other. Everyone else got glowers or disapproving glances, for existing in their line of sight. They were always eating at expensive restaurants and finishing half their plate. They honked, relentlessly. If they drove at all. And a cloud of cologne, or perfume, would follow them everywhere, enveloping their bodies like guilt. Because they knew. Because they saw.

On the other side of things were the street people. Living in plain sight, if you could even call it living. Most of them were missing teeth, or clumps of hair. Sometimes a limb. Their belongings were confined to a ratty backpack or blue Walmart bags. Or a grocery cart, which they'd push around hopelessly, rusty wheels screeching.

The worst of it took place on the downtown East Side, where entire city blocks had been transformed into tent cities, spilling over the sidewalks amongst the garbage. There was often talk amongst the higher-ups on what was to be done about the city's "homeless problem". This was always said in the same tone of voice reserved for pest infestations or a stubborn STI. Of course, nothing ever *was* done, except relocating them and complaining about their appearance. The ugliness of their existence. Thousands of people lived like this, with the number ever-increasing. It felt sick to see it, but worse to think about it. This city was only a tiny fragment of the world. A piece of a much larger, uglier puzzle.

Near where I stood under the eaves of The Odyssey, there was a group of street people huddled atop wet cardboard. They were wrapped in blankets, while one was smoking a cigarette. A mongrel dog slept dreamlessly at their feet.

I dug through my back pocket and strode over, five-dollar bill in hand.

"Excuse me," I said. I never knew what to say in these moments. How to express my sorrow. Or want for assistance, but inability to do so. A five-dollar bill was nothing.

I held it out and smiled. One of the people, a middle-aged woman with a black eye, took it without a word. Her face was riddled with red spots. I began to walk back to The Odyssey, but then turned around.

"I'm so sorry to ask, but could I…bum one of your smokes? I think I have a dollar on me somewhere…" I started to pat at my front pockets when the man smoking waved his hand.

"Don't worry 'bout it. Here. Enjoy." He let out a shuddery laugh, scarred with smoke. He pulled a pack from his jacket and shook out a single Belmont, before holding it up to me like an unlit torch. I took it gratefully.

"Thanks. I don't normally smoke, but..."

"And don't you start! Nasty habit." He coughed, eyes gleaming. "But if you're going to do it, gotta do it right. Only Belmonts for me. They're the best."

"Don't I know it," I replied. My grandpa had sworn by Belmonts in his final years, after smoking Camels for all his life. He had brought them to the hole in his throat with glee.

"How have I *ever* lived without these?" Grandpa had marvelled. In the end, he didn't.

I thanked the man again and walked back to the eaves covering of The Odyssey. I was just about to light up when I realized: I had no fire. Cursing myself, I prepared to approach the group again when a woman's voice came from beside me.

"Hey, could I have one of those things?" she asked. I turned to look at her and had to catch my jaw from dropping, lest it send the cigarette flying to the gutter from my gaping mouth. I was unprepared for such a sight.

The woman standing before me looked like a painting. Not something you'd find in today's museums of modern monkeycrap. And definitely not in a kid's classroom, unless a young Michelangelo was in attendance. I mean *art*. Living, breathing, staring up at me. She had abundant black hair that seemed galvanically alive, an entity onto itself. Her lips were full and swollen, like ripe stone fruit that had been split open by a tongue. Skin the shade of summer. She was taller, around five-foot-eight or nine, coming up past my chest. But there was something about her that seemed...larger. An extension of being invisible to the naked eye.

She was staring at me in the most peculiar way, with sea-coloured irises composed of harsh greens and blues. I felt looked-over, examined. A specimen under a microscope. I cleared my throat and turned away.

"Um, sorry, but, it's not mine. I bummed one from them." I jerked my thumb in the direction of the street people huddled on the sidewalk, keeping my eyes firmly on the road in front of me. I could feel the woman's gaze boring into the side of my face. I felt the urge to scream at her. To tell her to look away. Stop fucking staring. I clenched my jaw and said nothing.

Suddenly, she obliged. I could feel her gaze slide off my body and elsewhere.

There was a subtle release of pressure, which seemed insane. Surely a person's eyes couldn't be strong enough to inflict *actual* sensation? That was just a myth. A hiccup of the synapses perceiving attention. Our gaze-detection system, I remembered it being called from a psychology book. Nothing more, nothing less.

The woman beside me let out a sigh. I snuck another glance at her, as if to verify her existence. Not a trick of the light, are you? When I looked a second time, she seemed different. Less intimidating, but just as beautiful. The feeling of something bigger had vanished.

"Sorry," I apologized, turning back to face her. I ran my hand through my chopped hair. "That was kind of rude. I'm just having a shitty night." I thought for a brief moment. "Here," I mumbled, offering my unlit cigarette. "You can have this one. I don't even really smoke. I just…"

"Felt like you needed one?" she finished. Her voice had a lyrical quality to it, like rainfall on smooth stone. Or an underwater harp. "Yeah, I get that. Something about drinking alcohol always makes me crave it. I don't even really smoke, either."

She was smiling now, but so slightly it was hard to tell. Maybe it was just her mouth shape. She held it open a sliver, enough that I could see the glisten of saliva on her inner lips.

"Yeah, exactly. Like what are they putting in booze these days?"

"What are they putting in *anything* these days?"

A reasonable retort to my stupid question.

"You're right. I hate living in a time when everything feels like a lie. Everything that's sold to you is *actually* something else. Nothing's true anymore. There's always a scam or some dark side to shit. Fast food made out of plastic. Children mining for diamonds just so people can get married. Or all those side effects from pills and stuff. At least with these—" I held up the cigarette. "There's some authenticity. They tell you it's bad and we know it's bad. It's up to the person if they want to take the risk."

I finished talking, painfully aware that I had been rambling. The woman looked bemused.

"It's funny that you think life today is any different," she said pensively. "Humans have been lying to each other since...forever. It's what separates us from other animals."

"You think so?"

"I don't think. I know. Is it okay if we share that?"

She pointed to the unlit cigarette pinched between my fingers. I nodded.

"Yeah, of course. But I..."

~ ~ ~

Before I can get the words out, she has turned on her heel and is walking over to the bouncer. I watch as his face flushes, showing off his gums in a grin, and produces a plastic lighter from his vest pocket. The woman is back a moment later, looking pleased.

"I'll light you up," she commands, to which I obligingly allow her to do. The flame winks into existence and sears the tip of the cigarette, transforming white paper into a bulbous, red ember. I draw in the fumes and exhale.

"Thanks," I say, stifling a cough. I take another drag, feeling the onset of a head rush coming on, and pass it to her.

She takes it and inhales eagerly, with all the gracelessness of a hamster sucking the nipple of a water bottle. It takes me by surprise. So far all of this woman's movements have been languid and fluid, a flag rippling in slow motion. Her sudden aggression with smoking comes as a visual shock.

"So," she asks, after reducing half the dart to teetering ash in two puffs. "Who'd you come here with tonight?"

She looks up at me expectingly, and again I have the overwhelming urge to look away. Escape the knife-like gaze that are her eyes. I resist and hold my face her way.

"Just a friend. It's her brother's 19th birthday, so she asked me to come with him and his friends."

"I see," she says, leaning her head back against the building. The din of club music beats its way through the wall without cease. "So is this a girlfriend, or just a friend who's a girl?"

"I guess the second."

"You guess?"

"I mean, yes. Definitely. The second." I am tripping on my words, my head fuzzy with nicotine and street noise. The club lineup grumbles impatiently. A steady trickle of water falls from the eaves above, like a curtain separating us from the world beyond.

"What about you? Who're you here with?" I ask, turning the tables. She smiles at my obvious pivot.

"Some girlfriends. They're here to meet some new guys to take home."

"Are you in the same boat?" I question, more daring than usual. She shakes her head.

"No, no. I'm just...here." She gestures to the air. To nothing. Passes me the cigarette, which I tentatively take.

"Gotcha," I reply. Silence takes over the conversation, which is oddly not unpleasant. It feels comfortable to stand and smoke with this stranger, not saying a word.

As the cigarette nears its death, I break the lull.

"What did you mean by that comment earlier? About lying being the thing that separates humans and animals?"

She laughs. "Well, first of all, humans *are* animals. We just like to pretend that we aren't."

"I mean, I guess."

"You don't agree?" She turns so her full torso is facing my way, challenger-like. "If we aren't animals, then what are we instead?"

"People," I say. "We're people. If we were animals we'd be living outdoors, hunting for our food and fuc—mating wherever. That's what animals do. But we're more sophisticated. We've got grocery stores and houses, and like, doctors and stuff."

The woman gives me a patient smile.

"Fair. But the only reason we need those things is because we're weak. We're smart, sure, but we have nothing else going for us. Our bodies are clawless, wingless, fangless. We have no fur or coat to keep us warm. We can't see in the dark or run fast or climb trees. We can barely even swim. The only reason our species has survived for the past 300,000 years is because we're clever." She passes me the cigarette and keeps going.

"I mean, sure, we can build stuff and solve problems. But we still need the Earth for everything. We're not actually self-made. We rely on the plants, sun, rain, and yes, other animals, just as much as they do. If not more. Why? Because we are greedy bastards who are never satisfied with what we already have. But even more importantly, we are liars."

"Okay," I say, silently agreeing with her. "So what about that? Where does lying fit into everything? How does that make us different?"

"Lying," she begins pointedly, "is the cornerstone of our success as a species. Humans would never be where they are today without it. Without the ability to lie, we wouldn't be able to organize. How do you think societies were formed? Or religions? You can't get tens, hundreds, thousands of people to cooperate without something unifying them. Good will is not enough. You need a purpose. A fear. Some sort of cause. A belief that what needs to be done, *has* to happen. What you need is a lie for people to follow. Do you seriously think men dragged millions of two-ton blocks to build the pyramids because they were bored? What about the women who spent their whole lives in the fields, growing food that would feed complete strangers? How have leaders raised armies to slaughter little children? Built cities out of dust? And who planted that first seed of racism? Classism? War? A liar. Always a fucking liar."

By the time she has finished, the sense of bigness is back. An aura of formidability seems to have enveloped her, enchanting her words with a sacred, ferocious power. But what has not changed is her face. No mask of anger or frustration adorns her features. Rather, there is simply this look of quiet assuredness. A storm raging beneath ice.

I am left speechless by her onslaught of words. The flame consumes the last of the tobacco and goes out with a whimper. I let it fall from my fingers and onto the sidewalk.

The woman watches the cigarette butt fall to the ground, and turns her attention back to my face. Studying my expression. I feel that I must say *something,* but I cannot think of anything to say. For the first time in my adult life, I feel very, very small.

"I have to go back in. My friends will be looking for me," she says drily. I get the sense that I have failed some sort of test. "Thanks for the smoke. And the conversation."

She turns to leave, and has a foot on the first stair when I call out for her to wait.

"I never got your name!" I plead, miserably. Internally, I am already spiralling with regret.

She pauses for a moment, eyes gleaming.

"Genevieve. Or Gen, for short," she says. A second later and she's gone.

CHAPTER EIGHT

I spent the next 7 days in a manic state of desire. My bedsheets became permanently drenched in sweat, as I masturbated violently in the hopes of reprieve. *Nada.* Something had come into being, had laid its sticky hooks into my tissue with no intentions of letting up. I began to feel very afraid. My favourite trait, *autonomy,* had been abruptly evicted from within me. Ripped out like a healthy tooth. In its place was now a gaping cavity, begging to be filled.

I've always been a naturally curious thing. In the wild, I feel that curiosity is a boon. It takes you to all the good spots. The hidden ones. It shows you what others, so wrapped up in their own routine, have accidentally passed over. Some secret nook tucked in the fabric of the world, revealed just for you.

But there is another side to curiosity. If you aren't careful, it won't just show you what others have missed. Oh no. It'll show what's missing in *you.* A hole in plain sight. A hunger you didn't know you had.

By day 8, there was no denying it anymore. I wanted Jack. I wanted this giant man who had issues. I wanted him for reasons I couldn't quite understand.

He had the aura of an inverted sea urchin: hazardous but only to himself. Next to no friends or self-confidence. The blackest eyes I had ever seen. Eyes that looked at me with reverence, with awe. And yes, a touch of fear. I won't deny my awareness to it.

Outside The Odyssey, I'd discovered that I greatly preferred this version of Jack over the first one I'd met. Initially, I'd thought it was his emotional openness that stirred want within me, along with his ignorance to his own physical potential. The second remained certainly true, as he'd stood hunched under the eaves, as if to thwart his own bones.

In the past, I'd been attracted to the types of men who showed no hesitation with me, or *near none,* as the former didn't really exist. Now I could see what that really signified. It was a flaw of idiocy, a lack of self-awareness in the presence of a dangerous animal. That just wouldn't do.

Jack, in all his sober glory, was not half as stupid. He was deliciously reserved, kind, and a bit awkward. But more importantly, he was afraid of me. Anyone could smell that. It reeked off his skin like a fine perfume.

What I hadn't expected, however, were the repercussions that my desire would have on me. I'd always prided myself for my detachment, which came as naturally as breathing. Always leaving a foot of space between me and the other person. Freedom for us both to coexist. Or depart, in my case. Should the reason arise.

I did not feel like this at all with Jack. I wanted, without hardly knowing the man, to collapse into him. And him into me. I wanted to fuse together into a single entity, to know everything about him. To tell him everything about me.

Including the stuff I had told no one. Especially the stuff I had told no one.

In between shuddering orgasms brought on by my own hand, my head spun elaborate fantasies of us living together, eating together, doing *everything* together. I pictured him emerging from his shell with fledgling confidence, to stand by me as a partner in this life. The yin to my yang. I could hear all the wonderful words we would share, the full-bellied laughter filling our home. I moaned at the size of his body and the inevitable length of his cock. Our wedding day. Honeymoon. His last name, stolen from his caller ID, tacked onto mine. Dahlia Donner. Jack Donner. The Donners. It felt right in a way I could not shake.

Yet I was disturbed by these rapid-fire fantasies, as equally as I was enthralled. I recognized the lunacy of it all. Everything was happening too fast, before anything had *actually* begun. And did I really, truly want this? Did I genuinely want to surrender to the feeling of love?

~ ~ ~

By day 8, it was apparent that such questions were pointless. Motion had been introduced, and there was nothing in the way of stopping it, unless I wanted to deprive myself of what I wanted.

Temperance. Not a fucking strength of mine. Not then and not now. With a mixture of excitement and nerves, I fished out my cell phone from the kitchen drawer. All of my calls were forwarded to the landline, so I was forced to deal with the nasty thing as infrequently as possible. All my friends had come to accept that I was just someone who was hard to reach. “Elusive,” they’d say, with a knowing smile. Oh, if only. They wouldn’t be smiling if they did.

I punched through my sparse call history until I came to January. There, in capital bold letters: **JACK A. DONNER.** My thumb hovered above the redial button, not out of hesitation, but amusement. A great wave of calm, that my fate was already sealed and written to be, had overcome me. Suddenly everything seemed very trivial, and very much out of my hands. The cavity inside me opened its mouth and drank deeply. I sighed.

"Don't make me regret this," I muttered to the name on the screen. My thumb pushed down squarely on the redial symbol. Three rings. A click.

"Hello? Who's this?" That low, powerful voice. A storm cloud on the horizon. I imagined that voice right by my ear, telling me everything I wanted to hear. Begging for me. Worshipping me. Loving me.

Yes. I choose you.

"Hey. It's Dahlia, that girl you met at that party a few months ago. The fucked up one, where you blacked out." A beat. "I wrote my number on your arm."

"Oh shit, yeah. Hi. How've you been?"

"Good. I've been thinking and...I've decided to take you up on your offer for coffee. What are you doing tomorrow afternoon?"

~ ~ ~

I'm waiting with my back to the door when he comes in. I can't see him, obviously, but I can *feel* him. Two meetings and two phone calls and I've already attuned myself to his frequency. Wonders never cease.

The café I've chosen is called Elysium, situated right on the cusp of the downtown core. From where I'm sitting, I can see the harbour and mist-crowned mountains on the far shore, bordering the north like a terrestrial barricade. All that lies beyond are hundreds of miles of wilderness, peppered with remote towns and the odd ski resort. The rest is all trees. Nothing but trees.

"Hi. I'm, uh, here to meet someone," I hear Jack say to the host. Even though this place is technically a coffeeshop, serving no more than java and pastries, the format is more like a sit-down restaurant. Typical pretentious vibes, but perfect for a meeting like this one. There is hardly a soul in the building and the music is soft. Plus, look at that *view.*

Assumably, the host waves him over to my table. I still do not turn my head, but keep my face pointed directly out the second-story windows. I have to bite the inside of my cheek to stop from laughing.

There is the reverberation of heavy footsteps growing nearer, and at last I break gaze from the harbour, turning my whole body to face Jack. His expression is worth the world.

"Holy shit, it's you," he says, stopping in his tracks. His eyes, black as sin, look ready to tumble right out of their sockets. But he is smiling. And so am I.

"Hey," I say, the unfamiliar feeling of jitters twinkling inside my chest. Was this how men usually felt when they met me? I felt bad for those suckers. "Come sit."

He does, sliding into the booth with an adorable uncertainty. His body swallows most of the view from sight, not that I mind. Not at all.

"I thought...I thought you said your name was Genevier. When I met you last week."

"Gene*vieve.* And yeah, I felt kind of bad about that. She's my friend, actually. But she's not me."

"That's okay," he says quietly. "I like your name better anyways."

"Is that so?"

"Yeah. It's got a nice ring to it." His cheeks are tinged red, but he doesn't look away. An improvement. In fairness, I am also trying my best to diminish myself at this moment. Trying not to scare him needlessly. I know that I can if I want to. Just the knowledge is enough.

"Well, thanks. I like your name too. It's very classic."

"Haha. Thanks. You'd be the first to say that." He looks around at the café. "Fancy place you've picked here."

I glance around too, as if I hadn't been here several times before. "Yeah, it's cute. I thought I'd pick somewhere quieter for us to properly meet. Easier to talk with."

He runs a hand through his hair. "Yeah, I guess you're right. The last two places were pretty chaotic. And the first one I don't remember, and the second I didn't know who you were." He let out a laugh: a hard, pained thing.

"Hopefully this is better then."

"Yeah," he says. "It definitely is."

We sit and look at one another. I wait for him to ask me *why* I gave him a fake name, but he doesn't. It was a silly thing to do, really nothing beyond a drunken impulse. Some part of me wanted to keep the upper hand. But I can't help wondering what he thinks of it. Maybe nothing at all.

The waitress comes by, offering waters and two slips of paper for us to order off of.

"It's extra quiet in here today," I comment, referring to the dead café. Besides us, there is only a pair of old men slurping cappuccinos, and a young woman with headphones on and cakey makeup. For Saturday at noon, it's a ghost-town.

Our waitress, a rail-thin waif with fat teeth, shrugs.

"We've had some bad press," she replies disinterestedly. She floats off without further explanation, apron strings trailing.

I shake my head in confusion. "People are so strange."

"Thank you," Jack says. "I'm glad I'm not the only one."

We smile.

"So, how was the rest of your night last week? Did your friends have fun?"

"Oh, um, not really. My friend Li got in trouble for spilling Clamato juice on a girl, and then her brother got too drunk and threw up in the bathroom."

"Yikes. Well, it's a good thing it was on the main floor. He would've never made it to the basement." Off of Jack's confused expression, I elaborate. "That's where they put the women's."

"In the basement? That seems unfair. Especially with your shoes and stuff."

"Men's world 'til the end," I say, quoting Yvonne. Inside my heart is singing at his words.

"Fuck. Yeah, I guess you're right. That sucks." He takes a sip of his water, looking off.

"Why should it? You're on the winning side of things." Now I'm just testing the waters. Baiting him. He stares me straight in the eye.

"Not really. I don't really want to play for a team that's the cause of all the world's problems."

"You think men are the cause of all problems?"

"Well, yeah. I've taken a couple history courses. I watch the news, read books. It doesn't take a genius to see the pattern. Men are the common denominator."

I can't tell if he's being earnest or just trying to impress me. All physical tells point towards sincerity.

"Well," I say slowly, "you're mostly right. Men have been the root of most problems, some more than others. The lying type."

"Right. As you were saying."

"Uh-huh. But the blame can't fall wholly on their shoulders. There's been some pretty evil women in history too."

Jack laughs. "Oh, yeah? Like who? I can't even think of one."

"Well, that's the thing. No one usually bothered to write their names down. A, because they were women, and B, because…that's how women work with that sort of thing. They stay in the shadows. And more often don't get caught."

"But that's just speculation. You don't know that for sure. No one does."

I pause, decide, then agree. "Yes, I suppose you're right. I can't prove that for certain."

Our waif of a waitress returns empty-handed, stopping to stand at the side of our table. She looks at us expectingly. Jack clears his throat.

"I guess I'll just have the…maple flat white with an almond pistachio croissant."

"K," says Waif. Her lips hang ajar, giving clear view to the elephantine chompers she calls teeth. They're so distracting and fat that I forget that it's my turn to order.

"Hello?" the waitress asks with a voice like fried gravel.

"Oh, sorry. I was just admiring your necklace." Fuck! She's not actually wearing one. My attempted cover-up falls flat on its face, but she doesn't even react. Doesn't check her neckline to see if jewelry has miraculously appeared, doesn't give me a weird look, doesn't question, nothing. Waif could've had a lobotomy before clocking in to work today, judging by the way she's acting. I look down at my menu and choose randomly.

"Ahem, I'll get…a praline butter americano and a meringue gooseberry tart." Jesus.

"With whip?"

"Pardon?"

"With. Whip," Waif punctuates.

"Oh, without. Actually, can I just get a drip coffee? Medium roast?"

"We can't do that here."

"Seriously? I find that hard to believe."

All I get is a blank stare.

"Okay, nevermind. I'll change my drink to a lavender latte actually. But keep the gooseberry thing."

Without a word of confirmation, Waif plucks the menus from our hands and heads for the back.

"I hope she's not making our drinks back there. I'm afraid we'll get something extra with them," Jack says, once she's out of earshot.

"What do you mean?"

He mimics spitting into a cup. I snicker.

"I'd like to see her try."

"Oh yeah? And what would you do about it?"

I arch a single eyebrow dramatically. "Might have to become one of those evil women you've never heard of."

This makes him laugh. "I bet. I'll be sure to write your name down, though. For the history books."

"Promise?"

"Oh, absolutely."

We both cackle like jackals.

In the 20 minutes since he's sat down, I've already noticed a shift in Jack's attitude. His shoulders are pushed back and his focus is forward. Right on me. Some of that inverted sea urchin energy has dissipated. I feel vindicated. The boldness that I witnessed outside Henry's party is making an appearance, slowly but surely. All I have to do is keep teasing it out. Coax, coax, coax. I take a sip of water and lean back in my seat.

"So are you at UBC? How did you know Henry?" he asks. Subtle mind-reading. I like.

"Henry's just a friend of a friend. *Was* just a friend of a friend. And no, I'm not. I haven't ever taken any university courses, actually. It's not really my thing."

"How come?"

Because I already know enough.

"I don't know. I just don't really like the scene. Academia and post-secondary and all that. It's too stuffy. And most of it is bogus, anyhow. You spend all this money to take classes you don't want, to get a degree you're half-passionate about, all to do a job you don't get paid enough for? That seems absurd." I was regurgitating the same whiny spiel I'd heard from various friends, strangers. Jack's face, however, lights up with validation.

"Damn. I know exactly how you feel. I'm in my third year and...I'm so sick of it. Like some of the courses are pretty interesting, but I hate my main degree. And it's so fucking expensive. My dad's using all our savings to put me through, plus student loans, so I'm going to be indebted to him *and* the government when I'm done."

"What's your major, then? English? Psych?"

Jack blew a raspberry.

"Nope. Electrical engineering."

"Really? You? Did not strike me as the type."

"That's 'cause I'm not. It was my dad's decision. He wanted to be an engineer when he was my age, but my family couldn't afford post. So he's been working different odd jobs over the years instead. Farmer's hand, bartender, mechanic. Now he's working as a mail carrier since we moved here. Says he hates it but I have my doubts. He's best when he's left alone."

"Since you moved from Saskatchewan, yes?"

"Yeah! How did you know?"

"You told me already. First night we met," I say with a warm smile. Jack, however, tenses.

"Fuck, I keep forgetting. You probably know all sorts of shit about me, and I…know nothing about you." He chews his cheek. "So what did I tell you that night? Anything bad?"

I laugh. "Oh yeah. You told me all your darkest secrets. First kiss, most embarrassing date, biggest fears, the full shabang." I expect a laugh from this, or a smile, but Jack does neither. His face has gone very white.

"You okay?" I ask, suddenly guilty for joking.

"Are you serious?"

"What? No, of course not! I'm just kidding. We talked about random dumb stuff, and like…what we thought about the universe, what happens when we die. And the weather. Nothing too personal." Lie.

"Are you sure? 'Cause…" He trails off, his demeanour dipping dangerously back into old territory. Without thinking, I grab one of his hands on the table. It's nearly twice the size of my own.

"Hey, hey. You didn't share anything you would regret. You were very happy the whole time we talked. And honestly, you know as much about me as I know about you. Seriously. I promise." I pat his huge hand and let go. "Sorry for playing with you just now. I know this whole situation is pretty weird."

He lets out a laugh, which sounds relieved. Mostly.

"Yeah, that's putting it mildly."

The two of us sit in silence for a minute. Our drinks and pastries arrive, and we both sip from our respective mugs. The hot liquid seems to warm us both, and pretty soon we are back on track.

"Well," I say, washing down a bite of meringue with lavender latte. "Since neither of us know much about each other, we should probably fix that, shouldn't we?"

"I guess you're right," he says, a line of foam anointing his upper lip. "So what do you want to know about me, Dahlia?"

I pause, savouring the flavours on my tongue, the sensation of height before falling. I have to be smart here. Anything asked can be turned on its head, pointed back right at me. And despite assumptions, I really do hate lying. By omission or forthright. So instead of plunging deep, like I desperately want to, I start easy. A gentle swim in the sunlight zone.

"Tell me everything you like, Jack," I say. And I mean every word.

CHAPTER NINE

When I first heard about the 2004 tsunami in Thailand, it was hard for me to wrap my head around. The descriptions of carnage, catastrophe, of pulverizing force: all brought on by an insurmountable wave of water that transformed everything in its path. How quickly tropical paradise became tropical hell. I couldn't imagine the feeling of that upheaval. The totality. The sensation of being swallowed by the sea.

Falling in love with Dahlia felt like that. Her presence decimated me, consumed me entirely. One minute I was standing, minding my own business. The next…BAM. I was sucked under the onrushing ocean. Helpless as a tourist without swimming trunks.

The difference, of course, was how my landscape changed. Instead of destruction, my future wife brought nourishment to the desert. Rain to dust. Everything that was dead in my world opened its lips to drink from the heavens. Everything began to flourish. And all of a sudden, I was very, very happy.

We spent the next several months conjoined at the eyes, ears, and lips. She was an atrocious texter, worse than I, and seemed allergic to technology in general. The only time I could reach her was when she was home, via the landline. I'd lock myself in my room and listen to her voice, twisting like a lark in summer, for hours. We'd talk incessantly. Or sometimes just breathe heavily, as we touched ourselves miles apart. There was a lot of that, too.

The rest of the time, however, we were together. It took the better part of an hour to reach her home, way out on the westernmost tip of the North Shore. I was less busy now that my semester had finished up, and was lying to my dad about taking extra shifts at the auto shop. I ignored Li's calls and messages, demanding my time and attention. I had none to spare her. And she could frankly go fuck herself. I was giving everything I had to Dahlia.

After several dates out on the town—including dinners, a sea-wall stroll, three movies (*Jennifer's Body, Triangle,* and *Carriers*) and an art gallery—Dahlia had finally invited me to her place. I obviously couldn't reciprocate the favour, with my father stalking around our duplex every afternoon and weekend. So I was grateful that she had initiated the next step.

What I was not prepared for was her home. Dahlia had told me about her parents, how one was dead and the other gone. She'd inherited her family's money and house, along with her mother's two cars.

"And a speedboat," she'd said cheerfully, while we gawked at splotches of red paint and chewing gum at the gallery. The abstract exhibit was called "Death of an Apothecary". I'd seen more riveting artwork in the toilet after taco night.

"That's crazy," I'd said, a tinge envious. My own father had inherited the duplex we shared from his dead brother, who'd hanged himself 6 years ago. It was a ratty, rundown place in the poorer southern suburbs, where the trees had been mowed down in place of cement. The living room, where Uncle Mark had done the deed, had a dense energy that made it impossible to sit in for long. It felt like sinking into a bog, only that bog was depression, victorious after eating my uncle alive. Clearly, it was still hungry.

~ ~ ~

Nothing could be further from the shitpot I lived in than Dahlia's home. Sorry, *manor.* After following the squawking GPS through the downtown core, then along ever-narrowing roads once I'd crossed the suspension bridge to the North Shore, I arrived at her wrought-iron gates, crusted in rust, for the very first time.

Unlike the area I lived, the neighbourhood I found myself in was so heavily overrun with greenery that you could mistakenly believe that humans had failed to colonize it. The sky was choked out by pines, maples, cedars; engulfed in creeping ivy and moss. Ferns ruled the Earth. Each property was tucked behind a high wall of shrubbery, either hedging or some other natural composite. The wall of green that blocked off my girlfriend's house, however, was by far the most impenetrable. It looked like no one had pruned the onslaught of flowering branches in half a century. Maybe more.

The gates were locked. A meaty iron chain was bound tight around the middle, sealed shut with a padlock the size of my fist. Dahlia had said to call her when I arrived, so I flipped open my phone and punched in her number. She picked up after half a ring.

"Hi! I'll be right out," she said, sounding out of breath. She hung up before I could say a word. I stood awkwardly by the gates, peering down the long curved driveway, trying to get a glimpse of the house. I could see nothing. My stomach turned anxiously in on itself. I wondered why I hadn't dressed up more.

A few minutes later, and there was Dahlia, running full-speed down the driveway. She was barefoot and wearing a knee-length dress the colour of fresh cream. When she arrived at the gates, she shoved a key into the padlock, then tossed it and the chain to the ground with a clatter. The gates swung inwards with a whine as she leaned in on her tiptoes to kiss me.

"Hey, handsome," she said, when we finally pulled apart. Her face was blushed like a strawberry, hair wild. It was the end of May but still cool outside. The sunshine had still not arrived for its season.

"Hi. It's nice to see you," I replied. I still found it difficult to articulate myself with her, when the topic wasn't philosophical or topical. Directly acknowledging my feelings, my astonishment of her, came stiffly. Or not at all. I was determined to show her my desire in other ways.

"You can drive on up to the main house. I'll just lock up behind you." She pushed open the gates to allow my dirty brown Mustang to heave its way through. I drove slowly down the rest of the driveway, lined to the heavens with green.

There was a popping sound as my jaw snapped open, rounding the bend to see her house. Before the hood of my car towered a beast of dark wood and glass. Three stories high, with large panoramic windows and black tiled roofing. It sat, rectangle-shaped, like a fortress. Or a warning.

"Shit," I said to myself. I had not anticipated *this.* A place like this was surely worth upwards of ten million dollars on the market. And it belonged to my girlfriend. Solely.

I switched off the engine and got out of the car. Dahlia materialized beside me, causing me to jump.

"Wow! You're fast," I laughed, trying to mask my racing heart. I turned and faced the mansion. "You didn't tell me you were this rich. Like this is…next level. I've never been in such a nice house in my life."

"Well, you still haven't. You're still standing in the driveway," she replied, smirking. "Come on, let me show you my digs." She grabbed hold of my hand and pulled me inside.

~ ~ ~

The first thing that strikes me is the silence. We step through the front door and into a tomb; a gorgeous, expensive tomb, but a tomb nonetheless. The singsong of birds, rustling leaves, all of that dies when Dahlia locks the door. Only our breathing survives.

"It's so quiet," I say, sliding my sandals off one by one. The entranceway features a sweeping staircase to the upper levels and a deadly-looking chandelier. Dahlia smiles.

"Yeah, it's one of my favourite things about this place. I feel like I'm on another planet."

She takes the lead into the kitchen, which is conjoined with the living room. An enormous mantle straddles the fireplace, flanked by mammoth windows that look out onto the trees. A cutout between the trunks frames a view of the nearby ocean, churning away.

"Can I get you something to drink? How was the drive here?"

"Uh, yeah, some water would be nice. And the drive was fine. Traffic, like usual."

"Aw, I'm sorry. You sure you don't want something else? I have wine in the fridge."

"No, no, water's fine."

She pours a tall glass from a Brita container, gestures for me to sit down at the kitchen counter on a stool. For herself, she pulls off the cork of a half-empty red wine, which echoes with resounding zest throughout the house. She fills up a glass and holds it up.

"Cheers."

"Cheers," I say, clinking cups. We both drink, holding eye contact. For once, she doesn't specify what exactly we're toasting to.

Dahlia gulps down her wine, then tops off. She is noticeably flightier today, her hands darting to and fro, eyes shifty. This secretly calms me. I am feeling nervous myself. I sip my lukewarm water and look around.

"This really is a beautiful house. I love the view," I comment redundantly. It's impossible not to ignore it, though. Not once have I been face-to-face with such opulence.

"Thanks. I feel very lucky to be here, let alone by myself. But to tell you the truth..." she lingers on her words, index finger stroking the wine stem. "I'm actually thinking about selling it."

"Selling it? This place? How come?" I ask, incredulous. Dahlia shrugs.

"I know, that's the same thing my girlfriends said. I think I'd just like a clean start. Something new. This house reminds me a lot of my mom and when...like, I was a kid."

I ponder what she says. "Yeah, I guess that's fair. I know how you feel."

She looks up at me, again with those sharp, marine eyes.

"Right. Fuck. I guess you do."

Neither one of us have fully divulged about ourselves, or our past traumas. Meanwhile, our two dead mothers crowd the room, unspoken for. I haven't told a single soul about what happened to mine, besides my dad and the police, of course. Dahlia has been equally tight-lipped about her own. We've crept around the subject, mutually agreeing to keep that door of pain closed.

A part of me wants to keep that door closed forever. Another part of me knows that that's impossible. If we are to really know each other, then eventually, all things must be revealed.

I change the subject before things get dark.

"So...are you going to give me a house tour? Miss Moneybags?" I kick myself for the last comment, a joke that sounded funnier in my head. Out loud it comes across as an insult, underscored with insecurity. Which is the sad truth. I feel like a candy ring stuck on the finger of a queen. Displaced and inadequate.

Dahlia doesn't acknowledge my slight, intentional or not. "Of course. Let me show you." She stands from leaning on the counter and begins walking out of the kitchen, her footsteps silent on the white tile. I follow suit.

The main floor holds many rooms, each fully furnished yet obviously underused. Two guest bedrooms, an office, a "den", and a mudroom sit in various degrees of darkness and dust. The bedsheets look so stiff that you could break bones if you hit them hard enough. The den, which is really just a glorified sitting room without windows, clearly used to host some sort of animal. There are two ceramic bowls, a basket of toys and a plush floor bed, with a rack of rope and leashes hung above.

"You used to have a dog?" I ask, looking around at the room. She nods.

"Yes. A golden retriever. Her name was Mango."

"That's a cute name. When did she pass?"

"About 8 years ago." There is a flicker of something—sadness, or something more—that crosses her face as she says this. Then it is gone, as quickly as it came.

"Well, I'm sorry about her. Losing a pet is tough."

I'd never had one, not a dog or cat or even a fish. My dad didn't believe in that crap. His words, not mine.

"Yeah, me too. Worst day of my life."

She laughs humourlessly and closes the door. The tour continues.

As we ascend the curving staircase, her comment stews in the back of my brain. I can't understand how the death of an animal, beloved and all, could still ever supersede the death of a *mother.* For me, there was no comparison.

By the time we have rounded off the second floor, filled with more bedrooms, bathrooms, and living spaces, I am feeling very unsexy. All this thought of dead moms and dogs has killed my lust. The drive here had been the complete opposite, with the seatbelt holding my cock down as I imagined all the things I was going to do to my girlfriend when I arrived. *Finally.* This moment had been building for weeks, the air between us on our dates growing increasingly charged and suggestive. We had inched, glacially, to hugging, then handholding, then kissing. It was maddening.

I felt shot back down to 13, when the most action you could get was a mutual brushing of cupid's bows after 2 months of "dating". Since the dawn of April, I'd often found myself alone in bed, body stiff and angry with desire, unable to find any meaningful release. The thought of being with someone else had become repulsive. All I could think of was being inside of Dahlia.

"And this is the master, but I don't sleep in here. It used to be my mom's room so it feels kind of weird," she is saying, with a voice that is edging boredom. Meanwhile, my stomach has begun to knit itself together. My brain is spit-firing thoughts and questions I have no answer for.

"Hey, um..." I swallow laboriously, "I don't feel so good. Could we go back downstairs?"

"Why? What's wrong?" she asks. Her eyes, which I have grown to adore and loathe, puncture me.

"Oh, nothing. I just feel kind of lightheaded." I feel the opposite. My head feels like it's full of lead. But I play it off with a smile. "I don't think I ate enough today."

"Or you're dehydrated. It's probably that. Here, let me get you some more water." She thrusts open the master bedroom door again and strides in.

"Uh, isn't the water downstairs?" I ask. I tentatively step into the bedroom and look around. The room is four times the size of my own dirty quarters. A big, pillowy duvet covered in birds envelops the king-sized bed, which looks out onto floor-to-ceiling windows. Behemoth wood furniture squats against the walls, untouched for years.

From this vantage point, you can clearly see the ocean waves glinting from the sun, which has emerged from the clouds like an answer. An army of leaves ripple in the wind, dominating all else. The beauty of it has an immediate cooling effect on my boiling brain. Suddenly, I feel a lot less like running away.

"Here you are, handsome," comes a voice, and I turn to see Dahlia brandishing a cup of water. There is concern in her eyes, which softens them considerably. I look past her, to the far corner of the room, and see a fully-stocked wet bar with enough liquor to kill an Irish village.

"Thank you," I say, sitting down on the foot of the bed and accepting the cup with gratitude. I drink deeply as Dahlia sits down beside me, her hips pushed lightly against mine. The water is refreshingly cold. It awakens me from the inside out. I polish it off and then carry it back over to the wet bar to refill. Dahlia stays sitting on the bed.

"Your mom liked to drink too, hey?" I ask, the words spilling out without thought. This happens a lot when I'm around Dahlia. I find myself saying things that would normally kick and scream from my lips, not stroll out without care.

"Yeah. She did. Yours too?" I lean against the wall beside the bar to drink my second glass, facing the bed. Dahlia is holding her hands in her lap and looking very small.

"No. Not my mom. But my dad…yes." I pause, debating how much more to say. The words, however, decide for themselves. I keep talking.

"He was an alcoholic since I was a kid, after his own dad died. I think it started as a coping mechanism, and then grew into something worse. He wasn't like…abusive or anything, but he was very out of it. Nearly lost his job a couple times. We'd find him passed out in all sorts of weird places, stuff like that."

"So does he still drink? Or did he get better?"

"I mean, yes and no. He doesn't drink anymore. Not since the accident with my mom. But I don't think he's better now. He's very angry about everything. To be honest…I feel like he hates me."

She frowns at this.

"I don't know how anyone could do that."

"Do what?"

"Hate you. I don't see how that's possible."

"Well, you haven't known me for that long. Only a couple months."

"Yeah but…I can tell. I know when someone's a good person or a bad one."

"And I'm a good one?" I ask, half-jokingly. Dahlia replies with flat earnestness.

"Yeah. You are."

"Well. Thanks. But people still hate other people. It doesn't really matter whether they're good or not."

"I guess. But I still don't understand it. I mean, you're his son."

"Yeah, I know. I don't really understand it either."

I put the glass on top of the wet bar and cross the room. Sit back down beside her. It's the most we've ever spoken about my dad or my feelings surrounding him. The first time I've acknowledged my mom's death as an accident. It's barely scratching the surface, but still, it's a start. And instead of regret in my chest, I feel something else. Release.

"Hey," I say, after a moment of silence. "Could we open a window?"

"Yeah, of course. One sec." Dahlia ambles over to the glass, turning a crank on one of them to crack it open. In rushes the gentle choir of birds, trees, and breeze. A minute later and the stale air of the bedroom feels invigorated. Even though the ocean is too far away to hear, for a moment I swear that I can hear the waves.

Dahlia walks back over to stand in front of me. With me sitting down, she is exactly eye-level. She takes my left hand in hers, and lifts it up. Her touch is warm, as if she's got the heat of summer hidden under her skin. With her eyes steadily locked on mine, she brings my hand to her lips and kisses my knuckles.

"Are you feeling better now? Not lightheaded?" she asks, her voice barely a whisper. Her face is backlit with sunlight and shifting trees, the ocean perched on her left shoulder.

Robins and starlings sing their songs of gratitude. I sing mine.

"Yes. I feel perfect," I say. With my right hand, I grab the back of her body and pull her close, into a kiss. She folds—tall grass in the wind—and draws both arms to encircle my neck. Our lips meet: first soft, then hungry. Then ravenous. I fall backwards onto the bed, with Dahlia attached to my face like a leech. There is no turning back now.

We do not move slowly. My shirt strips off and tumbles to the floor, followed by her cream-white dress and matching bra. For a moment, we take in each other's nude torsos, panting lightly. The weight of her straddling me like a missing piece, back in place.

Her strength takes me for surprise as she suddenly pushes me down by the neck. With our lips locked in a kiss, tongues teasing each other, I feel her free hand slide down past my waistline. She grabs my sex with confidence and gives it a squeeze. Pulls away, to undo the front button of my pants. My body clenches in her absence, and I roll us over onto her back so I am on top. With my face pressed against her breasts, refusing to break body contact, I push my pants down, off, 'til we are two bodies separated only by underwear.

There is too much want between us to be graceful. I ease my face down the length of her torso, slathering it with kisses. As I do, Dahlia twitches and squirms, reacting to every sensation with lightning rapidity. Neither of us says anything, only heavy breathing. We are too focused on our work. I pull her panties off and—without ceremony—stick my face into the mound of her cunt.

My tongue begins to work its way around, exploring and flicking each little fold, her inner thighs pressed against the rough of my stubble. While I do, her hands stroke through my hair, fingernails scraping along my scalp and upper neck in a way that makes me shiver. This spurs me on, as I lap at her naked, trembling body, which is *still* agonizingly quiet. After several minutes, a word is born: shaky and wet with thirst.

"Please."

I stop what I'm doing and look up at her. I can feel liquid dripping down my chin as our eyes meet. Her gaze has never looked more intense than in this moment, nor this needy. I look away.

"I want you," she says, with almost no sound. But it is enough. I release her thighs, which I have been gripping hard enough to leave red marks, and stand up from the end of the bed. I dig through my fallen pants pocket, rip open the condom wrapper, and slide it onto me. I spit on it for extra measure and then climb back onto the bed, back onto Dahlia.

I am just about to push myself inside of her when she stops me, putting a hand to my chest. Her whole face is flushed rose.

"Wait, wait. Not like this. Lie on your back."

I comply wordlessly, stretching out onto the bed with the ends of my feet sticking off the edge. Dahlia sits up and straddles me again, bringing her face close enough to kiss.

With one hand over my beating heart, the other stroking the length of me, she kisses my lips, cheeks, eyes—closed in surrender—forehead. Down the sides of my neck, pausing over my ears. All the while sliding her hand up and down, squeezing and twisting. I flex and stiffen beneath her, trying to hold back my enjoyment. But after a few moments, I begrudgingly submit. A moan escapes my lips and burrows into her ear. She pulls her face back and smiles at me. Victory.

"Gotcha," she says, before sitting up straight atop my pelvis. My hands fall down the sides of her body and cup her bottom. From behind her, the windows have filled with light, as the sun brazenly undresses itself from the clouds to shine with absolute power.

Dahlia rises up to her knees. With her hand tucked behind her back, she eases my cock into position. Her eyes are blazing, and, despite their intensity, I refuse to look away. I let myself fall into their waters without fear.

As I do, Dahlia lets gravity do the rest of the job, letting herself sink down slowly onto me. Her whole body quivers as she does, taking in my entirety. And at last, she lets a cry of pleasure fly free from her open, glistening mouth.

CHAPTER TEN

Time is a strange animal. It wants to be your friend, but it can't help itself in biting you every now and then. That's just its nature: to eat. I understand time the way a hunter and a tiger might understand one another. Our relationship is founded on respect. One, however, only feels any true fear of the other. And I am not the one with stripes.

That first summer, time and I were best friends. As good friends as two predators can be, that is. There was no painful slowness or disquieting speed. Everything unfolded as smoothly as an orchid opening its face, certain that its season for reaping had come.

The season in question, of course, was love. Falling in love with Jack was like growing into a great, serene tree. An oak, perhaps. It felt like after a lifetime of wandering—tripping shoelessly from here to there—I was finally, *finally,* able to stand still. I felt like I could hold the world and its worries with infinite oak-like strength, and love every second of it. All my hunger for things I couldn't name seemed to evaporate. I was content. I couldn't believe a person could ever feel so happy. And yet here I was, within one who could.

By July, we were inseparable. There was rarely a moment when I was not with him: physically or mentally. My thoughts seemed to be filled by an unending barrage of his name, breaker waves beating against my shore, again, again, *Jack, Jack, Jack, Jack, Jack.*

It was embarrassing. But also new, so I relished it. Novelty had always been my first love. And now I had a human one: a breathing, living, flesh and bones man who I adored and who adored me.

There seemed to be no end to topics we could talk about. I loved this aspect most of all; besides the physical, of course. Jack had big questions and not a lot of answers, so we made a perfect fit. He produced queries with such consistency and magnitude, it was like being in the presence of a colossal 6-year-old. Always:

"Do you think we remember everything about our lives when we die?"

"Why are humans so obsessed with hurting each other?"

"How can people see what plastic surgery does to you and *still* want to get it?"

Or my personal favourite:

"How have I ever lived without you?"

How have I ever lived without you? He would ask this only after sex, after being wrung dry by the carnal. Walls down, eyes fluttering between open and closed. *How have I ever lived without you?* A lesser person might have felt insulted that such a question would only come after being fucked out of your skull, and vice-versa. Such a person might think that was all the other was after. The body. The flesh. But not me.

After half a year's time, I understood Jack profoundly. He was a king living in a moated castle, and the only time he would fully step beyond that moat was when he, and it, were drained dry. Like I said, walls down. I didn't take this personally. Not in the slightest. I understood, equally profoundly, what it was like to protect oneself from the world with high walls and a pit of water. Out of pain. Or necessity. Or both.

I knew how I had lived without Jack. In need. *Something* was missing, and had been missing, for quite some time. The trouble with having everything—on paper, at least—is that when you sense something is missing, it can drive you insane trying to figure out what it is.

I had dated before, and each time, I was left irritated and disappointed. I found most eligible men my age to be stupid dogs, which is only an insult to canines, and only true to the word "stupid". Most were sloppy, lazy lovers with thick wads of used toilet paper stuck between their ears. All of them were obsessed with me.

They'd wait around in their sports cars waiting to pick me up and take me to the most expensive restaurant they could fucking conceive of, only for the food to be a sweaty pile of overpriced noodles drizzled with quail semen and truffle pesto, served by a stick-in-the-ass server named Phill. They all wanted to work in finance and wore musky cologne that stank. Many of them were "third, fifth generation" Canadians, a fact they wore proudly on their pressed, black lapels. This comment would make me gag. To me, it only meant two things.

The first was that they were rich. Or rather, they *came* from money, which isn't much of a difference, but perhaps even worse. If you make your own money in life, you're less likely to be corrupted by it. Especially if you came from humble beginnings, saw life from the bottom before seeing the view on top, and all that. I, of course, am an exception. An extraordinary exception. But even I have felt the toxin slip into my character, all from having access to everything and anything I've wanted since birth.

When you are born into money, that's what happens. You're taught that you are entitled to the world and its gifts. And if you're not careful, this will rot your soul from the inside out. By the time most of those privileged rich children are sent out into society, it's already too late for them.

The second thing is worse. If you're a descendant of this continent and you *aren't* of Indigenous blood, I've got bad news for you. Your ancestors were directly involved with the violent theft and destruction of a rich cultural tapestry that was too evolved for their settler minds to understand.

To become intertwined with the land, with the world, is the ultimate point of being human, not the flaw. It is not the wrench in the cogs. Being one with the Earth *is* the cogs. The culmination of the human species at its finest. Indigenous people not only understood that, but they made it their way of life. And still do to this day.

Of course, I couldn't start spouting off about such things as I sat finger-trapped during another Tom Cruise movie with my latest catch. Although most of the time, I couldn't figure out why I was even doing it. Why was I dating these men I had no interest in? It seemed like all that anyone else was interested in doing. Not to mention, it had been drilled into my head since I was a child, was asked about by complete strangers: Do you have a boyfriend? Are you seeing anyone? What's a girl like you doing without a man?

A girl like me was sleeping in the woods at night. A girl like me was missing her dead dog and dead mom. A girl like me was taking her boat out under the cover of stars and staring into the blackness of the Pacific Ocean, wondering how it would all end. A girl like me was wondering if it ever *would* end.

And yes, she was also sleeping around. Going to parties. Making friends and dropping them just as quickly. Dating these insufferable men because they were all my friends would introduce me to. Or because they were the only ones dumb enough to approach me. The rest were all chickenshit scared. In the end, they all seemed to be.

By mid-summer, Jack's fear hadn't gone away entirely. I could still smell it, simmering in the back corner of his mind. But he fought against it, and for that, I commended him. He willed himself to hold my gaze, even when he was itching to look away. His eyelids would start to twitch, or his fingers would curl. It was cute. But I found myself losing interest in it all the same. It was far better to be loved than to be feared. This is what Jack taught me.

All my life, I had been surrounded by people who just…wanted me. They wanted my attention. My approval. My body. My energy. The only exception was my mother, who never quite seemed to pick up on what she'd given birth to. Too drunk, too air-headed. Bless her. The only other time I had ever felt true love was Mango. And look how that turned out.

So with Jack, this was a brand new experience. The thing, the unnamable thing that had evaded my essence for as long as I'd known, was here. It was love. All this time, all this *time,* all I had wanted was to be truly, honestly loved.

Or maybe that's not quite it. I didn't just want to be loved. I wanted to be understood.

The second part was taking its time. Occasionally, when it was late at night and Jack had fallen asleep in my bed—his huge figure pressed against mine like a promise—I would be hit with a bolt of fear. The love wasn't going to be enough. The *understood* part would never come. There would always be some distance between us, some lack of acceptance, and that gap would grow from a fracture into a canyon, and I would be back, right back to where I'd always been. Alone. Our love was finite. It was conditional. It lacked the *un*derstanding, the true understanding that comes from knowing everything about a person, to ever evolve into being *unconditional.* And what then? After tasting the fruits of love's paradise, how could anything ever measure up?

I would shake the fear from my brain and press myself harder into Jack's body. No. I would not, could not, allow it. The love would *have* to be enough. Unconditional or not. The risk of telling him everything to gain that completeness of understanding…it would be to risk losing him. I couldn't bear the thought.

In the darkness of my bedroom, as I'd squeeze my eyes closed and force my body into slumber, I could hear the sound of time, faithfully stalking my every move. Seeing just what I'd do next. We have been at this game for a long time, time and I. No pun intended. And in the darkness, I can hear the sound of that big cat, purring at the back of its throat.

~ ~ ~

So. July. After existing in a vacuum for weeks, carting from different dates to the depths of my mattress, it was time for Jack and I to enter the social world. Like it or not, I had become strangely attached to my current group of friends, and I felt bad for just vanishing out of nowhere. Most of them I hadn't seen since early spring. Except Yvonne, because…well. She was special.

I had kept the extent of my relationship with Jack largely hush-hush. The girls knew there *was* a man I was seeing, but not anything about him. The unspoken expectation was that all romantic relations in our group had an expiry date of 1-3 months. This ensured that all potential partners were held at arm's length, lest the relationship evolve into something more serious. And permanent. The only one who broke this rule was Stephanie, who was—gasp!—back with Brandon once again. As the confirmed weak link, her actions didn't come as a shock to the rest of the group. Mine, however, inevitably would.

"When are we meeting this mystery man?" Yvonne asked, her voice amplified over the speakerphone. I was cooking lunch: hard-boiled eggs and boxed quinoa. I had inherited my mother's talents in the kitchen.

"I was thinking we could do something this week, maybe drum night at Third Beach? That's always a fun time. Plus, everyone can bring whoever they're seeing."

"Well, I'm flying solo, so don't have any expectations," Yvonne said. I could tell she was irritated that I had distanced myself from her. "But I guess that could be fun. I know most of the girls have already caught a fish or two for the summer."

"Poor things. And don't you worry, there's always hot men at drum night. You'll find a guy to scoop up. Then we can all get drinks or something afterwards."

Yvonne went silent on the line. Meanwhile, I began to crack the eggshells, letting their encasing fall off in flakes into the trash. The patio door was open to let the air, muggy with heat, flow through the room. I felt divine.

"Yeah, you're right," she said finally. "I'm sorry, I just miss our…time together. It was fun. Men can be so annoying to deal with."

I stopped what I was doing and walked over closer to the phone speaker.

"Hey, we can still have some fun together. I've just been caught up with this guy recently, and some personal stuff. So I'm sorry I haven't made time to see you."

"It's fine, literally, it's fine. I'm just saying it was nice…y'know, and I wouldn't mind seeing more of you again. That's all."

"Okay, well, let's make some time then. For us."

"Cool. Cool. I'd like that."

I smiled, and went back to shelling my eggs.

"So, this guy. It's not serious, then, is it? Like it's just a summer fling."

"No, Yvonne. Nothing serious. I wouldn't be seeing you if it was."

"Okay, good. Just checking. You're too young to think about settling down, Dahlia."

"Well, thank you, Mother Goose. So you've said."

"Mother Goose? What the fuck does that even mean?"

We both laughed. The last of the eggshells fell into the trash.

"Alright, well, I'll tell the other girls about drum night. Honestly, that'll be fun. I need something outside of a bar for once, they're making me go crazy."

"Cesspools," I agreed.

"Right? I can't stand it. Ugh, whatever. What can you do."

"Seriously."

"K, I'll let you go, pretty lady. What time should we meet you there?"

"Let's say 7?"

"Perfect. 7 it is."

I hung up the phone and began eating my lunch, feeling a twinge of guilt. Of course, I didn't view Jack like that. And I actually had no intention of sleeping with Yvonne. But I did value our connection and her friendship, and I wasn't willing to part with either just yet. So it was easier to tell her what she wanted to hear. I'd let her down easy little by little. Slowly is the fastest way to get to where you want to be.

A few minutes later, Jack came in through the patio door. He was shirtless and shiny with sweat after running down to the ocean for a jog. He saw me and lit up like Christmas.

"Hey babe."

"Hey you. How was your run?"

"Amazing. It's so beautiful over here. You having lunch?"

"Yeah, I am. You want some?"

"Sure. What's on the menu today?"

"Uhm...boiled eggs and quinoa."

"Mm. Love it."

"I know you do. And that's Chef, to you," I said, swallowing a mouthful of yolk.

"Of course. Yes Chef."

He kissed me on the forehead, sat down, and opened his mouth. I speared an egg and gently slid it inside. He chewed thoughtfully, a hand on my bare thigh. It felt comfortable. Life was good.

~ ~ ~

Drum night was exactly what the name suggested: drums at night. Or rather twilight, when the sun was sliding off the windshield of the world and into oblivion. It took place at Third Beach, a remote tuck of earth on the western corner of Stanley Park, which in itself was a thousand-acre temperate rainforest right on the fringe of downtown. Untouched by man.

Third Beach was the crowning gem of the city. It faced the expansive inlet harbour, with the mountainous North Shore to the right and the far-reaching peninsula of Kits and UBC to the left. Both were separated by miles of water. Since Third Beach was bordered by the lush offerings of a rainforest, a person could have the distinctive feeling that they were on an island, yet close enough to civilization not to feel isolated. Coarse yellow sand met the foaming ocean, which in turn met hundreds of feet of beachgoers. On drum night, the place was packed.

Jack and I held hands in the taxi as the car wound itself along the solitary road through the forest. Solitary, besides the three-lane highway that sliced its way through the middle of the park, conjoining the downtown core with the Lion's Gate suspension bridge, which in turn connected to the North Shore. Okay, so maybe not as untouched as I just said. Sue me. Along this stretch of road, however, the trees encroached upon us like emerald demons, reaching out to strike the moving vehicle with untrimmed branches. Above, the sky was melting into caramel gold.

"They should really cut down these branches. It seems dangerous to drive through," Jack commented to the driver. The man let out a grunt.

"Budget cuts, my friend! The city's always putting money where it shouldn't be. Just look at the downtown East Side. You call that successful city managing?"

"No, I guess you're right. It's pretty messed up."

He squeezed my hand and gave me a smile. I returned the gesture.

"Messed us doesn't begin to cover it. People sleeping in their own filth, dying on the sidewalk. If it was up to me, they'd all be taken care of. It's disgusting to see."

"What would you do, then? If you were in charge?" I asked. The man found my eye in the rearview mirror.

"Whatever it took. It's a disgrace to this city. Having all those druggies on the street. Taking over whole neighbourhoods. Things never used to be like this."

I resisted the urge to disagree.

The car pulled into the drop-off zone and started idling. Jack hopped out and grabbed our bag from the trunk, while I paid the cabby. As I did, I offered him one final thought.

"You know, poverty isn't a new thing. It's always existed, as long as people have. The only thing that's new is your exposure to it."

The man just gave me a blank stare.

"What the hell are you talking about?"

I shrugged and flashed a smile.

"Nevermind. Have a good evening."

~ ~ ~

I press the money into his hand and step outside. Immediately, a wallop of hot summer air hits my senses, overwhelming them. The scent of old growth trees and salt water, doubled over with the aromatic cocktail of several hundred humans, slaps me upside the nostrils. Jack comes around the side of the car and takes my hand.

"Ready?" he asks. I can tell that he's nervous. I'd be lying if I said I didn't share the same feeling.

"Yup. Ready."

The two of us join the throngs of people funnelling towards the stairs down to the beach. As we breach the crest of the hill to descend, the vista of the sunset scene and backlit mountains yawns into view. Along with drum night in all its budding glory.

"Holy shit," Jack says, to no one but me.

As far as the eye can see, there are heads: every shade and texture of hair you can imagine, all being kissed by the setting sun. Over the din of a thousand languages being spoken comes the heavy rumblings of drums. Dozens and dozens of drums.

Leading the way, I guide us down the stone staircase to the sand. Once at the bottom, I lead us closer to the heart of it all. The girls had told us to meet them over by the northern beachside where it's quieter, but I can't resist the stew of activity before me.

There is an enormous semicircle overtaken by bongos, tambourines, djembes, congas, tars. A flurry of hands beat the taunt skin of instruments with ecstatic vigour, alternating between simple rhythms and complex syncopations. It is electrifying. The sound of drums seemed to have a hypnotic effect on the crowd: people flailing, shaking ass, dancing like prophetesses possessed by the divine, tongues waggling, voices hollering. It is a pagan, primal sight. For a moment, a person could forget where they were in time.

Those who aren't dancing are clapping their hands, smoking heartily, drinking dark liquor until the bottles run clear. I turn back to look up at Jack, who is wearing a thin mask of shock. I don't know what he had expected before coming here, but I can imagine it wasn't *this.*

"How have I never heard about this?" he asks, turning on his sandy heels to take it all in. Most of the beachgoers are stripped to the barest of fabrics. I join suit, peeling off my T-shirt to assimilate with the other bikini-clad dancers.

"It's wild, right? They do this every 2 weeks during summer. Come on, let's dance!"

The frenetic pounding of drums has infected me. I can feel it, as my body responds with anxious twitches and jerks. This is my one place to let loose, beyond the privacy of my home. And that is not nearly as much fun, dancing alone. Here, you feel like you are part of an entity. A superorganism of moving, sweaty parts.

"Wait, what about the stuff? And your friends?" He holds up the beach bag in protest.

“Just drop it! There, put it there!” I point to a pile of other bags over to the side of the main circle. “And take off your shirt!”

“But...” I do not wait for Jack to finish his sentence. I take two bounding leaps into the thick of the dance frenzy, and begin to move.

The magic of the drum is this. There is no music more ancient than rhythm, and with a drum, rhythm is *everything*. In the absence of melody, harmony, chords, modulation, blah blah blah, you are left with the bones of our most ancient art. Music stripped of its jewels and clothes, laid bare for your ears to hear. Rhythm. Beat. The original song.

It is the same song the tides have been performing since their birth. The same song the waves have always sung, beating into themselves. The splintering of volcanic crust. Magma cooling. Tectonic shifts. The fall of hail. Thunder. Mudslides. Avalanches. Even wind, which we have personified through our simple human lenses, performs in a kind of sonic rhythm. All the Earth knows is the original song.

Nearly a hundred drums now performed this enchantment. And for those who were willing to open up and let it in, there was nothing to be lost except your sense of self. You could—not theoretically, but truly—dissolve into the music of the Earth. Just for a moment.

I knew Jack might be disturbed by what he saw next. And I wasn’t talking about the riotous atmosphere that had overtaken the shores of Third Beach. Nor what the meeting between my friends and him would bring. I had made peace with the latter, regardless of the outcome. But at some point or another, Jack would have to see me let loose. He would have to see me in an instant of authenticity. This shedding of niceties in favour of freedom. Only then—if he still told me he loved me—would I ever really believe it was the truth.

CHAPTER ELEVEN

There was a commotion of excited chatters and remarks. I turned from the pile of bags and back to the dance circle, feeling exposed in my bare skin. The word "wild" was an understatement. The energy of drum night was *unhinged.*

The crowd had tightened around the perimeters of the dance circle. Even from my high vantage point I couldn't see what was so damn interesting. A second later, I registered that Dahlia was nowhere in sight. Suddenly, I had a pretty good idea.

I moved through the crowd of partying beachgoers, stumbling across the sand and towards the edge of the circle. There, in the centre of it all, was Dahlia.

Most of the other dancers had stopped their movements and stepped back to watch. This left an abnormal pocket of space in the midst of an immensely populated area, a bald patch conquered by one. And that one, my girlfriend, was moving with the ferocity of a rabid animal.

Her arms and legs jutted and spasmed in eerie synchronicity, her hair flayed and whipped into a frothing black cloud. It rendered her face almost invisible, as if she was being mauled by some voracious black beast. Her bare skin was wet with perspiration, as puffs of sand became airborne as she scissored and kicked, alternating between high and low movements. But most noticeable of all, was the space around her. The bigness. It was back. This hurricane of a woman seemed to be filling a solid six feet with her energy alone. I had never seen anything like it.

The flock of drummers seemed ecstatic to have such an electric performer. They had begun to beat their instruments with phenomenal force, while their rhythms see-sawed between unity and divergence. Slowly the crowd began to participate, clapping in-line with the drummers, egging Dahlia on.

By now, her movements had reached a feverous pitch. She seemed to be channeling all the drumbeats simultaneously, a different body part embodying each sound. As she curved and turned her head, glimpses of her face shone through, the flash of white. Teeth. She was grinning from ear to ear.

As if to test her, the drummers began to play faster and faster. More and more people contributed their voices, whooping and urging the spectacle to do more. Impossibly, she complied: her dancing quickening in its reactiveness to the thundering of percussion and cheers. I was left marooned in awe, unable to equate the *force* I was witnessing with my girlfriend.

And that sphere of energy that seemed to surround her. The same one I had sensed outside Odyssey, or in little flashes, here and there. It was mesmeric. Hypnotic. *And all mine,* I realized. Without shame, I felt a tug at my shorts, as I grew hard at the thought.

The pitch was reaching its breaking point. Everyone could sense it. Sweat streamed down the drummers' faces as they moved their hands, the crowd's sounds growing like a growl. All the other dancers, even the ones too drunk or high to know what day it was, had realized that something extraordinary was taking place, and had moved to the side. Dahlia took full advantage of the free space, becoming entirely aerial for brief moments of time, before returning to the sand with newfound vehemence.

With a grand, exhaustive bar of deafening pounding, the drums all came to an end. An echo of music filled the summer air and rushed out to open sea. In perfect symmetry, Dahlia concluded her mad performance, striking a final, triangle-shaped pose with her body. Her chest heaved with exertion. But she was smiling, face tipped to the sky.

The crowd erupted into applause. Drunken voices exclaimed disbelief and amazement, and the drummers patted their instruments in appreciation. Dahlia broke pose and rose to her feet, waving and soaking in the appraisal. Her eyes found mine and she ran towards me, beaming even brighter.

"Did you see? Did you see?" she asked with child-like enthusiasm when she reached me. Her face, however, seemed hesitant; as if unsure of how I'd respond.

In another life, I would've played it small. Told her yes and given her a smile. Or less. But that life was dead. I had both feet firmly planted in this new one. I picked Dahlia up by the waist and brought her into an impassioned kiss. With ease, she wrapped her legs around me and returned the gesture. My world turned dark and all I could feel was her panting, slippery body against my chest, her lips planted against my own. And a flame inside me. Burning with nothing but awe and desire and love.

The drummers had started to play again by the time we pulled our faces apart. To my surprise, there were tears on the lids of her eyes.

"Hey, hey, what's wrong?" I asked. My hands cradled her body, holding it up against mine without strain.

"Nothing," she replied, still smiling. She gave me another peck on the lips. "Absolutely nothing's wrong."

"Then why are you crying?"

There was a pause, as she stared at me with her marine-rich eyes. From behind her, a backdrop of sun-black mountains and golden skies hung in contrast to the howling crowd.

"'Cause I love you," she said finally. "Because I love you."

I kissed her again, feeling grateful that her body was covering the front of my shorts. I squeezed her closer, relishing the heat of her, the scent of her, the power of her. All mine.

"I love you too, Dahlia," I said, feeling my own eyes grow wet. We kissed again. People around us oohed and aahed. The drums played on.

~ ~ ~

After gathering our stuff and composure, Dahlia took the lead to go meet her friends. By now it was almost 40 minutes after the agreed meeting time of 7 o'clock, but she didn't seem to care. Both of us were giddy with joy. Hands locked, we weaved our way through the crowd and headed north to the quieter section. After about 15 minutes of walking, a group of people up ahead started to wave excitedly.

"There they are. I was worried they might have left," Dahlia said, sounding nothing of the sort.

"Yeah. That would've been a shame," I said. We gave each other a look.

"Yoo-hoo! 'Bout time you showed up!" a woman with fried blonde hair yelled.

She had her back leaned up against an enormous log, her head framed between the legs of a tan, thick-jawed jock. There were five girls and three guys in total, all bunched together with coolers, beach-towels, and a sand-sunken stereo playing Sean Paul. The women were smiling. The men were not.

"Hi, hi, sorry, we got caught up in traffic," Dahlia said, as she exchanged hugs with each of the girls. They seemed thrilled to see her. "Everyone, I'd like you to meet Jack."

"Well fuck, you didn't tell us you were seeing Andre the Giant!" one of the women, hidden behind huge sunglasses, said without venom.

"Stephanie, you can't say that! God. Sorry about her, she grew up in a barn." The fried blonde smirked, and strode over. "It's nice to finally meet you, Jack. I'm Genevieve."

My eyes flashed up to meet Dahlia's for a split second.

"Nice to meet you, Genevieve," I said, shaking her hand. "And don't worry Stephanie, I've heard worse."

"Oh yeah? Like what?"

"Um. Freak. Sasquatch. Big bird..." I began.

"Big bird? Ha!" Genevieve threw back her head and let out a single laugh. Her breath smelled like warm beer. "That's so fucking retarded. I can't believe someone actually said that."

"So dumb," another girl chirped.

"Yeah," I agreed sheepishly. "Pretty stupid."

"Well, don't listen to that shit. People are haters. You won the jackpot, Jack. No pun intended," Genevieve said, with a drunken wink. "Come on, come sit! We've got coolers, beer, some Malibu, and kush. You smoke?"

"Uh, no. Not anymore." I sat down on an empty towel, where Dahlia joined me.

"Hey, sorry, I wasn't trying to be rude with that comment. I swear," Stephanie said, pushing her sunglasses up to her forehead.

"It's fine, don't worry 'bout it. Seriously," I said. Dahlia patted the inside of my thigh.

The rest of the girls introduced themselves with varying degrees of enthusiasm. Hottest in temperature were Genevieve and Stephanie, whom the latter I suspected was just trying to compensate for her initial comment. Anita and Joanna were amicably lukewarm; the two of them each paired up with a man who stared me down like the devil. Both guys were built like balloon animals who'd skipped a growth spurt. Even sitting down, it was impossible to deny they were both stubby dudes. I didn't take their glares to heart. I was just happy to be positively received by Dahlia's girlfriends.

All except for one. Sitting alone in a foldout chair was Yvonne. She offered nothing but her name and a stiff nod when her turn came, mimicking the other men who had had to be introduced via their respective female partner. She was stretched out like pulled black taffy with a right to kill, her eyes piercing my skin with chilly hatred. Except she wasn't looking at my face. I followed the point of her gaze to Dahlia's hand, which was resting contentedly on my leg.

"You know we were in the same history class, right?" Joanna was saying, her fingers wrapped around a sweating cooler. "The one taught by that weird German prof?"

"Professor Brau…I mean, Klein? Oh, yeah! I thought you looked kind of familiar."

"What a weird fucking class. She went way too heavy on the inbreeding and slavery stuff." Joanna sighed and rolled her shoulders. "So, what're you taking at UBC?"

"Electrical engineering. You?"

"Oof. That must be rough. My friend James was in the engineering program for a couple semesters. He ended up offing himself."

"Oh my god, what?" Stephanie cried, whipping her head around.

"I'm kidding! I'm kidding. He's fine. Well, not actually. Just super depressed. I heard that program's stressful as hell."

"Well, I wouldn't blame your friend if he did. I've been thinking about taking up some late-night knitting myself." I mimed hanging myself with a noose. This earned an awkward laugh from some.

"Ha! I bet. Although I took a textiles class in my first year, and they definitely did not teach anything like *that,"* Joanna replied with a wicked grin.

"What are you taking yourself?"

"Oh, just business. That's where the money's at. But I might be joining you and James pretty soon if I don't finish up." She pulled a mock trigger to the side of your head.

"Jesus, you two. That's so dark."

"Uni will do that to you," Joanna said wistfully.

"Are you guys in school too?" I said, offering the question to the group. Two of the guys were sharing a joint, while the third was mushing face with Stephanie. None of them had hardly contributed a word. In the distance, the far-off sound of drums galloping across the sand.

"No, none of us are. Joanna's the baby of the group. I'm working at my father's company, and Stephanie's in marketing. Anita...wait, babe, where are you working again?"

Anita gave us a guilty look. "I'm a dog trainer."

"Aw, that's so cute!"

"I love that for you," Genevieve agreed.

"Yeah, but it's...only for pugs."

"What?"

"Yeah, it's like a whole thing. Apparently pugs are one of the most stubborn breeds, but they're also super popular with rich white ladies, so my boss started a whole side-business for training them."

"Aren't those the breed that can't breathe through their nose?" Dahlia inquired.

"Uh, yeah. That's the one."

"Yikes. So what's your boss's main gig, if that's just her side-business?" Joanna asked.

Anita took another sip from her drink.

"She's a pug breeder," she answered, shamefully.

This sent the group into laughter. Even Yvonne cracked a smile. I glanced over at Dahlia, who had moved to lean against the huge log. The dense rainforest stretched up behind her, as clumps of people began to trickle off the beach. I looked from her to the ocean, which had turned the colour of a bruised apricot and was growing darker by the minute. The sun had fully hidden itself behind the mountains, transforming the sky into a pink, pumpkin, oxblood swirl.

"What about you, Yvonne? What do you do?" I asked, extending the olive branch. Yvonne repositioned herself to square me head-on.

"I'm a legal assistant. I'm actually going to the States for grad school in the new year."

"That's awesome. Which school?"

"Vermont," she replied brusquely.

"Wait, what? Since when? I thought you decided to stay here," Dahlia asked. She sat up straight from her relaxed position against the log. The other girls followed suit.

"You're actually going?"

"What? Yvonne! Why didn't you tell us?"

Yvonne regarded the group with a steely gaze.

"Well, I changed my mind. You all knew I got into that school. It would be stupid of me to pass it up."

"Yeah, I know, and we're happy for you," Dahlia replied, sounding hurt. "I just didn't know you changed your mind. You seemed pretty adamant about staying here for a little while longer."

"What can I say? Things change," Yvonne said, leaning back against her chair headrest.

The girls all shared a look with one another.

"Yvonne, what's going on? You've been acting weird since you got here."

"Yeah, what's up?"

Sensing tension, Balloon Animals Number One and Number Two excused themselves to go join a nearby game of volleyball. Stephanie and her boyfriend Brandon even stopped making out to see what was happening. Yvonne laid there, staring at the sky. She let out a reluctant sigh from the depths of her chest.

"Dahlia, why'd you lie about traffic?"

"What?"

"I said," she pronounced, sitting up to face her, "why'd you lie about getting stuck in traffic?"

Dahlia shifted her position.

"I didn't. It took forever to get across the bridge to this side of the water. Right, Jack?"

"Uh, yeah. There was traffic," I agreed. I could tell this wasn't what Yvonne was getting at, but technically it was the truth.

"Right. Okay, so why did I see you dancing when I first got here?" Yvonne countered.

"Well, I did that too. I just didn't want to use that as my excuse for being late. It was a combination of both."

"That can't be true, because I saw you when..."

"Wait a sec, you two! Chill! D, it's fine if you did some dancing before coming over here, nobody cares. Yvonne, you're late all the time for shit, so come on. Why are you *actually* pissed?" Genevieve asked, her hands raised up as if to offer them a high-five.

Dahlia and Yvonne sat and stared at one another. Both of them had expressions that were impossible to read.

After several uncomfortable seconds, Yvonne let out another sigh. She reclined back into her chair. "Literally, it's fine. I just didn't want to be the third wheel for everyone tonight."

"Yvonne, we *just* tried to introduce you to that guy who—"

"Yeah, I know!" Yvonne snapped. "But men are bugging the fuck out of me right now. I'm just so sick of all their bullshit and goddamn mind-games." She brought a hand to her head and began to rub her forehead.

To my surprise, Dahlia rose from her spot to go comfort her. She went and put a hand on Yvonne's shoulder, who flinched at her touch.

"Hey, hey. I get it. It's tough, trying to find the right guy."

"I'm not trying to meet the right guy, Dahlia..."

"Well, *whatever* or whoever you're trying to find, you will. Don't you worry. I promise."

"That's right, gorgeous!" Anita called out. "What you seek is seeking you!"

I felt a cold stone in my stomach at the words. They were so familiar, yet I couldn't place where I'd heard them.

"Yeah, you're fine, Yvonne! You've got us. We're not leaving you for no man," Stephanie said. Brandon looked at her, bewildered. Stephanie just shrugged.

"Ugh, yes, yes, I know," Yvonne said, un-shielding her eyes. She looked up at my Dahlia and gave a half-smile, patted her hand. "Sorry for being a bitch. It's this heat, I swear. I've been baking in it all day."

"There we go! Best friends again," Genevieve said, bringing her palms together with a single clap. "Hug it out, you two."

Dahlia bent down to embrace her friend, who accepted her without hesitation.

"Yes! And then let's get out of here. I'm hungry. I totally skipped lunch."

"Fuck, you're right. Me too. What time is it?"

"Too late, that's when. Look, everyone is clearing out."

I turned to where Joanna was pointing, back to the main crowds and drums. It was true. The hoard had splintered into factions, who were fleeing the beach at rapid speed. The spectacular show in the sky had commenced its performance and died into a pitiful wash of blue. Only a few stragglers remained, beating their instruments with weary fingers. I shivered slightly, the air changing seasons by the second without sunshine.

By the time I turned back, everyone had started to pack up. I contributed the best I could, gathering empty cans and shaking sand from towels. Joanna went off to the side and stuck four fingers in her mouth.

"Yo! Boys! We're packing up!" She whistled with locomotive force at the two balloon animals, who were eating sand at volleyball. They dusted themselves off and began to plod over.

"Are they…related?" I asked Genevieve, helping her fold a towel. Her eyebrows went up.

"Yup. Twins. Fraternal. Jo and I decided to try something a little different, but so far it's been a bust. They're great lays, but otherwise…hopeless. I think tonight is their last night before they get the chop. Right, Jo?" She tipped her head back to catch her friend's gaze.

"Uh-huh. I can't deal with one more of their stupid questions. Like the other day…"

Joanna didn't get to finish her sentence, nor need to. Balloon Animal Number Two opened his mouth and shouted:

"What time are we getting picked up again?"

"We drove here *ourselves*, dumbass! Now help us clean the rest of this shit up!"

A ripple of giggles passed through the girls, as Number Two turned rust-red. I smiled despite myself. It felt good to be included.

As I grabbed the last of the garbage, I bumped into Yvonne.

"Sorry, didn't see you," I said. She looked up at me.

"It's fine." Her eyes met mine like crosshairs, locked in, and then moved on. I felt discarded, dismissed. She turned and started walking up ahead, where she was quickly accompanied by Dahlia at her side.

I picked up a cooler, two bags, and joined the group, wondering if the flicker of jealousy I'd thought I'd seen was correct. And what it meant.

CHAPTER TWELVE

Like all things, the summer had to end. Notice I didn't say 'good'. *All* things must end: good, bad, and every fucking shade in between. A teacher told me this back in elementary school, when we were learning about outer space. One of the other boys—a gentle, soft-spoken one, the best kind—had asked what happened to stars during science class.

"Do they keep burning forever?" he'd asked, with all the light of innocence.

Our teacher, Ms. Delora, had thought for a moment before responding. Of course, she must have known the answer right away. But she had decided to tell the truth about the whole matter, not just the fate of stars. Even if she didn't know the truth from the get-go.

"No, they don't," she'd replied. "One day, each and every star that you see, including our very own sun, will die off. They will burn out of gas and turn into something else. Same as everything. Isn't that amazing? We're just like stars, each and every one of us! So there's no need to worry. One day, we will also turn into something new. None of us are exactly sure *what,* but it has to be something. Does anyone remember what the rule of energy is?"

The class was silent for a minute. Finally, a single skinny arm inched its way up. Ms. Delora pointed.

"That energy can't be destroyed?"

"That's right, Constance! Energy cannot be created *or* destroyed. The most basic rule of our entire universe. *Energy cannot be created or destroyed.* So what does that mean, really? It means that, at one point, all of the cells in our bodies were bits of a star. Then, when that star burned out, it turned into gas and bits of rock and atoms, and eventually, after millions and millions of years, it became Earth. Tiny microbes evolved out of the sea into plants, which turned into animals, which then turned into people. And here we are!"

Ms. Delora smiled cheerfully, looking pleased with herself for tackling such philosophical questions in grade-six science. The class seemed equally pleased (and bored) by the answer. No one was really old enough to fully grasp what she was saying.

Of course, I couldn't just stay silent. I'd learn this lesson later on, the art of inaction. But for now, at age 12, I had no reason not to. Mostly.

I stuck my hand up.

"Yes, Dahlia?" Ms. Delora asked. Her eyes averted to a different spot in the classroom.

"Does that mean we'll live forever? If our energy can't be destroyed, does that mean we will never really die?"

A couple students started to whisper to each other. Ms. Delora regarded me with a hint of irritation. I had poked a hole open in her freshly-sealed can of worms.

"No, of course not, Dahlia, we won't live forever. That would be awful. We just..." she trailed off, trying to find the right, age-appropriate words. I sat waiting with my fingers laced atop my desk.

"Well, we don't know, like I just said, what happens when we die. Nobody does. But I can promise you it isn't *that.* So don't worry, everyone. Now, let's get back to talking about our solar system. We've already wasted enough time as it is."

She strode over to the whiteboard and began speaking louder to smother out the voices of the classroom. Eventually, the flat droning of Saturn and its many moons worked like a tranquilizer. Everyone fell silent, except me. My mind, the eternal student, kept chattering and chattering with questions that neither Ms. Delora nor myself could possibly ever answer.

~ ~ ~

September sank its teeth into us before we even realized it was dangerous. Suddenly Jack was gone: off to school, back to work. I was left to my own devices, with the ugly realization that none of them worked anymore. In his absence I was soul-crushingly bored. Unsatisfied. I wanted to share my experiences with him. Doing things alone had lost their charm.

"When can I see you this week?" I asked the landline, trying to sound less desperate than I felt. There was a sigh on the other end.

"I don't know, probably Sunday." *Today* was Sunday, so another week. He kept going. "My classes are all early, so I can't be staying over at your place on weekdays. It'd take almost 2 hours just to drive to campus. And my dad would get so pissed off if I started disappearing again."

"But you were gone all the time in the summer. Not to mention you're literally a grown man. Why the fuck does he care so much?"

"He just does, okay? Technically it's his money, or my parents' money, so I don't have much of a say. Living with him is bad enough. I don't want to make things worse."

"What about your auto job though? Can't you rent a place that's closer to the school?"

"Babe, I work 2 days a week. I can barely pay for my own gas. Forget about rent."

I felt a flash of anger. I knew it was directed at reality: the limits of money, Jack's dad, distance. But it felt because of that word. *Babe.* In the context of things, it felt wrong and miscast.

"Don't call me that."

"What?"

"Babe. I don't like it."

"But…I've called you that for months."

"Yeah, and I haven't liked it for months. Just call me by my name. Please."

"I don't understand. Why didn't you tell me before?"

"Because! I was trying to be nice. I don't fucking know. Why didn't you tell me your dad was such a controlling prick? Or that I wouldn't be able to see you more than once a week?" My voice was sharp, high-strung. I started to pace the kitchen, feeling out of my depth.

"Woah, where is this coming from? You were fine just a second ago."

There was a pause, in which his register dropped.

"I thought you liked when I called you babe."

"Well, now you know I don't." I sighed deeply into the mouthpiece. "Look, I'm sorry. This is so fucking stupid, Jack. I don't understand why you're doing this. If you hate your dad and your major and your dumb job at the mechanic's, why don't you leave it? Why don't you just come live with me?"

The words are out before I can even think them over. One moment, a thought. The next: hurtling down miles of wire at the speed of sound. Too late to bite back.

Jack went silent on the line. I leaned onto the kitchen counter, feeling dumb as day.

"Hello?" I asked, after he didn't say anything.

"I never said I hated my dad," he replied quietly.

"Right. Sorry. I shouldn't have said that."

More silence met my ear. I covered my eyes with my hand, pushing hard enough to see flickering stars.

"But you're right," he sighed. 'Why the hell do I keep doing stuff that I hate?"

I wished I could see his face at this moment. I wished this conversation wasn't happening with a whole ocean in between us.

"Are you serious about that, by the way? Me coming to live with you?"

"Of course I am," I expelled. It felt good to say. I'd been wanting to for weeks.

"Well, for the record, I'd love to. But I can't. Not with the ways things are right now."

"Yeah, I know. I had a feeling you'd say that."

~ ~ ~

The month dragged on. I went back to doing things with the girls, with Yvonne. They had come to not only accept Jack, but actually like him. I'd done my part in convincing them he was A Good Man, and they had done their part in recognizing that. Even Yvonne had inched her way around. Glacially, but still. Movement was movement. She seemed less possessive now that I carved out some solo time for her.

With fall in full swing, Jack finally asked me to go on a date with him, to do something outside of my bedroom. Our time together had been reduced to Sundays, the occasional Friday. We fucked like demons. The whole week seemed to lead to when we were together, a steadily simmering cauldron of desire reaching full boil by the time his car pulled up. We could barely wait to get through the front door before ravaging each other.

One time his initial greeting was to push me hard against the side of his car, before then sliding two fingers up to the knuckle inside me. I yelped. He asked if I'd missed him, which was a silly question. Why else would I be wet before he even showed up?

When I told him this, he'd smiled and pulled his fingers out. Then stuck them into his own mouth. He held my gaze while he did, something he'd become a master at.

"I guess you're right," he said, before picking me up in a fireman's carry. I screamed out with laughter and mock-beat his back, all the way up the stairs to my empty, waiting bed.

The date Jack planned took place out in the valley. From where I lived, it was well over an hour and a half drive east, where the urban sprawl dissipated into farmland and rolling green hills. Only now, in the crux of October, most of the green had transfigured itself into a work of gold, crimson, and orange.

I picked up Jack on the way before switching places, letting him take the wheel of my mother's Audi as we drove into the countryside. It was Friday, with an unseasonably warm breeze blowing through the cracked windows. Clear cobalt skies. From the stereo came the hum of folk music, soft and fuzzy like sepia.

"So where exactly are you taking me, handsome?" I asked, resting my hand atop his on my thigh. He had kept all details a secret, besides the general location.

"You'll find out. You've never been outside the province, have you?"

I thought about my answer before replying.

"No. I've never left the city."

"That's wild to me. How come your parents never went travelling? With all that money, it'd be the first thing I do."

"Well, my mom developed a fear of flying, so that was the main reason. And my dad was gone by the time I was 6. Plus, he would've been embarrassed to be seen with a crying child."

"You remember that? Seems specific." He looked over at me.

"Yeah, I do. It's one of the only things I *do* remember about him. He hated when kids acted like kids. He wanted me to act like a grownup from day one." Or something like that.

"Damn. That sucks. I can't even imagine you as a child."

"Oh yeah? Why not?"

"Because. You're you. How could all of this..." He gestured to my physical self. "Fit into a little kid's body?"

I laughed.

"Is that what you think, hey? Well, for the record, I was a very cute kid. The cutest."

"I bet. You still are," he replied, squeezing my leg.

"Smooth. Very smooth," I said, patting his hand. The highway raced on.

After another half-hour of driving, Jack pulled off the main road and onto a gravel one. The car vibrated along the way, kicking up a cloud of dust. Jack rolled up the windows to stop it from seeping inside. Finally, he turned the wheel again and switched off the car.

"We're here," he said proudly. I squinted my eyes out the window as the dust cleared.

Before us stretched a sea of corn. We'd parked on a rise of earth with a few other cars, high enough to see the extent of the thing. Rows upon rows of hunter-green leaf blades; stalks stretching up into splayed brown tassels, decorated with ears and silks of ripened corn. Black lines cut through the crop like arteries. Above, the sky held steady: a canvas with only one shade. It hurt to look at. The openness of it all. The expanse.

"Is that a maze?" I asked. I hadn't seen one in person before. Jack nodded.

"Yup. The biggest in the province. It used to be my favourite thing to do in autumn when I was growing up in Saskatchewan, so I thought we could give it a try. I had a feeling you'd never done one before."

"Well, you're right. I haven't." My heart was beating strangely fast, but I couldn't figure out why. "So…what do we do? Is there a goal or do we just get lost inside?"

Jack squeezed my hand. "Kind of. We have to try and find the centre. Come on, you'll see." He clambered out of the car, ducking his head on the way. I followed suit.

The two of us walked past the parked cars and down the grassy slope to the check-in. The welcome area consisted of a few buildings—all rustic and whitewashed and sagging—with a smattering of people milling about. A tinny overhead speaker played country tunes about broken hearts and hard times. Over to the right, a pen of goats trumped around, butting heads and the occasional child. Chickens roamed free. All in all, it felt like we hadn't just traveled to another world, but another time period.

"It's so…" I failed with my words, trying to articulate what I was seeing.

"You hate it," Jack said. "I don't know what I was thinking, bringing someone like—"

"No, no! Not at all," I corrected. "I love it. It's so peaceful. That's the word."

"It's peaceful where you live too, though."

"Yeah, but it's different. People around there are so pretentious, usually. There's this feeling of…tightness. Arrogance. Everything feels so simple here."

This made him smile. "I know what you mean. It's probably the only thing I miss from back home. The simplicity of it all. So I'm glad you like it too." He poked me in the ribs. "Maybe you're actually a country girl at heart."

"Ha! We both know I'm too lazy for that. I like the vibes, not the chores."

We both laughed and took each other's hand. The sun beat down.

The women running the check-in greeted us with a gaping smile.

"Hey there, you two. My, you're one of the tallest fellas I've ever seen! Any taller, and you'd be looking right over the corn!"

"Haha, I bet. I actually had to call beforehand to check that it was tall enough this year. It's happened before," Jack replied, grinning.

"Oh yes, this year's a doozy. Haven't seen heights like these in over a decade. Last we measured, this year's coming in at ten, eleven feet. Without heels," she added, with a wink my way.

"Jesu…I mean, wow. That's impressive."

"Yup. You lucked out."

The woman took our wrists and slipped a paper wristband onto each, then offered us a map.

"Some folks like to have a backup in case they get tired of being lost. But personally," she said, leaning over the front of the counter, "I don't see the point in that. It's called a maze for a reason. Half the fun is getting lost. *Most* of the fun is getting lost."

"I agree with you there. Dahlia, what do you think? Map or no map?"

I gave each of them a look.

"No map. I believe in us."

"'Atta girl. Now, once you find your way to the middle, follow the signs that'll point you to the path out. It'll save you a heck of'a time more than trying to find your way back. Oh, and be back before sundown. Otherwise we'll have to come get ya."

"What's in the centre?" I asked, my curiosity getting the better of me.

The woman sat back into her chair and laced her fingers behind her head.

"Well," she said slowly, "I guess you'll just have to find out for yourselves."

~ ~ ~

The sky shrunk to an overhead ceiling once inside the maze. We were enveloped in rustling, the stalks leering over us like judgement from the soil. I let Jack take the lead, forging ahead with the blind confidence of a European explorer. There was only the sound of our feet, unseen birds singing pastoral hymns, and the corn, moving with indignation for having been disturbed. Who could blame it? I wouldn't want a bunch of chatty humans crawling around inside me either. Yuck.

"This is wild. I've never been in a maze this tall before. Usually they max out at six to eight feet. Must have been a good growing year," Jack was saying.

"Uh-huh."

"Like, look at this shit! This one has to be almost twelve feet!" He was pointing to a particularly gargantuan stalk that seemed to defy the rules of gravity. I had never seen someone so excited about a plant before, vegetable or not.

"Yeah, it's crazy," I replied. Jack turned to look at me.

"You okay? Are you having fun?"

"Yeah, I'm good. I'm having fun."

"Then why do you have that look on your face?"

"What look?" I asked, genuinely surprised. He was getting so good at reading my expressions that it sometimes freaked me out. I'd spent years perfecting my mask, so to have someone penetrate it with such ease was unsettling. I smiled as authentically as I could.

"Nothing. I'm fine! Don't worry."

"I don't believe you." He walked over and took my shoulders in his hands. "What's up?"

I let out a sigh, and shrugged out of his grip.

"Okay, honestly? I'm feeling a bit anxious."

"What? Why?"

"I don't know, I think it's… the corn."

Jack squinted his eyes at me.

"You're afraid of the corn?"

"What? No! I said I'm anxious, not afraid."

"Isn't that the same thing?"

"Um, no. Well, kind of. It doesn't matter. And it's not the corn, it's like…how close it is."

I demonstrated with my hands, two flat palms slowly closing in.

"I'm a bit claustrophobic," I admitted. Jack's face fell.

"Oh, fuck. I wish I knew that beforehand."

"It's fine. You didn't know."

"I also didn't ask."

"Well, it's not usually something I tell people anyways. So even if you had, I probably wouldn't have told you."

Jack turned in a circle, looking around at our surroundings. Nothing but green stalks and invisible songbirds.

"So what do you want to do? Should we go back to the car?" he asked.

"No, no! It's fine. I need to get over it anyways, so this is good practice."

"I don't want you to feel like shit the whole time, though. This was supposed to be fun."

"It *is* fun. Honest. Anything's fun with you," I said. It was the sad, sappy truth.

This did the trick. He took my hand and gave it a squeeze.

"Alrighty. Let's face these scary corns together, then."

"I told you, it's not the corn…"

"I'm just teasing, D. I know." He leaned down and planted a kiss on my forehead. "I'll keep you safe regardless. Don't you worry."

I opened my mouth to reply, but thought better of it. We carried on.

After about 10 minutes of backtracks and left turns, Jack broke the silence between us.

"So…what other things are you afraid of?"

"What do you mean?"

"Well, you said you don't usually tell people what you're afraid of. So I'd like to know all of your fears. That way, I can make sure you don't ever have to deal with them."

Oh, sweet Jack. I wanted to correct him, to tell him my fears weren't the *only* things I didn't tell people. That would've been suicide. We were moving into darker depths, bit by bit, with each other's psyches. I wanted the descent to be a smooth one. Too much at once and the pressure might kill both of us. Or at least, him.

"Well," I began, taking my time with my answer. "Tight spaces, as you now know. Men, obviously. Everyone should be a bit afraid of men. It's just common sense. Otherwise…baboons. Box jellyfish. Hippopotamuses. Giant hornets."

He nodded thoughtfully. "Lots of animals."

"Well, I've seen a lot of documentaries."

"Fair enough."

"Torture. Bombs. Oh, and childbirth. The thought of it makes me sick."

Jack slowed his walk, turning to me. "So, you wouldn't ever want to have kids?"

"I mean, maybe. If it was a surrogate, or adoption. But from my own body?" I blew out air. "That sounds like a nightmare."

"Yeah, but like...I'm sure lots of women feel that way. It's a scary thing, I can only imagine. But it's part of life. Plus, don't they have drugs and stuff for the pain?"

I stopped walking altogether.

~ ~ ~

"Jack, have you ever seen what childbirth looks like?"

"Of course not," he says.

"Well, it's disgusting. There's blood and stretching and so much screaming and—"

"Okay, okay, I get it. Yeah, I know, it's not *great.*"

"Not great?"

"Fine. Bad. Horrible. Whatever." He starts walking, no longer holding my hand. I hurry after him.

"Wait, Jack! Hold on a sec." I catch up to him and stand in his path. "Why are you upset?"

"I'm not."

"Well, yes, you are. What is it? You can tell me." He stares down at me, the stale brightness of afternoon light rendering his face in shadow.

"Look, let's just forget it. I'm sorry I brought this whole thing up."

"No, no. Just talk to me. Please."

He sighs.

"Okay. Fine. I guess I just..." He turns his head, looking off to the side, the dirt. Anywhere but me. "I've always wanted to have kids. At least two, one of each. And if I'm with you, I...well, fuck. I'd want to have them with you."

His words take me by surprise. I didn't expect such emotional honesty out of him. And if it weren't about having kids, I'd be feeling pure elation. Instead, I feel a twinge of dread.

"I didn't know they were so important to you," I reply.

"Well, now you do. But you're right, I mean." He rubs my shoulders with his hands, "There *are* other options, if we get to that point. Surrogacy. Or whatever."

Relief.

"Right. Of course. I'm glad we're on the same page, then." I rise to my tiptoes to give him a kiss. "I'd like to get to that point with you, Jack."

Now it is his turn to flush. Even in shadow I can see his cheeks change colour. "Yeah? Really?"

"Yes, really. Now come on. We have to finish this maze. I feel like we've been in here for days." I tug at his arm to keep walking. Jack laughs and checks his watch.

"It's been just over half an hour."

"Tell that to my stomach. I'm famished."

"Well, maybe there's a five star restaurant in the middle."

"Mmm, right. I'm sure."

We meet another dead end and have to turn around. The sun lights up our faces.

"Hey, Jack?"

"Yeah?"

"What's some of your fears, then? Now that you know mine."

Out of the corner of my eye, I see Jack's mouth twitch.

"Um, I dunno. I can't really think of any off the top of my head."

"Oh, come on. There must be something."

We walk several rustling paces before he replies. Even the birds seem to have quieted, as if to hear his answer.

"I mean. I guess I don't like blood."

"Blood?" I ask naively. He grunts.

"Yeah. Shit's gross."

I nod without looking his way.

"Fair enough."

~ ~ ~

It's another 40 minutes before our sweaty bodies emerged into the maze's empty centre. Both of us let out a whoop of relief, grateful to have found our way to freedom.

"Alright, let's see what all the fuss is about," I said, cracking my knuckles. "I definitely don't see a restaurant, that's for damn sure."

"Nope. Just *that* thing," Jack said, holding back laughter. I followed his finger to where he was pointing.

There, sagging off by the exit sign, stood a scarecrow. Actually, 'stood' was too strong a word. The scarecrow was slumped pitifully atop a bale of hay, wearing a checkered vest and a bowler hat old enough to predate the dinosaurs. The hat was so tattered, it looked like it had been through a garburator. Spats of bone-white bird shit covered the ancient threads.

The scarecrow was in no better state. Crows had ripped the fucker to shreds. It had coaster-sized eyes with huge, painted lashes. Someone had stuck a beet in its burlap head to represent its mouth, giving the impression that the scarecrow was pursing its lips in a silent, juicy kiss. Its two arms were outstretched: spindly birch branches spotted with leaves. A squirrel, or maybe a rat, had made a nest where the scarecrow's stomach was supposed to be. Not that anyone was home right now.

"Oh my *god!*" I screamed. I clutched my stomach and keeled over with laughter. Jack had already beet me to it. Pun intended. The two of us clutched each other and killed ourselves laughing over something that wasn't even that funny.

A nearby flock of crows, annoyed from having been stirred by our ruckus, took flight and inevitably flipped us the middle finger. In whatever way crows do, that is. We'd spoiled their silence with joy.

CHAPTER THIRTEEN

My birthday gift was waiting for me on the kitchen table. It was the crest of November and I was exhausted: the toll of commuting, school, work, and home life had sucked me dry. My only reprieves were my weekly visits with Dahlia. Sometimes they were the only motivation I had to keep pushing forward.

As per Dahlia's encouragement, I'd quietly switched a few of my courses to English and philosophy electives. The work was hard, but nothing compared to the electrical universe I was still wilting away in. Now I felt a thrust of enthusiasm for some of my education. It was nice to be learning something of genuine interest. I was sick of linear oscillators and bipolar junction transistors. Give me food for thought and let me chew.

The gift was small and poorly wrapped. Dahlia stood off to the side as I inspected it, staring at me with a look of bemusement. I picked it up and shook it by my ear. Nothing.

"Let me guess. Table napkins? A tie?" I asked, jokingly. The thing had weight to it, despite being noiseless. I prayed it wasn't expensive.

"As if. Go on. Open it."

I obliged, pulling at the paper to unveil a patch of green. Then, golden trim, and…

"Oh, fuck. Dahlia. You shouldn't have."

I cracked open the plush emerald box and unveiled the treasure inside. A Platinum Rolex winked up at me. My brain immediately started counting zeros.

"Happy birthday, handsome," she said, coming to give me a hug. I embraced her half-heartedly.

"Wow. Uh, thank you, I appreciate it. I really, really do. But, Dahlia, I…can't accept this." Dahlia pulled out of our hug and looked up at me.

"Why not?"

"Because! Aren't these a couple thousand dollars? I mean, for your birthday, all I gave you were flowers and took you to dinner."

"At a *beautiful* restaurant," she replied. Two fingers poked my ribs. "And that's not all you gave me, mister. If I remember correctly." Her face was warm and smiling as she spoke. How did she always look so bright?

"Yeah, but still. This doesn't feel right. I don't want you spending money on me like this."

"Why not? It's not even mine. I inherited it."

"Doesn't matter. Technically, it's yours. I just feel bad."

"Well, stop. I have nothing else that I want or need. So what am I supposed to do, just let it sit and rot in the bank? Instead of spending it on the person I love the most?"

I let her words hang in the air for a moment.

"I mean…you could donate it."

"What?"

"Like, some of it. If you have enough money that you don't know what to do with it, couldn't you donate it somewhere?"

"Who says I already don't, Jack?"

"I don't know. I've just never heard you talk about it." I held up my hands in defence. "It's not really my business. Just a suggestion. I'd feel better about that instead of you wasting it on me."

"You are not a *waste.* Literally nothing could be further from the truth." Dahlia let out a sigh, her mouth curving down. "Please, just...take the watch. I spent a lot of time choosing the model." Her voice shrunk really small. "Do you even like it?"

"Yes, of course! It's perfect. I just..." I returned her air with a sigh of my own. "I feel bad."

"Will you try it on, at least?"

I looked down at the watch. Its dial, the colour of ice-cold water, stared back at me like an eye. Gingerly, I removed it from its velvet boxing and—after removing my digital Casio—slid it onto my wrist. A perfect fit.

"Wow," I repeated, rotating my forearm to admire the thing. The platinum band picked up the afternoon light and winged it back at me with force. I could feel its heft. Its expense.

"Please keep it," Dahlia begged, leaning her head against my shoulder. "I really want you to have it."

"How much was it?"

"I'm not going to tell you."

"D, I can just look it up when I get home."

"Do you promise you'll keep it if I tell you?" She peered up at me, her chin digging into my skin. "There's an engraving on the bottom, by the way."

I unhooked the clasp and pulled off the watch. Sure enough, there were two initials on the underbelly. J + D. With an infinity symbol beneath. My stomach fluttered.

"Okay. Yes. I'll keep it."

"Pinky swear?"

I laughed and rolled my eyes. Locked pinkies with her. "Fine. Yes. Pinky swear."

Dahlia smiled brightly again. She squeezed my ribcage and let out a sigh.

"Alright, I'll tell you. But don't be mad. It was around eighty thousand with engraving."

My mouth dropped open in pure shock. At my lack of reply, she pulled her head back to look at me. There was a hint of satisfaction in her eyes.

"You're joking."

"I'm not."

"Dahlia, I…"

"Nope! You promised! You're keeping it, and that's final." She pulled away from me and repositioned herself in front of the counter. Threw me a wink. "Just try not to lose it, okay?"

~ ~ ~

Losing it was not going to be a problem. The watch grabbed me like a python. Once it had its grip around my wrist, there was no letting go. I started to hate taking it off. Plus, it was designed to survive actual Armageddon, so there was no reason I ever *would* need to take it off. I could dive three hundred feet deep into the Arctic sea if I pleased, and still, it would tick. It would keep telling me the time 100 years after I became a frozen corpse.

Suddenly I felt branded. Not by Dahlia, but by wealth. I now carried big dollars, huge dollars, on my person at all times. It was impossible not to fixate on it. My skin under the metal would tingle incessantly, demanding my attention. The platinum picked up light like a thief. I had to sheath it beneath my long sleeves as much as possible to avoid detection from strangers. And my father.

The two of us were at odds more than ever. He resented the fact that I was dating, that there was happiness in my life. I tried to see him as little as possible, which was hard. Every night when I came home, he'd be waiting. He barely read or watched TV, which would've done him some good. Instead, he drank sparkling water and played Beatles records on non-stop rotation. And thought. Whenever the weather was bad or he was tired—which was almost always—he would spend the time sitting in his recliner chair, thinking whatever storm of thoughts filled his brain. I couldn't have imagined that they were anything good.

We didn't use to be like this, Dad and I. We were never close, but there was never the dynamic that it was now. The hatred. The anger. That came after the accident. Before that, Dad was a drunk, and had been since I was 6 years old. A sloppy drunk, yes, but never a cruel one.

He passed through jobs like seasons. He'd arrive home to Momma and I with excitement that *this time,* he'd found a good one. A keeper. The bartending gig at O'Leary's. Helping out at our neighbour Mike McKenna's pig farm. Shopkeep assistant at the general store. It was a mid-sized town, and my dad used to smile lots, so it wasn't hard for him to find work. The trouble, of course, was keeping it.

In the first couple of weeks of new employment, Dad would clean up. Start shaving, dressing better, eating breakfast. The house would brighten. He'd lose the stink of liquor and go back to wearing cologne. Old Spice Classic. Sometimes I think it was the reason Allan used to make me feel on edge whenever we'd hang out. He smelled just like my father.

Momma and I loved this time the best. Life would become easier, the wrinkles of worry all ironed out. Our fridge would fill back up from having a steady flow of income. We didn't have to think twice about bringing people over to the house. The air felt lighter. But there was also a certain tension about those weeks, too. The same tension that must have accompanied the ancients, as they hurried to collect the year's harvest before the frost of winter. Because we knew. It was only a matter of time.

It would start slow. Suddenly we would find him asleep in inappropriate places. The sitting room. The porch. His office. His words would lose their crisp edges and start to blend together like watercolour. He'd begin to laugh at things that weren't funny, such as Momma burning her pinky on the stove. Then the smell would come back. The liquid stink.

And then one day, inevitably, he'd be waiting at the house when I got back from school. Playing his records. McCartney, Harrison, Starr. And of course: good old peace-preaching, wife-beating Lennon. This was always how we knew he'd slipped fully back into the habit. The addiction. Most times he was wet-mouthed and goofy when I came through the door, crossing the floorboards to embrace me in a drunken bearhug of happiness.

"Y're 'ome, Jack! Where 'ave 'ou been?" he'd ask, squeezing me so hard that I'd have to tap him to break free and breathe. When I'd say that I'd been at school, he would roar with laughter. Tell me that was a waste of my god-given time.

"A boy like 'ou shud be outsside," he'd say, before cranking *Sgt. Pepper* to even greater heights. Our closest neighbours, the ones with the pig farm, were over two miles of prairie away. There were never any noise complaints from the wheat or wind. And any attempts from my mom and I to turn down the volume would result in a belligerent rant demanding to know why we were silencing the greatest band of all time.

"I just wana kno' why '*ou* should get tu deciding who plays the music round 'ere," he'd shout, guarding the speaker dial. "This is thu best music ever made and 'ou want to turn it *uff?*" Further attempts to explain that we were just trying to preserve our eardrums were pointless. Because if the Beatles were blaring, it only meant one thing. Dad was fucked up.

Nowadays I didn't know what it meant. Not entirely. We had nearby neighbours here, including a Korean family on the other side of the duplex wall. The father, Bong Chul, did not take shit from anyone.

The first time my dad tried blasting the Beatles, Bong Chul came and pounded on our door until he turned it down. Chul had commanded my father with his sonorous voice that if he didn't play his music quieter, he would happily call the police to deal with him. Dad's protest that the Beatles *needed* to be played loudly did absolutely no good. Bong Chul had scrunched his brows in disapproval and told him that "no music needed to be played that loudly". And that he hadn't even heard of "those beetles," before shutting the door in Dad's gobsmacked face. I'd watched the scene go down from the dinner table with a half-smile.

This did not stop my father. He had tracked Chul's car and noted the times he was home, and more importantly, not. Then he would go right back to blasting the golden boys. Unfortunately, Chul's wife and two kids did not share their father's outspokenness.

Dad's sober misery had been going on for the past 8 years. Since Momma's accident, Dad had stopped drinking entirely. He'd quit cold turkey in the aftermath of grief, gone emotionally rogue. I didn't even recognize him. In the weeks that followed her death, he had transformed into a fire-breathing parent of anger and misplaced hatred. His temper had only intensified after our move to the coast. The only thing that still reminded me that the man I shared a roof with was, indeed, my father, was the Beatles. Besides that, he was a complete, terrifying stranger.

~ ~ ~

By the time I come home from work, it is well past 9 o'clock. My hands are dog-tired from holding a pen and typing for hours, my mouth sore from fake smiling. For the past 2 years, I'd been working at a mechanic's shop, not as an actual mechanic, but as a glorified receptionist. I answered the calls, hung up keys, and explained to overworked moms that their oil change was going to cost a lot more than expected because *someone* had poured washer fluid in the oil tank by mistake. Though no one was pointing fingers, of course. And here's a complimentary calendar for Gobert's Auto Shoppe. Have a wonderful rest of your day.

Dad is sitting at the dinner table when I close the door. Right away I can tell something is off, because he never sits there. Usually he is welded to his recliner chair or his bed. And there is no music. Only silence and the sound of falling rain.

"Hey," I say, pulling off my wet clothes. I try to keep my gaze elsewhere, my tone light. A moving target. Neither does me any good.

"Come sit down, Jack," Dad says roughly. He has a voice like unpolished granite, like shark skin. It physically hurts to listen to. I hang up my coat and reluctantly come over.

There is a letter sitting on the table. It has been torn open and restuffed with whatever is inside. On the front of the envelope is my full legal name. And a return address to UBC.

"Is that for me?" I ask, stupidly. Dad scowls at me.

"Don't be fucking thick, Jack. Sit down." My stomach winces. I lower myself into the seat across from him.

As I look at my father, the first thing that strikes me is how old he looks. The hanging overhead light casts a pallid, overcast wash upon his features. His hair has largely fallen out, leaving only sparse clumps of wiry grey. Dark bags the size of islands reside beneath his eyes. Eyes that are staring at me with quiet, seething disgust.

"Is there anything you'd like to tell me?" he says, less of a question than a threat. I rack my brains, trying to think of whatever I've done now to upset him. Besides the usual crime of existence.

"Um. No. I don't think so."

"Then what the fuck is this?"

He smacks the letter with his open palm. The whole table, a cheap particle board thing, trembles violently.

"Open it," he commands, turning his face away from me.

I sit there, feeling unable to move. My whole insides feel like they have turned to rot. But there is another feeling, too, simmering on the surface. Atop the fear, there is a fine foam of fury bubbling inside me.

I lean forward and take the letter from the table. He does not watch me do this, but keeps his gaze planted on the wall. I pull out the letter and unfold it for the second time that day.

It's what I'd expected, and now feared. A billing summary of my tuition for university. Details for course costs, administration fees, student union offsets, et. cetera. The financial blow of learning, laid out on paper. But I know this isn't what has enraged my father. Not quite.

The summary includes the costs of specific courses, as they often vary from program to professor. The course costs and their *names.* And for the first time since I'd started school, words like "Circuit Analysis" and "Electrical Systems and Control" are almost absent from the page. Abbreviations denoting science and engineering classes have been replaced by the harsh red ink of **ELECTIVE**. English 200: Beowulf to Baudelaire. 191: The Mechanics of Poetry. Philosophy 203: Ethics, Virtue, and Consequentialism. And most embarrassingly, a course titled Sexuality and Eroticism in

Literature. Which had quickly turned into my personal favourite. Now, however, I felt nothing but shame as I stared at those damning words on the page.

I didn't know what I'd been thinking. Something like this had been bound to happen sooner or later. In the moment, I hadn't cared. I'd felt nothing but reckless joy when I'd marched into the registrar's office late September, spurred on by Dahlia's persuasion to take control of my life.

She'd been right, of course. Despite my exhaustion, it felt good to be learning something I cared about. It felt fucking great. It was a feeling I couldn't imagine being replicated from a career I despised, no matter how high the salary. The two concepts couldn't coexist in my mind. Plus, I'd figured if things worked out with Dahlia, I wouldn't even *need* to make a high salary. Just to earn enough to contribute. All of a sudden I'd felt free enough to pursue something I was passionate about. Or at the very least, curious.

Only now, as I sit staring down the barrel of my dad's gaze, all of those good feelings have died away. I feel myself right back under my father's thumb. I feel the weight of expectation. And the cross of disappointment.

"You're turning into a sissy now? Is that it?" He reaches over and snatches the letter out my hand. "What the fuck is this shit, Jack? You tell me what the fuck you think you're doing with my money? You pissing away your education 'cause you're turning into a goddamn cocksucker? Is that it?" His face is bulging, a trail of spittle staining his chin.

"Dad, it's...not your money." Another bad habit I've picked up from Dahlia: speaking without thinking. I regret the words before they even finish forming on my tongue.

"The fuck did you just say to me?"

"Nothing. I..." I run my hands down my pant legs. My heart rate has doubled, tripled, a thoroughbred thundering away in my chest. This isn't goddamn *fair.* Why am I still afraid of this miserable old man? Why should I be made to feel like a helpless child?

I clear my throat.

"I said, it's not your money. It's Momma's. And we both know that."

For a moment, he simply stares at me, unable to comprehend my defiance. I usually sat and took his berating with a bowed head, silent except for short words of agreement, apology. He'd make me feel like I was 17 again. Like I was the same boy being screamed at for causing his own mother's death. The one who would never amount to anything. The biggest mistake of my father's life. His greatest shame.

For 8 long years, I'd felt stunted, trapped at that age. Only now, I was stepping into my own as a man. Shedding the past and its grip on me.

My father turned his chin and spat on the floor beside me.

"You're a fucking disgrace. You know that? You make me sick to even look at. How dare you disrespect me after everything I've done for you. Dragging you across the country for a new start. Paying for *your* education, so you don't have to struggle like I did. Letting you sleep and live in my house without paying rent, without demanding a *cent* from you. And this is how you thank me? You blow my fucking money on this, this…sissy shit?"

I shake my head. He shreds the letter in half and keeps going.

"3 cunt-sucking years of tuition and *now* you couldn't care less about making a living, you just want to read books and stick your head up your ass because the view's nicer. You want to go live on the street? Is that it? You want to be one of those fucking junkies 'cause you can't afford to have a roof over your head?"

Outside, the rain has started to downpour. The symphony of water droplets hitting shingle is only second to my father in volume. I refuse to look away.

"No, Dad. I—"

"I'm not finished. You think it's funny bringing your mother into this? After what you did? I'll tell you what I fucking think of it. I think you should be ashamed of yourself. I think you—"

"I don't give a fuck what you think!" I shout, raising my own voice against his. The effect is immediate. He stops mid-sentence, mouth agape like a trout. I take full advantage of his shock.

"Momma would've wanted me to be happy, Dad! She would've wanted me to use that money to learn something I actually liked! Because I hate engineering, I fucking...*hate* it. That was your dream. Not mine. If you didn't succeed with it, then too damn bad. So stop punishing me with your failures by also making them mine."

There is a scraping sound as my dad stands up from his chair. He is a big man, my father: inches shorter than me, but not much. Two steps and he is looming atop me. His open palm winds back and slaps me with unrestrained force.

The sound is like a whip striking flank. One moment I am sitting on my dead uncle's dining chair, and the next I am off, my head colliding with the nearby wall. A hot flash of pain sears across my face and seeps into my brain.

For a moment I am stunned, unable to comprehend what has just happened. In all the years, through drinking and anger and everything in between, my father has never raised a hand at me. His words have always been more than enough.

He is screaming down at me. I realize I am on the floor, the chair flipped over beside me. My body is leaned against the wall, slumped in the pocket of space between the dining table and the bookcase. My father stands above me and screams down, in the same living room his own brother hanged himself in. The gloom of the place seems more alive than ever.

"You fucking faggot! You disrespectful, ungrateful child! You don't know what the fuck you're talking about! How dare you speak to me like that! How fucking dare you!"

The bloom of pain on the side of my face continues to grow. And so does the anger inside me. By now, it is rising to a boil.

I pull myself to my feet. The action causes a momentarily change of expression—fear—as I rise up before him, standing to my full, cursed height. Now I am the one looking down at him, if just by a bit.

"Don't talk to me like that, Dad," I say. My mouth feels weird to move after being hit.

"I'll talk to you however I like! This is my fucking house, and you are my fucking so—"

I rob the last letter from his lips. I put both of my hands on his shoulders and give him a shove. The surprise of such an action takes him off guard, and he falls like Babylon, a plank of hatred falling flat on his back. There is a cracking noise as he hits the floor.

Now he really starts screaming. Not words anymore. We are past the time for words. He is foaming and spitting at the mouth like a demon, trying to pull himself up from the floor and *failing.* I realize that part of his shrieking must be pain.

The sight invigorates me. I feel a torrent of vindication rise within me, a phoenix of rage. I think of every time my father laid into me, all the insults and jeers and accusations and threats and filth spouted from his lips. I think of the man passed out on the kitchen floor of our old house. I think of Momma, and her sad, brown eyes.

I straddle my father with my feet and lean down to face him. His head is blood-red and veiny. Something drastic must have happened from his fall, because he can barely speak. A herniated disk? He's been complaining about his back for years. And he's old. So goddamn, pathetically *old.*

He tries to grab onto my shoulders, to pull me down to his level, but I stand just high enough that he can't. He beats at my legs and howls the word "fuck" like a broken prayer, because he can't seem to get another word out of him. There is so much hatred spilling out of his eyes that his pupils change colour. And he is crying. Yes, for the first time in my life, I see what my father looks like when he cries.

I open my lips and let a fat glob of spit fall out of my mouth. I watch it splat onto his bloated red face, watch it mingle with his saliva and tears. I can see the unbelievable shock in his eyes. And I realize: I am happy.

Then I have an idea. The living room, cramped with its ceiling fan, recliner chair, bookcase, and dining table, has one more piece of furniture. Dad's record player. It sits atop a cabinet of vinyls, with two mammoth speakers on either side. He had lugged them across the country during our move, unwilling to part with them because of their rich sound. Although his speakers aren't what I'm interested in.

I move across the room, kicking my father's grasping hands off my ankles. His shrieking has dissolved into a sort of profanity-laced gurgling. Shot with intermittent threats to kill me.

My insides feel like they've been charged with a thousand volts of pure anger. It is an anger so titanic and whole that there is only calm. I feel perfectly rational, level-headed, despite it all. I cannot hear my heartbeat, hammering in my chest.

The hinges squeak as I open the cabinet and remove my father's most precious things. His albums. First edition, special edition, collector's edition. It doesn't matter. On each is the name of my sonic nemesis, the soundtrack for almost all the worst moments of my life. You already know their name.

Dad begins to make a strangling sound, and I turn to look at him. He's craned his neck to look at me, his eyes shot with mortal terror.

"D-don't, don't, puh-lese..." he is stammering. I carry the stack of records over and lay them on the floor above his head. Take my place next to them.

"Shut up, Dad," I say flatly.

I grab the top record off the pile. *Rubber Soul.* The bandmates stare at me with their bowl cuts and big noses. Egging me on.

I slide the vinyl out of the sleeve, lift up my knee. Hold it aloft out of my father's claws, as he tries to grab my leg to stand up. Dad begins to scream blue murder, and I say a brief prayer that Bong Chul and his family are out for the evening. Then I bring the wax down hard, shattering what my dad loves most into pieces.

~ ~ ~

By the time I was done, the room had gone very quiet. My dad had managed to turn himself onto his side and was sobbing silently. He still couldn't bring himself to stand up.

A graveyard of black shrapnel surrounded his crumpled body, as well as torn-up album sleeves like confetti paper. Now the sound of rain had reclaimed its title as the loudest. No neighbours had intervened with bangs on the door.

In the aftermath of the last record being smashed, a wave of exhaustion swept over me. I realized my whole body was slick with sweat. I poured myself a glass of water and saw, too, that my hands were shaking. And that I had crossed a line—no, *desecrated* a line—and there was no going back anymore. I had to leave. Right now.

I left my father's body on the living room floor and went upstairs to my room. Pulled my suitcase out from under my bed and began to fill it. My whole body was quaking, and a dark shadow of guilt fell upon me. I couldn't stop hearing the sound of my dad's back as he smacked the ground, the spluttering of his screams and tears, his manic wide-eyes as I destroyed his prized possessions. And with it came the memories of our old farmhouse. And of Momma.

I grabbed everything I could and stuffed it into the suitcase. My room, albeit not the cleanest, was relatively sparse. I had left most of my furniture and childhood belongings back in the prairies, and had accumulated little since moving to the coast. My entire wardrobe easily filled a large suitcase. I grabbed another two duffel bags from the hall closet and started filling them up with my books.

As I worked, I moved faster and faster. The urgency to leave, to get out, was feverish. I wasn't worried about my dad calling the cops. I knew he was too proud to be seen in that state. To recount his humiliation at the hands of his son. Regardless, the need to extricate myself was blistering. I could not seem to pack fast enough.

Before long, my room was stripped bare. I doubled-checked that I had my birth certificate, passport, documents. Every knickknack and memory that I held dear. And of course, tucked in a secret safe place, the last thing I owned of Momma's.

I took two trips down the stairs, the duffel bags jangling with their mixed cargo, the Kit-Cat Klock's tail stuck out of a worn backpack. I tried to keep my eyes off of the living room as I did. However, when I came down the second time, I saw that my father had moved. He'd eased his way into a sitting position, with obvious strain, against the wall.

He watched me with a look that was impossible to read. Not that I was trying to. My back was turned to him as I pulled my coats out of the entranceway closet, my shoes. All my belongings had been isolated to those two places, as far as I could remember. I had no desire to look elsewhere in case I was forgetting something. All I could think about was leaving.

I pulled my raincoat on and opened the door. The downpour was torrential, a divine lashing of water from above. I staggered out into the storm, and loaded my car with all that I owned. My dad stayed silent as I moved from the entranceway to the vehicle, and back again.

At last, the trunk and backseat were loaded, ready to depart. But there was one last thing I needed to do.

I walked back into the house and closed the door, bringing the room back to relative silence. My dad was breathing in short, ragged breaths. I sighed and looked elsewhere.

"I'm sorry," I said, feeling the extent of my guilt. The carnage of the living room was hard to take in. As was the sound of my father's pain-ridden breathing.

"I didn't ever want things to be like this, Dad. I hope you know that."

I stuck my thumbnail into the groove of my keychain, and pulled off the house-key. Placed it on the small table by the door.

"You don't have to worry about me coming back here. I don't want to see you again. And I'm sure you don't, either."

My father's expression was quite easy to read now. Even from the edge of my vision, because I couldn't bring myself to look at him full on, I got the message loud and clear. There was nothing but honest-to-god hatred in his eyes.

I cleared my throat, and turned to the door to leave.

"Take care of yourself," I said, without meaning it much. He let out a broken laugh at this.

"I hope you and that whore you're fucking get everything you've never wanted. I hope your lives are hell on Earth," he hissed. His words punctured my guilt and infused me with fresh anger. I looked back at him, one foot out the door.

"Have fun dying alone, Dad," I replied. His eyes widened ever so slightly. A sick feeling began in my soul.

~ ~ ~

50 minutes later, and I was at Dahlia's, unlocking the chain on the gates with my own key. I drove down the pitch-black driveway, parked the car. As I ascended the front steps, she opened the door with a smile, well before I even got a chance to knock.

CHAPTER FOURTEEN

After 5 months of living together, Jack proposed. He tried his best to ambush me with a surprise, but of course, I saw it coming from miles away. That doesn't mean I was any less ecstatic about it. In fact, I was even more so, knowing it was going to happen. I despised being surprised. By anything. Even love.

He does it on a road-trip down the coast. We'd crossed the border into the States, with Los Angeles as our destination. We never reach it. Instead of taking the atrocity of asphalt you people call a four-lane highway, we wound our way down the seaboard on side roads. After living by a relatively tame ocean for so long, it felt good to see the wild sea again.

Back in the city, there was an island many miles from the mainland, which protected the shores from battering waves and hurricanes. I could see its shape from my house, off on the horizon like a child's drawing of mountains. When the clouds were low, it vanished entirely. The main island—half the size of Ireland—resided about an hour's boat journey away. Along with its two hundred smaller gulf offspring, it served as a buffer between the city and the open ocean.

On the rugged coast of Oregon, however, the waves rushed in to meet the sand with abominable hunger. Jagged black cliffs, some reaching eight hundred feet high, bordered the sea with impunity. The water brewed itself into a frothing blue stew of turquoise and kelp, torn up from the ocean floor by cold, merciless currents. No smidge of land lay in sight. Only an infinity of saltwater and sky.

I knew something was up from the minute Jack asked me to go. He'd posed the trip under the guise of a post-semester change of scenery, a chance to travel somewhere new. Just the two of us. We could take a few days to travel to Los Angeles, and another week to explore it when we got there. Wouldn't that be fun?

When I asked him why we didn't just fly, his eyes turned shifty. He offered some excuse that his uncle had taken him and his family down the Oregon coastline as a kid, and now he wanted to show me the same spots.

"You've never even left your own province, let alone country," he'd said, in disbelief. "I want to change that. I want us to travel around, to see the world together."

I agreed, while silently concocting reasons to change his mind. I didn't want to see the world, thank you very much. I wanted to stay here, at home. Safe. Quiet. Peaceful. And in love.

Ever since he'd moved in, we'd established a routine that was practically matrimonial. He would leave early for university 4 days a week, with his degree officially transferred to the English department. During the days when the lengthy commute to campus proved too much, I would taxi him across the harbour in my boat. Drop him off at the peninsula, then putter around on the water until he was ready to come home with me.

Those hours were the only time we were ever apart. We spent the rest of the week in constant companionship. We'd go for hikes up into the mountains, where the forests were awakening with the warmth of spring. We'd do all our errands together. Grocery shopping. The gym. A different date night each week, ranging from dinner at the rotating restaurant of a skyscraper to boozy mini-golf. We made love as often as the sun set. I'd squeeze in the odd visit with Yvonne and the girls, just enough to keep them satiated, but they were really just an afterthought. I really only had one thing on my mind. Jack.

~ ~ ~

I let him drive the car so I can look out the window. As testament to his understanding of me, the drive is exactly what I could ever want. Curving thin roads that are underused and flanked with vegetation. The bouquet of salt, humidity, travel-worn wind in my nose, while I watch pinwheeling gulls and eagles speckle the sky like daystars. At times, the road dips so low to the ocean that water threatens to spill over the median and into the vehicle. For other parts, we rise up onto the crown of grassy buffs and exposed rock-faces. And I'd cry out, demanding that he pull over so we could get a better look. And each time, without annoyance or question, he would oblige.

The sights are so extraordinary that I don't need to fake awe about seeing them again. Each time, I feel it like the very first time. When we emerge from the vehicle and venture over to the cliff ledge, the view sucks the soul right out of me and replaces it with its own. Suddenly my being is all sun-dappled breakers and fresh air. My insides are the colour of rough seas, of clouds splitting into celestial gatherings: spun up high and fluffy like cotton candy. My breath is sea spray, flung from the base of volcanic rock by seven-foot waves. I am free. I am no longer just a woman in the world. I am the whole world in a woman.

Mostly, we are alone in these moments, standing by the parked car at a pull-off spot or road shoulder, looking out at something too beautiful to even comprehend. Our hands are locked. And I can feel his heartbeat, pulsing away down his wrist.

We spend the first night in an old motel near Cannon Beach. The place is squat and musty, but the view of the ocean is unbeatable. After dinner at the only restaurant still open, we stumble back to our room in the dark and take off our clothes. Our movements are slow, as we unveil each other's naked bodies for only our eyes to see. We do it in near-silence, until the act of entry. Jack stands me up against the window, and I watch the moon hang as a saucy gibbous above the wave-heads. Then I watch my breath grow deeper and deeper, fogging up the glass. I listen to the sound of him. The way his hips collide with the backs of mine, his member mining its way to my heart from my pelvis. When I feel him quickening, tauter than ever, I slide my finger down the front of my body and tease my clit into surrender. We cum within a minute of the other, as usual. Then fall asleep the same way.

Dawn arrives and proclaims itself like the second coming. Jack and I lounge in the morning heat, the sunbeams showering the bed frame. Outside, the gulls harmonize with the incoming tide. But something is up from the minute he awakes. His heartbeat is faster. He doesn't look me in the eye. But something also tells me, there is no need to worry. And for once, I listen.

~ ~ ~

By noon, we are on the road again. The radio jockey announces “Everybody’s Talkin’” by Harry Nilsson, which is ironic, since the car is otherwise silent. Every passing minute confirms my suspicion that something is coming, as does his twitching jaw. And the slight clamminess of his right hand, resting on my knee. I keep my eyes fixed to the passenger window and drink up the scenery. My molars chomp down on my cheek to stop myself from grinning.

The road slopes upwards, climbing higher and higher into the spring sky. Cottonwood branches replace the ocean, as we are thrust into a world of shadowy green. If for a moment. Abruptly, we emerge on the summit, and the world opens itself up to us again.

Jack slows the car to a murmur and pulls over. There is a stretch of pavement for cars, small enough that the average person would miss it if they weren’t looking. A wooden sign with the words “Phaon Point” stands, swinging in the wind. Blocking the ocean from sight is a thicket of soft-leafed trees and a solitary dirt pathway.

“What’s this place?” I ask, stepping out of the vehicle.

“Somewhere my uncle showed my parents and I when we drove down here. I’ve never forgotten about it, after all these years.” He laughs. “Although I was a bit worried I’d miss the turnoff.”

I smile and take his hand. “But you didn’t. Smart guy.”

“Mm. We’ll see. I may have overhyped it, in hindsight. ”

“I trust your judgement. Past, present, *and* future you.”

He laughs again, and starts down the path.

The path unfurls under the cover of canopy, overridden with exposed roots and shoe-smoothed stone. All we can see are trunks, branches, leaves. The call of seabirds invites us further.

As the path turns downhill, the vegetation gradients into a high wall of bramble bushes. Only the bravest of flowers have debuted, their pink heads standing alone amidst the crowd of sheltered relatives. Jack and I walk single-file between the thorny walls, prickles snagging our bare skin and leaving irritated red lines behind.

Finally, after several minutes of quietly cursing thorn-pricks, the brambles all fall away. The wind picks up. And we have arrived.

The place where Jack has taken me is beyond beauty. It is heaven on Earth. The sky is a dynamic oil painting of azure, cloud, and sunshine, resting atop the vast horizon of blue water. From the way the cliff point protrudes—overtop the ocean—a person has the distinct impression of flying, as if they'd just risen out of the depths and into the world above. The ground under our feet is soft, spongy with moss and wild grasses. Where the path ends, there is a flat slab of stone to sit on. As close to the edge as any sane person would dare.

"Oh, Jack," I say. My tongue feels useless in my mouth. Nothing I say can capture my feelings. My gratitude. I give him a hug instead.

"Do you like it?" he asks.

"It's the most beautiful place I've ever seen." And I mean it.

We sit on the stone bench and take it all in. On both sides, miles of cliffside stretch on, as explosions of whitewater collide with their black roots. The cliff we sit on, Phaon Point, is not only the highest, but juts out the farthest. When I peer over the edge, I can barely see any rock. Only deep water, churning hundreds of feet below us.

"I was worried this might've been too much for you," Jack admits. He has his arm protectively around my body, as if to shield me from blowing away in the wind.

"Nothing's too much for me," I retort.

"Well, that can't be true. Weren't you the one scared of some corn?"

He smiles down at me, his big handsome face lit up by the sun.

"Oh, shush. You know what I mean."

"Yeah, yeah. I know I do."

We kiss. Just a peck. I press my body closer to his.

"You're shaking, Jack."

"Am I?" He laughs, a bit too heavily. "I didn't notice."

"Well, you are. I can feel it." I nestle deeper into him. "Honestly, you've been acting a bit funny all morning."

I am choosing my words carefully. Softening my tone. I want to make sure he doesn't chicken out now, after all this. If I expose the fact that I suspect something, he'll have no choice but to follow through.

"Well," he starts, clearly a bit lost for words. "I guess I'm just really happy. To be doing this. With you."

"I am, too." I pat his leg and catch his eye. "You have no idea how lucky I feel to have met you, Jack. You make..." I look out to the open ocean. "You make this life make sense. For once. I finally feel like I know what I've been looking for all this time."

He takes my hand in his. Squeezes it.

"Yeah. I know exactly what you mean."

I hold my breath, waiting for him to continue.

Jack unwinds himself from me and sits back. Clears his throat.

"So, Dahlia, I've been thinking, and I...well, this past year with you has been the best of my life. Easily. You've brought so much excitement and good things into my world, and I just wanted you to know how much you mean to me. I can't imagine my life without you."

"Aw, Jack. That's so sweet."

"Yeah. Which is why..." He moves from his position beside me, dropping one knee to the mossy cliff edge. Digs a hand into his pocket to pull out a jewelry box. The box is old, weathered, but when he snaps it open, the ring inside glints with new hope.

My heart is cartwheeling inside my chest. The sound of water and birds are drowned out by the rush of blood. I feel buzzy, light-headed, yet so grounded in the moment that I cannot move a muscle. Jack continues.

"I know we haven't known each other for that long. Just a year is nothing in the grand scheme of things. But when I'm with you, D, I feel like we are catching up after 1000 years apart. Like I've known you longer than I've been in this body, that there has never been a time where my soul hasn't loved you."

He looks down at the ring, which is shaped almost like a raindrop.

"This was my mom's. She'd always told me to fall in love with someone who feels like home. To find someone who understands me as I understand them. And to treat them like the ends of the Earth weren't too far to go for them. Dahlia...you feel like home to me. You make me feel like I can do anything, be anyone. I want to keep you safe, and to experience the world with you. I want to come home to you each day, and to love you, always. I want us to grow old together, and have kids, and be so fucking happy it hurts. And I want to go to the ends of the Earth if you'd ask me to. Just as long as you were here when I got back."

Overhead, the seagulls are screaming. Wind pulls at my hair, possessing it with a life of its own. Jack holds the box and exhales. Looks into my eyes. There is no fear behind them. Only trust. Only love.

"Dahlia, will you marry me?"

For a second, I am worried I won't be able to reply. That's how strong the paralysis has set in, despite knowing all morning this was going to happen. I just can't seem to break free from the shock that this is really happening. He is asking the question.

I swallow. Nod.

"Yes. A hundred times, yes."

My words wash over his face with quicksilver suddenness. He snaps the box shut and places it on the stone slab, leans forward to kiss me. I take his face in my hands and pull him closer. His body falls onto mine, the weight of him pressing down on me like gravity.

I welcome it, all of it, the sensation of rushing air, of sun-warmed stone and love, bursting inside of me like an atom bomb.

When the two of us finally pull apart, Jack rolls onto his back beside me. We both look up at the clouds, which are metamorphosing before our eyes. He leans over and grabs the box, and pulls out his mother's wedding ring.

"I didn't get to resize it. I wasn't sure what size you were," he says apologetically.

"Don't worry about that. We can do it when we get back."

I sit up onto my elbow and offer a hand. "Can I try it on?"

He passes it to me, and I slide it on. The band catches on my knuckle, before hurdling it with ease. It fits almost too well.

"I don't think we'll need to resize it," I say with a laugh.

"Damn. I guess you're right. Lucky us."

"Lucky us, indeed."

We kiss again. My insides are flush with desire again, and for a second, I think about mounting him, right there on the cliff. But I settle for the crook of his arm, and his hand within mine. The ring digs into my skin, pleasurably.

~ ~ ~

I don't know how much time passes. Nor do I care to. Eventually, the sun slips behind the clouds, and the wind sharpens its fangs. We make our way up the path back to the car.

Both of us sway in step, woozy with joy.

"So, what now mister? Do we keep going south or what?" I ask, doing up my seatbelt buckle. I cannot stop my lips from lifting.

"I was going to ask you the same question. Do you still want to go to L.A. or should we just...I don't know, hang around here? Do some exploring?"

We look at one another, already knowing the other's answer. A tire-shrieking big city or the magical serenity of the coast? The winner is clear as day.

We both burst out laughing. Jack pulls the car out of park and starts to drive north, without another word from either of us. There is no need to say a thing.

I switch on the radio, and the jockey begins to announce the next song. I crank open the window to let some air in.

"Next up for ya, we have one of my all-time favourites. Here is the iconic 60's track "Michelle" by The Beatles, for *your* cruising pleasure. This is 101.5 FM Classic Radio."

Music starts to pour through the speakers. I start to hum alongside the melody, and I notice that Jack tenses slightly. Then, as our car winds down the hill, he relaxes.

As we drive on, he slowly joins me in song.

CHAPTER FIFTEEN

The suit I've chosen is a shade lighter than black. I finish tying my tie around my neck and inspect myself in the bathroom mirror. Outside, I can hear the clamour of our guests, milling around their seats on the lawn. I have about 20 minutes before we're supposed to begin.

A knock at the door, then a man's voice, asking if I'm almost done in there. I splash water on my cheeks, cursing the heat, and crack open the door.

"All yours," I say, giving him a nod. The man looks at me with uncertain recognition.

"Hey, you must be the lucky guy!" He extends a hand. "I'm Hale. I used to go to high school with Dahlia."

"Hey. Nice to meet you." I shake his hand, wincing at the force of his grip. The man has dirty blonde hair and eyes that linger. He's void of any dress jacket, just a collared shirt that is hardly buttoned.

"It's a fucking mother out there, right? Christ. I can barely stand it."

"Yeah, it's been a hot summer."

"You're telling me. I run a construction company and some of the guys were literally passing out. Funniest fucking shit I've seen in my whole life. Big two-thirty-pound dudes dropping like flies on the tarmac. Of course, not so funny for business, but you gotta take the piss out of things, am I right?"

He slaps my shoulder and steps into the bathroom.

"Nice to meet you, Jack. And congrats on bagging Dahlia. She's a slippery one."

One wink later and the door is closed. I'm left standing alone in the hallway, feeling bewildered. Who the hell was that?

I shake it off, then go back downstairs to greet the rest of the party.

~ ~ ~

Dahlia and I had picked her house as the location for both ceremony and reception. The grounds were big enough, and there weren't enough wedding guests to justify renting out a whole church. Most of the guests were Dahlia's friends, anyhow, a few extended family members.

I'd invited the handful of people I'd befriended at UBC, some old work colleagues. Even Li had agreed to come, responding to our first text correspondence in years with a flurry of exclamation points. Meanwhile, my invitation to Allan had gone unanswered. And for my father, I hadn′ t even dared try.

"So happy to hear from you! Of course, I'd love to come!!!!" Li'd replied. When she'd first arrived at the property, I had hardly recognized her. She was tanned from the summer and chipper. She'd brought her partner, Lisa, who'd followed in her wake with a bashful smile.

"Jack! Hoooooly shit, nice place!" she'd exclaimed, embracing me in a half-hug before pointing out that my tie was crooked. I'd slunk off inside to one of the upstairs bathrooms, chuckling to myself. Perhaps people don't really change after all.

While Dahlia had taken on the bulk of wedding planning over the past 15 months, I'd doubled down on coursework, cramming in my requirements to become a schoolteacher. One brain-breaking year later, and the finish line was in sight. By next December, I'd be a free man.

The time had flown by. Another round of birthdays, holidays, and seasons erased by the unrelenting march forward into the future. The two of us ate up our happiness with greed, each good day devoured with unwavering certainty that another would always come. We were very stupid in this aspect. Very stupid and very in love.

Neither of us had wanted to wait so long to get married. At that point it was hardly more than a technicality, an official stamp on a connection carved in stone. But there had been the social hangups of a wedding so soon into the relationship, and the scheduling logistics with school. In the end, we'd decided to wait a year and tie the knot in August. Then just like that, we were here.

Since the world had been cruel, neither Dahlia nor I had parents present. Or, in my case, any family. The scattered remains of the Donner clan all lived back east, and there was certainly no one I was close enough to invite to fly out. As for Dahlia, she'd asked her widowed, childless great-aunt Grace to come, alongside her godfather, Paolo.

In a surprise turn of events, 80-year-old Paolo had shown up with a hot young date whom he'd proudly introduced as "Misty". Misty looked fresh enough to be in high school, but with none of the doe-eyed naïveté. She'd snatched a glass of champagne off a passing tray and asked Paolo why he hadn't told her the ceremony was happening on *grass.*

"I would've never worn these shoes, you old freak," she'd snapped, hiking her boobs to greater heights. When I'd countered that the dance floor and reception would be on a floor the organizers had built, and that only the ceremony was on grass, she'd squinted her eyes and told me I had no idea what it was like to be a woman. Then dragged Paolo off with his cane to their seats.

Aunt Grace was a quiet spectre. She wore a black dress with jam-red flowers, which clung to her sweaty legs as she walked. When I'd introduced myself to her on the lawn, she'd held my hand and spent a good time looking at me.

"How long have you known Dahlia, dear?" she'd asked.

"Coming up on 3 years now, ma'am. I feel very lucky to be with her. And I hope she feels half as good about me," I'd joked. Grace had not reacted.

"She's a strong girl, that one. Doesn't take after her mother, though, that's for sure. Or her father."

"Did you know them well? Her parents?"

"Well enough. My niece Sharon was a lost woman, I'm sad to say. Bless her heart. She married a man who couldn't keep himself in check and fell in love with the bottle herself. But she was always very sweet, very kind. That one, however—" She'd pointed off to the house, where Dahlia was getting ready. "She's a strange one for sure. Never did let me get close to her, no matter how hard I tried."

She'd smoothed out the folds of her dress and started fanning herself with a hand. "Gosh, it sure is hot, isn't it? I've never seen a summer like this. The poor trees. Look, they're already dropping dead in places."

It was true. The summer drought had brought the city to its knees. Water restrictions were in full effect, and the lawns, including ours, were crispy brown. Tree leaves, so used to constant moisture, had fallen in ranks. Great clumps of orange and yellow covered the foliage like a plague. It looked as though we were in late October, not the height of August.

~ ~ ~

I took my place at the altar. The assortment of guests—barely forty, fifty people—sat on plastic chairs and perspired. Over to the far right, I could see the white-roofed tent where the dance floor and DJ booth stood, along with tables being tweaked by the catering staff. There were enormous displays of exotic flowers deposited around the tent, ornamenting the aisle and ceremonial archway. Dahlia had had to pay extra to fly them in because of the drought. The displays stood out as vivid splashes of green and petal against the dulled dryness of their native family members.

To my left was my best man, Gabriel, alongside the four other groomsmen. The rag-tag quartet consisted of: Brandon—Stephanie's on-again-off-again boyfriend—as well as Max, who was seeing Genevieve. The other two men, Derek and Myles, were both friends I'd made during the past year at UBC. I'd had to ask if they would be my groomsmen with the flimsy excuse that I was new-ish to the city and still didn't know many people. Despite the relatively short time we'd been friends, they'd happily agreed to it, with none of the condescension or reluctance I'd dreaded.

Gabriel and I had met during a philosophy class last year, when he'd accidentally dropped scissors on me. I'd been sitting in the lecture hall, learning about free will and determinism, when several objects—a binder, metal water bottle, Cypress Hill sweatshirt, gum wrapper, and an open pair of scissors—had fallen from the heavens. The last of these had landed on my forearm, slicing open the skin.

I'd looked up in shock to see a man sitting on the row above me, his curly black hair half-covering his worried, widened eyes. A backpack lay sideways on the desk in front of him, stripped of its contents.

He'd followed me to the bathroom to wash off the blood, apologizing profusely. I'd been so distracted by his presence, by his relentless attempts to lighten the mood, that I had hardly been bothered by the sight of red.

"Looks like we're scar brothers now, *mano*," he'd said to me, as freezing tap water rushed over my forearm. Gabriel had then rolled up his sleeve and showed me his arm. Along the same stretch of skin: a thin, jagged scar.

"Although, I got mine from falling off the roof of my sister's dollhouse when I was 6. Which is a million times cooler than what happened to you," he'd said, with a grin. Since that day, we'd become fast friends.

~ ~ ~

Now we all stood and waited for the woman of the hour. The officiant tapped his foot idly, as people fiddled in their chairs and chatted quietly. Looking out at the guests, I was struck by the fact that I was getting married in the presence of complete strangers. Besides Gabriel, the groomsmen, two guys from my old mechanic job, Li, and the bridesmaids still preparing inside the house, I didn't really know a soul.

After several minutes of waiting in the stifling heat, there was a stirring of movement on the front steps. The crowd turned in their chairs to look back at Yvonne and the other bridesmaids, in varying blue-shaded dresses. Their movements were slow as they crossed the dead grass. Following them was Dahlia.

Dahlia acted as her own flower girl, casting out fistfuls of ivory petals for her bare feet to step upon. She'd insisted on this peculiar detail, to be barefooted for the ceremony. A train of white fabric trailed behind her like a bleached shadow. Her veil was so thick that it was impossible to see her face.

The wedding guests all rose to their feet. Off to the right side, a string trio of a cellist and two violinists began to bow their instruments, filling the air with amorous music from the past. I stood up to my full height, chin held high. My heart pattered away, eerily calm.

The procession of women made their way down the aisle. As they walked, I caught the cold eye of Yvonne. Even after all this time, she still hadn't warmed up to me. No amount of flattery or back-scratching could bring the thaw. And the news of the engagement had only worsened things between the two of us. She would hardly acknowledge me if we were in a room together.

When the procession reached the front, Joanna stepped forward and took the basket of flower petals from Dahlia. The five bridesmaids then filed into position, opposing my motley group of groomsmen. Dahlia continued to creep atop the grass, until she was standing directly before me. The music swelled. With great care, I lifted the veil.

My fiancée was as brutally beautiful as the day I first met her. Or rather, *remembered* meeting her. Her skin had darkened in the summer sun, causing her eyes to stand out like beacons of marine. Her wild hair had been bridled and tamed into a cascade of intricate knots and flourishes. White flower-heads had been interwoven into her curls. Her whole face seemed to glow from underneath the veil, her smile pulled into that permanent grin.

"Do I look silly?" she whispered, barely moving her lips like a ventriloquist.

"Like a fool," I muttered back.

We both had to hold back giggles as the officiant began his spiel.

"Welcome, everyone, welcome. You may all be seated." A unified squealing of plastic chairs filled the afternoon. The officiant cleared his throat and dabbed his forehead.

"Folks, we have gathered here today to celebrate the love of these two people, Jack Anthony Donner and Dahlia…erm." He leaned forward and whispered privately to Dahlia. "Sorry, but there's no last name written here."

She rolled her eyes. "I know. Just carry on."

Someone coughed. The officiant continued.

"And Dahlia, who have come together to consummate their devotion to one another in the eyes of the law and their loved ones. Now, before we begin with the vows, I would like to read an excerpt of 'Song' by the poet Allen Ginsberg, at the request of the bride."

He shuffled his paper around and adjusted his glasses, which were slipping down his sweat-slicked nose.

"The weight of the world," the officiant said, "is love. Under the burden of solitude, under the burden of dissatisfaction, the weight, the weight we carry is love. Who can deny? In dreams it touches the body. In thought, constructs a miracle. In imagination, anguishes till born in human. But we carry the weight wearily, and so must come to rest in the arms of love. At last, we must rest in the arms of love. For there is no rest without love, no sleep without dreams of love. The final wish, without bitterness, is always love."

~ ~ ~

With a warm band of gold upon my finger, I stood off to the side of the dance floor with my wife and watched the wedding party. After a few rounds of alcohol from the open bar, the guests had found their groove to Dahlia's manifold music tastes. The DJ, poor guy, tried hard to accommodate her requests, ranging from dancehall to disco to doo-wop. I'd grown tired from introducing myself to strangers who already knew my name. But I was happy. So blissfully, extravagantly happy.

The sun had eased itself to the bottom of the horizon. It shone through the branches, illuminating the back lawn and open-aired tent with flaxen light. Dahlia and I watched as Hale, the guy I'd bumped into outside the bathroom, tried to drunkenly hit on Anita while Natalie Cole's "This Will Be An Everlasting Love" played on. She rebuffed his advances with a pout and flexed wrist.

"How do you know that guy?" I asked Dahlia.

"Oh. Hale. His dad was an old friend of my mom's. And we also dated for a bit. Way, way back when. I only invited him because I wanted to rub my happiness in his face," she replied, smirking. "If I'm being honest, about half of these people fall into that category."

"People you wanted to gloat over?"

"Yup. Let them see how I won the lottery." She jabbed a finger into my ribs. I laughed.

"God. You're wicked."

"Oh, didn't you know?" she asked mockingly, stepping forward to face me. She laced her hands around the back of my neck and looked up at me with her bright eyes. "Well I have news for you, buddy. I'm *your* wicked one now."

"Damn right you are," I said, and picked her up. Dahlia let out a scream of delight and twisted her body sideways so I could hold her. Her voluptuous white dress spilled out of my arms and onto the plastic-tiled floor.

A couple people nearby clapped at the sight. I kissed Dahlia hard, then dropped her back onto the ground. Took her hand.

"Come on. Let's dance." She followed my lead to the busying dance floor and started to move. Natalie Cole sang in a higher key. I took my wife's hand, spun her on beat. People clapped their sweaty hands and laughed with drunken glee.

Out on the water, the setting sun moved from the land of the living, and into the world below with total, tectonic silence.

CHAPTER SIXTEEN

December. The snow had returned, after a loveless marriage with the rain above. As a result, the city was blanketed with a thin layer of sleet, accompanied by a cold so black and powerful it bored its way into your marrow. Neither of us had wanted to leave the comfort of home. But we had, because it was Genevieve's birthday, and I was being a good friend. It was the last time I would make that mistake.

Jack and I sat at a table with the group. It was us five girls and our romantic partners, which made us ten bodies strong. Only Anita was absent. The rest of us passed around life updates about the holidays and laughed at nothing. Beer and sangria flowed.

"Next up, we have Stephanie and Brandon with a duet of 'The Piña Colada Song'," the announcer boomed. Stephanie let out a yip of excitement and grabbed Brandon's hand. He gave us a look of regret before being dragged up onto the stage. Two spit-riddled mikes stood waiting for them to sing into.

The karaoke bar cheered. Brandon tapped his mike and started to croak out the words atop a crummy backing track. "I was, uh, tired of my lady…".

Stephanie swayed to the music, utterly obvious to her chosen song's subtext.

I turned to Genevieve. "Do you think Steph realizes what this song is about?"

"Not a fucking chance," she cackled. "She just likes piña coladas."

Her and Joanna let out a whoop of encouragement as Stephanie started to belt the chorus, blisteringly off-pitch. "Come on, Whitney! Sing it!"

I looked over at Jack and smiled at him. He returned the gesture and waggled his empty glass. Pointed to the bar.

"You want another?" he called from across the table.

"Yeah, sure! Here, I'll come with." We excused ourselves from the crowded seating arrangement and made our way across the bar.

"We're not actually going to go up there, right?" Jack asked, yelling to be heard over Stephanie's caterwauling. I flagged down a bartender and looked up at him.

"Of course we are. Everyone has to. Plus, I've already put our names down," I said with a big smile.

"God damn. I *hate* doing karaoke," he grumbled.

"Why not? You've got a nice voice."

"Since when?"

"Since your last shower, hon. The walls aren't exactly soundproof." It was dark in the bar, but not enough to hide Jack's face turning red. I laughed.

"Oh, relax! No one cares. It's just for fun. And besides—" I leaned up on my tiptoes to kiss his cheek. "I'll be there beside you."

He squeezed my butt for a split second and pulled me tight against his chest. "Yeah, you better be. You got me into this, after all."

"Mm, true. Good thing I'll get you out of it, too."

The bartender strolled over and I ordered our drinks, then paid for them. Stephanie and Brandon finished their performance, much to the appreciation of everyone's eardrums. The next person was called up. A man with greasy hair and an oversized parka stumbled up the stairs, before launching into his rendition of "Gimme! Gimme! Gimme! A Man After Midnight". The crowd went wild.

This was our first night out in a long while. Jack's degree was finally behind him, and he'd been lining up teacher interviews for the new year. I knew I should've been happy for him, and a part of me was, now that he wasn't going to be pulling out hairs trying to finish school. But I didn't want him to work, or to have some fucking *job*. I wanted him to spend his time with me. I wanted life to be like it was during the summer, when we would wake up and do whatever we pleased.

No amount of persuasion could change his mind. He was dead-set on doing something productive with his life. Something of value for society. I couldn't understand it. Why would anyone waste their precious days policing ungrateful children to finish writing essays? I'd rather kill myself.

But instead, I'd let him pursue his decision to become a teacher. Hell, I didn't just *let* him. I'd paid for that decision to become reality. Every cent of his tuition these past years, siphoned straight from my bank account. Not that I cared about the money. No. Of course not. I wanted his time. I wanted our connection to be enough for him. Like it was for me.

"And next up to the stage, we have Jack and Dahlia singing 'Baby, I'm Yours' by Barbara Lewis." Our table cheered. Jack's eyes flicked at me with concern.

"D, I don't even know this song," Jack said as we made our way onto the stage.

"I've played it for you before. Don't worry, just sing the chorus! It's very simple."

We both took our place at the mikes. The backing music began and the lyrics started to roll across a lime-green screen.

I looked over at Jack and gave him a thumbs up. Then I started to sing.

"Baby, I'm yours…and I'll be yours until the stars fall from the sky…until the rivers all run dry…in other words, until I die…Baby, I'm yours…and I'll be yours until the sun no longer shines…until the poets run out of rhyme…in other words, until the end of time…"

~ ~ ~

To step outside was to emerge onto a different planet. I pulled my coat closer and clutched my prize between my fingers: a single Marlboro bummed from one of the girls. Jack followed me into the storm, still embarrassed from his time on stage. In the end, he had done little more than mumble and hum. But again. Nobody cared.

"Hey, you'll have to smoke over there. Six metres away from the building," said the bouncer, sticking his head out from inside the doorway and shooing us off to the side.

"Oh, okay," I said.

"Sorry. It's a heritage building, so they're fucking anal about that shit."

"It's all good. D, let's go over here." Jack gestured towards an eaves covering about half a block from the bar's entrance. I followed him, my mouth frozen in a drunken grin.

The bar we were at was Genevieve's pick, it being her birthday and all. Because places were swamped with holiday traffic, she'd chosen a shitty hole-in-the-wall in Gastown, with the hopes that it'd be less overrun by Christmas crowds. Gastown, with its gentrified, up-scale businesses and apartments, sat right on the fringe of the downtown East Side. Quite literally a few blocks away and the streets would transform from chic boutiques into a poverty-mangled horror show. There wasn't another place where the two ends of the spectrum came so close to dancing with one another.

By the grace of heaven, the sleet had stopped. Roads had become a skating rink of ice, causing most drivers to stay home and skip their holiday party altogether. In the reflection of the sheen black pavement, the steady pulsations of red and green lights flashed for only a few.

"Christ, it's cold," I said, my whole body shivering. I could barely hold the lighter still enough to light the cigarette.

"Hey, come here!"

"What?"

"Just trust me."

He pulled me into the mouth of the nearest alleyway, which was dark and stunk of fresh urine. Out of one of the building vents, however, flowed a thick cloud of hot steam. We both stood within it and were instantly warmed.

"See, this is why I love you. Such a smart man."

We kissed. I let myself grow toasty, then stepped out of the steam to light the cigarette with a steady hand. The tip glowed crimson in the shadows.

"Are you having a good time?" I asked.

"Yeah, of course. Are you?"

"The best." I passed him the cigarette, his single gloveless hand emerging from the steam. I stepped back in and joined him in the airborne warmth.

"I'm just glad that song is over."

"Oh, you were fine! Next time, I promise to pick something we both know."

"Next time?" he asked. "Once was enough, thank you."

"Don't be silly. There's always a next time." I poked his ribs.

"Ow. You're such a pest."

"Yeah? Is that what you think?"

"Yup. You're the biggest bug in the world."

"Oh, really?" I said, with exaggerated emphasis. I plucked the cigarette from his hand and smoked it luxuriously. "And to think, monsieur, all this time I thought you were a—"

"Hey! You got 'nother of those?"

~ ~ ~

The voice startles both of us with its proximity. We can't see the speaker in the haze of steam, but he sounds close enough to lick our ears. Jack and I both step out into the cold alley to see who has spoken.

There, a mere four feet from us, stands a middle-aged man. His cheeks are an ugly patchwork of red spots, whiskers, and what appears to be scratch marks from fingernails. One of his eyes is swollen, ringed in black. Instead of a jacket, he is wearing six threadbare sweaters—both men's and women's styles—all at once. But this is not what hits me first when I emerge from the cloud of steam. What strikes me first is the smell.

It is clear that this man has not had access to a shower in weeks. Maybe months. The ghost of piss, shit, and vomit radiates from his body, underneath the perforating stink of stale sweat. When he gets a good look at us, dressed up in our winter attire, he flashes a smile. Life has robbed him of most of his teeth as well.

"Well, look'it you two!" he exclaims. The waft of his breath hits the back of my throat and makes me recoil. Jack takes a step forward.

"Hey, sorry, man, but we don't have any more smokes."

"Aw, c'mon now. What's the matter, didn't 'ur mom ever teach you to share?" he asks. Far behind him, I can see a huddled pile of blankets and garbage, right beside the dumpster. The realization that he has been here the whole time, probably asleep, tugs at my insides.

"No, really, he's telling the truth. We don't have any more cigarettes. I got this from a friend." I hold it up as if to show him my sincerity. But it does nothing but wipe the smile off his face.

"Fuckin' rich bitch," he jeers. "You can't even give me a goddamn cigarette? Too good for that?"

"What? No! I'm serious, I don't—"

"Dahlia." Jack says my name with the weight of a stone hitting water. Sinking fast. "Let's just go back inside." He moves to step in front of me, but I shuffle over. I'm not finished.

"Look, sir," I say, sticking a gloved hand into my purse. "I'm not kidding. We really don't have any more. But I can give you some money instead, okay?"

The man's eyes twitch. He leans forwards, and then back, as if unsure if standing is the best option. Or if I'm bluffing. Jack stands right by my side, the heat of him almost palpable with nerves. I, on the other hand, am still very calm. I drop the spent cigarette.

"Okay," the man says. "That'd be good."

"Cool." I give him a small smile: something that conveys sympathy but not pity. At least I try to. I pull out my wallet and riffle through, squinting in the darkness to see. To my left, the glow of the quiet street shines pitifully. The alley walls seem to swallow all light.

While unzipping my wallet pockets, my eyes flick up and down from the man. He keeps swaying about and smacking his lips. One of his legs vibrates from the cold. Or something else. Suddenly it is crystal clear that he has not just woken up. Or slept at all recently. He is buzzing with uneasy energy, as if electricity is flowing through his veins. And something much worse.

As I thumb the empty folds of my wallet, I realize that I am void of solid cash. My last twenty was sacrificed in the name of booze, with the coin change newly re-homed at the bottom of a tip jar. I'm completely strapped. My heart starts to speed up.

The man mumbles something under his breath, his eyes fixed to the brick wall behind me. I look up at Jack and whisper without air.

"Do you have anything?" Jack checks his back pocket, his jacket. His movements break the man's daze. He jerks to life.

"You shor' changing me again? Playing poor?" he snaps. There is a steady fog building in his eyeballs. I wonder what it's like to be behind them.

"No, look, I'm so sorry, but I thought I had some change with me, but we—"

The man doesn't let me finish. He hucks back in his rotted mouth and spits. A wad of yellow phlegm smacks me on my right cheek. It's warm, like melted butter.

"Fuck!" he snarls. Jack and I freeze in shock as the man steps back, before smacking his head twice in frustration. He repeats the same word, then a few others that amount to profane, infuriated drivel.

Jack looks at my face and widens his eyes at the spit sliding down my cheek. Without hesitation, he wipes it off with his bare hand. As he does, the sleeve of his jacket pulls up. The platinum wink of his Rolex picks up the weak light from the street and glimmers.

The man abruptly stops spouting nonsense. Steadies himself. A new expression marks his face.

"Let's go," Jack says, taking me by the shoulder and guiding me towards the mouth of the alley. His voice breaks ever so slightly as he does, and I realize that he is terrified. This is probably the first time he has experienced something like this.

We both move towards the exit, but the man mad-scrambles ahead, blocking our way. He holds his arms out wide as if to give us both a hug.

"Hey, hey," he says in a low tone. His leg trembles more than ever.

"Get the fuck out of the way," Jack says, raising his voice.

Backlit from the street beyond, the man is cast in shadow. We watch one silhouetted arm drop from position, down to the belt of his waist. From beneath the bottom layer of his six ratty sweaters, something big and shiny is pulled from its sheath. His only form of safety, in the absence of a home. An old hunting knife, almost seven inches long.

"Gimme the watch," he growls. From behind us, the vent spewing steam suddenly stops. It makes a banging sound as it quits, and out of reflex, Jack and I both turn our heads. To the man, this must be perceived as us gearing up to run away. When we turn back, he is already mid-lunge.

The human body is many things. It is a container for incredible amounts of grief, and incredible amounts of love. It holds the memories of the past, experiences of the present, and dreams for the future, all at the same time. It is both animalistic and mortal, and the vessel for something much more. It is a resilient, enduring piece of meat. Hell, it can survive nearly anywhere on the goddamn planet. The human body is a *machine* of savagery and ingenuity, home to the greatest organic mind the world has ever created, accidentally or not. But it can also be very easily broken.

The knife tip sings its way through the air with a one-tune whistle. It's a short song. As Jack steps sideways, pulling me by the coat with him, he lifts his free left hand to shield my body. In reaction, the blade turns at the command of its unsteady owner, and severs two of Jack's fingers clean off. They bounce off the front of my white coat, then fall to the ground to lay amongst the litter.

The momentum of the man's lunge carries him forward to his knees, strong enough to send us reeling. For a moment, Jack doesn't even realize what has happened.

I turn to look at my husband. When he sees his hand, the deformity of it, *the blood,* he starts to scream. It is a sound that I have heard before, the sound of a person in the jaws of pure horror. Of disbelief. But I have never been hit in the same way than right now, with Jack. Because this time, it is him making that sound.

~ ~ ~

Fat spurts of blood gushed from the stumps where his pinky and ring finger had been. I could see the outline of his gold ring, the one I had slid onto his hand only 4 months before tonight. I watched as he staggered back, away from me, eyes splayed wide, and hyperventilating. At the same time, the man, who was sloughed down low between us, grabbed hold of Jack's calf. Jack tripped backwards and fell, cracking his head on the brick wall behind him. With a cry still stuck in his throat, he slumped to the filthy ground. His eyes fell shut.

"Jack!" I shrieked, my whole chest ablaze with something very hot and powerful. I rushed towards him and cradled his face, slapping his cheeks.

"Jack, Jack, wake up! Wake up!" He gave a moan but did not open his eyes. I felt the back of his head and felt the warm flow of blood, intermingled with his damp hair.

"Oh, fuck," the man behind me exclaimed. I whirled around at him, as he staggered up to his feet, knife in hand. A wild look of excitement and alarm crossed his face, looking at the sight of what he had done. Things had escalated far beyond his expectation. Far, far beyond. He turned to run away.

The hot feeling in my chest ruptured into two. I could feel it, splintering off into my bloodstream, filling my body with its power. A door inside my brain slammed shut. And something new, something old, opened. I charged towards him.

"YOU!" I howled, launching myself onto his back. He staggered under my weight but still kept moving. Without thinking, I sunk my teeth into his neck and bit him as hard as I could. His skin was taut like leather. The taste of iron filled my mouth.

"Agh!" he screeched. He stumbled, and waved the knife back towards me. I let go of his smelly body with one arm, leaned forward, and wrenched the moving knife from his hand. I was much stronger than him. Judging by the yelp of pain he made when I ripped his weapon away, he must have realized that as well. His balance gave way beneath us.

The man fell hard onto his stomach. I landed on top of him, my arm hooked around his neck, the knife in my right hand. But I was not ready to use it. Oh no. Not yet.

Instead, I uncurled myself from him. Then grabbed the back of his head and smashed the front of his face into the roadbed. There was the unmistakable crunch of cartilage and teeth. I repeated the motion.

"YOU!" I screamed again, rising to my haunches before heavily flipping him onto his back. It seemed to be the only word I could muster. My entire essence was ignited with pain, with rage, with *hatred* so profound and strong that I feared the seams of my skin would split. I would not stop until this man had suffered. Until his eyes wept blood.

By now, he was making a series of wheezing gasps. They sounded wet, as if he was drowning. Red, slick shadows smeared his broken nose, his toothless mouth. I straddled the body of my enemy and brought the knife high above my head. Waited for him to look at me.

After a moment of stunned blinking, his eyes finally rolled up at me with fear. Good. I slammed the knife down into the pit of his stomach, puncturing six layers of fabric and one layer of skin. I twisted the blade. He let out a bellow of pain, so hard that his whole body vibrated. I pulled the knife out. I did it again. And again. And again. And—

"Stop it!"

I whipped my head around at the voice. The voice I knew like the back of my hand. The voice I would kill for. The voice I would go to the ends of the Earth for, even if there wasn't such a thing in the first place. Jack. He was sitting there, slumped against the brick. Off to the side, his severed fingers laid amongst the garbage, tipped with red.

"Stop it!" he gasped at me. His eyes were shiny, and I could see tears on the crest of his cheeks. His whole face was plainly illuminated from the streetlight, weak-lit or not. I could see my husband's horror of me, clear as a summer's day.

I felt a liquid warmth against my legs as the man began to bleed to death beneath me. I felt his convulsing gulps. His hands smacking my thighs, trying and failing to push me off.

But what I could not feel was the desire my husband was trying to coax out of me. The desire to stop. Every single fibre of my being was screaming at me to continue.

I wiped my nose, which was running with snot, and gave Jack a weak, sad smile.

"I'm sorry, honey," I said raggedly. "I'm so, so sorry."

I turned back to the man, who was still very much fighting to be free. I pushed down the front of his head, so he could not raise his neck up off the pavement. He gurgled and coughed up blood and said the word *no. No no no no no no no no no no n…*

Up ahead, I could hear the sound of a woman yelling for help. A man, too. People had finally seen us. The police would be called. An ambulance. Everything would be okay.

But I could not stop. I did not want to stop. I would have my revenge for what had been done to me and my love. My sweet, sweet Jack. I would finish the job.

I leaned forward, right over the man's spluttering, bulging red face. My hair created a curtain of darkness, sheltering us two from the rest of the world. He started to thrash with all the might left in his miserable little soul, as I brought the knife to the side of his leathery neck. The bite mark from my teeth oozed on.

I opened my mouth and let out a scream, strong enough to tear my vocal chords. The sound buried the man, who looked up at me in terror, just inches away from his face. His body went limp from fighting. With my screaming mouth still wide with fury, I brought the blade down and across. One, two, four deep, rough strokes, bracing the back of it with my palm. Cutting off his fucking head.

Part Two

Rondo

ONE

The first thing to go was the house. We needed new perspectives. A new beginning. Of course, if I'd had things my way, I would've burned it to the ground myself. Taken a jug of gasoline to the frame and set it aflame. But instead, I settled for the real estate market.

I'd wanted to move from the house for years, to rid myself from the past once and for all. But after Jack came along, I'd foolishly believed I could paint over the bad memories with new ones. And it'd worked. Mostly. Until one day, the present turned as ugly as the past. So now there was nothing to be done but leave and start again.

I scoured property listings in the newspapers until I'd come across a real winner. 332 Marine Drive. The black-and-white photo featured a retro-modern home with tall windows and a central skylight the size of a mini school bus. It promised a "unique, unexpected layout for the seasoned homeowner". Best of all, the property was right on the water, with a private boat dock. "As close as you can get to the ocean without being in it," the ad said. You could open the window, any window, and hear the waves. That was all the convincing I needed.

2 weeks later, I'd signed the title papers. A For Sale sign went up on the front yard of my mother's house the same day. My grandparents, who were buried in Costa Rica after a freak catamaran accident, had originally built the place for eight hundred thousand bucks. The final sale price clocked in at twenty times that. Most of the cost had nothing to do with the actual house, but the enormous grounds it was built upon.

When the buyer's offer came in, I was ecstatic. Not only were we going to have a new house by the sea, but we were also going to be six million dollars richer. I'd rushed upstairs when I'd gotten home to tell Jack the good news.

"Isn't that fabulous, honey? And just wait until you see the new place! You're going to love it," I gushed, kissing his head.

He was hunched at his desk with a book: the same one he had been trying to read for weeks. The blackout blinds were drawn, with a dim lamp as the only light.

"I bet," he replied absently. He'd declined to come to the showing because of his head. 3 months later, he could still hardly hold a conversation. He squeezed his therapy ball and kept reading.

"Oh, you have no idea. This place is so quirky! It's got a conversation pit, and Spanish tiles in the kitchen. And the basement is built right into the bedrock! You can look out this little port window and be almost eye level to the water. " I laughed, cleaning up the room as I went. I backtracked to crack open the window to let some air in.

"Can you shut that?" Jack said, turning his back against the sunlight.

"Yeah. Of course, honey." I closed the curtains, plunging the room into near darkness again. I strode over to my husband and hugged his sitting torso. He tensed.

"How's the head today?" I asked.

"The same."

"And the fingers?"

Jack stopped squeezing his ball and held his hand out. Tried to curl his fingers into a fist. Three of them complied. The last two, scarred over and bumpy, stayed mostly inert.

"They're bending a little bit," I said hopefully. Jack didn't respond. He grabbed his ball off the desk and went back to squeezing it.

I let out a sigh and straightened up. His sadness was exhausting. It was like a vacuum of self-pity. And distrust. This second part hurt the most. I hated that my husband didn't trust me anymore.

"Okay, well, I'm going to go downstairs and make something to eat. Maybe do some more packing of the delicate stuff." I pushed my hair off my face and walked to the other side of the room. Stood in the doorway.

"I was thinking of getting movers to come pack things up in about a week or so. Get things over to the new house as soon as possible. What d'you think?" I'd already booked the movers for next Tuesday. But I wanted Jack to feel like he still had some input.

"Sounds good," he mumbled. He flipped the page back on his book, and tried to re-read it again. I nodded silently and shut the door. As I walked down the stairs, I felt the heaviness of Jack's energy lift off my chest. I breathed a sigh of relief.

~ ~ ~

The two of us had been sleeping in different beds since the incident. At least, *I* called it the incident. Jack called it the murder. I'd given up in trying to convince him otherwise.

At first I'd been interrogated by the police alone. Jack had to be questioned days later, after he was conscious enough to know where he even was. This time, it was both of us in the room. My hopes for Jack's memory to be a blur were in vain. For all his shortcomings of expression, his comprehension had not suffered in the slightest.

"Mr. Donner, I'd like to begin with confirming your wife's statement. Now, I want to be clear that neither you nor your wife are facing criminal charges for this situation. But it is imperative that we gather some more background on the night to better understand *how* things escalated so extremely. Am I making sense so far, Mr. Donner?"

Jack nodded. The whine of hospital machines filled the room, interrupted only by the occasional beep. Outside the door, I could hear the squeal of linoleum and rattlings of medical carts, as nurses walked back and forth.

Officer Walder proceeded to read my statement to Jack in his flat, monotonous drone. He had a face I'd grown to hate, which was pudgy and round like a sunburnt volleyball. So instead, I kept my eyes on my husband, who was propped up with several pillows. His expression remained unchanged, as Walder read out phrases like "extremely aggressive behaviour" and "threats to kill" and "heightened state of defence". Only after Walder concluded the statement with my account of the beheading had Jack's face twitched.

"I understand that this must be upsetting to hear, especially given your condition," the officer said. "But can you please verify for me, to the best of your abilities, that what your wife has issued forth in her statement to be true?"

Jack stared at the officer, then looked over at me. Then quickly away. His gaze remained fixed on the back wall as he answered.

"Yes. It's true."

"So you can confirm that your attacker, Shane Winnow, had every intention of mortally wounding you and your wife, and that the only solution was to retaliate?"

"Pardon me?"

Officer Walder cleared his throat. "Can you confirm that your attacker was trying to kill you and your wife, and that killing him in self-defence was your only option?"

There was a beat before Jack replied.

"Yes," he said. His eyes had still not moved from the wall.

"Thank you for your cooperation, Mr. Donner."

Officer Walder sounded disappointed by Jack's answer. He'd adjusted his sitting position on the stiff hospital chair and shuffled his papers around. I stared at him, wishing the floor would open up and swallow him.

"Now, Mr. and Mrs. Donner, I want to be clear in saying there are no criminal charges against y—"

"You've already said that. Twice," I said, cutting him off. Walder stared at me from the other side of Jack's bed.

"Of course. But I also must be honest that the *severity* of violence on display here has the department concerned."

"But this was an act of self-defence," I replied, trying to soften my broken voice. I felt sick to my stomach for having to suck up to this man for sympathy. "I've already told you and the other officers that I acted in total desperation. I had no choice. That man cut off Jack's *fingers*. He tried to kill him. And me."

I sniffed, hoping to sound weak. I reached out to hold Jack's right hand and gave it a squeeze. His left hand, bandaged beyond recognition, lay uselessly on the officer's side.

"So you've said. But, Mrs. Donner…" The officer leaned forward on his chair towards me, as if to tell a secret. Jack's blanketed body laid between us like a mummy. "We are talking about a beheading here. I have never encountered something like that in all my years as a police officer. Not even with Pickton."

Pickton was one of the most vile and prolific serial killers in the province's history. The association sent a bolt of anger down my spine.

I sat up tall in my seat. "Are you calling me a serial killer now, officer? A serial killer who raped and brutally murdered dozens of innocent women, before feeding their bodies to his pigs? Is that what you're saying?"

Officer Walder cleared his throat again and changed gears, realizing the implications of his suggestion. "No, of course not, Mrs. Donner. I was just making an example. I'm sorry to have insinuated something like that."

"Then what the fuck *are* you insinuating? My husband and I have just been through the most traumatic experience of our lives, and instead of comfort I have to sit here and be compared to the fucking pig killer? Jesus fucking Christ."

My explosive outburst surprised Officer Walder. And myself.

"Mrs. Donner, there is no need to raise your voice. I understand that this is a very upsetting time, but we are just trying to get a clearer picture of what happened here."

I wanted to rip out his eyes. The thought came to me, so clear and visceral: scooping out his beady eyes from his skull like bleached grapes. I wondered what I'd do with them. Squash them? Or stuff them into his idiot mouth?

"Of course," I said instead. I looked back at my husband, who had squeezed his eyes shut.

"Jack, honey, are you alright?"

He opened his lids blearily.

"Yes. Please don't yell. It hurts my head," he mumbled. It was the longest succession of words he'd said so far.

I felt awful.

"Of course. I'm sorry, honey."

Officer Walder looked at me with an air of triumph. Then back at Jack.

"Mr. Donner, are you able to continue this meeting? I can always come back another time."

"No. Just get it done."

"Very well, then. Only one last question."

Officer Walder shifted some more papers around on his clipboard. I breathed through my nose and told myself to stay calm. To stifle the anger stirring inside me.

"Mr. Donner. I have to ask. Are you aware of your wife's previous accounts of violence? I have two documented here. The first was reported at a nightclub 4 years prior, while the more serious occurrence happened when Mrs. Donner was only 13 years old. It says here that she seriously assaulted a family member in, I quote, 'self-defence'."

My mouth opened in shock. I knew the nightclub incident was on my record, no matter how many times I'd insisted that I was protecting a friend. Some creep had groped Joanna, and I'd returned the favour by pushing him down the club stairs. I'd been banned from the bar and legally threatened by the asshole who fell, but nothing more had come of it.

But the birthday party. I hadn't known that was on record. And neither had Jack. He turned to look at me: again, with that awful mix of distrust and fear. It broke my heart.

"Hold on, why is that even on my record? I was a minor when that happened. And it *was* self-defence. I don't understand why you're even bringing this up," I rebuked.

Officer Walden shrugged.

"Like I said, Mrs. Donner. We are just trying to get a clearer picture of what happened to you and your husband. *And* Shane Winnow, who is currently lying in a morgue with his head cut off. What I want to understand," he said, lowering his voice, "is how any normal person could do that to someone. Let alone a woman like yourself."

I stared at Officer Walden, wishing his smug face was in hell.

"I have nothing more to say to you," I replied, carefully controlling my voice. It had deepened considerably since I'd torn my vocal chords, become distorted. I didn't even recognize it. It was the voice of a stranger.

"All my life, I have only tried to protect others or myself from harm," I said, my words serrated like scissors. "Let me make that crystal-clear to you. I have done nothing wrong. Now or then. And frankly, officer, you can take your *mis*understandings and stick them up your slit. We're done here."

Officer Walden had gaped at me like the idiot he was. But I was right. Self-defence was self-defence. And there wasn't anything, really, that he could do about it.

Unfortunately, Officer Walden had accomplished one thing he set out to do. The can of worms about my 13th birthday party had been cracked wide open, and the stink of its mystery had filled Jack's nostrils. Only a day after he was discharged and back at the house, he'd insisted I tell him what happened. And because I loved him, I'd told him the truth.

~ ~ ~

My mother, I said to Jack, had invited my entire grade seven class, despite the fact that I hardly spoke to any of them. Of course, *they* often tried to befriend me, but I hadn't found a good enough reason to reciprocate their efforts. Nor had I needed to. I had Mango. And myself.

Regardless, about thirty kids ended up coming to the house. Along with all their parents and a flock of my mom's friends, whom she'd rallied together to witness her daughter's first party-planning attempt. I had gone all out.

A long row of tables held platters of authentic Hawaiian cuisine, served by caterers donning traditional hand-woven grass skirts. The pool had been filled with inflatable pineapples and bananas, while garlands of hibiscus flowers streamed from wooden posts, crisscrossing the clear blue sky. A wet bar serving tropical concoctions in coconuts stood off to the side. I'd hired a live band to play songs on the ukulele, pan drums, and lap guitar, as well as organized different activity stations. There was a lei-making table, limbo, and a Hawaiian-themed scavenger hunt that wound its way around the grounds and surrounding woods. People were floored.

"Dahlia, how on Earth did you arrange all of this, sweetie? I mean, the details are *incredible.* I feel like I've taken a trip right to Maui!" Rebecca marvelled, swirling her coconut in the sunshine. She was one of Mom's closest "frenemies".

"She's very talented at figuring things out," my mom slurred, answering for me.

"She made all the calls herself. I even heard her bartering with a carpenter on one of the islands to buy those authentic tiki torches. Isn't that brilliant?"

Mom had both hands on my shoulders, as she showed me off to her circle of friends like a prize pig vying for the blue ribbon. The group stared at me and pursed their blubbery lips, clearly envious.

"Truly. I find it hard enough to get Vicky to clean up after herself. Let alone handle something like…this." Rebecca waved a manicured hand at the party in full swing: kids screaming with laughter, the sound of clapping as the band finished another tune.

"Well, don't feel too bad. I'm sure Vicky will come around," I said, smiling sweetly. Rebecca clutched her coconut to her chest and studied me from behind her sunglasses. Then looked back at my mother.

"Say, Sharon, have you ever thought of getting her tested?" she asked, as if I hadn't just spoken.

"Tested?"

"Yes, for like…Mensa or something."

My mother scrunched up her nose. Finished her drink.

"Is that a disease?"

The group laughed.

"No, no, Sharon. God, you're a hoot," Linda said, brushing her bangs to the side. A child, some whiny turd named Reggie who picked his nose and rubbed it on the desk beside me in homeroom, came up and tugged on her dress.

"Mommy, I wanna go swimming!" he moaned. He pointed to the hoard of splashing bodies amongst the inflatable fruit. I'd reluctantly caved to the norm with the inclusion of half a dozen blow-up flamingos.

"Oh, Reggiebear, I'm sorry! We didn't bring your swimsuit."

"But I wannaaa," Reggie wailed, letting his weight drop to the ground and almost ripping a hole in his mother's Chanel dress. Linda smiled apologetically at the group.

"Sorry, ladies, just give me a minute." She began to haul Reggie away, who had given up on the ability to walk. He shrieked something about life being unfair, before being dragged out of earshot.

"What a brat," I almost said. Instead, I excused myself and said I was going to get some more punch.

"Of course, you enjoy!"

"Nice to see you, sweetheart!"

"Such a wonderful job with the party!"

The last thing I heard before walking away was Rebecca explaining to my mom that Mensa was an organization for people with high IQs.

"So she could be that," Rebecca sniffed, "or maybe she's on the spectrum. It must be something. I've never heard of a 13-year-old acting like this. It's weird, don't you think?"

"Rebecca!" one of the ladies chastised. The group tittered away.

I smiled to myself, before strolling over to the bar to order a passionfruit punch. Virgin, of course. I was still just a child. The bartender passed it over, complete with cut fruit and an umbrella.

"*Lealea*!" he said. I'd given instructions to the staff to use Hawaiian phrases whenever possible. It really added to the experience.

I replied with a brief *Mahalo* and strolled away.

Not two sips later, a boy had slammed into me, knocking me over into the grass.

"Oh, shoot! I'm so sorry!" he said, looking genuinely apologetic. The beachball he'd been running to catch bounced away. He extended a hand to help me up.

"It's fine, just watch where you're going," I said. Some people nearby stopped what they were doing.

"Are you okay?"

"What happened?"

"Nothing!" I assured. "Just bumped into each other."

I stood up and told the boy to keep on playing. He'd run off, grateful to escape any sort of repercussion. Only after I'd turned to go order a new punch had I realized my dress was stained down the front.

I groaned. This was one of my favourites: a flowing white sundress with sea-stars spotted across. Now it'd been desecrated with a splotch of red. I'd have to wash it right away.

Weaving my way through the running figures of my peers, as well as the mingling adults talking about upcoming trips and home renovations, I made my way up the back steps and into the house. Elvis Presley's *Blue Hawaii* record played on repeat, so as not to disrupt the atmosphere even when going inside.

As I headed towards the stairs, I passed my mother, mixing up a fresh cocktail at one of her personal wet bars. A line of people stood behind her, waiting for the bathroom.

"Oh, honey, what happened?" she asked, seeing my ruined dress. She did not stop in shaking up her cosmo.

"Nothing, just some boy. He ran into me by accident," I replied. "I'm going to change and get some stain remover."

"Of course. I should have some in my bathroom."

"Sounds good. Thanks, Mom."

I trumped up the rest of the stairs and made my way into my mother's room. Closed the door.

~ ~ ~

From her bedroom I could get a perfect view of the festivities. I felt a swell of pride for what I'd accomplished. It felt good to be at the centre of attention, but also, to be invisible. A kind of superpower, I thought to myself. Dahlia the Discreet.

Far off on the lawn, I watched as Mango trotted along the grass. The pair of Happy Birthday balloons I'd tied to her midriff trailed behind her. More kids leapt into the pool and screamed. My mom's blonde head rejoined her friend circle, bobbing in conversation.

There was a knock at the door. I turned at the sound, startled. Before I could say not to come in, it opened. In stumbled Uncle Charlie, who swiftly closed it behind him. His eyes opened wide when he saw me across the room.

"Dahlia! Oh, wow, look at you!" he exclaimed. His words were thick with booze, a habit he shared with my mother. Except where Sharon became bubbly with alcohol, Charlie let himself go rogue.

Also, I didn't like him.

There had never been a particular reason not to. Just a feeling I had whenever we were in the same room. A personality defect. He had a look to him, a lazy yet eager look, as if he wanted something badly but couldn't be bothered to go and get it. He was very thin and tall, like a pole. We hadn't seen one another in years, since he'd been busy travelling.

"Hey, Uncle Charlie," I said, standing awkwardly by the window. He crossed the room to give me a lengthy hug.

"Wow, it's so good to see you. It's been so long. You're practically a woman now!"

He chuckled, holding me in his arms. Finally, he let go.

"Yeah, it's been a while." I took a step back and looked up at him. His whole body stunk of liquor, but not the sharp sugary smell I associated with my mom and her friends. It was a darker, muskier scent. Whisky. Something that, when I was older, I wouldn't be able to drink without gagging at.

"I can't get over how much you've grown," he repeated, looking me up and down.

"That's what happens when people age," I replied. He howled with laughter.

"God! Always so quick with it, aren't you? I've missed you!" He squeezed me in another sloppy hug. His whole body pressed hard against mine.

"Right. Well I just—"

He cut me off.

"Shoot, are you here for the bathroom too? Sharon sent me up here to use hers, mind if I go ahead?" He gave me a wink. "I'll be fast, I promise."

Without waiting for my reply, he crossed the room, slipped into my mom's bathroom. He kicked the door halfway shut. The sound of gushing piss filled the air. Uncle Charlie let out a loud sigh.

"Ugh, that feels better! Breaking the seal, eh, Dahlia?" He laughed. I did not respond.

A very nasty sensation had begun brooding in my stomach. In my heart I knew I should leave, remove myself from the situation. I wasn't dumb. I knew what hid behind his gaze as he surveyed my body, sizing me up. I'd heard the underlying ways he spoke about women, about "adventures" in countries that weren't so "uptight". But I was also curious. I wanted to see what would happen if I stayed. So instead of leaving the room, I sat down on the side of the bed and waited for my uncle to finish up. On second thought, I stood up and drew the translucent cream curtains closed. Then resumed my position on the bed.

Uncle Charlie flushed and emerged without washing his hands. He walked out with an unnatural swagger, which almost made me laugh. I held my head tilted to the side, staring off to the far corner. Trying to look innocently bored. Charlie took the bait.

"You know, you should ask your mom to take you out for modelling. She'd be stupid not to," he said, trying to sound smooth. When I looked up at him, he was scratching his bald spot with shyness.

"You think so?" I asked. "That's sweet of you to say, *Uncle* Charlie."

I made sure to punctuate his title with venom. This was not a seduction, by any means. This was a test.

"Oh, yeah. Definitely." He flashed me a dopey smile and sat down beside me on the bed.

I stood up as he sat. He grabbed my arm.

"Can I say something without sounding weird?" he asked. His hand clutched the bones of my left wrist a little too tightly. From this vantage point we were nearly eye level. I could smell his liquored breath all the better.

"Of course," I replied. I let him hold my wrist without struggle. Inside my chest, my heart was pounding. I met his gaze with my full intensity.

He looked at me, then cast his eyes aside. Pathetic. He let my wrist go.

"Um, nevermind," he muttered.

"No, come on. Tell me."

"Promise not to tell anyone?"

"I promise."

"Okay, fine." He blew out air and looked at me again, his eyes slightly off from meeting mine. "I've travelled to a lot of places in the world, seen a *lot* of women out there. But you know what? I have *never* seen a girl look the way you do. Like you're so, just…"

In that moment of searching for a word, my uncle's desire got the best of him. He pulled me close to him and pressed his face against mine.

It was a terrible first kiss. His lips were stiffly puckered and sticky from drinking. A nib of tongue stuck out and entered my mouth, then retreated just as quick.

And then, just like that, it was over. He let go of me and leaned back. Actually *smiled.* My butt, where his hand had just grabbed, shivered from where he'd touched.

"I'm sorry, I just…" He let out a shaky laugh. "I've wanted to do that for so long, you have no idea. You'll have to forgive me. I've been drinking." He was leaning back on his hands now, thighs spread. I saw, with horrible definition, that he was hard.

I stepped back from him and resisted the urge to wipe my mouth.

So this was what would happen if I sat down on my mother's bed, if I was left alone with her creepy brother for more than 5 minutes. At my very own birthday party.

That's all it took. Nothing more than a moment of privacy and a few polite words.

My disgust could not be contained. I could not believe the look that was plastered on his face, the open smugness. The fact that his penis was erect. His expectation for *more.*

"You know, I'm not that much older than you, Dahlia. Like, not really. In some parts of the world, we'd be a perfect match." He laughed again, as I realized he wasn't just drunk. He was obliterated. He was having difficulty holding up his own torso on the bed.

"I know," I replied. "Millions of girls wind up as child brides."

I took another step back.

"Well, shit!" he said, grinning. He let himself succumb to gravity, falling back onto his elbows. The screaming of children outside carried on.

"I wasn't suggesting something like. Marriage. Ha."

"No?" I asked, taking a third, final step back. I could feel the edge of my mom's vanity table pressed against my back. "Then what were you suggesting, Uncle Charlie?"

His name flew right over his head.

"Just, you know. Some fun. Another kiss would be nice." He pushed himself a little higher on the bed. The head of his penis flexed beneath his white pants.

I turned from facing him and grabbed hold of the object sitting on my mother's vanity. My father, long before I'd been born, had brought it back from Turkey.

It was an obsidian globe, which he'd purchased at the Grand Bazaar in Istanbul. The detailing was absolutely astonishing. As a child, I'd spent hours admiring it, studying it. Trying to make sense of the whole wide world, which was now, neatly, reduced to the perimeters of a swiveling ten-inch ball.

The globe was heavy. But I lifted it up with relative ease, gripping its base with both hands and raising it above my head. I turned on my heels and rushed towards the bed.

Uncle Charlie's face crumpled before my eyes. His expression went from satisfaction to shock in a matter of seconds, as he registered through the gauze of inebriation what was about to happen.

"Wait—" he blurted, pushing himself into an upright position. Too late.

I brought the globe down hard, square to the meeting point of his open legs. There was a squelching sound as his testicles, presumably, were crushed. A red flower bloomed on his white crouch.

My uncle began to shriek. I let the globe drop from my hands and roll off the bed. It struck the floor with a bang, hard enough that I could feel the vibrations travel up my toes. Uncle Charlie twisted and shook, his body an instrument for a deafening performance of agony. It was hilarious. I stepped back and watched his face, feeling vindicated. Not just for myself. But for every girl that had been punished for having a body. For existing. There were, after all, millions of Uncle Charlies.

What was the world without one more, if not a better one?

My satisfaction was short-lived. A stampede of voices and footsteps could be heard from the stairs, and a moment later the door to my mom's bedroom was burst open. My mother entered first.

"Honey, I—" Her words fell flat in her mouth. Her brother's body laid writhing on the duvet, shrieking blue murder. The globe lay lopsided on the floor, the stone so black that you couldn't see the blood running down South America. And me, her daughter, a 13-year-old who seemed both too young and too old for that age, standing off to the side.

I did what I had to do. I burst into tears and ran into my mother's arms.

~ ~ ~

Jack sat in stunned silence after I'd finished speaking. We'd been sitting at the kitchen table, illuminated by nothing by a single taper candle. The shadows rippled across his face.

"Can you say something?" I asked, after several beats of silence had gone by.

It was an eerily quiet night: no rain, no wind, nothing. Besides our breathing, the only sound was of candle wax, slowly dripping.

"Like what?" he asked. He refused to look at me directly.

"Well, anything? Look, I know that it's a messed up thing to hear but—"

"That's fucked. So fucked," Jack said. His voice was expressionless, dead as tundra.

"Okay. Yes. But you have to understand. This was not a good person. He kissed me, tried to sleep with me. At 13! And I just *know* there were more besides me."

"How?"

"How what?"

"How do you know?" He cleared his throat, pushing forward to speak. "That there were more."

"Because, Jack. I just…I know. You have to trust me about that."

I sighed and rubbed my eyes. Leaned forward onto the table. Tried to catch his gaze.

"At the time, all I could feel was this…this anger. Because of what he had done to me. And his *expression.* His fucking cocky attitude. But also because…"

Again, I felt myself straining for words. Trying to express what I needed to, without saying too much. I was so tired of lying.

"Because, honey. There are so many bad men in this world. In all of history. All those creeps, and perverts, and fucking freaks who have touched their nieces and molested their own daughters. Whole armies who have raped innocent women and children just because they could. Because it makes me so angry that it's happened to *so many women.* And it's still going on, right now. Right this minute. Somewhere, some girl, whether she's 6-years-old or 60, they're being assaulted. By a man. Just think about that for a second."

Jack's face changed slightly as I told him this. A glimmer of horror made its way across his eyes. But he still refused to look at me.

"Okay," he said, at last. "You're right. I know. But…"

"But what?" I asked. Finally, he turned his face towards mine.

"How could you still do something like that? Or know all those things, at 13?"

I looked at my husband's face and felt a deep, indomitable sadness inside. He seemed so frightened. So confused. And there was nothing in that moment I could do to change that.

"I don't know, honey," I replied, deflated. "I just did."

That same night, Jack moved into a guest bedroom at the end of the hall. He cited his injured hand and concussion for the need for space, but I suspected that he didn't like the thought of sleeping in the master bedroom anymore. My mom's old room.

Or maybe he just didn't like the thought of sleeping with me.

Either way, I didn't argue with him about it. I set up his things and kissed his cheek goodnight. As I walked back to my own bed, I heard the distinct click of his door being locked.

And just like that, I felt completely alone all over again.

TWO

My physical therapist, Dr. Kimora, was not a kind woman. She had a lean, angular face, often donning a mask of open disdain. Her hair looked like it had been cut by Hellen Keller after a heavy night of drinking. To my great misfortune, I found myself—every 2 weeks—sitting uncomfortably in her client chair as she dipped my mangled hand in wax and scolded me for hunching.

"You should really sit up straight, Jack," she said, sounding bored. Her muscular fingers massaged the tendons of my hand. I bit the side of my cheek and tried not to wince.

"A man like you needs a healthy spine. Otherwise, you'll get a hump."

"A hump?" I asked.

"Oh yes. A big, fat hump." She paused and looked up at me behind her horn-rimmed glasses. "Like Quasimodo. Only *he* had the whole French thing going for him. You don't."

Ouch.

"Okay," I said, straightening my posture. Dr. Kimora went back to digging her thumbs into my flesh, willing "rejuvenating blood" to flow to my fingers. She had a remarkable way of making a person feel like they were a child again. She really should have been a principal instead of a therapist.

Several minutes of forceful poking and prodding went by. At last, Dr. Kimora stopped her torment and rolled away on her wheeler chair. She jotted some notes down on a clipboard and then rolled back.

"Flex," she commanded. I obliged, moving my reattached fingers as best I could. They quivered, looking like miscast actors in a play. The scars from where they'd been sewn back on looked comical, Frankenstein-like. You could see the zig-zag of healthy and severed skin, weaved back together with the magic of modern medicine.

Except, that's where the magic ended. In over 6 months, I had barely regained any movement. And even less feeling.

Dr. Kimora watched my pitiful attempt to move my fingers with indifference. Then wrote down some more things. Let out a sigh.

"Jack, it's pretty clear to me that your damaged members—" This was doctor-talk for 'fingers'. "—are making very little progress. While I cannot *actively* discourage you from continuing these therapy sessions, I *can* be honest in saying it would be a waste of time for us both."

Double ouch.

"Okay," I said again. "Are you sure?"

I put my left hand in my lap and touched my dead fingers with my other hand. They felt foreign, lifeless. Two alien bits of meat transplanted onto my stumps. I stopped touching them.

"Very sure. Most re-attached members will see a fifty to sixty percent return of usage, in the very best scenario. For you, I'd say that number is closer to twenty."

She checked her clipboard one last time and stood up. I followed suit, recognizing that this meant the session was over. A part of me was relieved that I wouldn't have to sit for another 45 minutes of therapeutic torture.

But another part of me was devastated. Because I knew what it meant, if she was giving up. This was as good as it would ever get.

Dr. Kimora must have seen the look on my face, because her expression softened ever so slightly. She led the way to the door and then stood in front of it, arms crossed.

"Look, Jack. I know you've been through a lot, and that an injury like this can really weigh on a person. Have you been to see a psychologist yet? Had the chance to talk things through?"

I nodded.

"Yes, but only twice."

"Why not more?" she asked.

"I...didn't find it very helpful."

It was true. The psychologist we'd been assigned, both Dahlia and I, had been a stiff-lipped man with a dingy office. He'd asked us to recount our feelings, first together, and then once alone. Because my concussion was so fresh, I'd hardly been able to express myself. Nor had it mattered.

The psychologist had prescribed "lots of darkness and rest" until I felt better. And the thought of opening up, actually opening to this stranger, had made me want to throw up.

"Well, you might want to look into it. If your initial experience wasn't very positive, I can recommend some other clinics that you could try. It's all about finding a psychologist you connect with. And, given your situation, I think it could do you some good."

I couldn't understand why she was being so kind all of a sudden. Not that her face had changed. No, she still wore that cold look of disinterest. But perhaps I'd assumed whatever lay beneath to match the surface.

I gave her a smile, and thanked her for the suggestion. Told her I would give it some thought. She nodded, before moving out of the way to open the door.

As I began to walk out of the clinic, she called out to me.

"Hey, Jack!"

I turned back to look at her. She drummed her nails against the door frame.

"Don't give up on your fingers just yet. Time can be the best healer. Remember that."

I held up my hand in thanks and turned away. Then headed down the rest of the hall, and into the sunshine.

Out of reflex, I flinched when I first stepped out into the light.

~ ~ ~

Dahlia drove me home as usual. She'd bought me a new car to replace my beat-up Mustang. Now I owned a brand new Porsche convertible, which she'd told me was so I could have as much headroom as I wanted in the summertime. It was a sweet gesture. Because of my concussion, however, it was still unsafe for me to drive. So Dahlia acted as chauffeur, driving me to and from different appointments, errands. There was hardly a minute when she wasn't around.

When I told her what Dr. Kimora had said, she'd frowned, staring straight at the road.

"That can't be right. She can't just give up on you."

Her voice was still fucked up. Just like my fingers, there didn't seem to be much hope in recovery. I still found myself unnerved by it: this harsh, raspy sound coming from my wife's lips. Almost metallic-like.

"There must be someone else we can see. A hand specialist, or something."

"D, Dr. Kimora *is* a hand specialist."

"Well, a better one, then. Someone who doesn't just toss in the towel. A quitter."

I watched her grip the steering wheel even tighter. Her knuckles flushed white.

"It's fine," I said. "I've made my peace with it."

Dahlia didn't reply. The speedometer ticked higher.

This was an outright lie. I hadn't made peace with anything. My whole world, which had previously untaken this dreamy, scenic quality, had revealed itself to be an ephemeral sham. My body had failed me. My brain had become my enemy. And the woman I loved scared the shit out of me.

Since I'd come home from the hospital, Dahlia had tried her best to return our lives to normal. I had to admire her effort. She ordered fancy take-out dinners and played Brazilian music on low volume. The house was always spotless, because she never stopped cleaning. Everything I asked for was supplied, performed, accepted. She wore a permanent, cheery smile, and dressed up for no one.

As I suffered away in the darkness, trying to train my brain to speak, to concentrate, to love the sun again, she waited patiently for my progress. On paper she had—and was—doing everything right.

But everything was different. Both of us knew that. I could not, no matter how much I tried, wipe the memories of what I'd seen and heard from my head. Quite the opposite. My foggy brain would replay them, as I laid in my pitch-black room for weeks, in jarring clarity.

I could not get rid of it. Any of it. Not the way my hand felt, drenched in steaming hot blood. Not the scent of human filth. Not the sound of the knife puncturing organs. Not the spluttering wet begs to stop. Or how she'd guarded the dead body like a dog.

This particular detail kept haunting me. In its strangeness. After Dahlia had finished, her earth-shattering scream still ringing in my ears, she had stripped off her bloodstained coat and covered what remained of the man. By then, the alley was alive with wailing sirens, yelling voices. She'd sat down on her bloody haunches and waited.

I had swum in and out of consciousness. Nothing I was comprehending seemed to be real. It couldn't be. The level of depravity I had just witnessed. The extremity. It couldn't have been my wife. My Dahlia. No. It just couldn't. None of this was real.

And yet, there she was: illuminated by red, blue, and blood. Her eyes were glued to me. Those eyes, too big and bright to be human. They'd looked like lanterns. Like blood-ringed torches.

This was the image that would not leave me. Sleepless night after sleepless day. Alone. In my room. For months. This image, stacked on top of all the other diabolical knowledge. The image of my wife, squatted beside the body she had just beheaded. For me.

It took me a long time to make sense of it. I couldn't understand why she'd stayed there, crouched on the ground. She had not risen or moved, even as paramedics came to take me away in a stretcher. Not when bystanders pushed to get a better look. Or when her own friends had screeched her name, demanding to know what had happened. Not when the doors of the ambulance shut on me alone, and I succumbed to my injuries.

Then one day, the answer came. I'd been kept in a relative bubble after being unable to read or watch the news. Doctors, therapists; they all kept dancing around the subject. Of what had happened. It was hard to tell what they even knew. What anybody knew about what had gone down. Besides the police, of course. Officer Walden had made that clear.

When I was finally strong enough to, I researched the news story myself. All that was written—which took me several minutes to re-read over, to force my brain to choke down—was of a mugging gone wrong. The perp had been killed in self-defence. The victims, us, were a young newlywed couple. This was all the media knew. Suddenly, it was obvious.

My wife had guarded her kill and hidden it from prying eyes for only one reason. She hadn't wanted the world to see what she had done. Or what she was capable of doing.

~ ~ ~

The car sloped down the driveway towards the new house. It still had not sunk in that I lived there. That *we* lived there. It added to the sense of surrealism that had shrouded my life, refusing to back off. Nothing I did or experienced anymore seemed tethered to reality.

Dahlia had been the first to call it Heaven. The name had stuck. There really wasn't a better word to describe the place. It was perfect, with startlingly white walls and pearly gates to match.

Unlike the previous property, there were far fewer trees and grass at Heaven. Instead, the house had been built right onto rock, suspended about twenty feet from the high tide. Arbutus trees, with their gnarled, soft-fleshed trunks, grew as close as dirt would allow.

As you drove down the driveway, the property opened to reveal an untainted vista of the ocean, angled in such a way that it was impossible to see any sort of neighbours. The only sign that human activity was underway were the lights of Kits and UBC miles away, on the other side of the strait. As well as cargo ships and the occasional cruise-boat, sailing close enough to hear the dance music and celebratory voices.

The house had a shape that was almost fluid. The construction was rounded in most places and resembled a Grecian island home, far more than a North American one. In the centre, an enormous glass skylight took the place of normal roofing.

It enclosed the indoor garden which had a man-made stream flowing at all times. The sound of water, either from the waves outside or miniature stream, was eternally present.

Dahlia pulled into the double-car garage and stepped out of the convertible. With the cold June weather and a headache looming, we'd driven with the top-up. Also, the roar of wind could be tedious to talk over. Not that we did much of that anymore.

She pushed a button to close the garage before going inside.

"How about I make us something to eat, and we can play a game or something?"

"That'd be nice," I said, slipping off my coat and hanging it with the others. The movers had, under Dahlia's direction, moved and unpacked all of our belongings. If I didn't know better, I'd say it looked like we'd been living here for years.

I followed her into the foyer, past the garden and gurgling stream, and into the kitchen/living space. Floor-to-ceiling windows opened onto the ocean and ever-changing sky. Since there was so much natural light everywhere, I had to keep my dark sunglasses on almost always. The only time I could take them off, besides at night, was in the basement.

While the previous house had been a towering fortress with more rooms than reason, Heaven was significantly smaller. It was a Mediterranean-style bungalow, complete with four bedrooms, vaulted ceilings, and the best view money could buy. The architect had leaned heavily into infusing the home with various idiosyncratic and artistic quirks. The most dramatic of these was the subterranean basement built right into the bedrock.

This was, by no means, a normal basement. In lieu of traditional building materials, the architect had embraced the original foundation and made the entire basement *out* of stone. Everything—stairs, flooring, walls—was all smooth granite. There were stone-made shelving units, sleeping area; even a bathtub, built right into the floor. If it wasn't for the embedded lighting strips that illuminated the ceiling edges with a warm glow, as well as the small port window that showcased the near-level water, the place would've resembled a cave. A fancy cave. But a cave, nonetheless.

I found myself spending a lot of time alone in Heaven's basement. It provided my recovering brain with the darkness it craved, as well as reprieve from the omnipresent sound of water. I never knew a person could feel stifled by the sound of liquid. Turns out, you could.

I set my briefcase down on the kitchen island and made a beeline for the stairs. Dahlia moved past me and popped open the fridge, started rooting around. It was always stocked full these days. Mainly with meat. She pulled out a pack of pepperoni and started chewing.

"I'll give you a call when everything's ready. Any requests?" she asked, my hand on the doorknob. I shook my head.

"Whatever you want," I said, slipping into the basement's cool invitation of silence.

~ ~ ~

I used the basement for another purpose. Because we were still sleeping in different beds, neither of us had had sex in half a year.

At first, this hadn't been an issue. I was so preoccupied with healing that being sexual hadn't even crossed my mind. But as weeks had turned into months, the bed became more and more empty.

The first time I tried jerking off was a disaster. Mentally. My dick still worked as well as ever, but my mind was another matter. This time, I couldn't blame my concussion. It was Dahlia. She had infiltrated my every desire. I couldn't stop thinking about her, no matter how hard I tried to focus on a past girlfriend or celebrity crush.

Porn wouldn't work either. The only time I had tried it, the screen-light gave me such a headache I couldn't stay hard. And forget about using a magazine. We lived in a digital age. Nor could I drive to buy one.

My problem was that every time I attempted to masturbate to the thought of my wife, another bad image would take over. Suddenly the memory of us making love on the sofa would involve her face, covered in blood. Or the time we laid on the lawn to stargaze, and we ended up screwing right there on the grass. Then the mental grass-blades would start screaming, and they wouldn't stop until I quit touching myself.

Every fantasy I had, every memory of sex we shared, became twisted into some new, nightmarish illusion. So, I was forced to train myself into thinking about nothing.

Which, if you've ever tried before, is very fucking hard to do.

As I made my way down the steep staircase, I removed my sunglasses and breathed a sigh of relief. The basement had become my sanctuary, my space of security. Dahlia almost never came down here.

I looked out the port window, onto the low tide. The waves, when they were irritated, could splash hard enough to soak the glass. Today they were calm, a murmuring of flat sea. A window to another world.

I stripped my pants off, climbed into the sunken bath, and positioned my body atop the tub drain. I'd purposefully left the lights turned off, so that the only illumination came from the port window. It cast a dim circle of pale June sunlight into the basement, leaving the rest in shadow. The sunken stone bathtub was located off to the side at the base of the stairs, in darkness. Just like I needed.

I closed my eyes and stroked myself until I was firm. Behind my lids, I started to focus on the world of blackness. Its wholeness. Its familiarity. I didn't try to make it something it wasn't. The darkness had no name, no motives. It was, simply, a void of everything.

A few minutes went by. There was no sound except for my palm, rubbing against the sides of my shaft. When I finally came, I didn't even sigh. I didn't feel much of anything.

THREE

The party was admittedly a bad idea from the get-go. I'd become overzealous with the idea of bringing everyone together under the banner of my birthday, Jack's recovery, and the new house. A triple-whammy of joy! What could possibly go wrong?

I'd told everyone to arrive around mid-afternoon. This gave me time to set up the food, the decorations. I'd been forced to go low-key this year, with Jack's godforsaken concussion receding at a glacial pace. He was still very sensitive to stimuli. Not to mention his equally slow thaw to love me again. In regards to that, I'd had to take matters into my own hands.

A few weeks before my birthday at the end of July, I'd knocked on Jack's door, long after he'd gone to bed. I knew he was still up because the lamplight was still on, glowing underneath the doorframe. Also, I had spiked his dinner with Ecstasy.

The drug had not been particularly hard to find. All it had taken was a rendezvous into the city, a quick asking around from some suspected dealers. You could always spot them. They walked with a particular bounce in their step, so as to draw attention, but not too much of it. Their clothes, whilst often unkempt, were unmistakably nicer than others. And most importantly, if you asked if they sold drugs, they would usually say Yes.

I'd dressed down for the occasion. Chugged espressos the night before to force myself not to sleep. The effect gave me a satisfyingly grungy appearance. After parking in the downtown East Side, I'd walked and asked around for hardly 10 minutes before getting a bite.

"Yeah, whatcha lookin' for?" the dealer had asked, who happened to be a she. She was sporting long strips of crimped hair, as if she had time-travelled, but only by half a decade. I'd smiled and told her what I needed.

An hour later and I was driving back to Heaven. In my purse, I had a few grams of crystal MDMA and a tester kit, swiped from one of the consumption sites where they let people shoot up safely. As safe as doing methamphetamines and heroin can be, that is.

The Ecstasy tested negative for lacing. Just pure love drug. I'd dabbled before and found that the experience could be summed up with those three words. Pure love drug. The original street name, I'd been told by a shit-faced girl in a bar bathroom, had actually been Empathy. Of course, that had sounded too soft and mushy for business, so the name had been switched to the harder, meaner Ecstasy. Or MDMA. An acronym of pleasure in the place of soft-hearted truth.

Because that's what it really felt like. Any tension within you—emotional, mental—could be melted away. You felt like there was nothing but love: big, juicy, delicious love flowing in your veins. Everyone was your friend. Your potential lover. All your troubles turned to ash in the place of smoldering contentment. It was truly marvellous stuff. And if all that was just a chemical mirage, mimicking the real thing? So be it. Just as long as I got Jack back.

~ ~ ~

I'd made gnocchi with red sauce and sprinkled it on top of his plate. I'd given him a purposefully small helping to make sure he ate it all. Every last bite. Then watched from the end of the table as he'd done just that.

"Is there anymore?" he'd asked, scraping the bowl clean.

"Lots. I'll get you some." I stood up to grab his dish before he could object.

"You don't have to—"

"Shush, it's fine. Just sit and relax." I sauntered into the kitchen and began to load up his plate with more. The sound of crashing waves filled the space. A record of Latin guitar played quietly on repeat.

I poured the pre-bottled red sauce atop the gnocchi, and then pulled the baggie of crushed powder out of my pocket. It was hard to know how much to use, since I'd always just taken what was offered to me in the moment. Plus, Jack was a big guy. He might need some more to topple. I stirred a sizable amount into the sauce and then topped it off with some grated black pepper. *Voilà.*

"Here you are, honey," I said, presenting the bowl with a flourish. Jack smiled wanly at me and produced a thank you, before shoveling a bite into his mouth.

"So, have you talked to Gabriel at all recently?" I asked, taking my place at the head of the table. Jack shook his head.

"Not really."

"Well, you should. It'd be nice for you to start seeing your friends again." I took a sip from my wine and smiled encouragingly. "I know how much he cares about you."

"Yeah. I know."

"Have you seen him much since the hospital?"

It was a rhetorical question. But I posed it as a genuine one.

"Not really. No."

"That's too bad. Although it's been hard, hasn't it? With the move and stuff. I'm just glad you're able to be outside more again. Back in the sunlight."

"Not without my glasses," Jack said dully. He took another bite of his dinner.

"Right. That's true. But still better than a pitch-black room."

"I guess."

There was more clattering of tableware. Waves. Guitar. I pushed my gnocchi around and prayed my plan was going to work. I couldn't withstand any more dinners like this. More awkward car rides, where I had to wrench a few measly words of conversation from my husband's mouth. The empty bed. The look. That fucking look on his face, whenever I got close enough to touch him. Like I was some diseased creature, coming to attack him. That look of fear. With a budding undercurrent of resentment. It made me furious.

At times, I wanted to grab him by the ears and shake him. I wanted to shout that I was hurting too, that none of this was easy on *me* either. All I had done was protect us, avenge him for what had happened. And this was the thanks I got? Three-word sentences dished out with disregard for my suffering? A constant attitude of self-pity and misery, instead of attempting to find solace in all this? I was doing everything I could to make things better. We were wasting such precious time. And Jack refused to play ball. Well, no more.

Dinner resolved itself without another word. He slunk away from the table and put his empty bowl in the dishwasher, then announced that he was going to bed.

"Sleep well, handsome," I said, but by that point, he'd already vanished down the hall. I grit my teeth, and poured myself more noir. Then took myself outside to listen to the water.

~ ~ ~

An hour and a half later, I was standing outside his bedroom door. I'd considered just bursting in, sneak-attack, but decided that would probably startle him. He was so jumpy now, always wincing at every little bump or movement. I found this deeply unattractive.

So instead, I curled my hand into a fist and rapped twice, gently, on his door.

"Uh, come in," he answered. I opened the door and quickly shut it behind me.

"Hey, I was going to…" I never got to finish my excuse.

Jack was propped up in bed with his shirt still on. A book sat unopened beside him. In the warm glow of the lamplight, I could see that his pupils were abnormally dilated. He was definitely rolling. What I hadn't expected to see, however, were tears. Jack was crying.

"Oh, honey, are you okay?" I did my best to cushion my damaged voice. For a moment I felt frozen. And deeply guilty. What the hell had I done?

Jack just stared at me, his eyes splayed wet and wide.

"No," he choked, very quietly. He looked like a little boy inside a giant man's body.

"Can you tell me what's wrong?" I asked.

I approached the bed slowly, and sat down on the far end. None of this was going to plan.

"I feel really strange." A hand swiped away the tear running down his cheek, which was quickly replaced with a new one. It suddenly hit me that, in almost 4 years, I had never seen my husband cry.

"Strange like…sad strange? Or, or what?"

"Yeah. Sort of."

"Okay."

I smoothed out my skirt. This felt like twenty-one questions, but with a concussed lover rolling on Ecstasy who was also scared witless. If it wasn't so sad, I'd probably be laughing.

"Could you tell me a little more of what you're feeling?" I reached out to pat his leg, but he had them curled up near his chest. Out of reach. I sighed.

"I…I want to help you, Jack. You have to understand that. I'm doing everything I can think of. But I need you to talk to me. Like...what can I do to make you feel better?"

There was a long pause as we stared at each other: Jack silently crying, and me, sitting awkwardly on the edge of the bed. Behind me, the long, silken curtains billowed from the cracked window. The night smelled of salt and heat.

"I…I…" Jack's bottom lip quivered, before his voice quietly broke.

"I miss my mom."

Now this was a curveball. The pit in my stomach sunk to the centre of the Earth. I'd come into the room with the preparation of *sleeping* with Jack, not talking about his dead mother. I didn't want to open that coffin tonight. But he left me no choice.

"Oh, Jack. I know."

At these simple words of validation, Jack fully broke down. He crumpled his face into his hands and started to sob. Instinctually, I crawled across the bed, close enough to rub his shoulder.

"Hey, hey, it's okay," I said, my gravelly voice sounding anything but soothing. I cleared my throat and tried a few more words of comfort. Nope. Still the same coarse voice, like sandpaper being stuffed into your ears. I hated it. And I knew Jack hated it, too.

I let him cry it out for a few more minutes. I counted the waves, breaking against the foundation of the house. I cursed Shane Winnow for all the trouble he had put us in, and hoped his skin was being peeled off in the afterlife. I prayed for everything to go back to normal again. For a miracle to save this love of ours.

When he finally slowed down his breathing, I left the room and returned with a box of tissues. Jack gratefully blew into them, then wiped his face.

"I'm sorry," he murmured, head bowed.

"Hey, there is nothing you need to be sorry about. Okay? This is a lot to go through. All of this. And trust me…I know exactly how you feel."

This got his attention. He looked up at me with those black eyes, now big enough for me to fall into. A great surge of adoration filled me up.

"Jack, you mean more to me than anything in the whole world. You know that, right? I would do anything for you. And I'm sorry that we're in this mess. I'm so fucking sorry. It breaks my heart to know that you're in pain, and that you miss your mom. I miss mine too. I feel awful that we've hardly even talked about it."

The words tumbled out of me before I could even think them over. Maybe it was the wine. But I could not stop once I started. My own voice began to crack.

"I'm sorry that you don't want to be with me anymore. Because I scare you, or you hate me, or whatever. And I'm sorry for all the shit you've gone through, and I *wish* I could erase it all for you. I wish I could fix everything. But I can't. I can't fucking fix this, Jack."

Now I was the one who was crying. And for once, it wasn't an act.

I stood there, cheeks wet, my heart laid out raw and torn to shreds. For a long, horrible moment, I thought he was going to turn away. Tell me to go. Or do absolutely nothing at all. I think that would've been the worst of all.

But Jack was not that kind of man. Deep down, I knew he wasn't. He rose to his knees on the bed and pulled me towards him. I crumpled into his embrace. An eternity of sadness flowed out of me and onto his shirt. I cried and cried and cried. And all the while, Jack held me, and took my pain. My mountain of hidden sorrow, transfigured into tears.

When my body was completely hollowed out, I let myself be held by him. The top of my head was wet, and I realized he had been crying more, too. We curled up beside one another and calmed our breathing. It felt so good to be close to him again. I'd forgotten how much I missed him. The heat of his body, his scent. I pressed my face closer to him and inhaled.

I could tell that he missed me too. There was no reservation in the way he cuddled me. Nothing like the timid, infrequent embraces I'd become accustomed to. I leaned up onto my forearm and gave him a kiss on the cheek.

He turned in slight surprise, his dilated pupils resembling obsidian orbs. I wondered what was going on inside his head. Although not for long. He leaned forward and kissed me on the mouth.

"I still love you, Dahlia," he said, when he pulled back. For a second I was worried he was going to cry again. "And I'm sorry too."

"I love you too, Jack," I replied, as sweetly as I could shape with my voice.

We kissed again. And then again. And this time, there was a reluctance to part. So we didn't. We pushed our mouths deeper into each other, feeling the stirring of that old desire that had been buried for months. Jack pulled me closer to him, and I willingly obliged.

With my free hand, I caressed the front of his torso. As I neared his pelvis, I felt the unmistakable bump of his erection. Turns out the Ecstasy was doing its job after all.

Our hunger for one another grew more intense. All the purging of emotion had cleared the path for lust—deep down inside our core—to rise up. I slid my leg up to straddle Jack's body, our hands loosely locked around each other's necks.

When we made love, it was very slow and deep. I had to bite into his shoulder to stop from crying out as I took him in after so much time apart. I didn't want my voice to ruin the moment. Jack moved laboriously but keenly, as if he was a starving man having his first meal in days. The room became filled with the depth of our breathing, as he worked himself to climax inside of me. And as usual, I wasn't far behind.

By the time we had finished, it was nearly dawn. The telltale sign of the rising sun came from behind the curtains, a sliver of golden glow. The emotional rollercoaster from the past several hours had exhausted us both, and we fell asleep, pressed up together just like we'd always done before.

Once I had broken down Jack's barricade against me, I refused any opportunity for him to put another back up. The Ecstasy had worked its magic once, but I didn't want to rely on it any more than I had to. I worked hard to keep the momentum going in the following days. And if I noticed a regression to bad habits, say, a withdrawing of the hand or turning of the cheek when I went to kiss him, I would do what I needed to correct him. Subtly, of course.

I didn't want to scare him all over again.

~ ~ ~

My first indicator that the party had been a mistake was the meat. I'd ordered too much of it. Far too much. The delivery driver carried in the gluttonous order, depositing it on the kitchen counter before pointing out each item.

"Those are the three racks of lamb, twenty-four Mediterranean breasts, nineteen Cajun Alabamans, five Pacific salmons, and four-dozen Wagyu skewers. The charcuterie platter with our best cuts, as requested. Oh, and I've already put the single tartare in the fridge."

I grimaced at the excess of it all. I had invited barely twenty people, and there were two more food deliveries on the way.

"Thanks," I said, forking over a hundred-dollar bill as a tip. The driver's eyes expanded as he took the cash and practically skipped out the door.

It was quarter-past 11 and the day was already sweltering. All the doors and windows were flung wide open, but the air was as still as a corpse. I pushed some of the boxes of ice-packed meat to one side, and then pulled out the tartare and one egg from the fridge. I cracked the yolk on top and mixed it in with the raw beef, then began to gorge myself.

A second doorbell ring announced that the personal chefs had arrived. I invited them both in and showed them to the kitchen. The taller of the two, Chef Kelsi, was a one-eyed giantess who quickly launched into the story of losing her left eye, before even taking off her shoes.

"If you're wondering about this," she boomed, pointing to her patch, "I can promise you it had *nothing* to do with the kitchen. Complete freak accident involving a cue stick and a bottle of olive oil. Nothing like them college parties, hey?"

She clapped a paw on my back, temporarily winding me.

"Mmm. So true," I replied, gasping for breath.

"How many people are you expecting? Fifty? Sixty?" the other chef asked, looking at the pile of boxes. His jacket revealed his name to be Chef Tim, and he sported a pencil-thin moustache that just pissed me off. It looked like someone had used a fine tip Sharpie to draw it on.

"Um, no. Probably closer to twenty. Or twenty-five," I added, going off their surprised expressions.

"Well damn! Are you inviting a bunch of Spartans over or what?" Chef Kelsi chuckled.

"No, just some...girlfriends mainly."

The two chefs looked at each other, stupefied.

"They're all big eaters," I lied.

"They better be," Chef Tim sniffed.

Before I could retort, the doorbell rang a third time.

"Oh, shit," I said, making a move for the entranceway. "That must be the other food orders, so you two can just get started with prep while they bring the rest in."

"There's more?" Chef Kelsi gasped, but by that point I was already out of the room.

A few hours later and the house was alive with activity. The two chefs had whipped the kitchen into a hurricane of aromas, as heaping trays of food manifested into being. Outside, on the wrap-around deck that overlooked the water and connected around to the front man-made yard, a DJ booth and wet bar had been erected. String lanterns rang along the sides, ready to illuminate the party once the sun had set.

Jack emerged from the basement about 30 minutes before the first guests had arrived. He'd elected to stay out of the way while I set things up, and was shocked to see the surplus of food being prepared.

"Woah, how many people did you invite?" he asked.

"Just over twenty. I may have gone a *bit* overboard with things," I admitted.

"Yeah, slightly."

"Oh, it's fine. It's better to have too much than not enough. You know me," I said, going to poke his ribs in jest. Instead, he pulled away from my reach, dodging my hand. I looked up at him, hurt by his rejection.

"I thought we were okay again?" I asked. Jack jerked his head down in my direction.

"Huh? What?"

"I said…nevermind."

"No, what is it?" he pressed, his eyes hidden behind his dark glasses.

"It's nothing. You just…y'know. Flinched. When I went to poke you." The words came out sounding childish and silly. They lacked the weight of the rejection entirely. Instantly I regretted saying anything at all.

"I did?"

"Yeah," I said. "Whatever. It's dumb. It just used to be our thing."

"Huh. I guess you're right. Well, sorry. Just out of instinct, I guess," he muttered.

I shrugged. "Doesn't matter. Just thought we were passed all that now."

"Passed all what, D?"

"Like, you being scared of me."

Jack let out an unconvincing laugh.

"Who said I was scared of you?" he replied, raising his voice from his now-typical mumble. Chef Tim looked up at us from the other side of the room.

I blew out air, deciding to let him win this one.

"Nevermind. That's not what I meant to say. Let's just drop it, okay?" I gave him my best smile, despite the seedling of irritation in my chest.

"Yeah. Sure."

He turned and walked out of the living space. His heavy footsteps caused miniature earthquakes as he rounded the corner and out of sight. I couldn't remember if he'd always walked so loudly. Or had that started after the incident? It was so hard to tell these things.

"Everything good?" Chef Tim called from the kitchen. He had an expecting look on his face, as he churned away at something suspiciously green and frothy. I gave him a double thumbs-up, a smile still glued to my lips.

"Never better!" I replied with my cavernously deep voice. I left to go sit out in the sun, thinking to myself that Chef Tim needed to learn how to mind his own goddamn business.

~ ~ ~

By 6, everyone had arrived. All except for Genevieve, who came stumbling around the deck an hour later. The cluster of girls let out a woo of joy upon seeing her face.

"You made it!"

"I thought you said you were too busy to come?"

"*Love* your skirt, where'd you get it?" Stephanie rounded off, clutching a watermelon margarita. The air was filled with the sultry sound of salsa music.

"Hi, ladies. Yes, I decided to come after all. And it's Valentino."

Her eyes skimmed the group and then landed on me. It was the first time we'd seen each other in months. She'd visited Jack and I only once in the wake of the incident, at the hospital, and that had been it. No effort since. There was a coldness to her expression that was never there before.

"I'm so glad you could come. It's great to see you again," I said, trying to sound warm and cheerful. Genevieve recoiled at my words.

"Holy shit. Yvonne wasn't kidding. You do sound like a different person." She hesitantly accepted my hug, before pulling back to get another look at me. Her breath reeked of wine.

"Yeah, I guess so," I replied. "I've been thinking about trying speech therapy, now that Jack's doing better. I've been so preoccupied with him and the move and stuff."

Genevieve's expression did not change. She looked at me intently, then let out a wine-rank sigh.

"Well, you should. You sound fucking awful."

Some of the girls gasped.

"Genevieve!" Joanna chided. "What the fuck?"

"Yeah, that's not cool."

I turned back and held up my hands.

"No, it's fine. I *do* sound weird. And she was just joking, right, Genevieve?"

Genevieve shrugged, and put her sunglasses on.

"Yeah, sure. Whatever, Dahlia."

I felt a fresh sting of rejection, only this time, I couldn't pinpoint it. What the hell was up with this attitude change? In all my years of knowing her, not once had I seen this bitter chill come from my friend. I pushed my hair off my face and pointed to the bar.

"Well, there's the bar, if you need a drink. I'm going to check in with the people inside."

I made my way back into the house, saying hi to people as I went. Besides Yvonne's girl-group, I'd invited a mishmash of old friends from the years, most of whom I'd never spoken to outside of the context of a party. For Jack, I'd made sure to invite Gabriel and his fiancée Irene, to make sure he didn't feel completely alienated. When I went back indoors, I could see him and Gabriel talking away, seated in the conversation pit.

The mountain of food the chefs had prepared sat, mostly untouched, on the kitchen island. The sight of it made me sick. Of course no one was going to come to a party with the expectation of eating an enormous meal. I don't know what the hell I'd been thinking.

As I began to gnaw away on a BBQ-seared Wagyu skewer, I felt a hand tap me on the shoulder. I turned to see Yvonne, standing beside me.

"Hey, could I talk to you for a second?" she asked.

"Yeah, of course. What's up?"

"Oh, I mean, somewhere private. If that's okay."

"Of course. Come with me."

I plopped the unfinished skewer down to lead her out of the main living space and around the corner. We walked past the indoor garden and down the hall, towards the bedrooms. I opened the door to the nearest guest room and shut it behind us.

"Wow," she said, seeing the bedroom. "This is gorgeous."

"Thanks. Yeah, it's pretty nice, right?"

"No kidding. The whole place feels like a dream."

"You have no idea."

The two of us sat down on the bed, each holding a cocktail in one hand. From the open window, the sound of salsa music, laughter, and waves came waltzing in.

"So, what did you want to talk to me about?" I asked.

Yvonne watched me with her large, golden eyes. Then let out a sigh.

"I don't know. I just wanted to make sure you're doing alright."

"Yeah, of course! I'm good. I'm *great,"* I corrected, sounding more eager than I meant to. The alcohol had loosened me up.

Yvonne frowned.

"Babe, I'm sorry, but I don't believe you."

"Why not?" I challenged, swirling my sangria glass. "Everything's fine. Honest."

"Okay, then why are you acting like this? All fake and bubbly. It's not like you."

Now it was my turn to frown. I felt like I was doing a damn good job of acting normal.

"Yvonne, I don't know what you mean. I'm good. Jack and I are doing great. I mean, yes, what we went through was bad, but—"

"Bad? Dahlia, you had to *kill* someone. That's not just bad. That's, that's..."

"Awful. Terrible. Fucked up. Yeah, I know," I said, finishing her sentence. I took a swig and kept going. "Literally, that's all I've been hearing from people for the past 6 months. So I get it. I know it's fucked, okay? Why do you think I've been keeping my distance from you guys? I'm trying to keep this mess to myself."

"Well, maybe you should be getting support from the people who love you instead of isolating yourself. We've all been worried about you, D. You never reach out, and you're impossible to get ahold of. Like, I know you've been busy with the move and everything, but Jesus Christ. Do you know how scared we've been for you about all this? It's been hard on us too."

I stood up in a huff.

"Well, Genevieve certainly has a funny way of showing that she cares."

"Oh, just ignore her. She's been off lately, dealing with some personal stuff. But I'm not just talking about the other girls. I'm talking about me." Yvonne stood up so she was eye level to me. Her perfume, amber and vanilla, saturated my nostrils. "I just want you to know that I'm worried about you. I still think about you, Dahlia. A lot. I want to make sure that you're okay."

"Okay, well you can stop worrying, then. I'm fine. Seriously. Everything is okay."

Yvonne regarded me with a sad look, one typically reserved for sick puppies and cripples. It made me want to slap her. Instead, I let her take my hand in mine.

"I hope so. You've been through so much, and I —"

A rapid knocking at the door interrupted her sentence. I whirled my head around, grateful for the interruption.

"Come in!" I called.

"Busy!" Yvonne shouted, at the exact same time.

Fortunately, my voice carried further. The door opened, and an uncertain-looking Anita peeked her head in.

"Um, hey, sorry, you two. Hope I'm not interrupting anything. Dahlia, I was, uh, hoping to talk with you. If you've got a minute."

"Yeah, absolutely. And no worries, we were just catching up. Right, Yvonne?" I turned back to look at Yvonne's face. Her eyes hardened.

"Yeah," she said, letting go of my hand. She made a move for the door, passing Anita brusquely on the way out. "I'm going to get a refill." Before anyone could object, she was gone down the hall.

"What was that about?" Anita said, closing the door behind her. She looked scared.

"No idea," I said, with a shrug. "So what did you want to tell me?"

~ ~ ~

20 minutes later, we emerged from the guest bedroom. I had to actively remind myself to breathe slowly and unclench my sangria glass to prevent crushing it to pieces. Anita excused herself to go freshen up in the bathroom and retouch her mascara.

"Just promise to keep this between us, okay?" she repeated for the fourth time, her voice thick from crying.

"Of course," I droned, before walking the other direction. In my chest, I could feel the unmistakable heat of fury rising. I shook my head, and willed myself back into host mode. This was *my* birthday party. I was not going to let a nasty shock ruin it for me.

As I rounded the corner, I could hear the distinct sound of drunken screams coming from outside. The DJ booth had cranked up the music and switched from salsa to rugged reggaeton. Jack and Gabriel were still sitting in the conversation pit, although now joined by a few other guests, including Irene. She gave me a polite nod.

"Hey! How are you guys doing?" I chirped, sounding fake as AstroTurf.

"There's the birthday girl! We were getting worried," Gabriel said, smiling broadly.

I let out a laugh.

"Seems like everyone is doing that these days." He gave me a perplexed look at my comment but didn't reply. I turned to the other two women seated beside them.

"Irene, Rida, how are you two doing? You guys want any more food?"

I gestured to the abundance of food on the island, growing colder by the minute. They both shook their heads.

"No, I'm good."

"Yeah, I already had some. But thanks, Dahlia."

I smiled and started to head for the deck. I didn't look at Jack because I was afraid of what I'd see. My mood didn't need to be ruined any more.

"Okay, well help yourselves! I'll just be outside."

None of them started to speak again until I had crossed the room, out of earshot.

~ ~ ~

Out on the deck, a cluster of fifteen-ish people stood awkwardly spread out. No one seemed to be having much fun. The thumping reggaeton beat seemed excessively loud, and I realized that the screams I'd heard had been Genevieve and Stephanie, who'd likely been doing cocaine bumps all evening. They were the only two people dancing.

"Shake your moneymaker, you fucking slut!" Genevieve shrieked, fanning Stephanie's rump as she waggled it in the air for no one. A couple of ladies I'd known from high-school watched the scene with discomfort.

I realized I needed to change the vibes, and change them *fast.* I had never failed in the role of party host, and I sure as hell wasn't going to let that change. I headed over to the DJ booth and told him to turn down the music. He happily complied.

"Hey, everyone!" I interrupted. "We're going to move inside for some party games!"

The group started to move for the door, as Genevieve turned towards me and jeered.

"Boo!" she said, her hands cupping her oversized mouth. Her and Stephanie stopped dancing, and joined the others as they funneled inside, although not before Genevieve shot me another look. I didn't react. Instead, I told the DJ and bartender to take a half-hour break, before following the rest of the partygoers into the house. The sun shone on.

"Alright, so first, everyone get into groups of four! We're going to start with charades," I instructed, moving past the crowd to stand in front of the fireplace, right at the centre of the conversation pit. People began to pair off into clusters, murmuring to one another. It felt eerily quiet after having music blasting non-stop for the past few hours.

"Ugh, why are we playing this? Isn't there a better game we can do?" Genevieve asked, lounging off to the side. There was a cruel smile painted on her lips, and with each passing moment I spent with her, I grew more and more unsettled.

"No, Genevieve. We're doing charades," I replied coolly. She rolled her eyes.

Once everyone had assembled themselves into groups, I distributed pens and paper for each group to use. There were five groups in total, spread warily around the living space. I picked Jack's group to go first, which consisted of Gabriel, his fiancée Irene, and my friend Rida.

Irene wrote something down and then folded it in half, before taking my spot in front of the fireplace.

I went over into the kitchen and grabbed an egg timer, then came back over.

"Alright, you'll have 1 minute to guess what Irene's thing is. Ready? Set? Go!"

I flipped over the timer. Sand began to fall.

Irene held up three fingers.

"Okay," Gabriel said, leaning forward onto his knees. "Three syllables."

She shook her head.

"Three words? Yes? Okay."

Irene clutched her throat and began to sing silently.

"A song! A three-word song."

She nodded excitedly. Then held up a finger.

"First word. Okay, um…uh…"

Irene had begun hitching her thumb over her shoulder. Jack snapped his fingers.

"Back? Backwards?" he suggested. Irene nodded again. Held up two fingers.

"Second word. No? Um, wait, two? To?"

Another nod.

"Okay, back to, back to…"

She pointed a finger towards black-skirted Rida, who had not said a word all game.

"Back to woman, back to Rida, um…"

"'Back to Black!' 'Back to Black!'" Jack said excitedly.

"Yes! That's it!" Irene exclaimed.

"Good job! Okay, that's one point for your team. Next group, go ahead."

Joanna rose from the couch and took her place in the centre. I gave her the thumbs-up to go ahead. She immediately started ducking her head like a chicken.

"A goose! Scoliosis! Giving a blowjob!" Stephanie yelled. Joanna shook her head and kept thrusting her face forward. Anita, who was part of their group, watched the scene with her knees curled up to her chest in silence.

~ ~ ~

A few rounds later, and a few drinks deeper, and the game was starting to heat up. I had had my doubts about stooping as low as *charades* for activities, but with my limited resources for entertainment, I'd been forced to improvise. Fortunately, everyone seemed to be having a relatively good time, and there were bouts of laughter as people tried and failed to guess their group's answer. So far, a dismal eight points had been scored in total. But no one really seemed to mind about that.

All things considered, I was even beginning to enjoy myself. My mind had wandered on from the ugly feelings I'd been stifling, and I was fully invested in the childish antics of the world's most clichéd party game. Which is when I felt Genevieve staring me down.

Unlike everyone else, she had left the room twice, off to excuse herself to the deck to do more coke bumps or steal hard liquor from the bar. I didn't care about that. But the look she kept giving me, the same one she'd been shooting my way since she'd arrived. Now that was bothering me.

Team Three failed at guessing Audrey's choice of the *Titanic*. She'd flailed valiantly on the floor to mimic a sinking ship, but the closest they'd come to guessing correctly had been the letter T and Movie.

"Ah, no points for Team Three, unfortunately," I announced. "Team Four, you're up."

Yvonne went to stand up, but Genevieve beat her to it.

"No, let me! I want to go," she said, practically tripping up to the fireplace.

"Girl, you need to write down your answer before you start."

Genevieve huffed and grabbed a pen and paper, turned around, and wrote something down. She looked back at me as she stuffed the folded paper into her bra. That cruel smile had not left her mouth.

She turned to the group and held up a finger.

"One word."

She nodded, then pointed directly at me. Everyone turned their heads, then back at Genevieve.

"Woman? Friend? Birthday?"

"Dahlia?" my friend Gillian asked.

Genevieve nodded again. Then circled her hand in the air. More words.

"Swirling?"

"Come on, give us an action!"

"Yeah, more! More!"

Genevieve looked at me once again, standing alone with the egg timer in my hand. Then she bent down and started doing a strange motion. It looked like she was using a handsaw.

"Um, uh, heaving, pushing, cutting down a tree—"

"Punching a midget!"

"Slicing, sawing—"

At this last word, Genevieve stood up and snapped her fingers. Her whole body swayed from inebriation as she did.

"Okay, so Dahlia sawing, Dahlia sawing what? What the fuck?"

I looked down at the egg timer. Less than 30 seconds.

Genevieve put a thumb to her neck and dragged it across. It was a crystal-clear action.

A couple of the girls gasped. Jack turned back and looked at me. I ignored him.

"Genevieve, that's not okay—"

"Girl, you cannot act out *that—*"

"Hey, hey! It's okay!" I proclaimed, louder than the rest. The room went quiet. I cleared my throat and looked Genevieve square in the face.

"What were you trying to act out, Genevieve?"

She met my expression with a smug one of her own.

For several moments, we stared each other down. My stomach started to turn inwards on itself, and I felt the dawning sense of dread a person gets, right before something really bad is about to happen. Genevieve opened her mouth.

"What did you really do to that man, Dahlia?" she asked. Joanna started to object but I held up a hand to silence her.

"I don't know what you mean, Gen," I replied, using the nickname I knew she hated. Her eyes narrowed. "And you're drunk. So maybe you should let someone else have their turn."

The whole room had fallen dead silent except for the sound of lapping water. I hoped that Genevieve wasn't as stupid as she was pretending to be. Unfortunately, I was wrong.

She reached into her bra and pulled out her answer. She unfolded it and held it up for everyone to see. In big, black letters, the words CUT OFF HIS HEAD were clearly legible.

There were more gasps as people read the words on Genevieve's paper. It was no secret about what had happened

6 months ago. Everyone here knew what I had been forced to do. The exact details, however, had been kept hidden. Until now.

"My cousin works for the police department," Genevieve slurred, looking triumphant. "He told me about what you did to that poor homeless man. How you stabbed him almost in half and then cut off his head like a psycho. And now you're just acting all la-di-da again, like nothing happened. What the fuck is wrong with you? Who does something like that?"

No one was saying a word at all. I looked around at the room of party guests, as they stared at Genevieve in shock, then over at me. I couldn't believe no one was defending me. Not even Jack.

A familiar feeling made its way into my chest. I felt like an outcast all over again. The goddamn pariah, kicked to the curb because everyone was too confused and frightened of me to know otherwise. Well, fuck them. I'd give them something to be scared of.

"Genevieve," I replied, keeping my voice nice and level. "I can't believe you would lie about something like that. No wonder your own mother gave you up. She must've been so embarrassed to have given birth to a fat little liar like you. Honestly, I feel disgusted to call you a friend right now."

In one swoop, I pushed all three of Genevieve's weak points. Weight, abandonment, and being a disappointment. It was very easy. Like all the people in my life, I knew exactly how to hurt her. Genevieve's response was immediate.

"You fucking *bitch,*" she hissed, throwing the paper to the ground. "You fucking murdered someone! And you're trying to make me the bad guy?"

"You don't need me to make yourself look bad, Gen," I said, raising my voice. "You already do that fine on your own. You're nothing but a sloppy, plastic-faced drunk who needs to ruin my birthday because I 'ruined' yours. By being violently *assaulted*."

My words echoed cathedral-like off the high ceilings. Genevieve's mouth dropped open as her face flushed even darker. I wasn't finished.

"The fact that you would *lie* to all these people, just for shock value, I mean…there's no words. There must be something really screwed up in that brain of yours, Gen, if you need attention on you that fucking badly. You should go soak your cunt in battery acid, since you're that desperate to feel something."

"You're sick, Dahlia. You're absolutely sick," she spat.

"Both of you! Stop it!" Yvonne cried, finally finding her voice. Everyone had been stunned into silence at the sudden viciousness of our exchange. She rose to her feet and held up her hands like a crossing guard.

"Yeah, Genevieve. Shut the fuck up," I sneered. Once the anger started flowing, I could not seem to turn it off. It felt too good not to keep going. Yvonne whirled her head at me, a look of repulsion on her face.

"Dahlia, stop it. You're being cruel."

"Oh, didn't you hear?" I asked, using a mocking tone. "Apparently I'm a murderer now, because I defended my husband after someone cut off his fingers. And then tried to kill us."

Several people had begun shifting uncomfortably in their seats. Yvonne continued to stare at me.

"Is it true?" she asked, voice low. Both of her hands were still raised.

"Is what true, Yvonne?" I replied, a threat more than a question.

"You know what she means!" Genevieve shouted. Her whole body had started to shake.

"Genevieve, enough. Just sit down," Yvonne snapped, before turning back to me. "Did you...did you cut off that guy's head?"

Jack, who had still neglected to intervene, continued to stare at me. His eyes were hidden behind his dark glasses, but I could imagine the look underneath. Anticipation.

In fact, everyone had turned to look at me when Yvonne asked her question. All the people I had grown to love over the years, my closest friends in place of family, gathered together in one space. Waiting to hear if I really was the monster Genevieve said I was. I took a deep breath and held up my head. I'd had enough.

"Get out of my house!" I snarled. My voice was so loud it shook my teeth right to their roots. Everybody flinched. The echo sounded like a thunderclap of stallion-hooves.

"Dahlia, I—"

"I said, get the *fuck* out of my house! Everyone, up! All of you!" I smacked my hands together and pointed to the front door. "Get out! If you all think I'm such an awful person, then you can fucking leave! I want you all gone!"

Despite my best effort to sound formidable, my voice began to break during those final words. And I felt, with great shame, the welling of tears in my eyes.

As if waking from a dream, all my friends began to rise to their feet. One by one, they filed their way out of the conversation pit and towards the door. Nobody knew what to say or do. A few people mumbled "sorry", too quiet to practically hear. Gabriel whispered something to Jack before heading for the entranceway, Irene pulled close to him as if they were walking through a dangerous neighbourhood. Meanwhile, Genevieve stomped past, giving me the finger and a curse as she went by. She looked like she was going to puke.

I stood off to the side, in front of the kitchen island, and let my cheeks run wet. I felt so embarrassed, ashamed. I couldn't believe how I had acted in front of everyone. Or of what had been said about me. None of what had just transpired felt real.

I watched as everyone pulled their shoes on and clunked out the front door. Practically everyone had cabbed here, so they would all have to congregate in the driveway until rides were called. I couldn't care less. I locked the door after Yvonne left, the last person to go. She walked out without saying another word beyond goodbye.

~ ~ ~

When I came back into the living room, I could feel my lungs on the verge of a panic attack. Jack had not moved from his position in the conversation pit. Like some oversized statue, too stupid to know what to say.

"You didn't even *defend* me," I exasperated. With great lethargy, he turned to look up over at me.

"What was I supposed to say, Dahlia?" he asked. His voice sounded drained of all its power. A limp dishrag of an excuse. This made my anger flash hot again.

"You were supposed to say that I'm not a bad person! That I was just trying to protect you that night! *That's* what you were supposed to say. You just let that, that cunt berate me in front of everyone, and you said nothing! Absolutely nothing!"

By now I was fully sobbing. It was a humiliating sensation, as I yelled at Jack with snot and tears flowing down my face. His expression remained impassive, conveniently hidden behind his sunglasses.

"Look, I'm sorry…"

"Oh, just shut up!" I turned my back on him and stormed to the kitchen island. I began grabbing plates of food and stuffing them into the refrigerator, which was already full. I felt like screaming, and if I didn't do something with all this food *right now,* I was going to start.

I marched to the deck door, flung it wide open, and threw the meat onto the ground. It landed with a splat on the deck: a ruin of chicken breast and herbs. I took the empty plate and tossed it into the sink with a clatter, then repeated with a tray of fish. *Splat.*

I kept throwing plates of fine cuisine onto the deck, waiting for Jack to say something in objection. Nothing ever came.

Pretty soon, the confused DJ and bartender tip-toed around the side of the deck. Before they could ask why all the party-goers were standing out on the driveway, I told them to go home.

"I'll pay you double, don't worry!" I promised through my tears. The DJ watched in awe as I unloaded the enormous charcuterie board onto the grotesque pile of meat. The moment I looked up at him, however, he quickly vanished around the side of the deck.

When I'd finished dumping the last plate, I shut the door, then slumped down to the sun-warmed floor. I kept my eyes on the glass, as my sobs gradually slowed to a murmur without any consolation from Jack. When I turned to look back at him, I saw that he had quietly left the room. Off to the basement, no doubt.

A few minutes later and salvation arrived in the form of a white bird. Then two, then six. Then the deck was completely overrun with seagulls, delirious with joy at the feeding frenzy they'd stumbled upon. They feasted on the expensive cuts I'd thrown out for them, screeching and clapping their beaks at their competitors. I watched: no longer crying, but not smiling, either. A pool of juice slowly grew beneath the gulls' dancing feet. By the time they had finished, the fronts of their white feathery chests had all been stained red.

FOUR

For a month, we hardly spoke to one another. Like magic, she would vanish for great stretches of the day, often before I even woken up. Now the first thing I saw when I rolled over was the outline of where her body had been: *Silhouette of Spouse,* an original sculpture composed of Egyptian sheets, pillows, and scorn. Sometimes I would go all day before seeing the woman who had made that artwork. And I certainly wouldn't get a response out of her.

"Listen, I don't know what else to tell you. I'm sorry, okay? Will you please just talk to me?" My pleads were met with a poker face that would give a Queen's Guard the creeps. Today was no different.

"I'm really not in the mood," she rasped. Her eyes flicked across me, then onto something more interesting in the room. A ceiling fan. Then a closed book.

"I know, you keep saying that. But we need to talk about what happened. I hate feeling like you're mad at me. And I…I feel bad that I didn't stand up for you."

"Do you have any appointments coming up."

"What?"

"Appointments. Errands. Do you need me to drive you anywhere."

Her eyes had taken on a dull, grey colour, their marine sheen wiped dry. I shifted on my feet and looked elsewhere.

"No, not really. And you don't really need to drive me anywhere. I've been feeling a bit better recently. So I can just take myse—"

"Great. I'm glad," she interjected, sounding anything but. Without another word, she left the room and disappeared out the side door. A few minutes later, I could hear the roar of the boat motor as she drove out to sea. I went to the window to watch her take off, before collapsing into the conversation pit couch and removing my sunglasses.

The truth was, I'd been feeling *much* better. I had been for longer than I'd been letting on. My sensitivity to light had regressed weeks ago, and the fog of disorientation had lifted as well. I felt more than well enough to drive a car again, and for the first time in several months, I was able to read a chapter without needing to struggle for hours over a single page. Even the immobility of my two dead fingers had sunken into relative obscurity. I hadn't realized how little I needed them, especially now that I rarely used a computer.

But none of that brought me much peace. All I could focus on was this horrible sense of guilt, needling into my gut.

At first, I had felt a far different emotion: relief. I felt horrible to admit it to myself, but there was no denying it. I was relieved that other people knew what had happened. Even if they didn't really believe it to be true, at least they'd *seen* the other side of my wife. I wasn't the only one who had borne witness to the thing inside her, the beast of rage. Only now, I felt like something had fundamentally changed.

There was no light behind her eyes. Her whole aura had caved in on itself, like a collapsed star. She didn't smile, or laugh, or do much of anything. I barely even saw her eat. When she talked, it was like listening to metal twine unspool. There was no effort to soften her voice, or perk it back up to its original warmth. And I knew, on some level, it was partly my fault.

With all my hours of solitude, I'd begun to replay my memories from that December night a bit differently. Originally, I had been so fixated on what my wife had done. Now I found myself thinking about what I *hadn't* done. I had failed—miserably—at protecting her in any way. And because of my inability to fight back, to do more, I'd forced my wife into a position of such extreme violence that she'd had no choice but to do otherwise. Right?

It was becoming harder and harder to think clearly about it. More than half a year had passed, and I'd recounted the night so many times—had told it to police officers, nurses, therapists, friends, all with conflicting details—that the memory had become tainted. Nothing seemed clear anymore. I couldn't recall what was truth or fiction, or a hybrid of the two. I couldn't remember what the man had even said, or how my severed fingers had wound up in the gutter in the first place. Most of the night was a hazy blur of fear. All that was still clear in my mind was how it ended.

~ ~ ~

About a month after Dahlia's party, I called Gabriel to talk things through. He agreed to meet immediately, after asking to see me for weeks on end. We decided to go for a walk on the seawall to take advantage of the August sun before it was gone. When I pulled up in my convertible, alone, he looked happy enough to burst.

"You're driving again! Ah, that's great!" he exclaimed, clapping a hand on my back mid-hug. He leaned back and looked the car up and down, letting out a low whistle.

"*Dios mío*, that's a nice ride."

"Thanks, she got it for me after..." I trailed off. Gabriel nodded.

"Right. Well, that's a damn good gift. Maybe if I get mugged too, Irene will buy me a Porsche." He laughed at his own joke, then quickly stopped.

"Sorry. That's bad taste."

"No, no, it's fine," I said, shrugging. My own sense of humour seemed to have dried up.

The two of us started walking along the paved path bordering shore and sea. Clumps of people strolled past, chatting amongst themselves. The water licked its lips against the wall, eating away at the granite fleck by fleck. Above, the sun beat down gratuitously.

"So, how've things been for you, my friend?" Gabriel asked, somewhat hesitantly.

"Not so great. I mean...I'm feeling better, so that's good. Been reading more, driving. And I can move these a bit better." I wiggled my two reattached fingers unimpressively.

"That's excellent! I'm glad to hear."

"Yeah. But things with Dahlia, well, they're shitty."

Gabriel frowned.

"Yeah, I was worried about that. Irene was pretty freaked out about the whole thing. And I have to be honest with you ,Jack, I've never seen anything like that. Just...the anger. Like a different person."

"I know. It's scary."

"Did you ever see that before? Back when you were dating?"

"No, never. She was always so calm, so patient. She never acted like anything close to that." I let out a shaky laugh. "Honestly, we didn't even really fight before we got married."

"Never? Well, that's your first warning right there. Couples have to fight. You have to let that anger out in little pieces. Otherwise..." He rubbed his chest area. "It keeps getting bigger and makes you sick."

We found a bench to sit down on and stretched out our legs. Or rather, Gabriel stretched out *his* legs. I kept mine tucked in to prevent tripping people over. A few beats of silence went by, as I thought about what he had said.

"Did something bad ever happen to her as a child? What was her family like?"

"I mean, I'm not really sure. There was this incident where she got like..." I dropped my voice down as a family walked past. "Molested by her uncle. And her mom died when she was younger. No dad. So, I don't really know."

"Jesus. That's awful."

"Yeah, it is."

"Have you guys tried therapy together? I mean, obviously you both can relate with, uh, trauma. But it might be good to see a professional."

"I don't know. Maybe. I don't really want to go back there though."

"Back where?"

"To like, what happened. With my mom and stuff. And I'm sure she doesn't, either."

Gabriel turned to look right at me with puzzlement.

"Wait a second, have you ever told her what happened?"

"About my mom? No. Not really."

He let out a sigh, rubbing his hands down the tops of his thighs.

"Man, why not? That's important shit. You've never told your wife about the worst thing that's ever happened to you?"

I wanted to correct him and say that it wasn't the worst thing I'd experienced *anymore.* But I just shook my head.

"It just never came up, I guess."

"Well, yeah, of course not. But you need to talk about that stuff. It's part of you. I mean, I told Irene about my dad on, what, our fourth date? How could I not?"

"Yeah. I guess you're right."

"How come you told me and not her, then?"

"I don't know. I just…"

In my head, I could think of several reasons. Gabriel was approachable and easy to talk to. He felt like someone I could trust. He'd brought up what happened to his father almost casually: how he'd left the house to go buy a coffee and wound up with a stray bullet in the head from a gang fight. On a random Wednesday morning, when Gabriel was only 14. It felt natural to tell him about what had happened to my mom in response.

With Dahlia, I dreaded the idea of opening up. Neither of us spoke about anything bad unless absolutely necessary. Even after the fight with my dad, I'd neglected to tell her the full extent of what had happened. It felt like rubbing mud onto a blank canvas, the idea of sharing all the shit we had been through. So for almost 4 years, we had danced around the periphery: never revealing, never sharing.

"Just what?" Gabriel asked. I realized I had stopped mid-reply.

"I felt like I couldn't talk about it. Because it would ruin what we had. It was so *good,* you know? It felt surreal how good things were between us. I didn't want to ruin that by talking about all the bad shit."

"I get it. I really do. But you have to understand, my friend, that pretending like those things never happened doesn't make them go away. They're still there, under the surface. Affecting how you act. You've got to embrace those parts of yourself. That's–" He jabbed a finger into my leg. "How you take your power back."

"Yeah. I guess you're right."

"I know I am."

We sat for a few more moments without speaking, watching the people pass us by. The world felt—for the first time in a while—very simple and straightforward.

"She's not talking to me at all right now."

"Have you tried to?"

"Yeah, of course. But she won't even respond. And she never has her phone with her. She just disappears for most of the day and then comes back at night."

He shook his head.

"Man, if this wasn't such a fucking mess, I'd say that's a pretty nice arrangement. If you know what I mean," he said, nudging my side. I smiled weakly.

"I guess. I just don't know what to do anymore. How to fix this."

"Well, just talk to her. And I mean *seriously* talk. None of that pussy shit, either. Be a man about it. When I screw up, Irene loves when I grovel a bit. Most of the time they just want to see you suffer a little before forgiving you."

"You think?"

"Trust me, *mijo*, I know. You've got to let her see that you're really sorry. Like, her friend was totally full of shit, right? Jennifer, or whatever?"

"Genevieve?"

"Yeah, that's it. I mean, she's the reason for this whole mess, right? Because she lied and you didn't say anything about it?"

When I didn't respond, Gabriel turned towards me, before repeating himself in a low voice.

"She *was* lying, yeah? Dahlia didn't actually cut off that guy's head?"

I looked at my friend's waiting face and shook my head.

"Yeah, of course. That was bullshit."

Gabriel let out a sigh of relief and chuckled.

"God, you scared me for a second! I thought that crazy drunk bitch was actually being serious. I mean, what the fuck. Making up a story like *that?* Women are on another level."

"Yeah," I said, looking back out onto the harbour. "You can say that again."

~ ~ ~

The whole drive home, I ruminated on what Gabriel had said. What I had to do was clear, which was to finally open up to Dahlia about what had happened. Maybe if we both shared our darkness, we could come to a place of resolution. And release.

When I walked through the front door, I was surprised to see her at the kitchen table, sifting through a stack of mail. She did not lift her head at the sound of my arrival.

"Hey, how are you?" I asked, going to grab a glass of water from the kitchen.

"Good."

"Just going through bills?"

"Yep."

I filled my glass to the brim and drank deeply. Sunshine poured through the towering windows, filling the house with golden heat. A warm wind blew through the house, as the steady song of waves filled the air.

I crept closer to the table to stand behind her and get a better look. Bank statements tattooed with ones and zeroes covered the table. I leaned in closer for a better look.

"Do you need something?" she asked, turned around to look up at me. Her gaze cut holes right into my skull. Immediately, I felt exposed without my sunglasses. I backed off.

"No, sorry. Just looking."

I moved away to go sit in the conversation pit. As I walked, I felt mildly sick to my stomach for what I had just seen. Now it was all I could think about.

After plopping down on the couch, I swallowed a mouthful of water, then another one dry for nerves. *Here goes nothing,* I thought.

"Hey, D, I have a question for you."

"Mhm."

"Your grandparents. They're how you got most of your money, correct?"

"Is that really your question?"

"Well, no, I just—"

"Obviously. You know that." Her tone was sharp as a scalpel.

I took another sip, irritated at myself for starting off so poorly. I tried again.

"Yeah, of course. But I guess I just never asked *where* that money came from. Like…how did they get so rich?"

There was a pause in the rustling of papers. Even though I had my back to her, I could feel the sting of her stare.

"Why are you asking me this now?"

"Well, because I just saw something and I wanted to ask you about it."

"So ask."

"Okay."

I turned around to face her halfway across the room. She was bathed in light, looking anything but sunny. The image of what I'd seen on the page, the name: repeated two dozen times, each accompanied with a multi-thousand-dollar deposit, flashed in my mind.

"Were they with the Trevi Company?"

Dahlia looked at me with that blank look of hers. No shock, no surprise. Just a void of emotion. She shrugged.

"In a way. My grandpa helped start it."

"What?"

"Yeah. He was one of the founders."

"So, that's where...all this comes from," I asked, gesturing to the house around us. She followed my hand, then looked back at me. Now she just looked bored.

"Yes. That's how money works, Jack."

I felt stunned. For a second I couldn't think of anything to say in reply. When I didn't say anything further, Dahlia went back to reading over her papers. I turned back and sunk lower into the couch.

"Wow," I muttered, to no one but myself.

"What?" she asked. I turned back to look at her.

"I'm just...surprised. I mean..." I racked my brains for how I could say this politely. "You know what they do. Obviously. What they've done."

A sigh escaped her lips, and she hunched over ever so slightly.

"Of course I do. Why do you think I've never told you?"

"I mean, yeah, but it's not like it was *your* idea. You just inherited the money."

"But I still benefit from it. *We* benefit from it."

It was the longest conversation we'd had since her birthday. Despite the ugly subject matter, I felt a stirring of hope to be making progress again.

"Yeah. I guess that's true."

We both stared at each other. She was still wearing that impenetrable mask of stoicism, but something had shifted. A layer of past dirt had been unearthed. And no lightning had struck us dead.

"Well, thank you for telling me," I offered. "I appreciate the honesty."

Her eyes narrowed at my comment.

"Why are you being so nice right now?"

I debated two options: the truth, and the half-truth. I decided on the latter.

"Because I feel shitty about what happened. That I didn't stand up for you in front of everyone. I know that was really lousy of me to do, but I was so caught off-guard. I didn't know what to say in the moment."

"Yeah? Well, imagine how I felt."

"Yeah, I know, but—"

"Well, actually you don't know, Jack," she said, raising her tone. "You have no *idea* what it's like for people to treat you like you're some monster. I'm so sick and tired of being seen as this horrible person when all I've ever tried to do is the right thing."

"You're right," I agreed, nodding my head. "I don't know."

"Damn right, you don't."

She glared at me, unmoved. All of my willpower was forced on holding her gaze. I took a deep breath.

"I think we need to talk about what happened when we were younger."

This took her by surprise. She twitched her head, eyebrows raised.

"What do you mean?"

"I mean, like, everything. I want to tell you about my parents. And I want to hear about yours." Off her silence, I kept going. "I was talking to Gabriel today and he—"

She let out a short, hard laugh. It was an ugly sound.

"Oh, great. So now your friends want to hear more about how fucked up I am, so they can have more to talk about. Nice. Good one, Jack."

"What? No! That's not what he meant at all. He just said that we should know that kind of stuff about each other. I mean…I've told him."

"Told him what?"

"About my mom."

"Really."

"Yes. And to be honest, I don't know why it's taken me this long to tell you."

I was going to leave it there, but I changed my mind. No more bullshit.

"Actually, no. I do know. You know what, Dahlia? You scare me. You always have."

Her mouth dropped open, and she stood up in anger.

"Fuck you, Jack. That's the last thing I need to hear right n—"

"Let me finish!" I shouted, standing up myself. My own voice boomed in equal strength to hers. I raised my hand and repeated myself, quieter. "Just let me finish."

Dahlia stood and watched me as I walked up out of the conversation pit to her level. Even from across the room, I towered over her.

"I don't mean that I'm scared of you as a person," I lied. Then back to truth: "I mean that you scare me because of how much I feel for you. You've taken over my whole world, made me someone I don't even recognize. And that's a good thing. I feel so strong when you're around. Like I can do anything."

A flicker of softness flashed through her eyes. I continued talking.

"You aren't a bad person, Dahlia. I know that. What happened in the alley that night was fucking awful, but I…I can't help but feel that it was mostly my fault. I should have done more to stop it from happening. You should never have had to do something like that. Ever."

She kept her eyes on me, studying me. I hoped that I sounded as sincere as I meant to.

Finally, she placed two hands on the table and sighed. She let her head hang.

"I'm so tired, Jack."

I took a step towards her, then two more.

"I know you are."

"I just want things to be good again."

Another step.

"Me too."

I paused, a few feet from her. Waited for her to reply.

"You really don't think I'm a bad person?" she asked, her guttural voice barely audible. I took the final steps towards her, close enough to touch. I put my hand, the good one, on her shoulder.

"Of course not."

At the sound of this, she turned and folded into my chest. I wrapped my arms around her and held my wife in a hug, her face planted right above my racing heart.

"I'm sorry," she said, her words muffled into my shirt.

"Me too, D. Me too."

Neither of us said anything more for a few moments. We stood and held one another in a hug, the chorus of waves ever-singing. From my vantage point, I could see the spread of bank statements, declaring our fattening wealth. The words **TREVI COMPANY** were branded more times than I could count.

The Trevi Company, as it was well known by everyone, was the largest development group in the city. Their name was intrinsically tied to the housing crisis that had crippled most of the city's population. Their approach was simple. In the 80s, they had mass-bought affordable housing units, then steadily evicted the tenants and tore down the old buildings. In their place, the Trevi Company would erect luxury apartments complexes: half the number of units, but triple the price.

By the time the city had caught on, it was already too late. The Trevi name had been stamped as OWNER on more than sixty percent of housing across the city. It didn't take a genius to trace the unlivable cost of living or growing population of the homeless to the Trevi Company. Or companies like it, who had followed in their footsteps.

People worked 50 hours a week just to keep a roof over their heads, their children's heads, and still, it was hardly enough to make ends meet. Because of them, the city had turned into a playground for the rich, and a prison for the poor. It meant that every time Trevi tore down an old building or hiked the rent of a current one, people suffered.

And Dahlia and I grew richer.

As I held my wife, I raised up my left hand to look at it. My discoloured fingers looked especially grotesque in the cold light of day. I moved them, to little effect. Dahlia squeezed me tighter, desperate to be close again.

"Let's talk more tomorrow," she said, pulling back to look up at me. "I still have lots to go through here."

"Yeah, for sure," I replied. She leaned up on her tiptoes to kiss me. I let her.

"Love you, Jack."

"Love you too, Dahlia."

She wiggled out of the hug wearing a small smile and sat down again at the table. I left her and ventured out onto the deck.

The afternoon had cooled off, as the Earth moved on to the next season. A cool breeze licked my bare skin. I frowned. I'd hoped to feel better after talking things out. But instead, the needle of guilt in my gut only seemed to have dug in deeper.

FIVE

The next day, I awoke to the sound of rain. Jack was still snoring softly beside me, like always. And like always, I left him there on his own.

I flipped the bedroom calendar over to September, then went to the kitchen. Turned on the kettle. In a matter of hours, the outside world had chilled considerably.

The ocean was blanketed in white mist, as beads of rain pelted the surface from above. Bent shapes of seabirds spiralled in and out of view, nothing more than stray M's in the sky. I stared out the tall windows as a mug of ginger tea brewed to fruition. I dreaded what was to come.

Truthfully, I wasn't interested in telling Jack more about my life. As time went on, the feeling had only grown stronger. I wanted him to know less about me, not more. Already, I felt so goddamn exposed in front of him, like a magician forced to keep performing for an audience that knows he's a fraud. There was no fun to the show anymore. No more awe. I couldn't see how talking about the past would bring anything but more harm to us both.

An hour later, he emerged, slinking around the hall corner in his boxers and tee. He looked disoriented as he saw me sitting in silence in the conversation pit.

"Hey," he said, rubbing sleep from his eyes.

"Hey."

"How long have you been up for?" he asked, going over to start the coffee maker.

"Not long. I thought we could talk before I go out for my run."

His mouth creased in a half-smile as the beans started to grind into powder.

"So that's where you go in the mornings."

I shrugged.

"Sometimes," I replied, deciding to leave it at that.

He didn't say anything further. Nor did I. Hot water trickled through bean dust and was reborn brown. I watched as he poured himself a large mug, then topped it off with cream and three spoons of sugar.

"Are you hungry?"

"Not particularly."

"Yeah. Me neither."

He drank from his mug and came over, sitting down on the opposite side of the circular pit from me. I clutched my own mug of cold tea, legs folded up to my chest.

"So you still want to talk about things, then?" he asked, looking elsewhere.

"I mean, I guess. This was your idea."

"Yeah, but I want to make sure you're okay with it."

"Of course. I wouldn't be sitting here if I wasn't."

"Okay. Just checking."

We both sat in awkward uncertainty, unsure about how to proceed.

"I guess I'll go first," Jack said. He set his mug down and leaned forward onto his knees. His hair stood up in wild tousles. "I kind of just want to get it over with."

I didn't respond. I pulled my knees tighter to my chest and sipped my bitter drink.

"Is that okay with you?" he asked, looking up with his black eyes.

I nodded.

"Of course. Go ahead. Just take your time."

"Okay," he said, taking a deep breath like he was about to free dive underwater. "Okay."

Outside, the rain pattered on, steady as a thousand heartbeats. The house was imbued with grey light, as if filtered through a smokescreen. I sat and stared at my husband, feeling a new kind of worry. I did not want him to say another word, or hear what he had to say. I wanted only silence. But I did not stop him when he opened his mouth and started talking. I let him speak, uninterrupted, for what felt like an eternity.

"What you have to understand," he said quietly, "is that storms in the prairies are different. They're not like the ones on the coast. They're brutal. They come on very fast, then leave just as quickly. So we didn't know one was coming. Otherwise I would've just stayed home."

He took another drink from his coffee. His eyes swung from the floor, to the window, the fireplace mantle. Anywhere but me.

"So," Jack swallowed. "Momma died in the—"

~ ~ ~

Summer. At the time I was working my first job at the neighbour's place, the pig farm. It was hard, smelly work, but I was happy just to have something to do. This was when I was

17, so my last year of high school. And Dad was drinking worse than ever.

The house we lived in belonged to my mom. She wasn't rich or anything, but she had money. Dad had nothing. Apparently, he used to be a handsome man, although I never saw any proof of that. That's just what Momma would say when I'd ask why she'd married him.

"'Cause he was a handsome man." Towards the end, she always sounded sad. All she ever seemed to do was clean up after Dad. Or sit on the porch and stare out at the flatness. You could see for miles, nothing but fields. That particular summer, because we'd had no rain, everything was dried-up and brown. It looked like some featureless dusty wasteland, somewhere where nothing grew and no one was happy.

So having the job at the farm was a blessing. Even if that blessing stunk of manure and pig fear. The owner, Mike McKenna, was one of Dad's few friends, and even *he* didn't like Dad much. But he'd agreed to take me on as a farmhand for the summer. I spent the time shovelling slop and cleaning out pens. Listening to the sows squealing as their babies were taken off to be turned into meat. The air was always thick with screaming, but after a while, I actually got used to it. It was like white noise, but of animal misery.

Most of the time, I worked with Mike's son Jacob, who went by Jake. Jake and Jack. My dad thought this was hilarious. Whenever he picked me up from work, he would yell out for us like a hog caller, repeating our names interchangeably with a "Heeeeere pig pig pig, Jake-Jack-Jake-Jack! Soweeeee!" Nobody found it funny. Especially rendered in my father's drunken bray.

Jake thought my father was an asshole. He was 4 years older, had never finished high school. When he swore, which was often, he'd make a hissing sound with his S's. Both of his front teeth had been knocked out by a shovel handle when he was a kid. In a town so small though, he was one of the few friends I had.

On the day of the accident, Jake's dad had left town to visit his family up north. Which meant that Jake had the house to himself, so he invited me over to drink and ssshoot the ssshit. I hung up the phone and asked my mom to drive me over there. Even though I knew how to drive myself, I didn't have enough money to buy a car of my own. And Dad never let me use his truck.

"I could really use some help around here, Jacky," she said. "Your grandma's coming in a few days and the house is such a mess."

I think I replied with something about the house always being a mess, which was true. No matter how much she cleaned, it transformed into chaos by morning. Dad was always more active at night. When he was on a drinking binge, he'd spend the days passed out because the sunlight hurt his head too much. That summer, he was practically Dracula.

"Doesn't matter if it's always a mess," she said. "Someone still has to clean it up."

In the end, she drove me off to the McKenna farm. Neither of us said much on the way there. I left the car and promised her that I'd be back by dark. I'd get Jake to drive me back home. She barely looked at me when she said bye.

Jake opened the front door with a bottle of rum in hand. He seemed thrilled to see me. We sat in the front parlour room of his house, which smelled of cigarette smoke and lemon cleaner. Watched TV. I drank rum from a tumbler and listened to Jake talk about this girl he was seeing. Mostly he talked about how much he loved fucking her and the yipping sounds she made when she came. As he talked, he'd smack his lips and grin, flashing the hole that framed his smile.

Eventually, Jake got tired of talking about ejaculating on his girlfriend's stomach and got this look in his eyes. He stood up and abruptly turned off *Jeopardy!*, mid-contestant answer. Then he stood there in front of the television set and asked me if I wanted to have some fun.

At first, I didn't respond. I didn't like the look he had, or the way he'd asked me. But I said yes. Because I was curious, and definitely bored. Jake practically ran out of the room and up the stairs. When he returned, he had an oversized sock in hand.

"Check thisss out," he said, pulling out something long and glassy from the sock. Along with a plastic bag of crystalline powder.

"What's that?" I asked. It was a stupid question. I'd seen pipes before, broken in half outside the school, in alleyways. Although never in one piece.

"It'sss good, isss what it isss," Jake promised. He sat down beside me on the couch and started telling me how one of his buddies, Cody, had let him buy it off him. As he talked, his voice got more and more excited, as he waved the pipe around like a conductor.

"You don't have to be ssscared. I'll jussst pack you a little one," he said, pouring white powder into the glass bubble of the pipe. It was all happening so fast. I'm sure I must have said something, said no. But honestly I can't remember if I did. I think I just sat there and let it happen.

I knew meth was bad. But I didn't know *how* bad. Nobody really talked about it, except to say not to do it. But then again, people said cigarettes were bad. And drinking. But there were plenty of people doing those things. So I guess I didn't see much of a difference. At the time, I didn't really give a shit about what happened to me. Or know enough to care to.

Jake took a hit first. The meth crackled like sizzling bacon, foaming away in the glass bubble. When he sucked in, he coughed almost immediately, filling the parlour room with sour smoke. He hacked away and started swearing. The whole couch seemed to shake from the force of his coughs.

A few moments later, he started laughing at nothing. He slapped his legs and told me he felt *amazing.*

"Fucking Chrissstmasss!" he yelled. I burst out laughing when he said that. My chest felt loose and warm from my third glass of rum.

So I let him pack me a hit. I had no idea if it was big or small, but he assured me that it was enough to fly on. I didn't really know what that meant, but I let him light the pipe from the bottom as I took the skinny end into my mouth. When I sucked in the smoke, it tasted like rotten eggs and bleach. I gagged instantly, expelling a cloud of smoke from my lungs.

At first, I couldn't even breathe. All I could taste was that flavour of chemical regret. For a minute I thought I was going to die. I could not stop coughing. And Jake kept slapping me on the back, telling me I was a fucking baller, a fucking baller, and I couldn't speak to tell him to stop hitting my back. 'Cause it was making my cough worse.

When I finally could breathe again, I realized that Jake hadn't been lying. I did feel amazing. My whole body was buzzing and my heart was pounding. I felt like I could lift a whole car over my head. I was almost horny, I felt so good. I started laughing, and Jake did as well. The two of us fell back on the couch and laughed like two baboons gone mad. Then we both took another hit each.

Here is where I start to forget parts. I know at some point we went outside, because the thought of sitting still seemed like torture. Jake ran up ahead and howled gibberish. As the drug set in, I felt more and more like I was coming out of my skin. I had this idea about trying to peel it off, like you would with a banana. I was just about to try when Jake yelled:

"Look at that ssshit!"

I looked over in his direction. He was pointing excitedly at one of the pig corrals. When I got close enough to see what was inside, my stomach dropped out from under me.

In the middle of the corral was a dead pig. It wasn't an unusual sight. There was lots of death on the farm, either intentional or accidental. This pig, however, was being eaten by a hawk. The bird had split the belly of the animal and was feasting on its entrails, spilled out onto the dirt. A group of pigs stood off to the side and watched as the hawk tore off a hunk of flesh and swallowed.

Jake started screeching with laughter. He laughed like it was the funniest thing he had seen in his whole life. And the sound of him laughing was the worst part about it, because I felt for sure that I was going to throw up. It was so sick, to laugh at something like that. And the whole world was spinning. And my skin was itchier than ever.

I started scratching my arm like crazy. I left Jake, collapsed on the ground in hysterics, and started to head back to the house. Nothing felt fun anymore. In fact, everything felt the complete opposite of fun. And once I started feeling bad, things just started spiralling from there.

I yelled at Jake that I was going inside. When I turned back at him, I could see a storm brewing on the horizon. Black, temple-sized clouds were rushing towards us, eating up the blue sky and brown earth. Tar-dipped plums. That's the colour, I thought to myself. Those clouds looked like plums dipped in tar. When the storm is bad, the clouds turn purple.

When I got to the house, my whole body was shaking. I had no idea how long the high was going to last, but I wanted it to stop. Instead, it seemed to be getting more intense. My heart was pounding so hard it felt close to exploding. I locked myself in the bathroom and sat on the floor. There was this wallpaper of green apples covering the place top to bottom. It made the light look all sickly and green, as I sat and scratched my arm and prayed again and again that I didn't want to die. There seemed to be no other outcome. I was sure of it. My heart was going to explode. I was going to die, right there on the bathroom floor.

I have no idea how long I was in there. It felt like forever. Jake came back into the house and started banging around in the kitchen. It sounded like he was cooking Thanksgiving dinner. The wind was picking up outside. It made the whole farmhouse creak and shake. And approaching thunder. I could hear that, too.

The rain had just begun beating against the roof when the phone rang. Jake swore to himself and dropped a pan on the floor. I was still clutching my body, rocking back and forth, trying to stay calm.

The phone was too far away for me to hear what they were saying, but a moment later Jake started shouting for me using his own name.

"JAAAKE! JAAAKE! WHERE ARE YOUUU!"

This freaked me out. Because now I wasn't sure who I even was. Was I Jake? Or Jack?

I didn't have time to really think about that, because he started pounding a fist on the bathroom door.

"Hey! Hey! Open up! It'sss your mom!"

I told him to go away. He would not.

"Ssshe'sss freaking the fuck out, man! You need to talk to her."

It took a few more rounds of convincing for me to move and unlock the door. When I stood up, I had this crazy feeling of vertigo, as if my legs were hundreds of feet below where my head was. Like I was a floating mountain. I staggered past him and into the kitchen.

The phone receiver was sitting face-up on the counter.

"Momma?" I asked. My voice sounded alien in my ears.

"Jacky! What's going on?"

"Nothing, Momma."

"That's a lie. I can hear it in your voice. What did Jake do to you?"

Mom had a superhuman power when it came to me. She knew I was getting sick before I even started coughing. This one time, when I fell at school and sprained my ankle, she was already in the car before the principal called her. There was no use in trying to hide from her. I started to cry on the phone.

"Momma, I'm sorry…I messed up."

"What? What? What happened?"

"I took something, and I, I feel really sick."

"What did you take? Jacky! Honey, what did you take?"

On the other side of the line, I could hear shuffling sounds, as she moved around. The storm had fully arrived by now, and the force of rain and wind was ferocious. I could feel my teeth vibrate from the intensity of the thunder.

"I, I, I don't know…" I sputtered. I couldn't get it out of my mouth. My voice broke down further. "I don't want to die! I don't want to die!"

Jake came around the corner and saw me crying. His face darkened.

"What the fuck are you sssaying?" he hissed. I turned away.

"Jacky, I'm coming to get you, okay? Just stay there and I'm—"

I never got to hear the rest of her sentence. Jake grabbed the receiver out of my hand and slammed it into the cradle. Then shoved me. Hard.

"What the fuck is wrong with you! Why would you sssay sssomething like that!"

I looked him in the eye and told him because it was true. His whole face seemed to be bulging out of his skull.

"You're not fucking dying, you idiot. I can't believe you told her that. Now ssshe'sss going to come over here. What the fuck!"

He started throwing kitchenware around. Pieces of plastic, metal and wood started to rain down on the floor. Against the wall. At me. He even picked up a knife—not a big one, but still—and threw it at the refrigerator beside me.

"FUCK!" he bellowed, again and again. I left him in the kitchen and went to the parlour room, where you could look out the window onto the road. Outside was a mess of rain and darkness.

Just the thought that my mom was coming made me feel better. It had never occurred to me that most of what I was feeling was my own anxiety. I was having a bad trip. I wasn't really going to die. But of course, I didn't know that then. All I could focus on was how bad I was feeling. When I looked at my arm, I realized I had broken the skin from scratching. I was leaking blood onto the carpet.

A few minutes went by. Then half an hour. I kept checking the wall clock to see how long had passed, because my own sense of time was so screwed up. Meanwhile, Jake kept stomping around the house, swearing to himself or at me. He sounded like he was talking in tongues. I tried my best to ignore him, and kept my eyes out the window.

It felt like years. The world grew blacker as night fell, sporadically lit up by a blinding flash of lightning. When the thunder came, it seized the farmhouse and shook it until the picture-frames toppled over. I curled up in a ball with my head in my hands. Jake broke a bottle somewhere in the house. Momma never came.

I never slept. My whole body still felt like it had been zapped with evil electricity, and my brain was racing with thoughts. Guilt. I couldn't understand why she had never come. When I tried to call her back, the dial tone just kept on ringing. Jake blasted TV from his bedroom, and shouted at the screen from time to time. The storm moved on and left the land quenched. I kept scratching.

Minutes felt like hours. Hours felt like centuries. But somehow, I made it through. I'd thrown up in the end, twice, but neither time had brought me any relief. Nothing but going home was going to make me feel better. Something had happened. I knew that, deep down. But I still was refusing to admit it. I told myself that she had gotten tied up with my dad somehow. Or she was so angry that she hadn't come. Even though I knew she would never do something like that. Abandon me.

Around 7 am, when there was finally a little light out, I started walking. In hindsight, I kept berating myself for why I hadn't tried sooner. Why hadn't I gone in the night? It was a straight road, even in the pitch black. But I think I was so ashamed about what I had done. And I was scared of what I might find if I went.

My head seemed ready to split in two from aching. I kept my eyes down, sinking into the mud at parts. I was talking to myself, too. But I can't remember what I was saying. I think something like "Please be okay," over and over again.

After about 20 minutes of slow walking, I saw the shape of Momma's house. It was a wide two-story with a single elm tree out front. Because there were prairies all around, it stood out like a ship at sea. Only now, something was missing from the silhouette on the horizon.

The elm tree was gone. I rubbed my eyes and squinted, sure that I was wrong. It was as tall as the house, impossible to ignore. But it was gone. There was a cavity of clouds where the leafy branches should have been.

That really bad feeling grew bigger inside me. As I got closer, I started to trot. Then I ran. I ran all the way to the property line, eyeballs jiggling in their sockets. Then stopped dead in my tracks at what I saw.

Underneath the fallen elm tree was Momma's car. It had been crushed right down the middle, obliterated. The windows were a ruin of glass, the roof crumpled metal. The trunk of the tree was scorched black from lightning. And the driver's door was open.

I started screaming her name. I ran towards it and looked inside. It was empty. The air smelled of burning. I stuck my head through the shattered window, and my heart froze its relentless beating. There was blood on the driver's seat. Lots of it.

I called her name again and again. There was a steady trail in the mud, a shallow trench filled in with earth, water, and blood. I stepped back from the car and saw where it led, to the front steps of the house. And there, lying facedown on the porch, was Momma.

She'd managed to drag herself by her hands all the way to the door. We found out later that her body had been broken in several spots from the weight of the tree. Her bones were mostly mush from the force of it falling on her. But she had managed to claw her way out of the car and across the yard. All the way up the stairs, to the front door. But she hadn't been able to open it. There were bloody handprints all over the white paint from her trying to pull herself up. Not that many, though. She'd already been near-dead by the time she got there.

I've never felt anything like that moment. It was like my soul tore in half. I rushed up the stairs and collapsed beside her, shaking uncontrollably. This horrible noise was in my ears, and I couldn't understand where it was coming from. But it was me. I was making that sound. I was shrieking at the top of my lungs.

I held her head and cried so hard that I threw up on the porch. But because there was nothing left in my stomach, I could only dry heave. A couple of chickadees started singing. The morning grew brighter.

When my dad came home, I was still sitting there, holding her. By then, I couldn't even speak. I felt like I was the one who had died. He got out of the car at the end of the drive and started yelling. I could tell by the way he stumbled that he was hungover. Or probably still drunk. It didn't matter. Nothing mattered anymore.

He came to the top of the stairs and just kept yelling. He wouldn't get any closer to us. He stood there, red-faced and frightened, waving his arms around like eggbeaters. But no matter how many times he shouted at me, demanding to know what had happened, I said nothing. I couldn't make a single sound to answer him.

~ ~ ~

There was a long drag of silence after Jack finished talking. He looked haggard, worn out. His mug of coffee sat, still full but cold, on the table. I had no idea what to say.

He had not cried once the whole time he told his story. Or looked at me. He'd delivered the entire nightmarish recollection to inanimate objects, with a dull, flat voice. For once, I understood his disconnection to sadness a bit better. It made all those months of seclusion make sense. He didn't have the ability to feel those emotions. So he shut down instead.

When I didn't say anything, Jack cleared his throat and kept going.

"We moved out here about a year later. Into my uncle's old place. My dad found out about the meth, because Jake had been dumb enough not to put it away before his father came back. And I admitted to it when he asked me. After that, he blamed me for the whole thing. Quit drinking entirely, and was so…angry all the time. He absolutely hated me from then on. Like, with all his heart. I never doubted that he did."

"But, wasn't he also out that night?" I asked, dimming my volume to a whisper.

"Yeah. He was. He'd gone out drinking himself and got so fucking plastered he couldn't drive home. He never actually said so but he must have passed out in the car somewhere. No one in the town would have let him stay over."

I let out a deep sigh.

"Hypocrite."

"Yeah. I know."

"Jack, I…I don't know what to say. I mean, everything. That's just awful. Beyond awful. I'm so, so sorry you went through that."

He shrugged, still refusing to look up at me.

"Yeah."

SIX

There was no relief to be had. In the aftermath of speaking, I only felt tired. Angry. I felt that old itch inside me, still impossible to scratch. The wound of regret. Maybe Gabriel had been wrong. Maybe this had been a bad idea after all.

Dahlia looked strangely unfazed by everything I had just told her. She was watching me with that piercing gaze of hers, and there were times when I had wanted to ask her to look away. But of course, I couldn't say a thing like that. So I just ignored her instead.

I excused myself to go to the bathroom. When I closed the door behind me, I turned the tap on high and splashed my face with ice-cold water. It felt good. It hurt. I did it a few more times, then stared at myself in the mirror. It was something I avoided doing as much as possible. I didn't look the way I felt. I was too big, too grown-up. My eyes were more like voids than irises. And I was starting to take on the look, the same one Momma always wore towards the end. The sad look. The hopeless one.

When I came back, Dahlia had vanished from the room. I looked around for her, then spotted her out on the deck. She was standing in the rain, leaning over the guardrail. I went out to join her.

"Hey."

"Hey. How're you feeling?"

I took my place beside her. The rain was meek, timid. It fell in a fine sheer that coated our skin like lotion.

"Honestly? Not great."

"Well, I can imagine how hard that was. To remember that stuff."

I nodded, keeping my head facing the harbour. The mist was thick enough to erase the world from being. It felt like we were the only ones in existence.

"I just wish I could change it. I wish I could undo it."

"Undo what?"

"Leaving her. The night in the alley. What I did to my dad. Just all of it. All of the bad shit."

"Well, of course. Everyone wants that."

She let out a sigh.

"I mean, I know I do."

"What would you change? If you could go back?"

There was a pause. A long one. I turned to look at her, but her eyes were firmly fixed to the sea.

"Probably every time I've hurt someone. Accidentally, that is. I don't regret the other times."

"So, what about what happened in the alley? Would you change that?"

Now she turned to look at me. Beads of rain christened her eyelashes.

"I would change us going there, anything to stop you from getting hurt. Of course. But I wouldn't change what I did, Jack. I don't regret defending you. Not at all."

I stared at her, her marine eyes half-hidden under a veil of water.

"Really? You'd do it again?"

She reached out a hand and squeezed my arm. Then let go.

"If it meant having you here beside me? Absolutely."

My stomach turned when she said that. Partially with love. And something else.

"I still want to hear more about when you were younger."

"Are you sure?"

"Yes." I turned to go back inside the house. "I want to get everything out. Today."

The deck door slid open on its well-oiled track. I stepped inside and looked back at her. A breeze pulled at her wet dress, making it flutter. She seemed scared.

"Please," I said. I offered my hand. "I think it's for the best. To get everything out in the open." And it was true, too. Despite my initial feelings of discomfort, I was starting to feel a bit better about telling her. Lighter.

Dahlia looked at my outstretched hand, then back at me.

"Okay," she said, before taking it. "I trust you, Jack."

I gently squeezed her hand before pulling her into the dry house with me.

~ ~ ~

The two of us resumed our places in the conversation pit, only reversed. Now Dahlia was the one with her back to the kitchen, legs curled beneath her. She had changed into a sweater and slacks, both shades of grey.

"What do you want to know?" she asked. I felt more comfortable looking her straight in the face, now that I wasn't the one talking.

"Anything you like. I mean…you could tell me more about your mom. And your dog. Melon?"

"Mango."

"Oh, yeah. Sorry."

"It's fine."

She was stalling. I could tell, because I had never seen her look so wary. It made me nervous to hear what she was going to say.

"Okay, well. Whenever you're ready."

The room fell quiet. I waited for her to speak. When she began, it was like listening to a century-old crone, not a freshly 28-year-old woman. Her voice swelled to the size of a wave, filling the room with its grating, rough texture. Sea urchins. Box cutters. My wife's voice.

"Before I met you, Jack, there was only one thing I loved more in this world. Mango. She meant everything to me. I loved my mom too, of course, but Mango was special. Pure."

I nodded, as if I understood. Dahlia pulled at the sleeves of her sweater and faced me.

"When I was younger, I found it very hard to relate to people. It's not something I've ever really grown out of. But when I was a kid, it was really bad. And I couldn't talk to my mom about it either, because I felt the same way with her."

"What do you mean by that?"

"Just…distant. She wasn't someone I could talk to. It felt like living with the idea of a mother, instead of an actual one. She hardly checked in on me, or asked how I was. And she was always drunk. It felt like life was one big party to her, and I was this sidepiece that could fend for itself. Which…she wasn't wrong about. But it would've been nice. To have a mom who cared. Or understood me a bit better."

She adjusted her sitting position, pushing her hair to the side.

"But Mango was different. Of course she was. She was a dog. Animals don't have all this stupid bullshit attached to love. They feel things unconditionally. But especially love. So I didn't feel like I had to pretend when I was with her. I could just be myself. And she would love me for that. Without being afraid."

I could have sworn her eyes flickered when she said that. But before I could ask more, she continued.

"After what happened with my uncle, Mom started acting really nervous around me. It made me feel horrible. Like *I* was the bad guy. And Charlie was caught with all sorts of porno shit afterwards, which came out in the investigation. So I definitely wasn't the only one."

"Jesus."

"I know. Fucking pig. Mom paid a *lot of* money to keep stuff quiet. And it worked, mostly. She got to keep her friends. I wasn't branded a psycho for attacking my uncle. It ended up being an unfortunate accident that no one really knew about. Except us."

"And the police."

"Yeah. That was a shock. I didn't think they still had that on file. But I guess if you do something as drastic as crush your uncle's balls, it doesn't really matter if you're 13 years old or not, hey?"

A shiver went up my spine when she said that. She sounded as remorseful as she would about spilling a glass of milk. I nodded, weakly.

"I guess not."

"Whatever. I'm not upset that I did that to him. Just that no one had beat me to it."

She sighed, rolling her shoulders.

"It just makes me so mad, y'know? That there's people like that out there. Men. And so fucking *many* of them, too. It makes me so mad that I feel like I'm going to explode. I mean, why? What the hell is wrong with people? How can so many of those, those assholes exist?"

"I don't know, D. But…is hurting them back the right thing to do?"

Dahlia's eyes hardened.

"Someone has to take out the trash, Jack. And if you have the opportunity to do that, I think you should take it."

"I mean, I guess. But look what happened to you. Things just got worse. I feel like it just keeps going if you sink to their level."

"What keeps going?"

"Violence, cruelty. All of it." I shrugged. "It's all cyclical, right? Like the more people try to hurt bad people, *they* just become bad themselves. It never stops."

"Are you calling me a bad person?"

"What? No, I…I don't know what I'm saying."

"I think you do."

I rubbed the front of my forehead.

"Well, kind of, yeah. I don't think revenge solves anything. I think it just perpetuates the original pain. That's what I'm trying to say."

"Well. I'm sorry you think that way."

She made a move to stand. I raised my hand to stop her.

"Wait! Please don't go."

"I don't want to talk about this anymore, Jack."

"Okay, okay. That's fine. But just…"

"Just what?"

"Don't just walk out. I want to finish this. I need to know. Then we never have to talk about this stuff ever again."

"I don't know why we're even talking about this in the first place."

"Because!" I said, my voice rising. "We should know this stuff about each other, D! Isn't it weird, just never talking about it? Aren't you tired of keeping everything inside?"

She blinked, expression unchanged.

"It hasn't bothered me before."

"I don't believe that."

"Well, it's true. And honestly, I don't see how this is doing us any good. Look," she said, lifting her palms up flat, as if to push me away from across the pit. "I'm glad that you feel better after telling me about your mom. But I'm not like you, Jack. Sharing stuff makes me feel worse, not better. So, please. Can we just leave it?"

I sat still, feeling oddly dismissed. Then shook my head.

"No. We can't. I need to know."

"Why? Why do you care so much?"

"Because I love you! And I want to trust you again!"

My words hung loud and opaque in the air. Dahlia didn't reply.

"Please, Dahlia. I need this. I need to hear everything. I'm so sick of wondering, of making up stories in my head. I need to know you better."

Her mouth twitched in a strange way.

"Fine. You want to know, Jack? I'll tell you. Here it is. I hope it makes you feel better."

"That's not what I mean—"

"Are you going to let me talk or not?" she snapped. I leaned back into the couch, stung.

"Sorry. Go ahead."

Now she just looked pissed. She unfolded one of her legs and tucked it beside her body in a triangle shape. Her position resembled that of a spider, green eyes aflame.

"When I was almost 16, Mango had a stroke. Not enough to kill her, but she lost almost all mobility in her back legs. So basically, she couldn't walk. But otherwise she was fine.

"My mom," she continued, "was at her worst. She was barely even a parent by that point. All she did was fucking drink. She stopped seeing her friends. Stopped driving me places. All she did was sit on her ass and watch TV and spill liquor on the couch. It was so pathetic to see."

As she spoke, her voice ground deeper into dissonance. I had the image of a mineshaft, drilled to the centre of the Earth. This seemed to be where my wife was speaking from.

"The only friend, the only *real* friend I had, was Mango. She was so sweet with me. And protective. Plus people were scared of her. Because of her teeth."

"What was wrong with her teeth?" I asked.

"She had two sets. It's a condition. She never lost her baby teeth, so her adult teeth just grew in overtop. It made kids nervous of her, even though she wasn't very aggressive."

Dahlia smiled as she said this. Then stopped.

"The point is, I loved her. With all my heart. I'd never felt so strongly about anything or anyone in my life. So seeing her in pain, unable to walk, it was...hell. Literally hell."

"I'm sorry."

She waved her hand, brushing my concern away.

"It's not your fault. It was no one's fault. Just one of those things. Bad luck. Or life."

As quickly as it had come on, her anger had dissipated. It startled me to see it flow and ebb so suddenly. An unpredictable current, ready to spike at a moment's notice.

"But still hard," I said. She nodded.

"Yes. Very hard. Mom sobered up just enough to drive her to the vet. Who told us there was nothing we could do. She was a golden, and oversized, too. Way too big for one of those wheelchairs they give to smaller breeds. Our only option was to put her down."

Dahlia's voice dropped further down the mineshaft. And in volume.

"I remember looking around the examination room, with those sterile overhead lights. The smell of sick animals and people's sweat. Feces. It was so uncomfortable. I couldn't let her die in that room. I just couldn't."

I wanted to ask how she could possibly smell those things. But I kept my mouth shut.

"My mom booked the appointment to put her down the next day. The vet who saw us couldn't do it that day, so we were going to have to wait 24 hours. I carried her back to the car myself. And then I started thinking."

My wife turned away from me and looked out the floor-to-ceiling windows. The world went on being nothing but white. As she kept talking, she held her gaze to the glass.

"I knew I had to act fast. That night. I had to do something. So, as soon as my mom had drunk herself to sleep for the evening, I went into her bedroom. I took a bunch of her pain pills that she didn't even need. Some sleeping pills. Anything strong. Then I crushed them up and put the powder in Mango's food."

Now she began to cry. It was completely without sound. Fat tears slid down her cheeks, as she struggled to keep going.

"I made her a special dinner. Chicken and rice with cheese. Something she couldn't resist eating. When she was done, I carried her to the boat. It was warm that night. And clear, too. You could see all the stars. It was so beautiful."

I felt glued to my seat in dread. I wanted to interject, to say something, but nothing would come to mind. Dahlia kept her face turned to the window.

"Mango was very excited. She loved the water. We would go out, just the two of us. Or swim by the shore when it was warm enough. I drove us far out into the strait, far enough that we couldn't be seen by anyone. I couldn't stop crying. But I was sure, I was absolutely sure that I was doing the right thing. I was going to give Mango the death she deserved. I was going to make it as peaceful and beautiful as I could for her. That's all I wanted to do."

Her tears began to flow even harder. They brought noise with them: sniffling, gasping. She sounded like she was choking underwater as she talked.

"But—but—I didn't know. I didn't know what happens in an overdose. I thought she was just going to fall asleep and never wake up. But that didn't happen. I was petting her, telling her how much I loved her as we floated under the stars. When she started to—to...convulse. And whine. And then she threw up. And I realized I had only made her sick. I'd put her in pain. I'd made everything worse."

Dahlia had to stop speaking. She wept without restraint, her body wracking with sobs. Even still, I could not bring myself to move from the opposite couch.

When she started talking again, I could barely hear her. We had reached the bottom of the mineshaft.

"I couldn't let her suffer like that, Jack. She was clawing at the boat, seizing up. So I...I lifted her into the ocean. And I held her under the water until she stopped moving."

It was so quiet in the room you could hear time pass. Dahlia had buried her face into her hands. She looked nothing like the woman I had come to love and fear. Instead, she resembled something very frail and broken. Like a torn-off moth wing.

I stood up and sat down beside her. Placed my right hand on her back. She flinched as I touched her. Then crumpled her upper body into my lap.

We sat like this, without speaking, for several minutes. There was no sound of crying anymore, but I could feel my pants grow wet with tears. I rubbed her back, clockwise. It seemed like the moment would never end. We would stay like this, in limbo, forever.

But then, after a long time, she sat up. Her face was swollen, red, impassive. She stared off into space, and then sunk back into the couch. Slumped her body against mine.

"When I told my mom," she whispered, "she said I was an evil, sick person. That there was something very wrong with me, and that she should have taken me somewhere, after what I did to her brother. A few months later, I came home from school and found her in the pool. She had mixed too many pills with alcohol. There was no note."

Lethargically, she turned her face upwards to look me in the eye. A tiny bubble of snot hung under her nose.

"When I inherited the house, I filled the pool in with cement. Laid topsoil down. It was right beneath the spot where we had our first dance. Do you remember?"

I nodded, my insides cast in ice.

"I do."

Dahlia twisted her mouth into a grimace.

"'Heaven is a Place on Earth'," she recounted. The memory of us, twirling in front of a whooping crowd, flashed in my mind.

I looked at my wife, tucked against my ribcage. A barrage of emotions and thoughts flowed through me faster than I could name. I could not grasp onto anything tangible long enough to form a reasonable reply. All the sorrow and pain that had been unleashed during the past few hours seemed too big, too vast to actualize. I felt drowned by it all.

Dahlia seemed to sense how I was feeling, because she turned her face away from me, taking the pressure off for me to respond. We both stared out into the whiteness.

"So," she drawled thickly. "Do you feel better now?"

SEVEN

We tried our best to rebuild paradise. No one could've disagreed with that. We really tried. We went back to doing things together, leaving the house more. We talked. Walked along the seawall and went for drives. But nothing seemed to work.

Instead of prattling on for hours, our conversations dried up after 15 minutes. We kept running out of things to say. I would rack my brain, trying to pull from the bottomless well of subjects that had kept us occupied for years. But the well was now empty. All my bucket brought was air.

It felt like life was being lived on the surface. Inauthentic. When we had sex, Jack would move almost mechanically inside me. None of the same hunger remained. When I'd try to initiate more intensity, more passion, he would cower in discomfort. So I stopped. I let him thrust away inside me. Then rolled out from under him when he finished.

"I love you," he'd say.

"I love you too."

Both of us would look each other in the eye. Then away. I think we felt the same thing. It wasn't a lie to say those words. But it didn't quite feel like the truth, either.

I didn't know what to feel anymore. Jack seemed so delicate. Skittish. I knew he didn't see me the way he used to, as this flawless force of nature. I was now a damaged girl, an unstable woman who might snap at any moment. And to some extent, he wasn't wrong.

Because this was the other thing. I could feel it, always at the back of my throat. The anger. It hadn't gone away. It took practically nothing for it to bubble up and spill out into the world. Jack would say something insensitive, or make a wrong turn with the car, and *boom*, out it came. I heard it. I saw the way he'd shut down whenever I snapped at him. But at the same time, it felt impossible to control. Like I was being puppeted by something else, and all I could do was let it take over.

The days turned into weeks. All the leaves shed their green clothes in exchange for autumn garments. The weather turned colder, the nights longer. I threw my cellphone into the ocean, once and for all. And with it sank all the connections and friendships I had built up over the years. I couldn't bring myself to bear their silence anymore. No one had reached out since my birthday. Except Yvonne. And Anita. I had replied to neither.

Now Jack was really all I had. Besides Gabriel—whom he talked to infrequently and saw even less—I knew I was the same for Jack. After everything that we had been through, it seemed like we should've been stronger than ever. Closer. We'd been through hell, yet both of us were still here. So why did it feel like we had never been further apart?

By late October, I was back to disappearing for most of the day. I spent hours in the woods, running until I couldn't breathe. Or far out at sea, where there was no one I could see anymore. I wanted answers. A solution. I pleaded for something to come. To save us.

~ ~ ~

Something else arrived instead. It had been approaching for over a year, despite the fact I hadn't prepared for it. But my ignorance wouldn't save me. Ready or not, said the world. Here I come.

The day started like any other. I awoke after mere hours of unconsciousness. Jack was rolled to the far side of the bed, still dressed. In the first years together, we *never* slept with clothes on. It just delayed being inside one another. Now we always slept in pyjamas.

I made a weak breakfast and took off by sunrise. It was a windy day, with low-moving clouds that resembled nothing. No amount of imagination could conjure a shape. I ran up the driveway, locked the gates behind me, and then jogged east up the road. Half an hour later, I was standing in front of the trailhead. The dense forest awaited me.

Running with music had never appealed to me. There was enough noise in my head to go off on, to spur me into motion. I liked the rush of my breath, the thuds of my shoes as I ran across dirt, roots, rocks. Not to mention the choir of tree-leaves, making out with their lover, the wind. And birds. Always the multilingual singsong of birds, warning others of my arrival. This was more than enough.

I also needed to think. Music only distracted me from that, as my brain poured over my problems, desperately seeking a way out. There had to be something I could do to change things with Jack. To make things better again. Yet days passed, either on the water or in the trees, and nothing ever came to me. I would return home to the same ruin of a marriage without any clue on how to fix it.

My legs took off on the trail. This particular path headed northeast, towards the snowy mountains and hundreds of miles of wilderness. Here was the border between civilization and ferality. Each time I ventured near, I felt the same ancient desire to cross that line.

Tree trunks swayed to and fro in the autumn wind. They made a creaking sound as I flew by, pumping my arms like pistons. I scampered across the rough terrain with ease, feeling more at home than I did at Heaven. The morning sun rose higher but no brighter.

As I ran, I thought over what Jack had said to me a few weeks back. About feeling ready.

"Ready for what?" I'd asked.

"I don't know. To be a dad. For us to start a family. I think it would help us both, D. It'd be a new start."

I'd been absolutely floored by this. Bewildered. I knew Jack had always wanted kids, but the thought of having a baby seemed like a terrible idea. Which I had told him.

"I just don't understand where this is coming from, Jack. Now?"

"Well, why not now? Babies bring couples closer together."

I'd crinkled my nose in disgust.

"I always thought the opposite."

He hadn't said much more after that. Just excused himself off to the basement to sulk. The whole exchange had seemed very out of the blue. It wasn't until days later, when I'd been forced to use the computer to search for specialized window-washers (damn seagull poop on the skylight) that I understood where it had originated from. Jack had forgotten to clear the search history. Fifth down from recently searched: 'best ways to help a marriage'.

When I clicked on the search myself, there were two answers that were repeated again and again. Therapy. And having a baby.

"Raising a child can help strengthen the bond between you and your spouse, reminding you both of the reasons why you first entered this union together," one website said. *"There are few things more meaningful or joyful than having a baby, nor hardly a better way to revitalize a distinguished marital flame."*

Reading those words had made me furious. I'd felt livid that he was resorting to such a cheap solution as having a *baby.* We were better than that. I knew we were. I refused to be reduced to a 'distinguished flame', reignited by something as common as pregnancy. There had to be another way. I was determined to return our love to its original inferno. Alone.

~ ~ ~

By the time I reached the upper level of the gorge, I was sweating through my shirt. The cool air had warmed considerably by the heat of my exertion. I stood to the side of the trail and took in the view, looking down into the valley below.

The splendour of mahogany, gold, and stale green was all around. I felt swaddled by the season, and I closed my eyes to take it all in. The smell of pine needles. October air. Simple peace.

Further down the path came an interruption to my bliss. A voice. A man's voice, on the move towards me. My eyes shot open as it grew louder.

"We'll need to work on our narrative, that's for sure. Yeah, I know he's a fucking prick, but we *need* him on our side. I can't keep scrounging around for data that Luis should be in charge of getting, especially with this new development on Lonsdale coming up..."

The running voice rounded the corner of trees, coming into view. He stopped short in his tracks when he saw me standing there.

"Oh shit! Hey, Alex, let me call you back. Just one sec, okay, bud? Yeah, okay. Make it ten. Talk then." He hung up the headset and pulled me into a hug before I could object.

"How are you, gorgeous? Fancy seeing you here."

My skin burned from where his body had touched me. I wriggled out of his grip.

"Hi, Hale."

Hale stepped back and flashed a shit-eating grin. His eyes looked me up and down.

"Didn't know you lived around here now. I thought you were further west."

"We moved. After the wedding."

"Woah. You sound different. Are you sick?"

I tapped my throat with two fingers. Inside my chest, my heart was pounding. Not just from running.

"Yeah. I have laryngitis."

"Fuck, that sucks. You sound like a smoker. Two packs a day, hey?"

He pushed me playfully on the shoulder.

"Yeah."

"Well, it's good to see ya. You look good, as usual. Things still smooth sailing with that chump you married? John?" He smirked.

"It's Jack. And yes."

"That's too bad. Honestly, I feel like you could've done better. But..." He shrugged. "As long as you're happy, right?"

I didn't reply. Hale started to frown a bit.

"I'm just kidding, Dahlia. You know that. Don't have to look so pissed off."

His eyes had narrowed in on my face. Studying it. I glared back.

"That's not why I'm pissed off, Hale. And I think you know that."

Hale let out a hard laugh. Took a step back.

"Dahlia, I have *no* clue what you're talking about."

"Really? You don't remember what happened with Anita?"

"Who?"

"Anita. My friend. She told me what you did at the wedding."

Now his whole face had darkened. The wind blew a gust that caused the leaves to jitter overhead.

"I don't know who you're talking about. Okay? I gotta get—"

"She told me," I repeated, blocking his attempt to walk away. "That you forced yourself on her. When she was in the house. *My* house. She described your hand on the back of her head, pushing her down. In the guest bedroom. You don't remember that?"

Hale's eyes twitched. There was, unmistakably, a glimmer of satisfaction behind them. Then it was gone just as quick. He straightened up.

"Your friend was drunk. I didn't do shit to her."

"Then why the fuck would she say that? She told me *exactly* how you pushed her into the bedroom, how you called her names, and the way you tast—"

"I didn't touch that Persian bitch! Jesus fucking Christ!" he exploded. Both his cheeks flushed jam-red. "You need to back the fuck off before accusing me of something like that.

That's so fucked up, Dahlia. I didn't assault one of your friends. You hear me?"

"I don't believe you, Hale."

"I don't give a shit if you believe me or not, you psycho."

He sneered, curling his upper lip.

"I heard about what happened, by the way. How you went apeshit on some homeless dude? I was going to be nice by not bringing it up. But obviously there's something wrong with you. And your friends. I didn't do fucking shit. So get that out of your head."

I stood very still, facing Hale. A current was flowing through my entire body, pulsing with blue-hot power. I lifted my chin up to him and made myself big.

Hale's eyes widened like camera shutters. He took another step back, almost tripping over an exposed root. The wind growled.

"What the fuck is that?" he asked.

"Hale," I appealed, "I'm going to give you a choice. You can go to the police and admit what you did to Anita. It's only fair. *You* were the one who assaulted her, yet she's the one who has to pay the price? I don't fucking think so. You need to suffer too."

"I didn't touch that slut! You hear me? I didn't do shit!"

"Option two is—"

"Go to hell, you crazy bitch," he spat. And with that, he turned and took off running. His headset bounced on his neck as he rounded the corner and disappeared into the trees.

For a moment, I was frozen. Enormous waves of anger surged through me, engulfing my body from the inside out. All I could think about was the look on Anita's face, as she'd told me what had happened to her. The shame in her eyes. Her tears.

She'd been so embarrassed for not fighting back more, for "letting it happen", that it had taken her almost a year to tell me. As if she was the one to blame for being violated.

I knew that Hale wasn't going to own up to what he did. A part of me, foolishly, had hoped that he would at least admit it. There would be some consolation in ownership at least. But to flat-out deny that anything had even taken place…to go further, to double down and insult the very person he had assaulted for even *saying* it had happened? Now that was unforgivable. Men like that did not change. They only kept hurting others.

Without any conscious effort to do so, I knelt to the ground and pulled a rock from the dirt. It was rectangle-shaped, like a block of butter. Loose bits of sediment and soil fell to the ground as I adjusted my grip on it. I began to sprint.

In my head rang a cacophony of voices. Women's voices, pleading for help. To escape. *No.* A rolodex of images, each more hideous than the last, accompanied the voices, filling my head with all that had been done to the female body over the millennia. All the acts that had been committed upon the female spirit, soiling it, defiling it, tearing it limb from limb with no other reason than *because.* And with that choir of voices, stretched across the arc of time itself, I heard Anita joining in with her own sour song of pain.

Hale came into view in front of me. He was a slow runner. He whipped his head back, saw me approaching with the rock, and let out a cry.

"Help!"

My feet quickened beneath me. I was no longer a mere body of flesh. I was a spiritual hurricane, a storm from another world. I was the death knell for this man. And he knew it.

"Help! Fucking help!"

Four more paces and I had him. I grabbed the back of his jacket with my left hand and swung the rock with my right. It connected, beautifully, with the side of his head.

Hale hollered. He buckled, folding beneath me like a house of cards. The two of us fell to the soft brown earth with momentum, my body landing hard atop his. He made an *oof* sound as he hit the ground, gut-first. I pushed up off of him, rose to my knees on his back.

Holding the rock still, I lifted and swung down again, aiming for the same spot.

Too slow. With a bleeding crown and desperation, Hale cocked his elbow back first, hitting me square in the chest.

I grunted and tumbled backwards. Hale crawled away, staggering to his feet again. He tried to run and only stumbled.

"HELP!"

I shoved myself into standing, grabbed the rock from the trail, and rushed towards him. Swung again.

This time my aim was way off. I only managed to hit the side of his shoulder. Hale spun around and tried to punch me. I scuttled backwards, out of reach from his knuckles.

"Get the *fuck* away from me!" he bellowed.

A smear of blood coated his right ear. I'd hit him with the corner of the rock, and a split of skin was clearly visible under his cropped blonde hair. Good.

The two of us stood, panting, facing one another. I needed to get him off the trail. Now. This was hardly an isolated spot, and a hiker or runner could be rounding the corner at any moment. From all around us came the rush of cold air, punctuated by the caw of crows and the murmuring river, far below in the gorge.

Hale had both arms up, as if this were a wrestling match. He looked like an idiot, with his lime-green windbreaker and bloody head, teeth gritted like a bitted stallion. Both of his eyes were bulging out of his skull with this ugly look of shock, fear, and confidence.

"You've lost your fucking mind," he gasped.

I jerked my head to the side, looking over his shoulder with mock panic. Hale turned his neck, certain that I had spotted someone approaching.

"Help! She's going to—"

He never got to finish his plea. I swung up and hard.

There was a crunch as stone met jaw and jaw lost. Hale's oblivious head snapped back, and he fell with a thud on his back.

A noise left his mouth that I had never heard before, which was saying something. It was a strangled *gah,* as if his larynx had been whipped by wet spaghetti. I wasted no time with him on the ground: I brought the rock down on his forehead.

This blow truly stunned him. His face flushed scarlet and his eyes teetered inwards. They fell shut, then opened again. He blinked, as his vision turned red.

I gave one quick look around to make sure no one was coming. Then I un-straddled his body, took my stance behind his head, and grabbed him by the shoulders.

Hale was broad, heavy. I hooked both my hands under his pits and pulled. He hardly moved. I tried again, making sure to keep my mouth closed, so as not to accidentally spit on the ground. I could barely breathe.

Once more I yanked him, dragging his weight to the side of the trail. Then I let go, sidestepped over, and gave the length of him a shove. With great reluctance, he turned over—once, twice, a third time—before starting to tumble down the gorge's embankment.

It was a noisy, graceless journey. Hale smacked jutting stones and rogue thorn bushes, as he log-rolled down the steep slope. He made it about twenty feet before colliding with the base of a maple tree. The branches shuddered upon impact. I'd have to help him the rest of the way down.

Overhead, the skies started to spit rain. Mean, rough wind ripped through the woods, as the trees moaned under duress. I kicked loose dirt around, smoothing it out from the fight. The small craters of blood filled in with soil, then falling rain. As I did my best to erase the evidence of a struggle, I came across a nasty surprise.

Waiting for me, amongst a clump of disembodied moss, was Hale's tongue. Or at least, the tip of Hale's tongue. He'd bitten it off when I'd hit him upside the jaw. Looking at it, sitting like a rouge mushroom head, I felt my stomach turn. I had done that. I had caused a person to bite off their own tongue. The cold awareness of it drenched me, sobered me up. But it was far too late to go back and change things.

Gingerly, I leaned forward and plucked the warm tongue off the ground. Then swiped a foot of dirt over where it had just been. I wound back and chucked it far into empty space. It flew out, a bloody missile, and disappeared down into the gorge.

Up and down, I paced to double, triple-check that nothing had been missed. The dirt trail, so rugged to begin with, was already turning to mud from the rain. To the untrained eye, absolutely nothing was amiss. Until you stepped over to the side and looked down.

Hale was madly trying to crawl his way to freedom. As he did, he let out little gurgling shrieks as he tried to claw up the embankment.

With great care, so as to make sure I didn't fall right down past him, I began to descend towards him. When he saw me coming, he started to scream.

~ ~ ~

An hour later, it was pouring. The air was thick with water, with hateful wind. I was struggling to breathe atop the riverbed, down at the vertex of the gorge.

Under my feet were hundreds of polished river stones, smoothed over from a thousand years of liquid kisses. This time of year, however, most of them were left out, exposed as the dwindled October current grew stronger with each passing day. By spring it would be a torrent.

Besides the rain, I was drenched in sweat. I could hardly catch a breath. My brain was barrelling with thoughts. Images. Sounds.

I felt close to rupturing. I had ruptured. I'd killed a man. An old boyfriend. My friend's rapist. I had become the thing I promised myself I wasn't. Not a protector. Not a woman, a girl, acting in self-defence. But a murderer. Me.

As I had buried his body with river rocks, I'd wanted to confess everything. I'd wanted to explain to him what this meant to me, how much bigger this feeling was inside. It was beyond my anger for Anita. Beyond Uncle Charlie. The night in the alley. Mango. Mom. Jack.

But I hadn't. Even though I knew Hale wouldn't ever tell another soul, I just couldn't bring myself to speak. To say the words out loud. So, I didn't. I'd covered every inch of his body in rock, with silence on my lips. His face had looked like a ruined pomegranate. And his eyelids were still fluttering, when I placed the final stone atop his head, vanishing him from existence.

In my pocket was his cellphone. I would have to dispose of it, far from here. I'd throw it off a bridge. Yes. I would cross the river, forge my way through the darkening forest, and get rid of the thing. Then go back to Heaven. Back to Jack.

"And then, and then?" my mind asked. "What will you do, then?"

I crouched down onto my haunches and held my head in my hands. I groaned. There was too much going on inside me. Too many things to see, feel, understand. Far too much. I had to forget it all, if for a second.

Shaking with nerves, I began to strip. I pulled the wet clothes from my body and folded them atop the bulging rock pile, which had finally stopped making sounds. On slippery wet stones, I crept across the ground on all fours, away from the embankment. The day had turned the colour of dried ink.

With practiced ease, I made my way to the edge of the river. Although low, it rushed on with formidable strength. Glacier-cold water splashed up at me. With my face locked on the gushing currents, I crawled, nude, into the freezing river. Slipping beneath the surface.

EIGHT

She came home after dark. Soaked. A bang at the door announced her return, along with a slew of swears.

"Ah, fuck! Shit."

I rose from the dinner table and hurried over to the entranceway. There she stood, dripping wet, still in her running gear. She was limping.

"Where have you been? I was worried about you."

Dahlia waved her hand at me, dismissively.

"Sorry, I…ran into an old girlfriend. We went out, lost track of time."

She was swaying on her feet, words overgrown and lazy. When I got closer, I could smell liquor radiating off of her breath.

"You went out like that?" I asked, gesturing to her outfit. She shrugged.

"Yeah, I mean. Whatever. Who cares, right?"

"You do. Usually." I checked my watch, to confirm the time. Quarter past 9. "D, you've been gone since dawn. How come yo—"

"Look, Jack. I don't need to be interrogated," she snapped, pulling off her shoes. They made a squelching sound as they came off her feet. "You should be happy that I was even *with* a friend. I don't have many of those left, y'know."

I put my hands up in defence.

"I know. And I am. I just get worried when I can't reach you. It's weird for me, not knowing where you are all day."

She didn't reply. She stripped off her jacket, her shirt underneath, and dropped them to the floor. *Plop.* Then she started to limp right past me, towards the bedroom. I stared at her, incredulous.

"Are you really not going to talk to me right now? Why are you so wet? And limping?"

Dahlia yanked her head back, eyes ablaze. She looked as though I'd just slapped her.

"Will you please fuck off? You don't need to know everything I do, Jack. I've had a long day. And the last thing I want right now is for you to pester me with your questions."

My chest flushed hot. Anger.

"Why are you acting like this? All I did was ask where you've been."

Dahlia blasted a gust of boozy air in my face. Stood up tall.

"Fine! You want to know where I've been? I've been listening to a childhood friend tell me that she has 6 months to live. I haven't seen her in over 10 years and now I find out that she has breast cancer," she shouted, her body shaking. Fresh water spilled down her face in the form of tears.

"D, I didn't—"

"No, of course you didn't. You just assume shit. That I've been doing something wrong. Isn't that right?"

"What are you talking about? That's not true."

"Of course it's true! I'm not an idiot, Jack. I see how you look at me. The way you—"

"Okay, stop it! Enough. You're clearly drunk, Dahlia."

My voice quivered as I yelled this. I felt a pang of hatred for myself, for being so weak.

Dahlia smiled: an ugly, loveless smile. She took a step closer.

"That's right. I *am* fucking drunk. And you know why? Because I just spent the past few hours trying to feel some goddamn semblance of relief.

"This whole fucking afternoon," she huffed, "spent thinking about how my friend is going to die of cancer, before her own daughter is old enough to remember her face. Or how my husband doesn't even love me anymore because he's so wrapped up in his fear, because he can't see I am still the same person I've always been."

"Now, hang on, that's not—"

"Let me finish!" she bellowed, jabbing a finger at my chest. "You know that's true. So quit lying to me! And quit lying to yourself. You're just like everyone else. You're fucking scared of me. I can see it in your eyes. Even right now, you can't even look at me!"

It was true. I had my eyes focused on the indoor garden, right past her shoulder. It hurt to look at her, to see her like this. But I forced myself to do it.

"That's because I hate seeing you upset. I hate seeing you—"

"Bullshit. Fucking bullshit. You hate looking at me because you don't know what to do with me anymore. You keep pretending that you're okay, being here with me. But I can tell that you're not. You can't stand to look at me."

"Because, Dahlia!" I exploded. "I saw you cut off a man's head! I watched you rip into your own friend and say horrible shit to her! I listened to you tell me how you killed your own dog—"

"I did not *kill* her!" she shrieked. The whole house seemed to tremble from her voice. "How dare you say that abou—"

"But you did, Dahlia! You did!" I took a step closer, monolithic in size compared to her. "You did those things. All of it! You did them."

She opened her mouth to rebuke but stopped short. Her lips trembled mid-fury, eyes splayed wide. I took advantage of this lapse to keep speaking.

"You did those things, Dahlia," I repeated, lowering my voice. "But you know what? *I still love you.* Do you hear me? I still do. Even though you scare me. I can't help it, okay? I don't want to be, and I'm trying my best to get over it. But it's hard. It's so fucking hard."

A deflation was happening somewhere in my ribcage. As if someone had punctured a balloon, pressure released the more I spoke. I kept going.

"But you have to know that I'm trying. I want to go back to how things felt at the start with you. And it's going to take time to see you like that again. But you have to be patient with me. You have to trust me when I tell you I still love you."

Dahlia stood, teetering in space, staring up at me. Her mouth opened and closed, as I looked down at her rapidly-changing facial expressions. It was like watching tides ripple.

I took both sides of her wet body with my hands. I felt good about what I had said. It was the truth. I still, almost inexplicably, loved her. I couldn't imagine being without her. Despite it all. I just couldn't.

Dahlia looked at my hands clutching her shoulders as if they were alien. She wriggled away, taking a step back.

"Don't touch me," she warned. "Just let me go to bed."

"Please don't be like this, D," I begged, moving closer to her again. She recoiled as I moved towards her. I let out a sigh, exasperated.

"Will you at least tell me where you were? It's going to drive me crazy not knowing."

"I already told you. I ran into a friend. Danielle. We went for drinks. I walked home."

"All the way from Ambleside?" I pointed to her leg, uncertain how she could've walked for over 2 hours with a limp. Through the pouring rain. "What about your leg?"

"I fell on the way."

"Why didn't she drive you?"

"Because I didn't want to be driven, Jack," she hissed. "I wanted to think. I needed to think."

"Think about what?"

"What to do. About us. About you."

Her words hung venomously in the air. Both of us fell silent, the rush of the garden stream filling the emptiness. I stared at my wife. She stared back.

"Well," I asked, "what did you decide, then? To do about me." I tacked the last part of the sentence on with a bit of malice. Dahlia kept staring, her expression still fluctuating in the most unsettling way. Rage. Shame. Adoration. Disdain. Apathy. I felt dizzy watching it.

"I don't know," she admitted, after a beat of silence. "I don't know what to do about anything anymore."

I nodded, understanding her better than I could put into words.

"Well if it you makes you feel better, D. Neither do I."

Stalemate.

I waited for Dahlia to say something in reply. Anything. This wasn't how I wanted to go out, with resentment and anger. There had to be more to us. To this life of ours. I couldn't let our love just die.

"I want to make this work, D," I started slowly. "I want to fix what we have. But I can't do this alone. Not when you disappear out of the blue or bite my head off about nothing. I can't be the only one trying to save us."

"You're not," she said. "I'm trying too."

"I know you are. I know."

The rain, which had dulled its falling, resumed its strength again. Underneath the huge skylight, the sound was tremendous. We both looked up at the noise, and started to move.

I came up behind her and put a hand on her shoulder, as we walked together into the bedroom. I realized, for the first time, she was shivering.

"You should take a shower. Warm up," I said softly. Dahlia nodded.

"Sorry for leaving you here all day," she confided. I sat down on the bed as she took off her remaining clothes, one by one.

"It's fine. I'm sorry about your friend."

"Yeah. Thanks."

The energy in the room felt very heavy. Like a funeral had just taken place. Without another word, Dahlia left the bedroom and disappeared into the bathroom, locking the door behind her. A minute later and the shower started running.

I sat on the edge of the bed, feeling strange. There was a sense of catharsis, yet also new discomfort. As if someone had uprooted something bad and planted something even worse in its place.

The shower went on. Dahlia did not sing like she had years ago. She never sang, since her voice had changed. A cloud of grief suddenly washed over me. I would never hear that voice again, the one I had fallen in love with. It was gone. Forever.

Then another thought came. Her friend, the one with cancer. Something about it didn't sit right with me.

I crawled across the bed to the other side, where my phone was charging. I plucked it off the bedside table, debating on if

I should even search this. But it was already too late. I had to know.

I searched "chemotherapy alcohol together" as quickly as ripping off a bandaid. The combination sounded abhorrent. Sure enough, the first several results yielded the same answer. Mixing poison and poison was an awful, terrible idea.

"*Since cancer treatment drugs are broken down by the liver, chemotherapy side effects are greatly worsened when alcohol is introduced to the system. Therefore, it is never a good idea to combine the two together.*"

The same answer was given by a dozen different websites.

I put my phone down, feeling a sensation of dread. Perhaps Dahlia's friend had quit treatment when she knew that she was going to die anyway. Or maybe Dahlia had been drinking alone.

Except that didn't make much sense. Dahlia never touched liquor unless someone else was involved. She swore she hated the stuff, the way it made her groggy and dumb. Unless she'd wanted to feel like that? I tried to picture the two of them sitting at a bar talking, and couldn't. The image wouldn't form.

But I had to make a choice. Either harbour my doubts for what she had told me. Or believe her, full-heartedly. I couldn't think of a good reason why Dahlia would lie about something like that, to make up a story about a fake friend/cancer-ridden new mother.

No. It had to be true, I decided. The alternative was too disturbing to even consider.

I closed my eyes and focused on the voiceless shower. Pretty soon, all my mental chatter washed away too.

~ ~ ~

Weeks went by without incident. Dahlia would still be home when I woke up. She was stuck inside, now that the weather had taken a turn for the worse and she couldn't run on her leg. It was fully sprained, a doctor revealed. Best thing to do was rest and heal.

My birthday came and went. No gift this year. The best she did was order an ice cream cake to be delivered, which ended up sitting mostly uneaten in the refrigerator. It'd turned to goo, chocolate ganache milk soup.

One day it was fine. The next: leaking out of the fridge and onto the floor. There'd been a power outage in the night and the fridge had turned off. The following morning, a lagoon of smelly ice cream awaited us on the kitchen floor.

"How are there still flies in November?" Dahlia griped, sopping up the mess with a rag. I watched her smack them dead with her cloth. By the time she was done, a cluster of black bodies floated atop the sea of melted ice cream.

She scooped up the slop with a dustpan and threw it into an empty bucket. Ice cream splattered the sides of the stove. Earsplitting classical music filled the room.

"What is that racket you've got on?" I cringed, going to turn down the record she had put on to clean to. The siege of strings and uproarious piano was giving me a headache.

"Racket? You call that a racket?"

"No, I'd call it a headache inducer," I replied.

Dahlia snorted.

"You wouldn't know good music if it hit you *on* the head."

I shot her a look, but she had her face down. She scooped up more liquid ice cream.

"That's not funny."

"I wasn't trying to be."

Splat.

"Well, don't say that kind of stuff to me."

Sploup.

"Hello?"

"Yes?"

Spladoop.

"Did you hear what I said? Don't say that kind of stuff to me."

"I heard you. I'm just busy cleaning up your fuc—

Spoolt.

"—king ice cream cake."

"I just offered to help yo—"

"It's fine! I've got it."

There were more vaguely toilet-reminiscent sounds, along with the sound of her heavy breathing, as she scrubbed down the sticky fridge handles. I'd stood, helpless and annoyed. Then without another word, I'd left the room and went down to the basement to read.

28 days into being 28 years old, I received an invitation. Gabriel and Irene were hosting a party at their house to celebrate their new marriage. They'd tied the knot in Paraguay a month ago. Now they were back on Canadian soil, ready to have a celebration with friends. Nothing fancy. *NO GIFTS!* forbade the email.

Dahlia initially refused.

"Absolutely not, Jack. I'm not going to some stupid party."

"D, it's my best friend's wedding party..."

"And I have a sprained ankle. Big whoop."

She was slouched, grouchy and overheated, on a bare deck chair. The temperatures had swung up to the peak tens. It was "unseasonably warm, record-breaking" weather. It was all anyone could talk about.

"God, it's hot for this time of year, isn't it?" grocery cashiers remarked relentlessly. All I could do was smile and agree.

"Look," I said to Dahlia, "it would be a lot easier for me if you came. I don't want to have to answer people's questions about how you are. I want them to see that you're okay for themselves."

"Sounds like it would be easier for us both if we *both* stayed home."

"Dahlia. Please."

"Jack?"

"Yes?"

"Can you please piss off? I said no."

It'd taken hours for her to concede. Eventually I had convinced her to do it by saying people would assume she was too scared to come out of hiding.

"They'll think you're ashamed," I said mournfully. I shook my head a little. "No one will believe me when I say that you're fine."

"Whatever. I don't care."

"Yvonne will be there. Irene invited her."

"And?"

"She'd tell everyone. Genevieve."

Dahlia readjusted her sunglasses. The December sun blazed on.

"I'll think about it," she replied flatly.

~ ~ ~

A few days later, we were driving there. I took the wheel.

Dahlia sat in the passenger seat, grumbling. Her crutches rattled in the backseat as we sped down the highway. We crossed over the suspension bridge spanning the two shores, then through the downtown core. Past office towers. Another bridge. Suburbs. Bridge. More houses.

"Jesus, where do these people live?" Dahlia asked.

We'd been wading our way through traffic-dense city roads for over an hour. Horns honked and blared at one another.

Clumps of people overran the corners. Everyone was shopping, talking, moving about. Off to a meeting. Pushing strollers filled with babies or aluminum cans. It was pure chaos.

I balked at the steering wheel, feeling overwhelmed.

"We're almost there," I said, lying through my teeth. This was the first time we had ever driven this deep into the city together. Normally, it was a frustrating but manageable drive. With Dahlia beside me, completely non-speaking, it became unbearable. I could feel her disgust at the endless human havoc we saw. It infected me like a virus.

By the time we'd arrived, both of us were raw. I got out of the car and hurried to get her crutches from the backseat. Somehow, she had already beaten me to them.

"Here, let me take that," I said, offering to hold onto her purse. She snatched it tighter.

"It's fine. I'm good. Let's just get this over with." She began to hobble her way towards the house. I hurried after her.

I debated asking her to behave, but figured that would only backfire. Feeling uneasy, we made our way up the stairs and knocked on the door. The sounds of laughter rang out on the other side.

A moment later, Gabriel opened the door. His face lit up when he saw us.

"There you two are! Come in, come in!"

He pulled me into a hug, smacking my back. Marriage had done him well. His whole energy seemed buoyant, jolly. A twinge of envy came from my gut.

"So good to see you, Dahlia. How've you been?" he asked, holding her hand for longer than usual. Dahlia flashed her blinding smile.

"Oh, can't complain," she said through gritted teeth. "Thanks for inviting us."

"Are you kidding? Of course! I would've invited you guys to the ceremony but it was pretty low-key. Mostly just family. Although Irene's parents flew down, so that was nice."

"That's great," Dahlia said, freeing her hand from Gabriel's grasp. "Glad to hear."

We followed him deeper into the small house. A smattering of people were crammed on every sitting space available, talking loudly. Irene came over from across the room to greet us, bearing a fresh tan and a smile. She slid her arm beside Gabriel and gave him a cheek-kiss.

"Hi, you guys! So glad you could make it," she said warmly. She gave Dahlia a little nod.

"Yeah, thanks. Us too."

"How've you been keeping? What's new?"

"Ah, not much. Just…staying busy," I answered.

"Oh, yeah? With what?

"You start teaching now, Jack?"

The couple beamed at us, conjoined at the hip. It was making me nauseous to look at them. Dahlia and I had a full foot of empty air between us. I shook my head.

"No, no teaching. I was thinking about it maybe in the new year but I…I don't know. It didn't feel like the right time."

Gabriel nodded understandingly. "That's fine, *mijo.* Take your time. It's been a rough year for you two."

"Yeah, of course. How's the hand?"

I held my left hand up for inspection. They both leaned in to take a closer look at the lightning bolt scars on my fingers. Dahlia crossed her arms and turned away slightly.

"Wow. That's amazing."

"Modern medicine, hey?"

"Yup," I said, tucking my hand away. "Amazing, all right."

The four of us stood in the living room, unsure of what to say next. From all around came snippets of other conversations.

I had to crane my neck so as not to hit the overhead track lighting.

"Nice place you've got here," I offered.

"Thank you! Irene's parents helped us with the down payment. Medical school doesn't pay for itself, does it, honey?" Gabriel said, squeezing Irene's sides. She laughed.

"You're going to be a doctor?" This was news to me.

"Well, eventually. I'm working as a nurse at St. Paul's at the moment. But getting my doctorate is definitely on the agenda."

Gabriel grinned at her, then back at us. "Yeah, she's been a busy bee with classes and work. And I'm working full-time at a prep school downtown, so we've been keeping busy."

"I know, I hardly get to see this guy," Irene said, pouting her lips. "We're always on the go!"

"My god," Dahlia said drily. "How ever do you do it?"

I shot her a look, but neither Gabriel nor Irene seemed to pick up on her sarcasm. Irene squeezed her husband's hand and turned back to Dahlia.

"We make it work, don't we, honey?" she replied, dripping with earnestness.

Someone told a loud punchline in Spanish and a group of people erupted in laughter. Gabriel and Irene both turned their heads at the sound.

"Excuse me, I'm going to get a drink," Dahlia said, then slipped into the kitchen before anyone had even registered what she said. When Gabriel and Irene looked back, she was gone.

"Oh, where did—"

"She went to get a drink," I explained with a shrug.

They both glanced at one another.

"How've you been, Jack? Honestly?" Gabriel asked, lowering her voice.

"Yeah, we've been worried about you two," Irene added. Her brows creased into a frown. "Yvonne told me she hasn't been able to get in touch with Dahlia for months."

I tried to make my voice light and cheery. Put on my best fake smile.

"Oh, we're fine. There's just been a lot to process, but we're good. Honest." I went to sip my drink, and then realized I didn't have one. I folded my hands awkwardly.

"And don't worry about her not replying. She got rid of her cellphone a while back."

"Got rid of it? What do you mean?"

"She threw it away. She said she didn't want one anymore."

"That seems a bit weird, doesn't it? Or at least concerning. Shouldn't she be staying in touch with her fri—"

"Look," I said, cutting Irene off. "I think she just needs some space right now. But I'm sure she's fine. The whole thing with Genevieve kind of shook her up, that's all."

"Right. Of course."

Irene looked up at me with a pitiful look in her eyes. *Poor you,* it seemed to say. *Poor Jack and Dahlia.*

I cleared my throat, taking a step back.

"Uh, I think I'll go get a drink myself."

"Yes, yes, of course. Go help yourself," Gabriel said, waving me to the kitchen.

"Thanks. And congrats, you two. I'm happy for you guys."

I left them holding one another in a loving embrace, grinning like fools. I couldn't stand to be around them any longer.

I stepped into the cramped kitchen, overrun with talking heads and red solo cups. An oversized punch bowl sat with citrus fruit floating on top. Everyone looked perfectly happy. Comfortable. I stood hunched in the doorway, scanning the faces.

It took me all of 15 seconds to realize that my wife was nowhere to be seen.

~ ~ ~

Time dragged its feet. I tried making small talk with strangers and failed miserably each attempt. Nothing felt right to talk about. Everything there was to say—be it the weather, or work, or plans for the upcoming holidays—just seemed like total fucking bullcrap. After my fourth cup of punch and fifth dead conversation, I took myself out on the deck. I still hadn't seen any sign of Dahlia.

Outside, the air was starting to cool off. Finally, the season was catching up to us; the stint of bizarre hot temperatures was receding. Before long, it would be just a memory, the time when it was almost warm enough to suntan in December. And after that, it wouldn't even be that. It would be completely forgotten about.

A couple other people stood chatting on the deck. Below us was a dingy, yellow grass yard that backed up onto an alleyway. All around were perpetual rooftops.

For the first time since I'd arrived, I was able to pinpoint my discomfort. I'd spent so much time in isolation, geographically, that it felt weird to be surrounded by people again. I'd grown accustomed to seeing the sea and trees as my neighbours, not actual houses. It made my head spin to look at all the chimney stacks, sticking into the air like fangs.

All those people with their own, fucked-up little lives, I thought to myself.

What a mess.

I dangled my arm and empty solo cup over the railing and stared down at the yellow grass. It looked like an army of

Chihuahuas had pissed all over it, killing off the vegetation. It was gross.

I looked back up at the deck, over to the side. A couple was gushing over one another, mouths mushed together. A full cup of booze hung from the girl's hand, and she paused to take a drink before going back to kissing her boyfriend. Equally gross.

The sky had turned wispy grey. Oceanic wind blew in from the west, boring right to my marrow. I shivered. I felt lonely. A bit drunk. I had an image of jumping over the railing and landing on my neck. I could picture all the people coming over, shrieking and making a big scene. The thought made me smile. Then when I realized what I was fantasizing about, I took a step back from the edge.

A particular strong gust came along, and with it, a snatch of voice. I jerked my head to the side. I recognized that metallic rasp, for better or worse. Dahlia. She was close by.

I strode over to the other side of the deck and looked down. Sure enough, over to the side of the house beneath me, was my wife. She was smoking a cigarette with her crutches propped against the house. She wasn't alone.

Leaned against the house was Yvonne. One of Dahlia's hands rested on her shoulder.

The scene seemed to be something out of a dream. Both of them were cast in shadow from the houses, as they stood in the narrow walkway between the two. I could hear little bits and pieces of what they were saying, but nothing in full.

Smoke curled up above my wife's head, as she sucked down the nicotine with greed. Then handed it to Yvonne.

But this wasn't what struck me most above the tableau. Even in the dingy setting of the two rundown houses and trampled lawn, there was an unmistakable glow coming off the two of them. Or at least, Dahlia. I could see her face clearer, as she watched Yvonne smoke and talk. She looked happier than I'd seen her in a long time.

I watched them talk to one another. At some point Yvonne said something funny, and Dahlia threw her head back in sparkling, rough laughter. I pulled my body back from the railing, out of sight.

Then, when a few seconds had passed, I looked back over. What I saw made my heart stop.

My wife had her lips pressed against Yvonne's. Hard. So hard, in fact, that Yvonne's head was pushed against the plastic siding of the house. Her hand holding the cigarette went slack, and she grabbed the back of Dahlia's neck with her other to pull her closer. They stayed like this for what felt like forever. Then finally, they parted.

Dahlia's face was flushed, giddy. Her mouth parted into a smile.

She looked like her old self. Yvonne passed her the smoking cigarette, and she took it. Inhaled deeply. Laughed.

I stepped back from the railing. In the time this had happened, the deck had cleared out. I was all alone. A roiling wave of fear had overtaken me. I felt like I couldn't breathe. My chest clenched up, refusing to release.

My brain started to spiral. Dahlia was going to leave me. My wife was going to leave me and be with someone else. Yvonne. A man. Whomever. She was done with me. She couldn't stand me. How many times had she made that clear? I was nothing but a disappointment, a weak man who needed to be saved.

I'd been blind to think there wasn't a chance this could happen. She was sick of me, her husband who couldn't fight back, couldn't defend her, couldn't *really* understand her. All the signs were there. The end was coming. I could feel it, definitive and certain, out of sight for so long but now: suddenly breathing down the back of my neck. Fucking stupid *stupid* Jack to think otherwise. To act like our love was set in stone.

It explained the short temper. The disappearances. The constant changes of mood, the lacklustre attitude in bed. Not that we even fucked or made love anymore. Oh no. What we did was far worse. Stale. Lifeless. Nothing like the kiss I had just seen. I couldn't even remember the last time we had done something that carelessly passionate.

And Yvonne. Of course. No wonder she'd never liked me. She'd wanted to sleep with Dahlia all along. If she hadn't already. All the instances of cold shoulders and glares came into crystalline focus. I felt like an idiot for being so ignorant.

And now, now what? my panicking brain asked. *If she's done with you, sick of you, that means that the only thing left to do is get rid of—*

The deck door slid open, disrupting my mental maelstrom. Gabriel poked his smiling head out.

"Hey! We're about to make an announcement, if you want to come join us in the front room."

"Oh, shit. Okay, yeah, I'll be right in."

"Irene wants to do it now, so better come quick." He studied my face, changing his expression to one of concern. "Everything okay?"

"Yeah. Yeah, I'm fine. Just a bit too much jungle juice," I said, shaking my empty cup.

He laughed.

"Okay, good. Glad to hear I haven't lost my bartending touch. Come on in, then."

I made a move to follow after him, heart racing. Then stopped. I stepped back outside and leaned my head over the side railing.

"Hey, you two! They're making an announcement inside," I yelled. I pulled my head back over and hurried inside before I got a chance to see the look on their guilty faces.

~ ~ ~

It was a long drive home. The radio played top-forties hits, all of them terrible. Ads for dandruff shampoo and mall Santa meet-and-greets interjected every few minutes. Most of the time, we sat in traffic, inching forward. Neither Dahlia nor I hardly said a word. About mid-way into the first hour, I switched the radio off.

"So did you have fun?" I asked, immediately regretting it.

"You already asked me that."

"Yeah. I forgot I did."

Silence. I drummed my fingers on the wheel and stared at the license plate in front of us. SHOOP2. Above the plate was a menage of stickers, all holding hands from biggest to smallest. A family. Inside the mini-van were silhouettes of children's heads, gyrating with excitement. It looked like there were four or five of them, crammed in the backseats.

I looked over to Dahlia, arms crossed. She had barely looked at me for the rest of the party. She'd sat beside Yvonne, as Gabriel and Irene had excitedly shared their good news. They were having a baby. Everyone had clapped, cheered. Except for her.

"Was it nice to see Yvonne again?"

"Of course. I missed her."

I bet, I thought. *And her, you.*

"Well, that's good. I'm glad you got to see ea—"

"Look, Jack. Can we just not talk right now? I'm getting a headache."

"Oh. Okay. Yeah, sure."

Dahlia let out a sigh and cracked the window. Gasoline fumes and horns slipped in. She quickly shut it with a grunt.

Ahead of us, one of the back windows of the mini-van mirrored ours. A small fist stuck out into the road, dangling a stuffed elephant. There was a flurry of motion inside the van as the adults in charge turned around to reprimand the elephant thief. Seconds later, the stuffed animal vanished from sight, and the window rolled back up.

"Brats," Dahlia said, almost inaudible. I resisted the urge to look at her.

~ ~ ~

After 2 hours of driving from Gabriel's, we pulled up to the gates of Heaven. I got out to unlock them, manually. We still used a steel chain and padlock, at Dahlia's insistence. She didn't trust those "automatic ones". I drove through before hopping out on the other side to reverse the process. The chain rattled as I pulled it tight across the middle.

Dahlia was up out of her seat the moment I parked in the garage. Once again, I hurried to help her with her crutches, but she had them planted in her pits before I could even get close.

"I'm fine, just go on inside," she said testily when I went to reach for her purse, still sitting in the centre console.

"Okay," I replied, stepping away. I turned and went into the empty house first. The sound of rushing water from the stream hit me like a train. It sounded louder than ever.

I slipped out of my dress shoes and stuck them in the hall closet. Waited a moment. My wife did not come through the door. I waited some more. Nothing.

When at least a few minutes had gone by, I walked back over and opened the door. Inside the garage were the two cars: my white Porsche convertible and Dahlia's black Lincoln SUV, motor still ticking. But no Dahlia. She was gone.

"Honey?" I called. I stepped into the garage with my socks. The cement was freezing on my feet. The double garage door was still wide open.

I walked between the cars, towards the outside. The temperature had chilled to an icy shiver. I looked around, up the sloping driveway. Opened my mouth to call out again, but then stopped.

Dahlia was sitting on the small wooden gazebo at the edge of the property line. It was a whitewashed, octagon structure, barely big enough for two. Moss had started to overtake the bottom half, giving the base a green tinge. Her crutches leaned against the side as she stared off towards the ocean.

For a moment, my breath was taken from me all over again. She looked so beautiful. Her black hair levitated half-heartedly behind her head as the wind blew stronger. I wasn't close enough to see the expression on her face. Not that it mattered. I already knew what it looked like by heart.

All at once, I felt homesick. For Dahlia. For us. I missed when we would talk until our tongues got tired. When the night was never long enough for us. When every day felt like a divine dust had been sprinkled upon it, making the world pop with colour and serendipity. I missed when she was a mystery to me. When our love felt new and exciting.

Now I just felt tired. And afraid.

Afraid of what she had told me. Of what she had done. Afraid that this feeling of loss, of *something missing,* would never go away. Afraid of feeling powerless, like I was a burden. Afraid of drowning in feelings, worries, and the past.

Or something even more horrible than the past. The future. What would my life look like if we split up? How would I be able to live?

All the experiences we had shared. The wealth. The trauma, binding us like insidious glue. Who could ever measure up to that? How could I ever be without her again?

The idea of such a reality made me want to die. I had a flash of memory, of Yvonne and her mid-kiss, and I had to physically turn away, clutching my gut. No. This couldn't be happening. Not after everything. This couldn't be the end.

With a racing heart, I walked back into the house alone. I went to the kitchen and got a beer from the fridge. It cracked open with a hiss, the cap falling to the ground. I didn't pick it up. I brought it to my lips, drank deeply. Then leaned over the side of the sink. Spit it all out. The rest of the bottle quickly followed down the drain.

Heaven was deadly quiet. With the windows all closed, it was hard to make out the surf colliding with the granite bedrock below. I paced around the room, stared out the walls of glass. My thoughts were back to being a cyclone.

Only now, a new element had joined the mix. Anger. I felt tired and afraid and angry. A vicious trio, nipping at each other's heels.

"What're you going to do?" my father's voice echoed in my ears. I hadn't thought about him in a long while. My teeth grit instinctually. He kept talking.

"You going to let that whore cheat on you? Why aren't you madder? What the fu—"

"Shut up," I told the empty kitchen. I threw the empty beer bottle into the recycling bin and marched out of the room, past the garden and gurgling stream, down the long hall decorated with doors. I opened one on the left. The master bedroom. Our room. Shut it.

A part of me knew my father, real or not, was right. Why wasn't I madder? Why wasn't I fucking pissed that Dahlia had cheated on me? Because I didn't feel mad at her. I felt hurt. Scared. Upset. But not mad when I thought of her and Yvonne. Why not? And if so, then *where* was the anger coming from?

Because it was there, brooding. Evading my grasp. I pulled my sports jacket off, tossed it on the ground. Picked it back up.

Nothing was helping. Nothing was feeling right. I had no answers, no solutions.

With shaking hands, I undid my shirt buttons. Took my navy blue shirt off and hung it up with my sports jacket. Goosebumps pimpled my torso, down my arms.

Maybe I'd take a hot shower. Maybe that would fix everything.

I started to walk towards the bathroom when I noticed the wall calendar hadn't been changed. November's photo of an overweight harbour seal stared back at me. A blurb at the bottom begged people to stop dumping garbage in the ocean.

"How would *you* like to live in sewage?" it asked in bold letters. I yanked the pushpin from the wall and flipped the page over to December. A carmine octopus, stretched atop a bouquet of coral, jumped out at me.

"Did you know? Most octopuses lay between one hundred thousand to four hundred thousand eggs! That's because they only live to be—"

I never did learn how old octopuses grew to live. I ripped the calendar in half and carried it into the bathroom. Threw it in the garbage. There. I'd never have to look at some stupid sea creature again, first thing when I woke up.

Which left me holding the pushpin in between my fingers. I looked down at its tip, a silver point dusted in plaster. I brought it closer to my mouth and blew. There. All clean. The sharp end winked at me in the light.

Then my father spoke to me again. Except it wasn't really his voice that I imagined. It was his dad's dad. My great-grandpa. The voice whispered something awful. Something truly unforgivable. It made my stomach lurch.

"No," I said to the mirror. It was just me in the bathroom. I knew that. "I can't."

"But," my long dead great-grandfather purred. *"It might be the only way to keep her."*

And in some way, I knew. He was right. *I* was right. My great-grandfather wasn't talking to me beyond the grave. It was my own subconscious who had, at last, cooked up an idea in the 11th hour. Something drastic. But something that would, maybe, possibly, work.

"No," I muttered out loud again. "No."

Silence filled the empty space my words left. An assault of mental chatter. Tight, sick feelings across my chest. A bellyache. And the hummingbird-light weight of the pushpin between my fingers. Too light to be a threat.

Somewhere deep inside my noisy brain, another word bubbled up. The answer to my previous question. Of where my anger was really coming from.

And the word was:

Brats.

NINE

Cold metal. All I could feel was cold metal. It was sliding inside of me, prying me open. And then, cobra-quick, it was gone. Yanked from my insides.

The doctor who was examining me, Dr. Erikson, let out a small gasp. I craned my neck up from the table to look down at him between my legs.

"What's wrong?" I demanded.

His face had flushed a strange colour. He shook his head slightly, flipped my gown over my exposed pelvis, and rolled away on his chair. Stood up.

"Nothing, Mrs. Donner," he replied. He kept his eyes just off meeting mine. "I'd just like to change gears here. Start with some other tests if you don't mind. I'll be right back."

"Wait, why do you nee—"

He did not let me finish my question. A wisp of fabric and he was gone, out the door. I laid in silence, alone on the patient table. My stomach ached.

I tried to keep calm. I laid my head back and counted the ceiling tiles. They were dirty, plastery. Speckled with holes.

The reek of sickness and disinfectant bore down on me like a plague.

As the seconds turned to minutes, I became more and more regretful that I had come. Nothing was *actually* wrong with me. I knew that.

It had been Jack's idea to get a checkup. In the past few months, he'd shape-shifted into a new man. Possessive. Almost aggressive. I couldn't decide if I liked it or not. It was both a relief and a concern. Relief because he was less boring now. Concern because I didn't know where it had come from. And, on some level, feared that I did.

He'd stopped treating me like a fragile thing around New Year's. No more coddling. No more tip-toeing on eggshells. He'd came over to me in bed, long after I pretended to have fallen asleep, and told me he wanted to fuck me. That straight. There was no lead up, no warning. And there was a coldness to his tone, a light in those tar-black eyes of his, that had made me excited. I'd said yes.

When I'd let him in, it had been borderline brutal. He'd handled me like a prostitute. But when he was done, panting from exhaustion, he'd curled up beside me and held me tight against his body. Fallen asleep holding me. It was the first time we had slept in each other's arms in ages.

The following weeks were no different. I'd catch him watching me from across the room. All of a sudden a prickling would alight on the side of my head. And I'd turn from whatever I was doing to see him staring from the couch. Not with an angry look. Or a necessarily kind one. Just staring.

"Do you need something?" I'd ask. Head shake.

"No, just admiring you. You look sexy today."

"Oh. Thanks."

I didn't know what else to say. I'd forgotten how to take a compliment from him.

My worry, of course, was timing. It seemed suspicious that right around the same time I started seeing Yvonne again, Jack started trying to control me. Dominate me. Brand me.

It was eerie. I racked my brain for how he could have known. Yvonne and I were very careful when we saw each other, ever since reconnecting at Gabriel's. I'd bought a special phone just to contact her. And we never met up more than once a week.

Yvonne was working at a law firm downtown, the same one she had been employed at for years. In the end, she'd never gone off to Vermont, or even finished grad school. Instead she had settled into the realm of mediocrity. And she hated it.

"God, I mean…I just don't know what to do anymore, D," she lamented one day, the two of us rolled up beside one another. "I can't stand work. I fucking hate it. All I can think of is when it's going to be over."

"So why don't you leave? Go back to school or something?"

"You don't understand," she said, "I don't want to do *anything.* Law, retail, business, all of it. I hate it. I'm sick of it. I'm tired of working, and paying bills, and worrying about rent. I'm tired of giving my whole life away to some stupid job that doesn't even care about me."

I would nod in mock understanding as she'd complain about work, before nudging the energy back towards the intimate. Sleeping with Yvonne was to fill a hole. A hole in feeling human again. And I needed that hole to be filled more than ever.

Of course there was guilt involved. How could there not be? I had never, ever wanted to be a person who had an affair.

But Yvonne was the only one who still saw me as my old self. She was in love with me. She had been for years. And that made her blind.

So blind, in fact, that she had cut Genevieve out of her circle, along with Stephanie for even believing "her fucked-up revenge story". Yvonne was convinced, absolutely certain, that I could've never done such a thing. I wasn't evil like that.

"Honestly," she'd confessed, "you had every right to lash out like that. It was fucked up of her to say that. Joke or not, it wasn't funny. Like, I knew she was an attention whore, but not to that extreme."

"It's fine." I'd shrugged. "I've let it go."

We'd meet up and be all over one another. True passion. Easy desire. Then she would look at me with those magic, golden eyes. Nothing like Jack's coal pits. Yvonne's were like sunflowers, like summer honey, drizzled into effervescent light. Oh, and the way that she looked at me. I'd forgotten how good it felt to be carelessly adored like that. It was exactly how Jack used to look at me. Before he knew me better.

So before long, we had fallen back into our practiced waltz with one another. It just felt so easy, being with her. I would come home after burying my face between her legs feeling more alive than ever.

Jack would be waiting for me when I got back. Watching me with those dull, black eyes of his, flat-faced. Would he ask how my day was? Yes. But not always. Most of the time he'd only be looking to fuck. And feeling generous, I would often say yes.

Until the pain started. First: an ache. Then a tenderness that wouldn't stop rising to attention. I tried to ignore it, to shove it far into the corner of my brain with all the other bad stuff, but it kept demanding to be noticed. With reluctance, I finally conceded.

I had to ask Jack to stop mid-sex. Then Yvonne. It felt like too many nerves had bundled in the same area, vying for attention. My genitals stung. My whole groin, in fact, had grown thorns from the inside. And there was a hotness to it, a warmth, that spread down my legs and up my belly.

Yvonne immediately blamed Jack. She accused him of giving me an STI, of cheating on me. Her dislike had escalated to full-blown hatred, and I knew, to some degree, that she was still secretly hoping I'd leave him. For her.

I'd had to gently remind her that if anyone was cheating, it was me. Jack didn't have the guts for betrayal. He spent the days twiddling his thumbs, watching TV, and reading. Going for drives to god-knows-where. As I'd told her this, the realization that I didn't really care bubbled into being.

It was an ugly revelation. I didn't care anymore what Jack did with his time. Not really. Partially because it was always the same thing. He'd refused to step in the future, to release the past. He didn't try to make friends or want to go back to work. All he seemed to do with his life was a fat load of nothing. It was driving me insane.

So no, I'd told Yvonne, he wasn't cheating. That couldn't be it. She'd silently agreed to disagree, and the two of us had spent the rest of the afternoon playing tongue tag. When I'd come home to Jack, however, and he'd passively pushed the two of us to the bedroom, I'd had to tell him no.

"That pain I had a few days ago," I'd said, "it's getting worse. I can feel it all in here."

I'd patted my navel area, unperturbed. Jack's eyes had both dilated, then shrunk to normal. Cleared his throat and looked elsewhere.

"Maybe you should go get it checked out," he'd said. "Go see a gyno or something."

"A what?"

"A gynaecologist?"

"It's gyna, not gyno."

"Okay, well, whatever. Just trying to help."

Then he'd stomped out of the room before he'd realized I was only trying to tease him. Like we used to do. And before I could tell him that I had never been to a gynaecologist in my life.

~ ~ ~

Dr. Erikson had been visibly horrified to hear those words.

"You've never been to a gynaecologist before?" His whole moustache had drooped into an oversized frown. If I had known he had that much facial hair, I wouldn't have called his number from the phonebook. He had been equally—if not more—horrified to hear this, too.

"People still use phonebooks?"

"Well, I do. When I can, at least." I'd felt degraded to be sitting on the examining table, feet dangling beneath me. "I've never been a fan of computers."

Dr. Erikson had nodded, still looking baffled.

"Fair enough. They're ruining people's brains."

"Mm," I'd said, pursing my lips in false agreement. "Exactly. Just trying to stay sharp."

"But why haven't you had a check-up before? It's very important for your health as a woman. Didn't your mother or, um, parental figure encourage you to see a doctor before?"

"I just…didn't think I needed to. I've never had any issues before."

I'd neglected to tell Dr. Erikson that, prior to my fucking sprained ankle, I had never really been to *any* doctor before.

My mother had always forgotten to make appointments for check-ups. And I never, ever got sick.

"Okay, well, that's a common misconception. You see, the female body is very sensitive, and it needs to…" Dr. Erikson had continued with a long-winded speech about the immense importance of vaginal health, and why women needed to be in tip-top shape before even *considering* having a child. I'd cut him off there.

"But I'm not trying to have a baby," I'd said. "My husband and I always use protection."

"Alright. Good to know. Can I ask why you aren't on birth control?"

I'd crinkled my nose.

"I tried that before. It made me nauseous. And gave me headaches. So no, thanks."

"Of course. Well, just so you know, those side effects are very common, so I think—"

"Listen," I'd interrupted, holding my hand up in warning. "I'm not here to have you sell me on that hormonal poison. I just came to get checked out. I want this pain to stop. So can you do something about that or not?"

Dr. Erikson had clutched his clipboard tighter, bobbing his head unconsciously.

"Right, of course, Mrs. Donner. My apologies."

He'd uncapped his pen and begun writing.

"So, what kind of symptoms are you experiencing?"

I'd told him what he needed to know. The pain during sex. The lingering ache that stretched from my thighs to my bellybutton. Dr. Erikson had jotted things down with a shaky hand.

"Right, right. Okay. And when was your last period?"

"Last month."

"Anything unusual? Discharge, or heavy flow?"

"No and no. Same shit as always," I'd replied with disdain.

"Are you regular?"

"What?"

"Are you—" He'd paused to cough wetly into his hand. "Regular? Do your periods arrive on a regular schedule?"

He'd made it sound like they were houseguests, my periods, dropping in every second Sunday to say hi. I'd regarded him with a narrowed eye, hoping he was telepathic enough to know that I thought he was a sorry excuse for a doctor.

"No," I'd said, after a beat of silence. "I've always been quite…irregular."

"With date or flow?"

"Both. Although I don't see how that matters to what's happening."

He'd coughed again, before continuing to scribble away.

"Just asking, Mrs. Donner. I don't want to miss anything. That's how I do things."

I'd resisted the urge to roll my eyes at his self-importance. Instead, I'd answered the rest of his silly questions. Then lied down to be prodded like some Thanksgiving turkey. Only for the doctor to up and leave me, deserted, on the examination table. A mixture of fear and boredom started brewing inside me. With a dash of perverted excitement, that something awful was about to happen.

~ ~ ~

15 minutes passed before he came back. He brought someone else with him, a female doctor. She regarded me with apathy, stretched out in my hospital gown. Dr. Erikson also had another new friend. I recognized it from seeing it in movies. An ultrasound machine.

“Mrs. Donner, I’d like you to meet Dr. Hill. She’s one of the other doctors on our team here at the clinic. She’s going to be overseeing your check-up, just to make sure everything looks all right.”

“Hello,” Dr. Hill said. Her greeting splashed on my ears like cold water.

“Uh, hi,” I said in reply. “Always dreamed of having an audience for this.”

Dr. Erikson laughed at my joke far too hard. He rolled the ultrasound machine over to the side of the table, parking it right next to my covered belly.

“Oh, that’s hilarious! Good one,” he wheezed.

Dr. Hill’s face didn’t move a muscle.

“Listen, um, why do you need that thing?” I pointed to the leering ultrasound machine. “Isn’t that only for pregnancies?”

“No, no. We use ultrasounds for cervix exams *all* the time. They’re very non-invasive, so I figured it would be best to use in your scenario.” Dr. Erikson spoke coolly, as casually as if he was forecasting rain. But something about his expression made my heart quicken.

“No need to worry,” he reassured, “we’ll have you right as rain in no time. Dr. Hill, if you wouldn’t mind?”

A full body chill swept over me when he said that. Rain. Rain. Go away. I laid my head down and went back to counting ceiling tiles. I’d counted them eight times already. There were sixteen of them in total. Fitted together like an aerial jigsaw puzzle.

Dr. Hill and Dr. Erikson started muttering to one another, using terms and vocabulary that I couldn’t make sense of. I tried my best to tune them out, which wasn’t very hard to do, because the sound of rushing blood had overtaken my eardrums.

"Right," Dr. Erikson said, after their discussion ended. "Mrs. Donner, I'm just going to lift up your gown now, okay? You're going to feel a slight coldness on your stomach as I apply some gel."

As promised, a coldness caressed its way up my exposed legs, privates, midriff as the gown was lifted. I shivered, as he squirted freezing liquid all over my stomach, rubbing it smooth across my skin.

The whirring of a machine, followed by screeching electronic beeps, filled the room. I closed my eyes and tried not to openly cringe. I would not show them I was afraid. No.

"Okay, Mrs. Donner. I'm going to start taking some images with the ultrasound here, so please hold still. Again, just a little coldness."

The wand pressed into my belly and began skating across the icy surface. I felt humiliated. Terrified. My skin had never felt tighter. All I wanted to do was burst out of myself and leave this horrible, sterile room forever.

Dr. Erikson and Dr. Hill hovered on either side of me, watching the screen. The plastic wand slid over my stomach. I alternated between squeezing my eyes shut, then up to the ceiling. Quick glance at the screen. Repeat.

Grainy, distorted shapes came into being. None of it seemed to have any real meaning. That couldn't be what was inside of me. This body couldn't be mere white lines and black landscapes. I was more than that. This body was more, so much more than what I saw on the screen. It made me sick to look at.

Dr. Erikson slowly dragged the wand across my gel-smeared belly. Neither he nor Dr. Hill were saying anything. Both of them were watching the screen intently. I realized, with a stark-straight clarity, that they were looking for something.

"Is something wrong?" I asked. My voice came out as a crunchy whisper.

"No, everything is fine, Mrs. Donner, we're just trying to see if..."

Dr. Erikson suddenly stopped moving his hand. His head jerked slightly at the image on the screen. Then, with great care, he pulled back half an inch to where he'd just been.

Dr. Hill leaned forward across my body with interest.

"I told you," he said, almost inaudible. Dr. Hill's brows turned in on each other.

"My," she muttered, "I haven't seen one of those in a minute."

"What? What is it?" I asked, pushing myself to my elbows. I stared at the screen with a sense of frustration. It didn't look like anything to me. Just another shapeless blob.

"How long?" Dr. Erikson asked, completely ignoring me. "What's your estimate?"

"I'd have to do some more tests, but that looks at least 16 or 18 wee—"

"HELLO?" I bellowed. Both of them jumped. Dr. Erikson dropped the ultrasound wand and clutched his chest melodramatically. The wand clattered to the ground.

"Jesus! You have a strong voice," he stammered.

"What the fuck is going on? What's wrong with me?"

My whole chest was vibrating with terror. Dr. Erikson opened his mouth to speak, but Dr. Hill beat him to the punch.

"Mrs. Donner," she said stiffly, "there's no need to be upset. You are perfectly healthy."

"Then what the *hell* is going on?"

The two doctors exchanged a look. Dr. Erikson stooped down to grab the fallen wand and Dr. Hill straightened her shoulders. Then began to talk.

"It seems that you find yourself in the rare percentage, Mrs. Donner," she quipped. "I personally have seen only two other situations such as yours." She paused, out of sadistic pleasure. Why else?

"This may be a bit of a shock to you, given the background you've shared with Dr. Erikson here. But..."

She gestured for Dr. Erikson to finish her sentence. He swallowed.

"Yes, well, cryptic pregnancies are quite rare," he muttered. "Really just a one in five hundred chanc—"

"Cryptic what?" I snapped. "That's impossible."

"No, it's not impossible," Dr. Hill said. "And by the looks of it, you're at least into your second trimester. We'll have to run some more tests so we can accurate verify that, but..."

The rest of Dr. Hill's words became a meaningless blur, a streak of sound with all the distinguishing qualities of static. I watched her mouth move, Dr. Erikson's head tremor, light shine on my gel-wet belly. My unchanged, normal body, which now had something alive and growing inside of it. A person. There was a baby living inside of me.

I pushed myself to the side and leaned over, before vomiting onto the linoleum floor.

~ ~ ~

My car roared down the highway, a chariot of silver grill and black metal. I could not stop panting. From toe to crown, I felt flush with an electric, buzzing heat, the kind you might see writhing atop a Tesla coil. I kept replaying what I had heard over and over, as I raced home to Heaven. To Jack.

A cryptic pregnancy. One in five hundred. Ninety-eight percent chance that the condom should have worked. The good news was that I wasn't like some women, who didn't know they were pregnant until labour. What would you like to do moving forward? Surgical abortion, that'd be the only option this late into the game. Although I wouldn't recommend it. No, I would not. Does your family have any history of abnormal pregnancies? Does your family have a history of unusual births?

This last part had made me huck laughter at the two of them, a mad, barking chuckle. They had both flinched at the sound. I was ushered out with a few pamphlets and a pat.

"Everything will be okay, Mrs. Donner," Dr. Erikson had said, hand on my back. "I can promise you that—"

"Get your hand off me," I'd threatened, before snatching the pamphlets out of his grip. With a sickly vertigo sensation, I'd stormed out of the clinic, and threw myself into the car. I'd driven so fast out of the parking lot I'd almost mowed down a woman and her stroller with my Lincoln.

Jack. Jack. Jack. Something wasn't right. Nothing was *right* about this. Somehow he had a hand in this. I knew it, in the depth of my gut. Somehow he was to blame.

The depth of my gut, where that pain was living. Where a fetus was sucking the life out of me. A curled-up parasite, as big as a ripe bell pepper. Living inside me. I had to put the image out of my mind to not throw up again.

I made it home in record time. 20 minutes of burning rubber and I was outside the gates of Heaven, ripping off the chain with my fist. I threw it to the ground without pushing the gates open, then raced back to the driver's seat.

The hood of my car collided with the gates, sending them flying wide with a bang. It felt good to hear that violent sound. To feel the shudder of the vehicle against white metal.

I parked the car in the driveway, killed the engine and tore towards the front door. It opened with ease. No one had remembered to lock it.

"Jack!" I yelled, the moment my feet crossed the entranceway.

My voice hit the skylight and ricocheted back at me, big and spooky. I still could not believe that I sounded like that.

There was no response. The garden stream gurgled away, running between fronds of fern and monstera leaves. Lush. Green. Perfect. Sun rays fell through the open windows, warming the home with late April comfort. No sound at all, except for the stream and sea, just out of sight. But nevertheless, still churning away. I tried again.

"JACK!"

I kicked my shoes off and strode into the house. I marched up and down the hallway, casting the doors open and sticking my head in. All of them came up empty. A ghost house. Again and again: office, bedroom, bathroom, laundry room, garage, closet. Empty empty empty. I swept back down the hall and into the living room, the kitchen. There was still no sign of my husband. I looked out on the deck, ready to investigate its full wrap-around self when it hit me. Of course. How fucking stupid of me.

The basement. Jack was in the basement.

With a bitter sense of satisfaction, I walked to the basement door. Pulled the stone door open. Upon opening, weak light trickled up out of the darkness.

I looked down and saw, dim-lit with candles, that Jack was having a bath. He had his head back, as he floated naked amongst pearly bubbles. I stepped down to the first stair and closed the door behind me. Hard. This woke him up.

"Hello?" he asked warily, sitting to attention.

"Hi, honey," I said through clenched teeth. "It's just me."

With a swish of water, Jack moved positions in the tub, craning his neck up the stairs. From his vantage point, I was entirely cloaked in darkness. He couldn't see me at all.

I took another step down towards him.

"Oh, hey," he said. "How was your appointment?"

Something about his relaxed tone set my bones on edge. He looked like he was at a spa.

The candles cast dancing shadows on the stone walls. The curtain covering the port window had been drawn, blocking out the sun. It was just us, with some fire and water as witnesses.

"Not good," I replied. "I got some bad news."

"Can you come down? I can barely see you."

I crept down the rest of the stairs, until I was almost at the bottom. Jack looked at me, pupils lit up by candlelight. He frowned.

"What kind of bad news?" he asked. His left arm was rested on the lip of the tub, built right into the floor. Even from this vantage point of the bottom stair, I was staring down at him.

I felt my lips curl at the ends.

"I think you know, Jack."

He frowned even deeper at this.

"Um, no. No, I don't." He cocked his head to the side. "Is everything alright?"

I sucked air through my front teeth. Tilted my chin up.

"No," I said. "I'm pregnant."

Both of Jack's eyes widened considerably. His mouth dropped open, making a small popping noise when he did. He sat back deeper into the tub.

"Wow," he said slowly. "That's a surprise."

"Is it?"

"What's that supposed to mean?"

"The doctors told me there's a two percent chance of that happening. With protection."

He gave a little shrug.

"I mean, yeah, but…stuff happens."

"I'm already in my second trimester."

This made his eyes pop. Onyx Ping-Pong balls.

"What? How?"

"It's called a cryptic pregnancy. They're rare, but here we are." I let out a harsh laugh at this, the kind of laugh reserved for hearing someone had died and not knowing what to say. Jack cringed at the sound.

"You seem upset."

This made me laugh again.

"Oh, do I?" I said. "Really? What tipped you off on that, you fucking genius? Does having my worst fear come to life sound right? What do you think?"

"Come on, D, don't be like th—"

"No, you listen to me," I hissed. "I want you to tell me right now how you did this."

"D, I have no idea what you mean—"

"Liar! Fucking liar!"

I stepped down the final stair and stomped over to the tub. Jack looked up at me with surprise. He retreated further into the bath water. I didn't give him a chance to speak.

"You expect me to believe, that after months of having to practically *beg* you to touch me, that all of sudden you want to fuck every day? And so aggressively, too. Like you were angry with me each time. And now, now I just happen to be pregnant. I don't believe that, Jack. You wore protection for years and nothing. So what did you really do?"

Jack glared up at me. He did not look pleased to be yelled at. Accused. For a moment there was only the sound of dripping water, of candle wicks burning shorter.

"Maybe I should ask you the same thing," he cautioned.

"Excuse me? What the fu—"

"I know," he blurted, "about Yvonne. That you've been sleeping together."

Now it was my time for shock. I had dreaded this, the fact that he maybe knew. But to hear it out loud, blunt and true, hurt me deeply. I took a step back from the tub.

Jack looked vindicated by my reaction. He moved closer to me, still submerged.

"Yeah," he said, "I've known since Gabriel's. When I saw you two eating each other's faces beside the house. And I'm not fucking stupid, Dahlia, even though you think I am sometimes. I can tell when you're lying to me. You'd come home freshly showered after seeing her. You were all smiley. And you tasted different. Your cunt tasted different after being over there. That's how I knew for sure."

His whole expression had blackened with gloat. He rose up higher out of the water and kept going.

"After all the shit we've been through, Dahlia," he said, "how could you do something like that to me? How could cheat on me like that?"

I didn't think long about my answer.

"Because, Jack. I was sick of playing this stupid game with you."

"What game?"

"The game that everything is alright! The two of us, pretending we still love each other. That we could ever possibly go back to the way things were. It's a bunch of bullshit. I know it, and you do too. So I gave up."

"You gave up? That's your answer?"

"Yes, *Jack,*" I said, punctuating his name with toxin. "That's my fucking answer. You are such a letdown as a husband. You know that? You do nothing with your life. You don't work or go out or make any friends. And you've never looked at me the same since. Never."

His eyes narrowed.

"You know damn well why."

"Yes, I do! You've made that crystal-fucking-clear why you can't get over shit. But you know what? I can't wait forever, Jack. This life is short. I don't have time to sit around and wait for you to figure out how to love me properly again."

"I can't believe you right now, turning this on me."

He stood up, naked and dripping, and got out of the tub. He towered over me as he wrapped a towel around his waist.

"You can be such a selfish person, Dahlia. You really have no idea how hard this has been for me. This whole year has been hell. Fucking hell. And all you can think about is yourself."

"That's not tru—"

"It is true! Listen to yourself! All you can think of is me me me! You're such a hypoc—"

I slapped him. I rose to my tiptoes and smacked his talking face as hard as I could. It made a crisp sound that echoed through the basement. Jack recoiled in shock.

Then he did something I didn't think he was capable of. He shoved me back in return.

My body went flying backwards from the force. With a thud, I crashed onto the floor, a bolt of pain searing up my spine from the unforgiving stone. For a second, my vision went grey as scorching hot nerves flared up in agony. I couldn't breathe.

Then, ever so slowly, I came back to myself again. I was flat on my back a few feet from Jack. More than a few. And he was staring at me, with a horrified expression on his face.

"You pushed me," I said, my voice coming out mangled and gaspy. I couldn't believe it. I was shocked mostly, and obviously angry. But a tiny part of me was also proud. That there was that side to him too, after all.

"Dahlia, I'm so sorry, I don't kno—"

"Stop. Just stop." I held up my hand to silence him, and then pushed myself to my feet again. I would not allow him to see me weak like that. With some strain, I made myself big. Jack responded with the desired effect. His eyes went white with fear.

"You—you can do that. I knew it, I knew I wasn't—"

"Jack," I said, digging into my low voice. His name came out like air escaping an opened tomb. "Just tell me the truth."

I put a hand to my stomach, eyes on him.

"Did you do this to me?"

My husband stared at me in disbelief. With a hawk's gaze I studied his face, watching his reaction to my question. His eyes didn't flinch. His features stayed inert. But when he spoke, his voice dipped ever so slightly, just like it always did when he was spooning a lie down my throat.

"No," he said, "I did not."

It was the final straw. With ease, I retracted back into myself. I shot him my meanest, coldest look, and made a move for the staircase.

"You're full of shit," I proclaimed. "I can tell. You're such a fucking coward."

I took the first couple of stairs in stride and then turned around. Jack stood there, a too-tall man in a towel, backlit by candlelight. He looked miserable. A freak.

"I never want to see you again," I said. "I want you out of my house. Right now. You can pack up a suitcase and leave. I'll get the rest of your shit boxed up. But I want you gone."

Jack's mouth dropped open again. He stepped towards the stairs.

"Dahlia, please, you're being craz—"

"I'm being smart for once, Jack. Not like when I made you my husband. No, that was probably the dumbest thing I've ever done. I mean, look at you." I gestured to his naked torso below me. "You're a sorry excuse for a man. And you'd make an even worse father."

Jack's eyes flared at this comment.

"Don't say that."

"I just did. And you know what? I mean it. I mean every goddamn word. You couldn't save your mother, or yourself, and you certainly couldn't save me. Now…" I paused to smack my stomach. "You wouldn't be able to save your own fucking kid."

"NO! What's wrong with you?"

Jack began to scramble up the stairs. I was standing in the middle, halfway between him and freedom. I took a few steps backwards, my hand on the railing.

"You can't get rid of it! You can't!" Jack faltered, before he reached up to my level. He put a hand out to my side, which I batted away.

"Don't fucking touch me!"

"Dahlia, please! Please don't say that!"

He grabbed onto my shirt again, and I realized with disgust that he was crying. Out of nowhere, he was tearing up, sobbing. He knelt his head and kept pleading.

"Dahlia, wait, please! You can't! Please don't—"

"I said get the fuck off!"

"Dahlia, I lov—"

I brought my foot back and kicked him square in the chest. There was the solid feeling of bone, as my heel collided with his ribcage. And then there was no sensation. Just air.

Jack tumbled backwards into empty space. As he turned, I got a good look at his face, wet with tears. Eyes glazed with a hurricane of emotion. Lips parted with words he would never get to say.

He crumpled backwards on himself, his high centre of gravity coming to fuck him over one last time. Like a drunken gymnast, he backflipped once, making a tremendous cry as he did: a popping of bone against stone, a swoop of towel being ripped from his waist.

Then, as quickly as it had begun, it was over. He smashed onto the basement floor with his full momentum. The sound of something being broken, of a skull connecting with stone. And then Jack was still. Blood, black under the candlelight, started to pool around his naked, twisted body. I couldn't see his face any longer. Only his chest, not rising and falling.

I couldn't move for several seconds. The world had frozen on its axis, suspended me in this moment of excruciating understanding. *I just killed my husband.* He was dead, or very near to it. The amount of blood coming from his body was vast, unimaginable for a living soul.

After an eon of silence, populated only by my shallow breaths, I turned away from his body and crawled the rest of the way up the stairs. When I got to the top, I shut the door. Curled up against the wall on the other side. The light from the sun went on shining. The ocean waves frothed away. Nothing had changed. Yet everything was completely different.

Then, on second thought, I stood up just high enough to reach the door bolt, sliding it into the locking position. Just in case. It snapped shut with a crack. *Fin.*

~ ~ ~

It didn't take long to pack. My mind seemed to be operating on ancient hardware, working on something close to autopilot. My suitcase filled itself up with the essentials. Clothes. Passport. Toiletries. Any cash I'd forgotten to deposit. I shed the ring from my finger. I had no mementos that I wanted to take. Everything I had ever truly loved was gone. Because of me.

I swept through the house, locking it tight. Opened up the electrical panel and killed it dead. All the crackling sounds of electricity, imperceptible to any human ear, went quiet. It was a relief to hear such emptiness. Too bad I wasn't going to be here to enjoy it.

Still sore from my fall, I lugged the suitcase to the garage with a series of grunts. Jack's white convertible sat waiting in creamy anticipation. I wanted to take his car instead of my Lincoln, which was a gas-guzzler and a beast to drive. Also, if people went looking for a car, they would probably start with mine. Not that it mattered. Not really.

I shoved the suitcase into the trunk, slammed it shut, then resurrected the Porsche's engine. It awoke with a purr, interior lights flashing. I clicked the electronic garage door opener and drove through the rectangle of light. Then I hopped out to drive my Lincoln safely into the garage, leaving the keys to sit on the seat. Once done, I carried on in the convertible up the driveway, pushing the button to close the garage door as I went.

At the top, I got out of the car one last time. The heavy chain laid discarded amongst the wild grasses bordering the driveway's entrance, rippling. With great care, I swung the gates of Heaven closed and wrapped the metal chain around the middle. The padlock teeth snicked together with delight, happy to be reunited again.

Then I gave one last look at the paradise below me. My home. Far beyond the rooftop, the ocean stretched out with a restless, sparkling fever. The air was rich with the scent of blossoms. I took in the sight of Heaven, sealed up once and for all. Then got into my dead husband's convertible, pushed the button that put the top down, and drove away.

I couldn't stop my hands from shaking.

Part Three

Lament

1.

Darkness. The Earth had died and left me darkness.

Pain. Something cold. Hard.

And sticky.

I opened my eyes and shut them again. There was no change. I was in the stomach of black, the gut of suffering. My whole body was made of broken glass, stuffed under skin. I tried to move and succeeded in only twitching. Copper. Pennies. I had eaten pennies and they had melted on my tongue.

"Heu-le."

The P wouldn't come out. Wouldn't form. I tried again, unkinking my neck. It cracked as I slid it out straight, against the crusty coagulation suckered against my left ear. Again.

"Heu-le. Heu-le. Puh."

Where am I?

I squeezed my eyes closed. Listened to my breathing. Shallow. Ragged. It didn't want to continue. My lungs were conspiring to kill me. I tried to move again. Roll out from over my arm, scrunched beneath me. Immediately a knife-shock of pain shot up my arm to my shoulder. But I managed, barely, to roll onto my stomach.

Smuck. My body rolled onto the sticky stuff spread out onto the floor. Old jam? It stunk, too, of pennies.

Blood. I was laying atop semi-dried blood.

With my chest flat on the floor, arms on either side, I stretched my legs out. My bones creaked. I greedily sucked gulps of air between my lips. Irregular. I could hardly muster up the strength to gasp, to take in—

where am I?

—those precious swallows of oxygen. My legs filled up with pins and needles. Blood. Something was still flowing inside me. Good. Somewhere inside, a heart was still beating.

WHERE AM I?

This time the question was a shriek. Almost audible. I closed my eyes again (or were they already?) and stepped back in time. More darkness. More black. More empty empty nothingness, where the sun did no—

Sun. Something about the word stuck out. Emboldened. I zeroed in on it, repeated it. Sun. Sun. Sun. The word bounced around the echo chamber that was my skull. It brought more nothing. And then slowly, *slowly,* a picture.

A skylight. A garden, too overgrown to be indoors. Water. Water flowing from a stream, in between bent-tipped leaves, over polished stones—

Stone. Basement.

Heaven. I was in the basement.

No.

Our basement.

No.

Her basement.

Her. Like a face floating through gauze, she swam into being. Black torrential hair, cast around the face like a halo. A medusa. The hair was alive, serpents flicking scarlet tongues and coming to bite me. Then gone. Then hair, once again, only hair. And a face. And eyes.

Eyes that hurt. Green eyes, scattershot blue. Fractured. Bright. Sharp. Staring out from a face that also seemed to hurt. It didn't seem like a normal face. It was a face to be feared, admired, watched from a distance. From a mile away. Or a lifetime. And yet:

Love.

There was a warmth rising within me. A dawn, happening at the back of my throat. It grew, swelled with heat and scorched the roof of my mouth. The name fought its way out of me. It hurt to say. But the moment I heard it echoed back from the cold basement walls, I knew it was home. My home.

"Dah-l-ia."

~ ~ ~

An hour or a century. It was hard to say. One of the two it took to stand. To my knees. I could still see nothing, absolutely nothing, so I had to crawl to rediscover the world. Only a few feet forward was a dip. A basin. I leaned my hand forward and recoiled. Ice-cold water.

Images of the bath, lit by an orange glow, flickered in and out of existence. My bare skin felt wrinkly, numb. The whole left side of me was caked in flaky slime. Moving took energy I did not have. I barely had been up for a moment before I collapsed again. My left shoulder screamed at me. As did I. The sound bounced around the basement, a trapped bird.

Something very clear spoke to me. Time. I did not have much time. If the blood on the floor was all mine, then I had very little time. My head was blurry with thoughts. Sounds. Questions. But the need to get out of this pitch darkness was by far the strongest.

The need yelled itself hoarse within me. To get out. Get up. *Hurry.*

I lifted myself up to my knees. I could not put pressure on my left arm, unless I wanted a jolt of agony to slither up my nervous system. I used it as a kind of counterweight, letting it dangle below me as I shuffled my right hand along, lugging the rest of my body with it.

As I moved, my mouth made all sorts of noises that didn't sound remotely like a real person. Choking, animalistic grunts. The enfolding of air in on itself, like some dilapidated bagpipe stuffed down a man's windpipe. And curses. Lots of curses.

"Fu-ack! Af-auck!"

I was moving away from the water. Towards, what I hoped to be, the stairs. The dark was inexpressibly whole. A void, a universe that I had awoken to: coasting adrift through empty space. Except this wasn't empty space.

There was a stone floor beneath me, gummy with blood. Somewhere forward, there were stairs. And at the top: freedom.

All I had to do was get to the top.

I could barely drag myself across a flat floor. How was I supposed to get up an entire staircase?

Be quiet, I thought to myself.

I meant to follow it with my own name, and for a second, it lapsed out of me. A chalk smudge where a name should've been.

Jack.

My name was Jack.

The loss of identity, no matter how brief, made me freeze up. It was like the emptiness that surrounded me had seeped into my*self,* was devouring my own persona. For a second I could not will myself to crawl another inch. I was on the verge of falling inwards. Back to the floor. And if I fell again, I knew

I might not be able to get up once more. My will would be dead for good.

No. Who are

You?

I dragged myself another inch. Again.

Again.

On the fourth, profane-laced movement, my fingers hit something vertical.

Cold. Stone. Stairs.

Yes.

Very slowly, I eased my weight to my right side. Just as I'd hoped, my shoulder bumped into the wall face, and I leaned into it. For a moment: relief. My body was half-supported by stone, as I caught my breath. I squeezed my eyes open and closed, to feel some sensation on my face. Otherwise, it felt like I didn't have a face at all. Nor eyes.

Who am I?

My name is

Jack. I leaned forward, harpooning the crown of my head towards stairs. I collided with the second step with a *thunk.* Using my skull as a kind of crutch, I pushed my right hand as close as I could to the bottom, distributing my weight between the wall face and my head. It hurt like fucking hell.

With a sort of gasp-scream, I lifted my hand up, as quick as I could. With a crash, I brought it up onto the first stair, whilst also collapsing my weight onto my left arm by mistake. It flared up with anger.

"Fuack!"

But I had made it. One stair. With my head still leaning forward, digging into the groove that was a higher stair, I pulled the rest of my body closer.

All the exertion was getting my blood pumping, which meant that my legs were starting to be of some use again. They pushed and slid on the viscous floor. What it also meant, however, was that my mind became foggier.

Something was very wrong with my head. That much was clear.

I repeated my mantra again. Added some more to it.

My name is

Jack.

Anthony.

Donner.

Each word felt like a resistant bottom feeder being pulled from the depths. But up they came, regardless. It spurred me on, this reclamation of title. Name. I knew who I was.

Head forward, body to the side. Hand up.

No crash. But another stair. My balancing act of weight paid off this time. No searing pain branded my action forward. Despite myself, I think I actually smiled. I tried again.

My name is

Head. Wall. Hand. Up—

JACK

And forward. Another godforsaken stair.

I was panting from effort. Beads of moisture had christened my forehead, were sliding down to sting my eyes with salt. I squeezed them shut, not needing them anyway. Repeat.

MY NAME IS JACK

And my confidence got the better of me. The front of my body smashed into the side of the stairs, sending razor-tipped pain up the side of my face, across my chest, all through my arm. I scrambled with my back legs to get a footing, to stop myself from sliding all the way back down to the bottom. I let out a howl of frustration.

"Agck!"

Everything was so cold. The wall, the stairs, the floor. Cold, cold stone. Yet my body was overheating, boiling up from the inside. Together, the two extremes were unbearable, too much for anyone to—

MY NAME IS JAC

Keep going. But something old and powerful had awoken in me, had begun its war cry for victory. I could not give up. No. I would not die here, not like this. I had to climb higher.

Another stair.

Pain. Gasps. Swears. Stone. *How—*

Another.

Old was I? I had to focus on something else, besides the journey that seemed impossible to summit, besides the raking talons of pain across my body, boring into my brain. The face from before was gone. The name that was not my own: gone.

Everything was as black and empty as the darkness around me. I was my only anchor against oblivion.

Who am I?

MY NAME IS JACK I AM—

Another motherfucking stair.

28 YEARS OLD

No? Yes. Yes. I am. *I AM 2—*

Grunt. Head. Wall. Gasp. Hand.

8 YEARS OLD. AND I LIVE—

Another.

IN CANADA. MY NA—

Another.

ME IS JACK. I AM—

And over. And over. And over.

Until there was, gloriously:

The top.

I reached up and smacked my hand against the stone door. The rapture of pain on my knuckles could've brought me to tears if I hadn't been crying already. My long body was sprawled down half a dozen of the stairs. I was just barely hanging on to hold my position.

I had given up on not using my left arm out of necessity. It sizzled and swore at me with pure hatred, but my labours were not in vain. I was here. At the top.

"Yus!" I babbled with relief. "Yus!"

As slowly as I could muster, I wiggled over to the other side, careful not to lose my grip and slide all the way to the bottom. With my weak legs, I kicked myself higher, just enough so I could reach the door handle. My heart was pounding, close to rupturing. It had taken every last drop of willpower to get here. Now all I needed to do was get to the other side, to a phone. Call for help.

My hand spider-walked up the door. I felt around for the handle, found it, pulled down. It jiggled easily. With my right shoulder leaned against the door, I pressed as hard as I could to open it. Nothing. I tried again, even harder. Nothing.

Now my heart was really racing. A shot of terror had been administered straight to the source. I must be pushing the wrong way. That must be it. How could the door be locked from the outside?

Again, I wriggled over to the other side, although not as far this time. Just enough to get out of the way of the swinging door. I dug around with my hand, scrambling for the handle. My whole arm was shaking, quivering from struggle and pain. The cold handle filled up my hand. With all my might, I jiggled the handle down, then pulled the door towards me. It had to open. It had to.

The stone door stayed locked tight.

~ ~ ~

I cried myself to sleep. I'd tried beating against the door, pushing, pulling it. Willing it to crumble off its hinges. I'd groped around, certain there must be a lock-switch for me to turn, to pull across. Instead, I'd found a light-switch. I'd flicked it up. Down. Up. Nothing.

When that didn't work, I'd yelled for help. My shouts were shredded, senseless pleas. They reverberated around the depths of the basement and came back empty.

Utterly exhausted and at my wit's end, I had finally slumped down on the top stair, leaned against the wall to stop from falling, and cried. The darkness drank up my tears.

Eventually, sleep came. Or rather, unconsciousness. I dreamed of nothing. Just more blackness and cold stone. When I woke, I forgot where I was all over again.

Once again, I had to calm myself down by repeating my identity mantra.

My name is Jack. I am 28 years old.

I live in Canada. On the west coast.

I am in the basement.

Whose basement?

My basement. No. *My—*

DA—

Wife's basement.

No. Our basement.

There's been an accident. A terrible accident.

And I am alone.

Why was I alone?

I couldn't think about that right now. The question started a new pain inside of me, an ache that seemed to go on forever inside my heart. So I shut it down. Stayed focused on the present moment. Which wasn't hard to do with my whole body screaming at me.

I had to try something else. The door wasn't going to open. Not without help. I closed my eyes and tried to remember the basement. *Our* basement.

First: stairs. The mental picture was hazy, like looking at an old photograph at twilight. I could see the stairs clearest because I had just gruelingly traversed them. But what was beyond them? What was at the bottom?

I squeezed my eyes even harder, willing my mental self to travel down the image of stairs. Room at the bottom. Rectangle-shaped. Sparse. Something strange here, unusual. What was it? Something on the walls, a bench, a sitting area? Shel—

water

Cold water! The basin. The bath. Yes, I could see that now too. Right near the base of the stairs was a bath, built right into the floor. Only that wasn't it. Not entirely. There was something else I was missing.

I tried to scan the mental basement, squeezing the image until answers were juiced. But nothing came. Not a drop. I opened my eyes again with a sigh and laid my head back. What the fuck was I going to do?

Pretty soon, it became obvious that I would need to go back down the stairs. It seemed like a spectacularly cruel result for all the effort it had taken to ascend them. But there was nothing to be had at the top.

No victory. No freedom.

With a great and heavy reluctance, I began to slide down the freezing cold stone stairs. Completely naked. In the pitch darkness. I used my right hand to steady myself, to slow my descent to a sluggish pace. I hated every single second of it.

Every now and then, I had to pause and pull my testicles out from under my pelvis, to stop them from dragging under me. They were unrecognizable to the touch, encrusted with dried blood, and shrivelled from the damp cold. I shivered at their alienness.

After several minutes of controlled sliding, I arrived at the bottom stair. The floor was as frigid as ever, practically gnawing into my skin. But there was another surprise waiting for me, which warmed me up considerably when I saw it.

There. On the wall. A little thread of light behind fabric.

Of course.

The port window.

~ ~ ~

With my back against the wall, I looked out at the basement from my position on the floor. After ripping the curtain to the ground, the basement had become illuminated by a buttery glow.

I could see the sleeping area, carved out with a single mattress. Wooden table and chairs in the centre of the room. A series of stone shelves to my left, and the staircase leading to nowhere on my right. It was a dismal scene. I scanned my eyes back and forth, trying to locate something I could use to break the window. Nothing jumped out.

A huge brown smear covered the floor. Dried blood. You could still see the outline from where my body had been. I could also see the purplish green tint of my left arm, broken in more than one place. I kept my eyes elsewhere. My vision ran filmy grey. Woozy.

Come on, I prayed. *Please. Something.*

Moving up and down the stairs had taken its toll on me. I could barely stay awake. My eyes fluttered shut, then jerked open again. More darkness. The sight of it scared the shit out of me. With my right hand, I slapped my face. Pinched my legs.

On my wrist, a faint sound that I hadn't noticed before ticked on. A Rolex watch, blue, the colour of ice. The glass was cracked, but the second hand moved on.

8 minutes past 9 o'clock.

Outside, the sun grew stronger. High tide. The ghostly splash marks of water speckled the window as the surf chewed against rock. Slowly consuming it over eternity.

Again, I scoured the room. There had to be *something.* The chairs were too big to wield in my state. Too heavy. The shelves, from my vantage point, all seemed empty. There were no cupboards or other furniture: everything besides the table set was all stone. I couldn't fathom why a person would ever come down here. It was so cold. Primitive. Unwelcoming.

My best bet, I figured, was the shelves. Gingerly, I eased my body into a crawling position and started to inch ahead. Pain everywhere. All my attention went straight to keeping my shaky frame from collapsing. My brain stopped boiling with thoughts that made no sense. The world shrunk to the size of a pinhead.

Pain. Shuffle. Breath.

Pain. Shuffle. Breath.

Bit by bit. Until I had reached the chairs. With my head, I pushed one to the side, and began plowing it forward. Mercifully, the chair slid. I repositioned myself over, to angle my body straight towards the wall. With the chair in front of me, I began to push it on with the top of my head, crawling on three half-working limbs.

Pain. Shuffle. Push. Breath.

Pain. Shuffle. Push. Breath.

It was exhausting work. My whole circuit of nerves was on hyperdrive, delirious with the call to STOP. To lay down and STOP moving. To STOP trying. To STOP. To die.

Pain. Shuffle. Push. Gasp.

Pain. Shuffle. Push. Gasp.

Pain. Shuffle. Pu—

Thunk.

The back of the chair hit the wall. I peered up, almost in disbelief that I had made it. Up above were the three stone shelves. They looked higher than stars. I blinked thickly, took a few deep breaths. Then tried to mount the chair.

My face planted into the chair's seat, which was made of wicker. It scratched at my cheek and tried to break skin. With my one good hand, I quickly transferred it onto the chair's seat beside my mushed face. Pushed up. My legs kicked beneath me, driving me forward.

By the grace of some god, I managed to get halfway onto the chair seat. It shook as I dragged the rest of my body up.

For a moment, I thought all hope was lost when it leaned forward on its front legs for a split second. And then it was back, *bang,* on all fours, and I was precariously crouched on the seat, knees bent under me, body in fresh agony.

YES! YES! YES!

I didn't want to celebrate out loud. Not to jinx the fickle scales of luck. With a series of rough breaths, I planted my right hand against the wall and straightened up. Reached for the heavens with my oversized torso. I easily collided with the bottom of the three shelves. I grabbed onto it, and used it to pull myself up a bit higher. My hand grasped around on the shelf-top, desperate and hungry.

Nothing. There was nothing on the fucking shelf.

I kept my head leaned against the wall for balance and reached up higher.

Second shelf. Grasp grasp grasp. Nothing.

Again. Higher. Only this time, my body wouldn't stretch that far. Not without failing and tumbling down to the floor. I could feel my limits overreaching. Defeat. I tried the second shelf, grasping around blindly. Nothing but nothing. And cold shelf stone.

Sinking deeper into horror, I brought my hand back to the bottom shelf, sliding my head down the wall as I did. The chair trembled beneath me. Last chance. If there was truly nothing for me to use, nothing to break the window, then I was screwed. Fucked.

No. Worse.

I was dead.

My hand reached around. Patted the surface of the shelf with militaristic precision. It came up with a fat lot of emptiness. There was nothing on the shelf. Absolutely nothing.

But the shelf. I was on my third round of anxious patting when I noticed something. A crack. A divot. Abnormal, given that the rest of the shelf was all dolphin-smooth. I cranked my head back, chin dug into the wall, and stared up. Squinted.

A worker's flaw. Maybe? Perhaps. It was too early to say. I looked up and saw a hairline-thin line, zigzagging like a lightning bolt from front to back on the bottom of the shelf.

Where the wall met the shelf was another line, except this one was straight, uniform. It ran from one end to the other, adjacent to the wall. It could only mean one thing.

The shelves weren't carved out of the stone wall. They had been made separately. Then added on afterwards. So it seemed. There was only one way to find out.

I turned my head back towards the wall, planting my forehead against it as a crutch. My third eye crinkled from the stone kiss. Then I moved my hand so it was clutching the centre of the shelf, grasping the front of it. Squeezed my fingers as hard as they could muster. Said a prayer to whoever was listening. Or watching. Then pulled back.

The shelf inched forward. Barely. Was it a trick? I let go, craned my neck up, and saw a miracle. The straight line running along the wall had widened. Become a crevice.

"Yes!" I cried. Superstition be damned. "Fuck yes!"

Once again, I jammed my forehead against the wall, grabbed hold of the shelf above me and pulled it away from the wall. And once again, it inched forward on its brackets: three iron rods, drilled into the wall to support the slab of stone.

When I finally saw them exposed, penetrating into the rock, I could've wept with joy.

"Yes! Thank you!"

My legs were cramping ferociously atop the chair, back muscles straining. I kept feeling close to blacking out. But I was nearly there. All I needed to do was:

Twist my legs to the side, so I was sideways to the wall. This meant leaning my left arm against the wall face, which brought more yells of pain. I reached up with my right hand to grab onto the shelf, to pull it off the brackets for good. My hope was that it would smash onto the stone floor, nice and hard. And the worker's flaw, or what I *hoped* to be a worker's flaw, would be my ticket to salvation.

Steady. I pulled the shelf out further, felt it teeter on the edge of the brackets. I yanked my hand towards my bare chest.

The shelf fell like divine intervention. It hit the floor with a stupendous crash and was still. In reaction, I instinctively closed my eyes. For a second, I couldn't bear to open them and risk seeing the shelf whole, still in one piece. I balanced on the chair, shaking with fear. Exhaustion. Hopelessness. Then, slowly, I peeked one eye open and looked.

Whoever had built this house had made a mistake. They'd broken one of the stone shelves, had cracked a third of it off accidentally. Instead of making a new one, they had sealed the two pieces together with adhesive. Then stuck it on the wall.

Or so I imagined. It didn't really matter why, or how the lightning-shaped crack came to be. It didn't matter if my imaginary story about a clumsy stonemason was full of shit. All that mattered was that when I looked down, a third of the shelf had broken off cleanly.

It was lying there, in a patch of sun, separated from the whole. And in my eyes, I had never seen anything more beautiful in my entire life.

~ ~ ~

With my underwear on and a shirt draped over my head, I was banging against the window with the broken shelf piece. I had to do it backwards, since I couldn't hold my body upright any longer without verging on blackout.

So instead, I had my back to the wall, directly below the window. With my working right hand, I was hitting backwards, smashing the glass as hard as I could. Which wasn't very hard. Doing anything, even breathing, seemed to take too much effort.

Lie down, my pain said.

Stop. Go to sleep.

Sleep meant death. Stopping meant death. Anything that did not involve breaking the window and crawling through it meant death. I had paused only once since starting, to go over to the bath and lap up water like a dog. The taps were in the far corner, out of reach unless I'd wanted to climb in. I'd had to settle for drinking soapy bathwater instead.

Then back to work. Shirt overhead to stop the (hopeful) rain of glass.

Bang. Bang. Bang.

My arm had gone numb from use. It was a stranger's appendage, moving on its own accord. Nothing my body did seemed to come from an active place of thought. I watched my arm swing up and down, a disembodied pendulum bearing a fistful of square stone.

Bang.

Bang.

Bang.

Ban—

Crack.

It was the sound I had been lusting to hear. My heart leapt to the top of my throat, and I leaned forward to glance up at the glass. A sizable fissure in the window was visible, neon white in the sunlight. A smile spread across my face. There was hope after all.

Bang.

Crack.

Bang.

Cra—

And the window was no more. A cloudburst of broken glass hailed down onto me. It made a tinkling sound as it clattered onto the stone floor, a glockenspiel of destruction. A whoop of triumph, weary and hardly audible, tumbled from my mouth.

"Ya!"

Too came the ocean. Suddenly the waves were loud, tangible. The sound of their heads butting against the other side of the wall was formidable.

Shaking glass from the shirt on my head, I threw it over to the side, to land on top of my crumpled pants. I was going to have to swim, and clothes would only slow me down.

Immediately after throwing my shirt away, I realized I had made a mistake. There were still shards of broken glass all over the floor. I could've used it as a thin layer of cover, as I turned around to climb out the window. Fuck. Wincing before I could even feel shards, I peeled away from my sitting position against the wall and turned around on my knees. My skin dug into glass dust, grinding it into further powder.

I swore again. But it didn't matter now. I was in the home stretch.

I positioned the wicker chair so it was directly beneath the circular hole. I repeated my manic climb atop it, using my head as a crutch. As I did, my feet inevitably pushed down into the floor, right atop chunks of broken glass. The sensation was horrific.

I let out a powerful shriek as I dragged my knees up and onto the chair's seat. Now I could see clearly out the port window.

The sea beyond was thrashing under the morning sun. Sharp glass littered the circular passage, which I blew on with queasy sighs. The shards did not budge. The realization that I was going to have to swim was hitting me with frightening clarity.

My body already felt like it weighed a ton. The idea of throwing myself into wild, frigid water seemed like madness. I had an image of jumping from the window and immediately sinking to the bottom of the ocean. It wasn't very deep so close to shore, but certainly not enough to stand on. And regardless, I would need to swim out, away from the foundation of the house, to get to dry land.

Once again, I clenched my eyes shut, trying to remember what was beyond the stone grotto I was emerging from. Was there a dock, just out of sight? To the left or to the right? Nothing was coming to mind, and the ceaseless splashing of saltwater was penetrating my mind. All I could see was bubbles and breakers. Bits of kelp. And a bloated, drowned body, which would soon be me.

NO NO NO

I couldn't afford to think like that. Not after everything. I would have to swim.

On a single trembling hand, I pulled myself up onto the lip of the window. The feeling of broken glass had sunken into obscurity, and all my attention was on the frothing water below me. I could do this. I had to.

I leaned forward, over the window's edge. Closed my eyes to brace for impact. Then I pitched my near-nude body forward into the ocean.

~ ~ ~

The water was colder than I could've dreamed. It swallowed me up, made the air in my lungs expel upon entry. A thousand, no, million blade tips all plunged into my body from every side. It was a revelation, to feel that much pain all at once. My vision went completely black, and I was sure I was dead. Nothing could come back from…

And then my twisted legs were kicking under me. And the roiling surf was pushing me, not down but up. A moment later, and I emerged: gasping, yelling, spluttering stinging cold water from my lips, my right arm clawing and digging at the surface to keep me afloat, my left dangling like an amputation.

The waves prodded and pulled, pushing me back towards the stone, then further into the depths. I mad-dog-paddled away from the stone foundation, out of the grotto. Then I was out, into the open water.

Blinding light scorched my eyes. It was so intense that my world was transformed into white, a ghostly sheen of spraying water droplets and sun. My mouth was wide, as I started screaming like never before. Seawater rushed in between my teeth, trying to choke me out.

"HE-*gul*-P! H-*als*-P!"

I couldn't see where I was going. I couldn't see anything but water and light, water and light. The cold: sucking my final remains of energy with each stroke of my cramping arm. Bare legs egg-beating. I squinted and shrieked and spun, directionless, alone in the sea.

And then. Bobbing just out of the corner of my left eye. A flash of brown.

A dock. A wooden dock.

With every last ounce of adrenaline, I began to swim-crawl my way left. The currents were enraged at this attempt of escape, and they slashed at me with liquid nails. I would not stop. I kicked and clawed at the sea, head bobbing up and below the surface, mouth shut, stopping the influx of brine down my throat.

It seemed like it was getting further away. The dock was floating away, and I was too: regressing into the ocean. No amount of violent thrashing was getting me closer. I was a lost cause. Dead. Dead dead dead in the water. I was dead.

From miles away, a boat was plowing through the ocean, due west. A ship, chartered for Asia, for the Panama Canal. As it blasted forward, leaking oil and battering marine life, a wake of water trailed behind. A reminder of what human power looked like. And as that wake galloped across the harbour, it swelled, grew in strength. Before colliding with a sort of aquatic vindication into me.

All of a sudden, my body was rising up with the tide. Then I was rushing, falling down and forward, back to the shore. Towards the dock. I did not waste this gift. I kicked with all the fight I had left inside me, towards the stretch of wood, and smashed into it. It sent electric pain through my torso, but I could not care less. I had made it. Almost.

With my right hand as guide, I pushed myself down the length of the dock. Towards the gleaming silver ladder, waiting for me. I grabbed hold of it, lost my grip, tried again. Got a clear holding of the metal. With my legs screaming blue murder beneath me, I hooked my foot on the bottom submerged rung and pushed up.

The top half of my body emerged from the ocean. I flopped forward and dragged the rest of me up, onto the wooden dock. It was dry and scratchy with splinters. Nothing had ever felt better.

Some part of me was laughing. Maniacally. I heard this laughter through waterlogged ears, certain it had to be someone else. Until I felt the ache of my chest, rising to the sound. It was me. I was laughing.

I rolled over on the dock and looked up. The sky was an empty blue that didn't look real. It was a paint job, a sham. The sun glared down, white as bird shit. Still. The warmth did feel nice.

My whole body was shaking. Shivering. I closed my eyes and tried to catch my breath, which was near-close to hyperventilating. Through the skin of my lids, the sun took on a red, haloed appearance. A blood-soaked eye. Staring down, right at me.

2.

A year is a little thief. When you aren't looking, when your arms are full of worries and your vision is nothing but short, it comes. Under the cover of moonless nights and denial, it comes. And before you can prepare, it has opened its jaws wide and swallowed a bite of your life forever. A four season, circle-shaped bite. With five or so degrees tacked on as extra. Meanwhile, Father Time watches and scratches his beard.

Where I live now might as well be on a different planet. The roads are dirt, overrun with a green, narcissistic grass that grows everywhere. Turn around and you can see forever. The mountains are far away, a memory on the horizon. It smells of earth and solitude. Manure, when the wind blows from the east. And the best part is: no one really knows who I am.

I've spent a year in a new house. An old house, really, but new to me. The finishings are entirely outdated: wood paneling lining the inside from top to bottom. Two stories tall, with a dusky-tan exterior and white roof trim. When the sun sets, the house turns caramel, as if to melt right then and there. But it never does. The old house, at the end of the road, holds.

At first, I had tried to return to Heaven. The word, like so many other things, had come back slowly. When it came, it carried the same hollow sound of a stranger's name. It meant nothing to me. I felt no attachment at all. Nor could I remember who'd thought of the name in the first place. Was it me? Or her?

Heaven. It didn't feel like heaven to me. It looked like it, with its all-white construction and oceanfront location. Its privacy, tucked beneath the main road: down a lush driveway that concluded with arbutus trees and a gazebo. And, of course, inside. The entranceway garden, staggeringly large skylight, vaulted ceilings. Windows everywhere. Rooms big enough to fit a rich man's ego. The carved stone basement, which I could not bring myself to re-enter.

I could understand where the name had come from. But there was a heaviness to the air, a profound sadness. No amount of invited sea-breeze could exorcise the house. Those first few weeks home after the hospital had been awful. I felt poisoned by the energy of it. So, after barely a fortnight of bad dreams and wandering down the halls, I had put Heaven on the market. Moved into a hotel room on the eleventh floor until some sucker snapped it up.

This is where I'd spent hours, entrenched in thought. Watching TV. Scrolling my phone, playing simple games. I'd wake up in the morning and lumber down to the lounge. Pour waffle batter onto a sizzling griddle, and then slowly chew it down with a tall glass of orange juice. Coffee made me too anxious. Then I would go back to my room, close the blinds, lay on the king-sized bed. To think. To try and remember.

Every now and then I'd get up. Stretch. Peek outside, where cars had piled up behind each other, blowing horns. I'd think about going swimming in the hotel pool, but never do it. Or Gabriel would call me to talk. Or rather, ask questions: the same damn question, over and over again in different forms. And I'd lie and say what he wanted to hear. That I was fine. No, no, I was okay. Seriously. I'm okay. Don't worry.

~ ~ ~

I'd remembered almost nothing when the ambulance came, called in by a fisherman who had seen my body on the dock. Same with the days that followed. A bottomless sense of horror accompanied those days, laying in a hospital bed with paper-thin sheets. The sense that life had never happened to me. A man without a past.

This had aggravated the doctors, then the police officers who came to interview me. How had I wound up, broken-boned and brain-damaged, at the bottom of my basement stairs? I didn't have an answer for them. I listened to their frantic questions with glazed eyes and the sneaking suspicion that none of this was real. I was in a very long, very bad dream. Any minute now, I was going to wake up. I would wake up and be myself again.

None of this happened. I slept: relentlessly, deeply, dreamlessly. But I would always wake up the same. Still in the extra-long, single hospital bed. Still with my arm in a cast, legs bandaged beneath blankets, head swaddled in tight fabric. Still with a scooped-out cavity of a brain and two names that meant almost nothing. Mine. And my wife's.

Dahlia. This was the name the officers kept using, coming every other day to see if I had improved. Do you have any idea where your wife Dahlia might have gone? What was the reason for your fight, if you can remember? Is she a danger to others? Where is—

Dahlia? The moment the first frowning officer had asked me where *Dahlia* was, I had a sensation close to déjà vu. Really, just a memory, but it felt more otherworldly. It was the same word I had used when I'd first woken up in the basement. And there had been a face along with that name. A mirage of piercing green eyes and black hair. The memory of that, no matter how frightening, had brought me a rush of hope. If I could remember that, then there was a chance that I could remember other things too.

I'd asked to see a picture of my wife. Nobody, of course, had one. My phone was still at Heaven, which was being investigated by forensics. Everything felt so absurd. How could a team of police be rooting around in a home I didn't remember, trying to find more about a wife I didn't know? Towards the end of that first interview with the officer, I had started to laugh. He hadn't understood what seemed so funny. Nor could I have been able to tell him.

2 days later, my cellphone was brought to the hospital. By the grace of muscle memory alone, I was able to unlock it with the four-digit pin. A nurse stood by the bed, watching me as I did. As did a police officer. I could never tell if they were the same one as before.

"Anything of note?" he'd asked, as I swiped aimlessly through my phone.

"Not yet."

He'd sighed. Annoyed.

"Well, let me know when you do. I'll need a photo of your wife as well. Of her face."

"What for?" I'd asked. The request seemed strange to me in my drugged-out state.

The officer had flashed a disgruntled look.

"For the investigation," he'd said, slowing down his speech to a condescending putter.

"Oh. Yeah. Right."

I'd been scrolling through text messages first, secretly dreading what I'd find in my photos app. My messages hadn't been much better. Clearly, I was a very lonely person. There was only one missed text from the past few weeks, from someone named Gabriel.

He'd asked me to grab a beer sometime. The rest were from mailing lists, spam requests. No sign or mention of a "Dahlia" anywhere.

With my uncoordinated thumb, I'd moved through the phone to the photos folder. One thousand, seventy-eight photos and fifty-nine videos awaited me. I clicked photos first. A smorgasbord of images filled the screen. I scrolled and tapped, feeling unsettled.

Puffy clouds. Trees in autumn. A group of people, squished together in a group hug. As I looked at the different images, a widening seemed to be occurring in the back of my head. There was a tingling sensation of distant recognition. A faraway bell, ringing clear.

My thumb scrolled up, further into the past. The camera roll flew past, rocketing me to the top. The end of the line in photographic memory. Upon arrival, a picture on the second row caught my eye, and I clicked on it. Immediately, my bruised chest clenched up.

It was us. Sitting side by side at a restaurant booth. The lighting was mellow, friendly. A pile of fluffy goo sat on the table, literally on fire. Curls of white were scorched brown.

Baked Alaska, my brain whispered, crossing the gap between mystery and meaning.

Yes. A Baked Alaska on the table. But what struck me far beyond the flaming dessert were the two people behind it, grinning ear to ear. I had my arm around her, squeezing her tight as if she might fly away any moment. There was a giddy ecstasy radiating off our faces, as we looked at the waiter holding the camera and smiled like a pair of fools. Unashamed to show how completely and blindly in love they were. We were.

I'd felt completely entranced by the picture. There was so much joy. Love. Bliss. And my wife, *Dahlia,* the woman spoken about through gritted teeth and downcast eyes, the woman I had been told was the reason I was even in this mess. How could this be the same person? This strikingly beautiful woman, crinkling her eyes in a smile too big to be—

"Found something?" the officer had asked sharply, interrupting my reverie.

I'd looked up from the phone to see him and the nurse staring at me in anticipation. I'd swallowed the lump in my throat and nodded.

"Yes. I did."

I'd handed him the phone with the photo of us at the table. He'd taken it, scrutinized it, then dipped his chin in a nod.

"This'll work," was all he'd said.

I'd laid uncomfortably in bed, propped up by lumpy pillows and the inclined mattress. The nurse had flicked her eyes across me. Then away, trying not to stare.

"Oh, and um," I'd started slowly, waiting to get his attention. The officer looked up from my phone.

"I think there's someone we could message," I'd continued. "As a contact. I saw a text from him."

"Good. Which one is he? I'll give the nurse his number to call."

The officer had looked relieved at this news. They'd been trying to locate an emergency contact for me for days.

There was a pause as the name failed me momentarily. Then came back.

"Gabriel," I'd said. "His name is Gabriel."

~ ~ ~

The next morning, I'd awoken to whispered voices. I'd opened my bleary eyes, brought myself out of sleep.

Two nurses and a young couple were standing by the doorway to my room. I'd heard a snatch of "significant memory impairment" and focused in on the conversation. One of the nurses was shaking her head, her back to me.

"…scans we've seen so far, his cranial damage is relatively moderate," she was saying. "What we believe to be happening is more of a psychological response. In some traumatic situations, we see the patient's brain's dissociating from reality, in an attempt to cope wi—"

"Oh, he's awake!" the young woman had interrupted, breaking away from the group to come towards me. The man, her husband, quickly followed.

"Jack! Oh my god, I'm so sorry, we just found ou—"

"Gabe, relax!" the woman had said, pulling him away from me. He had rushed to the bed, frantic-faced, words spilling out like water.

"He doesn't know who we are," she'd chastised gently, rubbing his shoulders.

The man's face had crestfallen, his whole expression crumpled with grief.

"*Ay dios*," he faltered. "How could this have happened?"

I stared at them, this flustered handsome couple, tentatively standing by my bedside. Out of the corner of my eyes I saw one of the nurses leave, while the other stood guard at the doorway.

When I looked back at their faces, an image popped into my head from the day before. From my phone. A group photo of twenty-something people, smiling away in a living room. I recognized the two faces in the middle of the frame. As I'd thought harder, focusing on the memory of the photo, it seemed to come to life. Suddenly the image was kinetic, a part of a larger, real memory of a party, a celebration for my friend, no, my best friend…

“Gabriel,” I’d choked, voice rusty from sleep. The corner of my mouth turned up.

“Irene.”

It was all that I needed to say. My two friends gave each other a look, and then came on either side of the bed to embrace me in an awkward double hug. I’d reciprocated with my one good arm. It wasn’t until they’d pulled away that I saw Gabriel was crying.

“Jack,” he’d said, squeezing my right hand. He’d shook his head in disbelief.

“I’m so sorry.”

I’d looked up at him, a memory of a house party playing in my head. I could see red plastic cups and a cramped living space. Latin music playing in the background. A group of people laughing.

My heart felt light for the first time since I’d arrived. For once, there was evidence that I wasn’t alone in the world after all.

“It’s so good to see you,” I’d mumbled. “So, so good.”

~ ~ ~

Over the next month, Gabriel or Irene would visit me nearly every day. Even for just a few minutes to check in. It was a time of great suffering for me, as I’d had to relearn my life and retrain my brain to work again.

The doctor assigned to my case, Dr. Morrison, talked repeatedly about flushing out my “islands of memory”.

“In extreme TBI and dissociative amnesia cases,” he’d said, “it’s important to build on any islands of memory that you may have. That is, any vivid or detailed moments you can remember.”

He’d paused to look me dead in the eyes.

“Do you understand what I’m saying, Jack?”

I did. With Gabriel as my primary guide, I'd recounted my life, piece by piece. I'd been a lousy cameraman, so my photos app offered little in the way of concrete memories.

But every now and then they would give me something, a crack at the door into the past that I would then barge through.

"Oh, yes!" I'd announced excitedly, looking at a pixelated image of bonfires and bodies. "I remember this one. Drum night. That's where I'd first met—"

Blank blank blank.

"—her friends," I'd finished, a bit disappointed. Gabriel had nodded enthusiastically. Any progress was still progress.

"That's great, *mijo*," he'd said. "That's really great."

The rest of the time, I would sit and listen. Gabriel would tell me stories about the times we'd spent together during university. The singular double date we went on with Dahlia and Irene. And then anything at all that I'd told him about my childhood. Or life with my missing wife.

"Some of the shit you went through," he'd said sorrowfully, "it's really fucked up, man. I don't know if it's good, if I should even tell you. Maybe it's better to just forget."

"No," I'd insisted. "I want to know."

Gabriel would grimace, scratch his cheek. Take long sips of water to stall. Then, quietly, he would tell me about what I had told him.

Of how my mom had died. My estranged dad, whom I'd left on the floor, surrounded by broken Beatles records. Of all the stuff that had occurred in between. Listening to these long-winded tales of anger and violence made me dizzy. They didn't seem real. Or feel like they had happened to me.

"Are you sure?" I'd ask, interrupting him now and again. "I told you that?"

"You did," Gabriel would say. "Especially when you got drunk, you'd open up to me a lot."

It was all so strange. I couldn't remember being a drinker. And when memories came back to me, they were mostly all pleasant.

I could see those good moments so clearly. Each one was like a gift being unwrapped, or a puzzle piece sliding into place. A chunk of blackness replaced by luminous memory. A fragment of happiness that I could fully submerge in.

The bad memories Gabriel told me were nothing like that. Slowly, they crawled back to me, one by one. But there was a distance to these memories, as if I was a spectator. I could watch flashes of blood. Loud angry voices. Rainy windshields, dusty fields. But there was a dreamlike, fake quality to them. These things had happened. But not, truly, to me.

And then there was Dahlia. She came back with a vengeance. Gabriel was limited to the things the two of us had done together, or stuff I'd told him. So the rest was up to me. I'd sit in silence with the hospital blinds closed tight, and let myself drift into a waking sleep. Eyes open, staring at the dark ceiling. Daydreaming into the past.

My whole life—out of order, juxtaposed, and unfiltered—floated back to me. Dreams of an old me. The good ones felt close and tangible. The bad: a far-fetched fantasy.

Dahlia often came back in these dreams. Our first date. Her mother's house. The hours of talking in bed, punctuated by sex and laughter. Wedding. Boat trips. Dinners. Heaven.

The daydreams were mostly happy ones. They were a welcome reprieve from the hospital room, the prison-like bed, as I pissed down a catheter and looked out the window to watch spring come and go. I'd lay there and dream of my wife, the two of us living a life that was too good to be true. There was no one to verify what was fact or fiction, so I had to accept that whatever I remembered had actually happened. Not long after I made that promise, the bad dreams started to occur.

Now my parents weren't the focal point. It was Dahlia. She was dark. Different. When she spoke to me in memory, there was a metallic rasping sound coming from her mouth. Not a woman's voice at all. I dreamed of fights about nothing, of days of disappearance. A hateful screaming match between her and another woman. And fear. And confusion. And guilt. Lots of guilt, which I couldn't figure out the source of.

~ ~ ~

The guilt, I decided, was somehow tied to how I'd gotten here. I had done something to upset her. When I had told one of the officers that, that I believed that I was the reason she had pushed me, he had let out a hard laugh.

"Mr. Donner," he'd said, shaking his head. "I think you have a very poor idea of what's going on here."

"I don't think that's true," I'd argued. "I've been remembering a lot more about—"

"About your wife?" he'd said, cutting me off. He wasn't an officer I'd remember seeing before, loitering around my room, asking if I'd recalled anything of note.

My answer was always *no*. No, nothing to do with what had happened right before I'd woken up in the basement. No, I didn't know where she, *Dahlia*, might have gone.

I couldn't understand why they cared so much, why a manhunt was even in place. It seemed that there had been a misunderstanding, a serious one, but nothing that couldn't be explained. The image of her, laughing and sunlit, kept burning in my head.

The bushy-browed officer with the name Noor stamped on his chest checked the file of papers in his hand and looked at me with a sort of disgust. Then continued.

"Have you ever been properly informed about your wife's history, Mr. Donner?"

I had not. I'd looked at him from my bed and shook my head.

"Not completely."

"Well," he'd said meanly. "Let me read it off to you."

Before I could object, he'd begun to list off a series of reports from her case file. Each one stung to hear.

"Aggravated assault of a family member when suspect was 13 years old. Questioned for the sudden accidental death of suspect's mother, 16 years old. Assault of a stranger at a nightclub, 23 years old. Lethal assault with a weapon in proclaimed self-defence, 27 years old. And now this, Mr. Donner," he'd said, shooting me a look before reading the rest of the file. "Attempted homicide of suspect's spouse. 28 years old." He had lowered the file and given me a glare.

"Your home," he'd ranted, "had every door locked and the power shut off. There was an iron chain on the front gates. No sign of your wife's passport or IDs anywhere. We've been trying to track down the vehicle she took for over a month, and nothing. The closest thing we've found were bank statements of multi-thousand-dollar withdrawals, halfway across the province. Any security footage showed only a hooded figure at the ATMs."

He'd paused to catch his breath. The room was filled with a deadly silence, save for the beeping of machines and birds, singing outside the window. The officer had let out a heavy sigh.

"Mr. Donner, she left you there to die alone," he'd said finally. "I'm sorry to say it like that, but it's the truth. Now, I don't care what kind of argument you two may have had, but there is nothing I can think of that could justify any of this. Your wife is a very sick person. And we need to find her before she hurts someone else."

I'd felt stunned into silence by what Officer Noor had told me. I'd blinked several times, shook my head slightly, as if to shake the words out of my brain.

"How...I don't..." I'd stammered, trying to find something to say. Nothing would come.

"Mr. Donner, if there is anything you can tell me that would help us locate your wife, that would be of great help. Otherwise, I'll leave you here to get some rest."

"What did you say?" I'd asked, suddenly grasping the meaning of what I'd just heard. "About lethal assault? You mean she killed someone?"

Officer Noor had frowned, sighed again deeper. Adjusted his pants with a free hand.

"Yes," he'd replied, sounding tentative. It was then that I wondered if he was breaking protocol by telling me any of this.

"What did she do?"

He'd looked at me with a mixture of pity and immense discomfort. All of the fire I had just seen seemed to have been extinguished. He opened the case file and turned to a new page.

"It says that there was an attempted mugging of you and your wife. Late December, at a friend's birthday party downtown."

A cold feeling had settled in my stomach. Brick. Steam. Blood.

"You," he'd said, gesturing to my broken left arm wrapped in plaster, "were attacked by a homeless man who was under the influence of amphetamines. He severed two of your fingers in an attempt to steal your watch."

Officer Noor paused, before paraphrasing the next sentence.

"In retaliation," he'd muttered, "your wife cut off his head."

~ ~ ~

By the end of July, I was in the hotel room. Sleeping. Thinking. Waiting. Hot summer nights rolled past with next to no updates. The police had nothing. I had nothing. Repeat.

I'd relayed my fragmented story to more than a dozen officers, counsellors. A single judge, sequestered behind a court desk. There was little I had to give. My memories were increasingly hazier and unreliable the closer they got to the basement floor.

"Mr. Donner, can you please think of anything that would have triggered such a violent response from your wife? Any arguments leading up to the day?"

Deep, deep down, I knew there was something. That prickling of guilt would flare up, tease me with an answer, and then burrow right back down into my subconscious again.

"No," I'd repeated, more than a dozen times. "I can't."

It soon became obvious that time and resources were being wasted. There were brand new crimes to attend to. Fresh rapes. Break-and-enters. Murders where the blood was still wet, not 2 months dried.

One by one, I stopped having to meet with strangers and answer their questions. My arm came out of its cast. I was anointed with a permanent limp in my right leg. My sense of smell and taste would likely never recover. A parting gift from my second brain injury.

As for my memory, there would be some degree of impairment. Forever.

"Even if you do remember most things, Jack," Dr. Morrison had professed, "the chance of recovering memories directly linked to your traumatic events are slim. Most patients incur some pieces, but the majority of the event will remain obscured. In cases like yours."

Cases like mine. Cases where the brain had seen too many nasty things, been battered one too many times, and shut down in response. Thrown the past into a locked box, then the box into the subconscious sea.

"Okay," I'd said in response. I'd taken to using that word a lot.

"Well, if you need anything, don't hesitate to call the number on my card. I'm usually pretty booked up, but we can schedule an appointment if things take a turn for the worse. How does that sound, Jack?"

"Okay."

The doctor had smiled, shook my hand, and ushered me out the door, happy to be rid of another hapless patient.

Out into the world I went. Off to answer more stupid questions that felt increasingly vapid, meaningless. Colour had been sapped from the world. I could see only in grey, speak only in mindless affirmatives. *Okay.* Okay, okay, okay.

Did I want to have a room with a balcony? *Okay.* How high should we list your property, sir, is ten million close to your last appraisal? *Okay.* Would you like your belongings sent to a storage unit on the North Shore or across the water? *Okay.* As the hotel manager, I'd like to offer you a free room upgrade. I…heard about what happened to you, that is just so awfu—

Okay. Now, I don't want to put too much pressure on you, Mr. Donner, but I do have a potential buyer who just submitted an offer that supersedes—

Okay. Hey, man, how're you doing? Haven't heard from you in a little bit. Irene and I wanted to take you out for dinner sometime, our treat. It's been a few weeks since we saw you and we just want to make sure that you're—

~ ~ ~

"Okay."

"Really? You'll do it?" Irene had asked, eyes widened.

The four of us had gone out to eat at the hotel lobby grill, which was a dismal excuse for "fine dining". My steak had come pre-dolloped with ketchup, laid atop a bed of onions which were fried beyond recognition. I'd had to clarify with the waiter that they were, in fact, not a bunch of cinder shavings.

"I guess," I'd said, stuffing another bite of fried onions into my mouth. The texture was like dust. Flavourless. You don't realize how much you live through your senses of taste and smell until you can't use them anymore. "I guess it could be good."

"I mean, only if you really want to," Gabriel had said, looking concerned. "It's just that—"

"That you have an incredible story and people deserve to hear it," Irene'd finished.

I'd listened to her gush a bit more about the interviewer, Sati Singh. According to Irene, she was the best when it came to true crime in the province. I'd be in safe hands.

"I just really think it would be good for you, Jack, getting that stuff off your chest," she'd said. "And who knows? Maybe it'll help with the investigation. Get some new leads going."

"As long as they catch that fucking bitch who did this to you," Gabriel said under his breath. Irene smacked his arm.

"Don't start that," she'd cautioned. "Not here."

All around us, crowded tables filled with hotel guests chewing their dinners. Generic pop music trickled out of the speakers. I pushed my tasteless food around and fantasized about taking a long, hot shower in my room upstairs.

"Look, *mijo*," Gabriel'd said, taking my hand and squeezing it. "You don't have to do anything you don't want to. I mean, maybe talking about everything publicly will just be for the worst, you know?" He'd turned to Irene and shrugged.

"I don't know. This might be a step backward instead of forward."

Irene had frowned, brows creased.

"I don't see how Jack sharing his story about how he's a fighter, a *triumphant* fighter," she'd emphasized, "could be anything but good. It's inspirational."

"Yeah, but—"

"But what? You were just agreeing with me that it was a good idea. It's not like I'm forcing—"

"It's okay," I'd said, nipping their argument in the bud. "I'll do it. I already said so."

Irene and Gabriel had looked back at me, Irene pleased, Gabriel less so. She'd smiled.

"Okay! Okay, good. I really think it'll be a good thing for you, Jack," she'd said brightly. "I wouldn't be suggesting this if I didn't think it was the right thing to do."

"Or you just want to say you know someone famous," Gabriel mumbled.

Irene had shot him a look but said nothing. Took a sip of her wine.

"I'll send you her submission link on the way home," she'd said. "I'd be shocked if she didn't take your case. Just shocked."

~ ~ ~

Irene hadn't needed to worry about that. The Sati Singh Show responded in less than 72 hours to say that they would love to schedule an interview. In the email, they asked whether I'd be comfortable supplying a few photos of Dahlia and I, and would August 29th work for a filmed interview? Here was a list of things to expect. Address to the studio. See you then!

As the days to the interview edged closer, I found myself see-sawing between calm and nerves. On one hand, I felt that

Irene was right. I actually *did* want people to know what I'd gone through. All of this damn suffering on my shoulders had exhausted my spirit, left me immobilized. The idea that sharing what had happened might, on some level, alleviate the pain I was in, filled me with hope. I wouldn't have to carry it alone anymore.

But there was also the other side. I knew what everyone thought of my wife, the near-husband killer. Talking about her in such a negative light made me feel ill, even though I could remember most of the bad moments. At least in fragments.

The alleyway. Her anger towards Genevieve. Her anger towards me. Our final months together were still fairly blank, but I could picture, however dissociatively, the stories she had told me. About her uncle. And Mango.

The more I thought about everything my wife had done, the worse I felt. Only, it was an ambivalent feeling. I could almost understand her. At times, her violent outbursts seemed to make an evil sort of sense.

I could picture myself in her shoes: a 13-year-old girl, lashing out at her molester. A heartbroken teen, trying to give her pet a peaceful death and failing. A newlywed resorting to revenge. A woman betrayed by one of her best friends.

The extremity of each situation still freaked me out. I couldn't fathom how things had escalated to *beheading* in the alleyway, nor remember. The night was an uneven echo, just like the rest of the bad memories. The good ones, stubbornly, blazed on with clarity.

This was another issue. I couldn't stop seeing my wife in a good light. I had a million snapshots of us, drenched in love. How the fuck was I supposed to equate this mental angel with the woman who had tried to kill me?

And this, this was the final problem knot. Me. All of those other situations where Dahlia had reacted aggressively had been triggered by some sort of friction. What did I do to make her push me down the stairs? The illusive guilt, swimming through my subconscious, knew the answer. But no matter how my hours I laid in my darkened room, slipping through my mental waters, I could never seem to catch it.

~ ~ ~

Sati Singh was glowing like a bronzed chestnut under the camera lights. Her studio set-up was cozy, simple. Two peacock-blue chairs sat facing one another, a hulking hot camera trained on her and her guest's face like a sniper. I'd sat with my fingers laced in my lap, my cane leaned idly against the armrest. Sati had insisted we leave it in frame.

"I think it demonstrates your resilience," she'd said before we'd started rolling. "Shows some vulnerability, too."

"Okay," I'd replied. A makeup person was dusting my nose with powder, trying to hide the sweat-shine betraying my nervousness. The suit I was wearing was a shade lighter than black. It felt stifling. Like a straitjacket.

"So, just keep your eyes on me throughout the interview, okay, Jack?" she'd said gently, just loud enough for me to hear. Her voice had a breathy musical quality to it, as if she had wind chimes for vocal chords. "And just think of this as a conversation. You don't have to do anything but be yourself. Okay?"

"Okay."

"Right. Okay, everyone!" She switched into a louder tone, bringing the studio to a hush. "We're all good to go. Whenever you're ready, then."

There was the sound of scrambling, as the crew filed into place to do their jobs. The twin red eyes of the cameras fixed their gaze upon us. Sati smoothed out her jacket, glanced at her top cue card. Then up at me. Big smile.

"Camera ready?"

"Ready."

"Sound speed!"

"Rolling."

"Action!"

"Good evening, everyone, I'm Sati Singh," she said, directly down the camera lens. "And tonight, I'm joined by a very special individual. Jack Donner, who has been to hell and back and lived to tell the tale. Jack," she asked, turning to face me. "How are you doing tonight?"

My throat muscles clenched up simultaneously. I swallowed and coughed out a reply.

"I'm, um…alright."

"Cut!"

I looked over to the crew, blinded by the lights. They resembled a bunch of silhouettes.

"Did I do something wrong?"

"We can't hear what you're saying," one of the silhouettes responded. "Gotta speak up, buddy."

"Okay, relax, Mark," Sati said sharply, before leaning closer to me. "Just project a little more, okay, hon? Otherwise the sound guys will be up my ass about it."

She said it maternally, *hon,* the way a middle-aged woman might try to comfort a young man riddled with fear on a studio set. But the word chilled me straight to the bone. Hon. I could hear it, replaying again and again, overlaid with a different voice saying the same.

It must have shown on my face, because Sati's expression changed to concern.

"Everything alright?"

"What? Oh, yes. Yeah. I'm okay."

I cleared my throat and gave a thumbs-up to the faceless crew.

"I'll be louder this time," I said, voice deepening into my chest.

The crew repeated their commands. Sati said her intro, tonally identical. Turned to me.

"How are you doing tonight?"

"I'm alright, thank you."

She nodded her head slightly.

"I'm glad to hear. So, Jack, you grew up in a small town in Saskatchewan. Cranby. What was that like for you?"

Sati had pre-prepped me with the questions she was going to give me. I thought back to my canned answer, hatched up before filming.

"It was pretty isolating," I answered. "We lived on a farmhouse about 20 minutes from town. From Cranby, I mean." The name tasted sour in my mouth. "My grandparents were farmers on my mom's side, and they gave her the house when they retired."

"Is that how your family made money, then? Through farming?"

"No, my dad worked odd jobs around town. My mom just stayed home."

I knew what was coming next. Sati shuffled to the next card and gave me a serious look.

"Now, speaking of your mother, she passed away due to a rather horrible freak accident. In fact, you were the one to find her body."

"Yeah. That's correct."

I proceeded to regurgitate the story of Momma, crushed to death by a falling tree. The whole time I spoke, I kept getting flashes of memory, blurred but there. Most of the details had been reiterated by Gabriel. Sati listened to my stumbling, patchy retelling with a frown, her head shaking as I did.

"What really hurts," I said, "is how it ruined any semblance of relationship I had with my dad. He blamed me for her death. And he never forgave me for it."

"You haven't spoken to your father in years, is that correct?"

"No. No, I haven't."

"So he has no idea that any of this has happened to you?"

"No. As far as I know, he doesn't."

Gabriel had driven me to the duplex, about a week after I first got out of the hospital. It had been resold. A young Ukrainian couple answered the door when Gabriel had knocked. I'd sat in the car and watched as they talked, shaking their heads. They'd bought the place from my father over a year ago. He'd left no forwarding address.

"How about your other extended family?" Sati was asking. "Do you have any uncles or grandparents you're in contact with?"

"Um, no," I said, swallowing thickly. "My mom was an only child. And my dad's brother committed suicide when I was 20. That's the only reason we moved here in the first place, because he left his place to my dad." I shrugged. "Otherwise, my grandparents have all passed. I never really knew any other family besides them."

"So, you don't really have anyone?" Sati asked. She said this the way a doctor might give a patient bad news. The tumour has spread. Kidney stones. You're alone in the world, Jack.

"I mean, in terms of family. No, I guess not." My eyes couldn't seem to meet hers. I felt very small all of a sudden. A grain in the Sahara.

"I have my best friend Gabriel and his wife Irene. They've been a huge help the past few months. But otherwise, I'm by myself."

"Your wife was a huge part of your world, then."

I nodded.

"Yes." I raised my eyes to meet hers. They were creased with kindness. "Dahlia meant the world to me."

"Cut!"

There was a release of tension as the crew collectively expelled their held breaths and started moving again. We'd reached the break in the interview, where Sati would feature a segment of photos and background info about Dahlia in post-production. We could relax again.

"You're doing a great job," Sati said, taking a sip of honey water. "How are you feeling about everything so far?"

"I'm alright," I said, mirroring Sati by taking a drink of water. My mouth filled with no sweetness. "It's just a bit weird. To be talking about this in front of cameras and stuff."

"Oh, of course. It takes some getting used to."

"Sorry to interrupt," one of the sound technicians said, stepping into the basking light of the film set. "But we need to change the battery pack on your mic. It's getting low."

"Sure. I'll be right back, Jack," Sati promised, before rising from her chair and following the technician beyond the border of light, into the darkness.

I was left alone, clutching my glass of honey water, blinded by stage lights. A flurry of voices could be heard, as the crew joked with one another, calling out requests before we started filming the next portion of the interview. The meat of why I was here. Dahlia.

My foot tapped away on the faux rug floor. I thought about the questions Sati was going to ask me. About life with Dahlia. The night in the alley. Anything I remembered leading up to her disappearance. What I had needed to do to escape the basement.

I'd prepared my answers best I could. I knew what I wanted to say. How the things she had done were awful, yes, but also reactionary. Horrific in execution. Honourable in intent.

And I knew, too, that this would lead to more questions. Raised eyebrows from Sati, or anyone else who watched the interview. How could I possibly defend the same person who had drowned her dog and killed a homeless man, mugger or not? How could I see the pattern of violence, extending all the way back to 13 years old and ending with me, left for dead in a locked basement, and not be horrified? Disgusted? Enraged?

This was the woman who had tried to kill me. Who had given me a permanent limp, no sense of taste. Spring would never smell like anything but air to me. I had lost pieces of my past, shards of memory that would never come back to me. How the fuck could I feel anything besides pure, burning hatred?

Because.

Because.

I could not get the thousand-and-one images of us, in love, out of my head. All the other memories paled in comparison. Tea candles next to infernos. When I closed my eyes and thought of my wife, the first things I thought of weren't beheadings, blood, and basements. It was an endless flip-book of love. Our love.

Sati sauntered back to the set, donning a new set of batteries on her back. She sank into her chair and gave me a sympathetic smile.

"Hey, you ready to get into the heavy stuff?"

I returned her smile with a flicker of my own.

"Yeah. I think I am."

"Alright, then." She turned to face the darkness and shouted.

"Listen up! We're ready to roll!"

~ ~ ~

The interview was posted a week before the first bombshell. I had just signed the deed to buy a house in the valley, beyond the city limits. A sightly hour-and-a-half drive from the ocean without traffic. Triple with. I'd felt an urge to return to flat earth, to a place of emptiness. So, after seeing it listed online one night, I'd bought the old farmhouse at the end of the road.

When I'd driven out to take a house tour in Dahlia's Lincoln, a wave of nostalgia had hit me. The SUV rolled past congested streets, rows of houses, until suddenly yawning open to the rural valley beyond.

The house, as promised, was off a stretch of cracked pavement, about 10 minutes from the closet town. The house came with a few acres of farmland, said the realtor. If I wanted the place. I did. I'd made an offer on the spot, a grotesquely generous offer, then gone out to the back porch and taken another look around.

My neighbours would be primarily grasslands and fields, groves of quaking aspen trees. There wasn't a sound to be heard, no cars, no ocean waves. Just the silent sunshine, falling on the dirt. It felt like where I needed to be. On my own.

Gabriel and Irene had tried their best to stop me. They'd offered to let me stay at their place, to help me find a nice neighbourhood in the city. The worst thing I could do, they decided, was be alone.

"You can't just go and move into the countryside, Jack," Gabriel had protested. "Not after everything. You need to be around people. Seriously. Going off and living like some hermit would be terrible."

"And what about your appointments? They don't even have a hospital nearby, what if you need to see someone?"

"Better yet, what if you need to see us?"

I'd calmly explained to them that it was already too late. I'd bought the house. There was nothing they could do to convince me otherwise.

"You have to understand, I grew up in the country. *That* feels like home. Not being in a city, surrounded by people and traffic all the time." I'd given them a smile across the table, trying my best to assure them. "I'm going to be okay. You can visit. Or call me anytime."

Gabriel had shaken his head in disbelief, while Irene had just stared.

"You're making a mistake, Jack," he'd said. "Please don't do this."

"And what if, what if..." Irene had dropped her voice to a low murmur. "And what if *she* comes back? You'll be all alone out there."

I'd said nothing. I hadn't wanted to lie to my friends with a fake reply.

The thought of Dahlia coming back didn't scare me. I had questions. Lots of questions. I wanted to ask her what had happened in those last few months, the ones obscured with a stubborn haze that wouldn't go away. It was where the guilt lived. And the answers.

"I'm going to be okay," I'd said instead. "I promise."

Neither of them had said much more after that.

~ ~ ~

The interview, on the other hand, had stirred up a lot of opinions from them both. I'd received a bewildered call at 11 pm from Irene, demanding to know why.

"How could you've *said* that about her, Jack?" she exclaimed, sounding out of breath. "I don't understand, after all the evil things that woman did, how could you defend her?"

In the background, I could hear Sati Singh asking me to clarify what I meant when I said that Dahlia wasn't a bad person. There was more baffled babbling from Irene when she was abruptly cut off by Gabriel.

"Give me the phone back, Gabe, he hasn't even said anythi—"

"Hello? Jack?"

"Yes?" I'd replied, rubbing my head. The call had woken me from sleep.

"What the hell, man? Why would you say some of that shit?"

"What shit?" I'd asked, naively. I could practically hear his eyebrows furrowing across the line.

"You know what," he'd grumbled. "Seriously, I just don't understand. This was sup—"

"Give me the phone back, Gabe!"

"—posed to be a way to tell your story, find some healing in this whole mess. Not get on there and make her sound like this misunderstood psychopa—"

"I'm not going to do this right now," I'd said, interrupting him. "I'm trying to sleep. It's done. Goodnight, Gabriel. Tell Irene the same."

"Just wait a se—"

The line went dead. I'd put my phone back on the bedside table and laid in darkness, thinking about the interview. I hadn't regretted what I said. And when I'd finished, despite Sati's confusion about changing my answers, I'd felt lighter. Freer.

After a few minutes of trying and failing to sleep, listening to my phone buzz twice from missed calls, I'd gotten out of the plushy hotel bed and opened up my computer. Searched for the Sati Singh show. My interview, titled "HUSBAND SURVIVES HIS NIGHTMARE WIFE! VICTIM INTERVIEW" had already a hundred thousand views in the past 16 hours.

The thumbnail showed me, sweat-skinned and humongous-looking in the blue chair, with Sati Singh's face PhotoShopped beside me, looking shocked.

I couldn't bear to watch more than the first minute of the interview. The sight of me hunched over with dark bags under my eyes, cane at my side, made me feel ill. My voice sounded pinched, like I was being choked by an invisible being. I'd paused the video and scrolled down to read the comments. Like an idiot.

Each one seemed worse than the last. Although there were a handful commemorating me on my resilience, the bulk seemed to target Dahlia. Calling her a murderess whore, the next Aileen Wuornos. Others seemed fixated on vilifying her looks, listing ways they would degrade her to "put her in her place".

"She deserves to be raped with a curling iron," said Apoj0n93. "Women think they can get away with anything these days. So f*cked up."

People also seemed hellbent on letting me know that I was pathetic for having any sort of sympathy for her. Pussy-whipped. A cuck. Beta. Retard. Delusional.

"Is he for REAL???" another comment asked, with a series of emoticons. "She stabbed a guy and he still went back to her. He DESERVES what happened 2 him."

In response to those comments were others, arguing in the replies. People defending my choice to stay with Dahlia, reminding them she had acted after my *fingers* were cut off.

"You have no idea what this guy has been through…shame on you."

"How does it feel making fun of a cripple online? WTF."

"Man's been through hell and u want to call him—"

I shut the computer. My hands were trembling, as I went to the mini fridge and pulled out a bottle of overpriced water. I sucked it half down in a series of glugs while sitting on the bed. The room was near black. From the window, the dim glow of a streetlamp seeped through the curtains.

The assault of comments replayed in my head. Obscenities. Irene and Gabriel's voices. The whole world felt like it was spinning. I'd suddenly staggered to my feet and stumbled to the bathroom in the dark, almost tripping on my bad leg on the way. I'd made it just in time to the toilet to vomit up my stomach contents, void of anything by water.

~ ~ ~

A week later, I'd received a call from the police department. They needed me to come in for some more questioning. A body had been found. My heart stopped.

"You found Dahlia? She's dead?"

The idea seemed impossible to be true. Nor was it.

"Not your wife, Mr. Donner," the voice said. "We'll explain more at the station."

My nerves were so shot, I'd had to call a taxi to get there. The week since the interview had dropped, my whole body had become riddled with anxiety. I couldn't sleep without a pill. Gabriel and Irene called me near-daily, apologetic but still confused.

"Just tell me why, Jack," Gabriel had pleaded. "What's going on inside your head?"

I'd danced around giving him a straight answer. It felt hopeless to even try to explain. He wasn't the one who had fallen in love with her. I was.

"I think I need some space right now, Gabriel," I'd said at the end of the call. "Just for a little bit. I appreciate everything you two have done. Honestly. But I need to be alone."

At the station, I received the first bombshell of September. Hale Donaldson had been found. Or what remained of him, anyhow.

After a year of exposure to the elements, the rise and fall of the river, a pair of hikers had found his skeleton. A piece of his lime-green windbreaker was seen under a rock pile. The rest was history.

"You don't think she killed him, do you?" I'd asked. There were three officers in the room, all staring at me stonily. I'd wondered how many of them had seen the interview.

"That's what we're hoping you can help us answer, Mr. Donner."

They'd questioned me about any suspicious behaviour I'd seen. Whatever I could still remember. I'd told them about her frequent vanishments during the day, when she'd go for runs or out on the boat. For drives. To meet friends.

"You mean you don't know where she was most of the time?"

"I mean, sometimes," I'd replied. "But not always, no."

The officers had shared a brief look. *Chump,* it seemed to say.

"Did your wife ever come home with any injuries? Evidence of a struggle?"

My lips went numb. The image of Dahlia, coming home after dark with a sprained ankle, played in unnerving 4k.

"Well," I'd started slowly. "There was this one night…"

~ ~ ~

This was all it had taken. No forensic evidence could be found linking Dahlia to Hale. A near year had passed since the body had been buried, and decomposers had feasted on his flesh until there was nothing left. They'd had to identify him by broken teeth alone.

Still, the best lead they had was the crazed woman currently on the run. Who had also been his previous girlfriend. An attendant at her wedding. The media went ballistic.

"The body of BC local, Hale Donaldson, was found earlier this month by police," news anchor Lydia Purrel had reported. I'd watched from my hotel room in abject horror.

"Friends and family describe Mr. Donaldson as a fun-loving, generous man. He will be greatly missed." A photo of Hale, grinning away on a golf course, flashed on the TV.

"As of right now, the investigation is looking at a possible lead of Dahlia Donner, who was our news story earlier in the year when she was charged with the attempted murder of her husband, Jack Donner."

Now my face was plastered on the screen. It was a still image taken from my interview with Sati. Then an array of photos began to circulate, depicting me and Dahlia. Dahlia on the beach, Dahlia kissing my check, us at dinner…

"In addition to attempted murder," Lydia Purrel said. "Dahlia Donner was previously involved with an attempted mugging that left her attacker dead. She is notably the only grandchild of Edgar Trevi, the wealthy co-founder of the Trevi Company, which has been accused as a major contributor to the ongoing homeless crisis within the city. Case details are still sparse."

Lydia had concluded the segment with a warning to viewers to stay vigilant until Dahlia was found. And to please contact the authorities if they had any additional information.

Someone watching the news that night took this personally. Because 24 hours after the story broke about Hale, a new bomb detonated. Some insider at the police department had leaked the report on the mugging. Just for shits? It didn't matter. The thing everyone cared about was the word, listed for cause of death.

Shane Winnow, age 58.

Charge: Attempted Armed Robbery

Status: Deceased

Cause of death:

Beheading.

~ ~ ~

At the horn of war, the world went wild. Dahlia and I achieved overnight cult status. The interview I'd given garnered a million views, as people weighed in with their thoughts of sympathy, vows of violence, and regrets of lust.

"if this bitch wasn't a fuking serial killer, she could've been a porn ★"

"It's the EYES, she's evil all right."

"CUNT CUNT CUNT CUNT CUNT CUNT!!!!!!!!!!!!"

"poor guy. I feel bad for him."

"The rich ones are alwaaays the sickest. No surprise here"

"Dahlia = satan's little cumslut (just like her greedy grandpa)"

"She DEFS killed that guy,,,,probably a bunch others too"

"gr8 tits, but what an absolute FREAKK"

"Long live the Queen of Hearts Killer!!"

"I'd give her something to cry about lmaoooo"

"WEAK ass man, defending a psycho like that"

"pussy bicth cant even walk now...serves you RIGHT dude"

"what the fuck is wrong with you people???"

In the midst of the firestorm, I moved into the old house. My furniture and belongings were unloaded and placed by movers, with next to no instructions from me. I couldn't seem to care. The entire universe seemed like it was crumbling around me.

~ ~ ~

One afternoon, I received a text message from an unknown number. The seasons had shifted to autumn, resulting in tepid rains prattling away on the roof.

I never left home unless I had to. I felt like I had a target on my back whenever I went out. Which, in many ways, I did. When I bought groceries at the general store, I'd wear a ball cap or hood, trying to hide my face. Sunglasses. My height, however much I hunched, was a dead giveaway.

"Hey, aren't you that guy on the news?" one woman asked me in the produce section. "John or Jack? That's really some story, about your wife—"

"No, sorry," I'd blurted, moving away with my cane. "Wrong guy."

There was slim margin for error when it came to my identity. If people learned that I was the same man whose wife was the nicknamed "Queen of Hearts Killer", the little slice of privacy I'd fought for would be ruined. All my efforts to be left alone would go up in flames.

With the TV on low volume, playing reruns and advertisements, I'd read the text on my phone. Peter Falk was asking "just one more thing" as I read:

"Hey Jack, it's Yvonne. I got your number from Irene, I hope that's alright. Look, I just wanted to say I'm sorry for everything you're going through right now, and for being bit of a bitch to you before. I had no idea about some of the stuff that happened to you. And sorry it's taken me this long to reach out, but I hope you're okay. Let me know if you hear anything about D. Take care."

I'd sat and stared at the message for a long time. Right at the back of my head, a moving sensation could be felt. Something unearthing, shedding layers of dust. Out came the image of Yvonne, glaring at me across the room, glued to Dahlia's side. I knew the room they were in: Gabriel and Irene's living room. At the post-wedding party they'd had last December.

That glare. It triggered an anger in me, a betrayal. Guilt. I'd clutched for the remote, turning off the television. My house went silent. I'd leaned forward on the couch, placed my hands over my eyes, and pressed. Darkness came to me. And the image. The memory.

I was swimming in darkness, hunting my own memory. I was close, I could feel it. I locked onto the image of Yvonne, sitting beside Dahlia with a glare, drink in hand and her other...

Around my wife.

There, like an awful resurrection, was the rest of the story. The missing piece of the puzzle. It rushed into being, filling in the slot of darkness after alluding me for months.

The vertigo flush in my stomach, leaning over the railing. Dahlia and Yvonne, mid-kiss. The abominable terror of being abandoned, being left. Resentment growing roots. Calendar torn in half. Pushpin. Doubt. Waiting. Christmas day. Then alcohol on a lonely night. The sensation of condom wrappers, all being punctured with a pin. Satisfaction.

Then sex. Rough, mean, sad sex. A chasm inside. Hopelessness. Certainty that there was nothing left that I could do. To fix things. Detachment. Self-pity. Solitude. And then.

I'd ripped my hands away from my face, plunging myself back into the world of now. I could remember. Right until the bitter end, I could remember. I could remember what I did.

And the bulb of guilt—planted on that lonely, impulsive night— finally pushed through the dirt of my brain. And bloomed.

3.

Winter. Spring. Another summer. As promised, the Earth kept turning. I settled into my new life and waited for an answer. Resolution. Anything.

At first, Gabriel and Irene would visit me at least twice a month. They'd bring pizza and a pack of beers, and we'd eat our dinner while watching TV. They kept trying to persuade me to move back to the city, back to the suburbs. It didn't work.

"I just don't think this is healthy, Jack," Irene had said one time, looking around at my near-empty old farmhouse. "You shouldn't be alone all the time. It's not good for the soul."

I'd assured her that I was fine. Then changed the subject: asked if they were trying for a baby again. Irene had gone silent. Then turned up the television.

Gradually, their visits started to spread out more and more. It was, after all, a journey to get to my place in the country, and gas was expensive. That's what I kept telling myself, as I noticed that weeks had passed without a visit. But I knew the truth. I wasn't fun to be around. I was a depressing sight. And I had let them down.

Our relationship had never been the same since the interview. There was a schism born from my decision to defend

Dahlia's actions as "almost justifiable". As human. So, bit by bit, phone call by less phone call, my last two friends faded into relative obscurity.

I didn't receive any more messages. Not from Yvonne, or any of the other women Dahlia had been friends with. Not from any of my university friends. Or my father, if he even knew this was happening. My cell stayed quiet, an empty husk of connection. I started talking to myself. And to Dahlia.

~ ~ ~

It started during the first winter in the new old house. A snowstorm had smothered the windowpanes with frost, wind trespassing anywhere it could. The insulation was abysmal. In late January, I could sometimes see my breath inside the house.

When I spoke, ghosts of mist hung in the air. My only company.

"I hope you're doing alright," I'd said one morning, wrapped in a blanket on the couch. I hadn't thought much about it. The thought, of hoping my confounding, crucified wife was okay, just came. Then it was aloud.

There was no reply. Of course not. But for a single, exhilarating moment, I had almost expected there might be. It would be *just* like her to pull a stunt like that. To appear out of nowhere, laughing sneakily, a great big "Gotcha!" on her lips.

The image had made me, abruptly, very lonely. I'd pulled the blanket closer and turned the television on. Watched TV movies with the swears dubbed over and genitals censored. Violent scenes edited, or completely cut out. It felt good to consume media like that: with all the bad bits wiped away. Almost wholesome.

By spring, I'd lost thirty pounds. The idea of eating had moved from the unpleasant to the torturous. Any sense of taste and smell was still nonexistent. Everything just slid down my throat the same. It was pleasureless. Pointless. I could hardly find the motivation to chew down a single meal, let alone three a day.

As a result, my cupboards filled up with powders, pills. Stuff I'd order online under a fake name, then hide when the delivery person came. Just in case. All the supplements I could need to keep a working body running on protein and vitamins and archaic minerals from shellfish. I'd grind the pills into dust and mix them with water and protein powder in a blender. Call that dinner. For the most part, it worked.

"Looks like I'm the worse cook now, hey, D?" I'd say to no one, filling the kitchen with blender music. Sometimes I would list off the ingredients from the label, one by one. Just for something to do.

"Spirulina powder. Pea protein. Acacia gum," I'd announce theatrically.

"Branched chain amino acids. Monk fruit. Vitamin C. Lecithin. Sea salt."

Maybe I would repeat the whole bloody list, but in an English accent. Russian. Italian. Or maybe I would just start crying, and the full blender would sit, untouched, for the rest of the day.

~ ~ ~

After months of heated discourse online—which I had watched despite my promises not to—the flames were finally dying down about Dahlia. A case with no updates, no leads, and no new victims can only run so far on novelty before collapsing from exhaustion. Or damn near it.

I was amazed by how much I could learn just from being online. It was like watching the world from above, like some disembodied falcon soaring over society's dumpster-fire. As time passed, the real world shrunk and shrunk, until it was no bigger than the size of a computer screen.

This warped my perspective on what the world really was. I didn't count my infrequent trips into town as entering the *real world.* It was town-world. Rural. It felt like an inland island, cut off from civilization. The world beyond: the giant, scary one where wars were starting and animals were dying and everyone was wrung through with stress, that world existed solely in the computer. It was where Dahlia—no, the Queen of Hearts Killer—lived. Where a version of me lived. The victim. The spineless husband. The man-betrayer.

Whatever masochistic desire I'd had to watch videos, chat-groups, online threads pick apart my marriage, eventually fell out of favour. I stopped opening the screen. The talking, shrieking voices of strangers became unintelligible. And once and for all, I was shut out of the real world for good.

Time assumed a shapeless form. Days of barely moving around the house. Reading the same books over and over. The muffled sound of television, permanently affixed in the background. If I was feeling particularly adventurous, I'd hobble down the front steps and along the dirt road that stretched south from the property. I never went far. I'd get tired too quickly.

Other days I would spend completely in bed. Laying in the largest of the two bedrooms, waiting for the sun to set. I'd watch the light change, as the sun moved through the sky and illuminated different parts of the bedroom. Floorboards. Back wall, side wall: both painted burnt yellow. Wooden dresser. Around mid-day I would take another sleeping pill, then fall into darkness. By the time I'd wake up again, it'd be night.

Through it all I thought, obsessively, about my missing wife. About Dahlia. Thoughts of longing or anger. Lust. Shame.

Guilt. Love. There was no part of our history that I couldn't recall, at least in part. But my mind kept circling back to the good moments. The supercut of our best times together.

I'd ask the empty rooms if she remembered them too. The motel in Oregon, under the moon? Our zip-lining date through the cedars in May? Or that old lady who'd spilt mustard on her blouse and was almost knocked down by her own poodles trying to lick it off?

We'd laughed so hard we'd cried: walking through the park after a dinner, wine-drunk, love-high; and here was this lady fending off her two mustard-hungry poodles, shrieking in Greek, waving her hot-dog bun in the air like a lasso. It was ridiculous. Uproariously stupid. But it was the sound of my then-girlfriend as she snorted with hiccups of laughter, doubling over, clutching my arm as we hurried past the woman to hide in the trees, to collapse into hysterics; this was the sound I could still hear, clear as day. The sound of Dahlia laughing.

I realized there was a good chance I was losing my mind. Sometimes I couldn't tell what was real anymore. I'd wake up and feel certain, dead certain, that everything was fine. Any minute now, she would come through the door. She would look exactly the same as before. Sharp-eyed, smiling, black hair tumbling over her shoulders like a wild animal.

Everything would be forgiven. Her me, me her. She would rush towards me, and I'd be strong enough to pick her up with ease, just like I used to. We'd kiss for an eternity or two. And when she told me she loved me, her voice would be the same iridescent cadence. Just like it used to sound. In the beginning.

More than once, I caught myself in a sort of trance: my chin resting on the back of the couch, staring at the front door. It felt like coming out of a dream, only to realize I'd been waiting for my wife to come home. Each time was a disturbing awakening, because I often had no concept for how long I'd been doing it for. How long had I been staring at the door? A couple minutes? Or hours?

With no one to tell me otherwise, I'd shiver at my dissociation and turn back to the TV. Brendan Fraser would be learning hieroglyphics from Rachel Weisz. Or Alex Trebek would be gearing up to reveal the true flying height of honeybees. The longer I watched, the less sense TV seemed to make. So, as I entered into my second autumn in my new old house, I turned that off too. Goodbye, last window to the world. Goodbye.

~ ~ ~

The dark miracle happened a few months after I turned 30. My birthday passed by with a bowed head. I wouldn't even know it had happened if Gabriel hadn't called to sing to me in Spanish.

"Thank you," I said, at the end of the last *Cumpleaños feliz.* There was a beat of silence on the phone, before I realized he was crying.

"Jack," he quavered, "I have some bad news."

His mother was sick. Very sick. She'd been given 6-8 months to live, and he and Irene were moving back to Paraguay to take care of her until she died.

"We leave next weekend," he said, taking back control of his emotions. "It's just been a nightmare, trying to find coverage for work and someone to look after the house. I feel so horrible that I'm not going to see you before we go."

"It's okay," I replied. I was sitting on the couch, watching the rain fall for the 4th hour in a row. Sheets of water wavered in the gale, creating ripple patterns as it fell to the fields.

"It's not okay, and…honestly I don't think you are either. You sound weird, Jack, and I don't want to think of where your head might be at."

"Gabriel, it's okay," I said again. "I'm fine. I'm at peace."

"Don't say shit like that. You're scaring me."

"Well, don't be." I dug my fingers into my neck, working at a kink that had been there for weeks. It felt like my head was screwed on wrong.

"Just go take care of your mom. Don't worry about me. Seriously."

There was another long pause on the phone.

"I'm really sorry to hear about that," I said, after he didn't reply. "It's so hard. Losing a parent."

Gabriel swallowed on the end of the line.

"Yeah. No fucking shit."

"I'll see you guys when you come back. Just focus on your mom. And say hi to Irene for me."

"Yeah, yeah. Of course."

"I'm really sorry, Gabriel."

"Me too."

A beat, then:

"And happy birthday, Jack. Sorry it couldn't have been a better one."

When I hung up the phone, a profound numbness had enveloped me. They were gone. I was really, genuinely alone. I hadn't realized how just the possibility of them coming over, stopping for a visit, had brought me comfort. Now that was gone, too. I'd gotten up from my place on the couch and moved closer to the window. Watched the rain. Feeling nothing.

December brought bitter cold and snow. The world morphed into a white desert, a dull wasteland of ice. My daily highlight was my hour-long shower, until the hot water ran out.

I had tried baths, but they weren't the same. I needed the cascade of scalding water over my ears, so there was nothing else I could hear. I'd feel held by the elements, curled up on the tub bottom with my long arms wrapped around my legs. Occasionally, I'd fall asleep and be awoken when the water turned to freezing. Then I'd wander around the frigid house in my blanket, talking to the walls. Asking questions. Giving answers.

Christmas passed. New Year's. I considered ordering myself a gift for the holidays, but couldn't think of anything I would want. I scrolled through online web-stores, looking at the offers for specialty mugs and VR goggles. Ski sets. Collectible hacky-sacks. Foreman grills. Everything was a bunch of junk. In fact, the mindless consumerism on display had left me nauseous. By the end of it, I'd seriously considered stabbing my computer screen.

And with that, I was into the annals of midwinter. Skies alternated between dove-grey and charcoal. Rain, constantly. Heavy spats of wet snow. The house whined from the cold wind's lashings. I spent most of the time halfway between sleep and waking. As the month of January sunk its icicle fangs deeper, I began to have new bad dreams. Of guns. Handfuls of pills. And a long, looped rope, swaying in the breeze.

~ ~ ~

In the dead of night, the phone rang. The clanging of bells intercepted my dreamscape like the voice of god. I came to, disoriented, tangled in the sheets of my bed. The bedroom was near-pitch black. Wind groaned, sifting through the rafters.

I laid in darkness, blinking up at the ceiling, confused about why I had woken up at all. As usual, the details of the dreams blurred at the edges. I could just make out a fortress of clouds, and the sound of…

Ring, ring.

Ring, ring.

Bells.

I sat up straight in bed and looked across the room. On the other side was a rectangle of light, laying on the floor. I kept it plugged in out of habit. Instantly, my chest started to seize up.

Ring, ring.

Ring, ring.

Very carefully, I stood up and crossed the room. I could hear, distinctly, the thumping of blood in my ears. I picked up my cellphone, where an unknown number was pulsing on the screen. My thumb pushed the answer button. Brought it to my ear.

On some deep level, I already knew who it was.

"Hello?"

My breath clenched at the back of my throat. There was a faint sound of static on the line. Of someone breathing.

"Hello?" I repeated. I pulled the charging cable out of the phone and went back to sit on the edge of the bed. Closed my eyes. Waited.

"Is that you, Dahlia?"

More crackling static.

Then.

"Yes," the voice replied. Worse than I remembered.

A grating, broken glass voice.

My wife.

"You're alive," I breathed, shock reeling through my system. "Oh my god. Where have you been?"

There was a shuffling sound on the phone. Spits of static.

"Hiding," the voice said plainly. "I've been hiding."

"I can't believe it's you," I said, relieved as much as I was startled. "I thought you were dead."

"Did you really?'

No.

"Yes," I lied. "I did."

The voice let out a sigh. It came across the phone like distortion, a mutation of air.

Haaaaaaaaah.

"Well, I'm not. I'm still here."

A beat.

"And I'm not alone."

My heart, tensing rapidly, stopped.

"What do you mean, you're not alone?"

There was more shuffling noise. And then, something new crossed the line.

Crying. Whimpering.

Unmistakably from a baby.

Then it faded away, replaced by more shuffling.

"Dahlia, is that—"

"Yes," the voice said. "Our daughter. She's here. With me."

"Oh my god," I gaped, clutching my forehead. "Oh my god."

"Listen to me, Jack. I need you to come. Right now."

"Why? Is something wrong?"

My heart had started again, sending a tidal wave of nervous blood through my body. All of this was too much to bear, all at once.

"Not yet. But there might be."

"What's going on, Dahlia?"

"I'll explain when you get here."

"Dahlia, how can I—"

"Do you have something to write on?" the voice interrupted.

"Please, you need to tell me wha—"

"Get something to write. I'm going to tell you where we are."

I opened and closed my mouth, struggling to concede. After a few seconds, I broke.

"Okay. Okay. Just hold on."

I stood up from the bed and staggered out of the room. Everything was moving too fast. The hallway rushed past me, light-speed, and I was descending the stairs. Living room. Grabbing a scrap page from the desk set, a ballpoint pen.

"Okay, tell me."

The voice complied. I scrawled out the address—only coordinates—with a trembling hand, then read it back to her.

"Is that right?" I asked, voice shaking. Cold sweat had broken out across my body.

"Yes. And you have to come alone. Do you understand?"

"But what abo—"

"Come as quickly as you can."

There was a click, as the line went dead.

~ ~ ~

Immediately, I tried to redial. The phone rang twice, three times. Then an automated greeting told me that the number I had called could not be reached at this time. Please try again later. I called again. And again. Nothing.

My chest was contracting with shallow breaths, as I began pacing around the darkened living room. Dahlia, alive. With our daughter. I was a father. A dad.

Shit.

I didn't even ask her *name.* I didn't know my own daughter's name! In panic, I tried to call the number one final time. This time it didn't even ring. It went straight to the greeting.

Shit, shit, shit.

For a moment, I considered calling the police. The logical thing to do. I couldn't go off to find my wife alone. After everything, it suddenly seemed very reckless, dangerous.

And that voice.

I'd forgotten the way it froze my bones. It destroyed my image of her, the effervescent shadow of the past. Dahlia wasn't that woman anymore. The one I had first fallen in love with. Or was she?

I couldn't tell anymore. My mind was overrun with voices, shouting all the nasty things my wife had done. Angry, hateful voices from the real world, calling her a slut, bitch, evil, murderer, sick, psycho, demon. The voices mingled with my memories: the good, the bad, slurring together into an indistinguishable soup of opinion.

Who was right? Who was wrong?

I couldn't. Fucking. Tell.

The phone call replayed in my mind. Every word. Every diction. Remorse? Vindication? What hid behind that voice? What was waiting for me if I went?

The answer sang out softly.

A baby crying.

My daughter was waiting for me.

What if she was in danger?

What if Dahlia hurt her?

I couldn't risk that. I couldn't risk anything anymore, except my own life. And if that meant following my wife's demand to come alone, then I would have to comply.

I would have to go alone.

The piece of paper was crumpled in my fist. I flipped on a light, smoothed it out and then, with unsteady fingers, punched the address into my phone's GPS. A winding trail of blue lit up the screen. An 8-hour drive. Depositing me right in the Rocky Mountains, miles away from the closest municipality.

Fuck.

I took a few deep breaths. Poured myself a glass of water and drank it down. It coated my throat with chill. The stove clock said 2:54 am. If I left now, I could be there by noon. Give or take. I'd have answers by lunchtime.

With a still pounding heart, I went back upstairs to get dressed for the journey.

~ ~ ~

The roads were vacant. Lines on the highway, illuminated by the Lincoln's headlights, snaked over black asphalt. The further I drove east, the more snow there was. I was driving upwards, little by little, rising away from sea level towards the Rocky Mountains. As I went, the temperature dropped from minus ten to minus twenty-three. Then lower. I put the car radio on shuffle, so it could only play a station for 15 seconds.

A snatch of Fleetwood Mac.

Traffic reports.

High-speed chattering in Mandarin.

Metallica.

Hockey game hosts, reporting a win.

Election predictions.

Static.

Back to Fleetwood.

And so on and so forth. I couldn't stand to listen to one thing for too long. And silence felt like death. I needed something to drown out the voices in my head. Warning me. Lying to me. Cheering me on.

Hours ticked past. A half-lit moon vanished and reappeared again. The terrain shifted from farmland to hills. Black mountains. Forest. Lots and lots of forest. Brown-trunked firs the size of small skyscrapers. Leering green pines.

An army of spruce, advancing onto the highway, bearing snow-smothered needles.

I envisioned a thousand different scenarios for when I arrived. Some where Dahlia was waiting at the door, baby in hand. A smile on her lips. Others where she drew a butcher's knife from her back. Plunged it into my neck.

Or others where she wasn't there at all. All of this was a trick. I would drive deep into the mountains and discover I'd been led to nowhere. And I would never hear or see from her again. Or my daughter.

This was the other thing. Our child. If all went well, the best it could go, what happened then? How could we go back to a normal life, ever? Dahlia could never go back into the real world again. Neither, barely, could I. What kind of life was that for a little girl, if her parents couldn't be seen by anyone?

And Hale. And Yvonne. And all the other shit that I had questions for. I needed to know before my head imploded. I deserved that, after everything.

At the very least, I deserved the truth.

~ ~ ~

6 hours in, the GPS told me to turn off the highway. The weak January sun had begun to rise over the mountains, backcasting them, making them taller. Deities of glaciers and rock. The car wound its way along unused roads, buried in snow. The wind had created drifts on either side of the vehicle, some as high as my rear-view mirrors. I shivered despite the hot air blasting from the AC system. The gas tank, refueled an hour back, sat at full.

Inside my head, I practiced what I was going to say. Changed it. Didn't like it. My words couldn't express how I really felt, the full spectrum of emotion raging away inside me, that had been raging for months. Years.

My fingers ached from clutching the steering wheel so tightly. So did my heart, although for different reasons. I snuck glances down at the GPS, as I inched closer and closer to my final destination. The morning grew pitifully brighter.

The robot voice of the GPS told me to turn left, onto a road that didn't even resemble one. It was suffocated by snow and fallen branches. Nobody seemed to have driven it in ages. The car wheels struggled to push forward, spinning at times. The engine revved and squealed. It became clear, after 30 minutes of minimal progress, that I would have to walk.

"Your destination is on your left in nine hundred metres," the GPS said cheerfully. I killed it with a push of my finger, then turned off the car. Took a deep breath.

I emerged from the driver's side and stepped down into the snow. My boots sunk in deep. I looked up ahead, where the road leaned left. Into darkness.

Teeth chattering, I grabbed my cane from the backseat and started the treacherous walk. All around me, old skinny trees creaked in the wind. I stumbled forward, painfully slowly, a three-legged beast blasting puffs of white from my mouth.

Besides the crunch of my feet and cane, the air was deadly quiet.

It was fearsomely cold. In just 10 minutes, I had already lost sensation in my fingertips and toes. Each step forced snow into the lining of my boots, where it would then melt and freeze over. It hurt, too, to breathe: the frost-lined air was an attack to the lungs. I couldn't bring myself to curse, even, for relief.

Crunch, crunch, crunch.

The further I got from the car, the more I realized what a bad idea this was. If things went south, I would have no quick way of getting out of the situation. Certainly not with a baby to hold as well. I could barely keep my body upright with my cane, let alone with a crying infant. I had to push the thought from my head.

Crunch, crunch, crunch.

Moaning trees. Robbed of branches. What had they done in a past life to deserve such a wretched existence?

Crunch, crunch, crunch.

Crunch, crunch.

Crunch.

There. Peeking around the bend, beyond the snowdrifts and shadows. The black forest opened up a little, allowing a clearing to take root. And in the centre—light-less, two-storied, and alone—was a small, wooden house.

Against the backdrop of the jagged mountains, the house looked like a doll's. A fragile, diminutive thing, surrounded by ancient trees and snow. With the flat light from the cloudy sky, everything looked black and white. No tracks were leading to or from the door. At first glance, it looked completely abandoned.

I stopped to lean on my cane, taking it all in. In another life, the sight might have been a beautiful one. But in the moment, I felt nothing but unfiltered dread.

The silence returned the moment I stopped moving. Even the creaking trees had quit their micro-sways. Nothing but heavy breaths, expelling from my tight chest.

I could go back, I thought to myself. There was still time. Go back to the car and call for help, real help. Professional help. There was no service out here, but I could drive to where there was. I didn't need to do this alone. I shouldn't.

Except, I did. This was still my mess. My Dahlia. No one but me could possibly be the one to walk through that door. Nobody understood, really understood, everything it had taken to get to this moment. And a part of me, stubbornly, blindly, believed. I believed in the love we had. I believed in the good of the woman I had married.

Sweating inside my gloves, I began the lurching walk forward to the house. The sound of crunching snow now seemed deafening. I felt completely exposed. If she was watching from the window, there would be no surprise to my arrival. Ready or not. Here Jack comes.

I reached the bottom of the front stairs and looked up. The house, really just a cabin, was not as run-down as it looked. Maybe 40 years old or so. The windows, both upstairs and down, were curtained. I closed my eyes and listened, trying to detect that sound of a baby. Nothing.

One hand clutching the railing, the other to my cane, I heaved my way up the snowy stairs. It wasn't until I reached the top that I realized how exhausted I was. My body was dead weight. My head felt close to falling right off.

Two steps forward, and I was at the solid wood door. No doorbell. I raised my fist to knock, but before I could, a voice heralded from inside.

"Come on in, Jack."

~ ~ ~

It was very dark inside the cabin. Musty, stale air, underscored by pine needles. I closed the door behind me, taking a moment for my eyes to adjust to the dim.

Sitting on a simple wooden chair was Dahlia. She was wearing a long, pale-moon dress that covered her arms and legs. Her hair had been shorn to the roots, now just a black fuzz adorning her scalp. If it wasn't for her eyes, shining in the feeble light, I wouldn't have even recognized her.

"Hi, Jack," she said. Voice perky as rotted flowers.

I just stared.

The room she sat in was large, square-shaped. A kitchenette to the left. Wood fireplace to the right. All along the walls, however, were heads. Half a dozen deer, caribou, a single moose. Fox. Elk. A bear. Glass eyes glowered down at me. Tangles of bone-white horns punctured the empty air. A jury of dead animals, here to bear witness to whatever happened next.

"What is this place?" I asked quietly. It was not the first question I'd had in mind, but I couldn't help myself. Dahlia turned her near-bald head to look up at the walls behind her.

"It was my grandfather's hunting cabin," she replied. "He was pretty passionate about it. As you can tell."

"Which ones are yours?"

I raised a gloved hand to the stuffed heads.

"Which ones did you kill?"

My wife turned back to face me and gave me a sad smile.

"None, Jack," she said. "He only took me here once. I never could bring myself to pull the trigger."

She looked back up at the heads. As she tilted her chin upwards, I could see the bones in her face jut out. Gaunt cheeks. Razor jawline. She looked near-starved.

"They're horrible, aren't they?" she whispered. "I wanted to take them all down. Burn them, or something. But I couldn't seem to do it."

"Where's our daughter?" I asked, raising my voice. My heart was rabbit-thumping away in my chest. I didn't like this feeling, growing inside me.

Dahlia whipped her head back towards me. Stared.

"She's upstairs."

"Is she okay?"

Dahlia regarded me with that sad, worn look.

"No, Jack. She's not."

My stomach dropped down. I leaned back against the door.

"What happened to her? Is she sick?"

The skeleton that looked like my wife sighed.

"Maybe it's better if I just show you."

She stood from the chair with some difficulty. Her frame swam in the folds of her dress.

"Wait, I..."

None of this was how I imagined things. I'd prepared for rejoicing, fighting, aggression. Anything. Not this empty shell of a person, eyes brimming with sadness. Not this heaviness, dampening the air like a cloak.

"I have questions," I confessed. The thought of ascending the stairs and seeing my sick infant daughter terrified me. I needed to know things first.

"Okay," Dahlia said, folding her hands in front of her waist. "Go ahead."

I swallowed. Which to ask? Where to start?

"Why did you leave me there? In the basement?"

She closed her eyes. Breathed through her nose.

"Because I was afraid," she said, almost too quiet to hear. "Because I was so angry, that I really wished you would die in that moment."

"Do you still want that? For me to die?"

She opened her eyes again.

"No. I don't want that."

"Then what do you want, Dahlia? Why did you bring me here?" I took a step closer, a swell of confidence filling my lungs. The reality of all that had happened, everything these years had taken from me, suddenly took hold.

"It's been almost 2 years, Dahlia," I said. "2 years of not knowing if you were dead or alive. Of me being the laughing stock. Because everyone knows about what you did. You know that, right? The whole fucking world thinks you're a monster. That I'm the idiot who married you. And *I've* been the one who's had to deal with that. All of it. How to walk and think again. How to live a life after what you did to me. And now this."

I gestured to the cabin around us. To her.

"You call me in the middle of the night, asking me to come help you. Begging. Telling me that I have a daughter, a fucking child, that all this time I've been a father and I didn't even know. And I want you to tell me why, Dahlia. I deserve that. I want you to tell me why you brought me to the middle of nowhere, why you made me come here. I need you to tell me why I'm standing here right now, what I'm going to do because I, I can't keep doing, I can't keep living like this, not knowing, I can't—"

My beratement crumbled inside my throat. I couldn't catch a breath, I was gasping for air and my words were falling apart, shedding tears, I was angry and furious and so fucking hurt and why couldn't I speak, why couldn't I breathe, why couldn't I…

I was having a full-blown panic attack. Or was on the cusp of one. My lungs were making a whistling sound, as I struggled to speak, struggled to suck in air. Dahlia watched me with a pitiful expression on her face.

"Jack, you need to calm dow—"

"Don't tell me what to do!" I blurted. "And stop looking at me like that!"

I gritted my teeth, forcing my heaving chest to slow. It fought back, viciously.

"Like you feel *sorry* for me," I hissed. A meanness was coming from inside me, a cruel streak. I wanted to hurt her back. I wanted to make her feel as bad as I did.

"I do feel sorry for you," she said, sneaking a nervous glance towards the stairs. "Jack, I really think it'd be best if we went upsta—"

"Did you kill that guy? Hale?"

I took another step towards her, close enough that I was looking down at her. My cane was clutched like a spear in my hand.

"Did you do it?"

Dahlia held her gaze as she replied. There was still, furiously, no anger in her voice. She spoke with the flatness of still water. And those eyes, piercing as ever. Sad, sad, sad.

"Yes," she said finally. "I did."

"Why? Why would you do something like that?"

"Because, Jack."

She took another deep breath.

"He raped my friend. Anita. At our wedding."

Now it was my turn for shock. I blinked: once, twice. The chorus of outer voices calling her murderer, sick, evil witch, faded to a murmur. My chest kept heaving.

"What? How?"

"It happened in the house. When everyone was dancing," she said. "He ran into her by one of the bathrooms and pushed her into a bedroom. Made her give him a blowjob while she cried."

She tipped her bony chin up higher, pointing it at me like a dagger.

"So I made sure he could never do something like that again."

I thought back to our wedding night. In the midst of celebration, under lantern-lights. A brief kerfuffle of Anita pushing Hale away on the dance floor. Her early, sudden departure.

My mouth opened and closed. I couldn't think of what to say.

"Jack," she said, taking a few steps away from me. "You really have no idea what life has been like for me. No idea."

Her voice, so stoic in its sadness, now fissured and split. Total desolation. It broke my heart clean in two to hear.

"I'm sorry," I muttered. All the rage had vacated my body. My breaths had returned to a ragged steadiness. "I didn't know."

Dahlia stood, watching me. Her expression was still impossible to read.

"It's okay," she replied softly. "I'm sorry, too. For everything."

She turned her cheek to look at the staircase.

"I've always just tried to do the right thing, Jack," she said. "As hard as that may be to believe. But this world has ruined me." She turned back. "I don't even know what the right thing is anymore."

A hush settled over the cabin. The two of us looked at one another.

"You should go upstairs," Dahlia whispered. "I can explain everything to you. I want to. But you need to go upstairs first."

A cold stone of dread plunked into my heart's waters. Rippled outwards.

"What's upstairs, Dahlia?"

I waited for her to say my daughter. Our daughter. But she didn't.

"Just go look," was all she said instead.

There was a long moment of silence. The air around us was so thick, it felt like we'd been buried alive. My thoughts spun and chattered with warnings, with pleads. I didn't listen to any of them.

I set the tip of my cane onto the wooden floor, and began to hobble towards the stairs behind my wife. She had a subtle limp herself. When I reached the bottom, Dahlia stepped aside.

"After you," she said.

~ ~ ~

The stairs went up, five at a time, before a hairpin turn to face the other direction. I lurched up the wood, legs stiff, heart broken. Dahlia trailed behind me, the wisp of her dress professing secrets in the language of thread. I kept my head down, all my attention on the climb upwards.

Clump.

Clump.

Clump

Clump.

And then the final step, rounding the corner. It was equally dark up here, only slivers of silvery light sneaking through the cracks of the curtains. The upstairs landing opened up to a short hallway, with three doors facing me. All were closed.

"Which one?" I asked, craning my head back to look at my wife.

"The furthest to the left."

Clump.

Clump.

Clump.

Clump.

Clump. The top.

I straightened my spine and stared at the closed doors. A faint line of light from the window above the stairs illuminated doors one and three. The middle was in complete darkness.

I began to move towards the door on the far left. Number one. I had the distinct feeling of being in a dream again, just like I used to have at the hospital or in my house. None of this, surely, could be real.

My hand grabbed the brass handle, icy to the touch, and turned.

Bleak sunlight filled this room. A crescent window was open, showing the view of the snow-dense trees and domineering mountains in full glory. A single bed, right under the window, sat across the room. On top: a bundle of blankets.

A baby-shaped bundle of blankets.

I didn't speak. I didn't dare to. I stepped into the sparsely furnished room. Besides the bed, there was a drawer set on the back wall. A mop bucket. A package of diapers. Shelves with old books. A single lamp on a knee-high table. And now, me.

Without breathing, I crept across the hardwood floors with my cane, coming to stand in front of the bundle of blankets. Behind me, I heard the sound of Dahlia closing the door.

With my free hand, I reached out and poked the bundle.

There was nothing inside. Except more blankets.

No.

"Her name was Iris," Dahlia started. "She was premature. Stillborn." A pause. "I had to bury her myself."

No.

I grabbed the empty bundle and shook it, unravelling the folds. No miracle occurred. My daughter was dead.

"No!" I cried.

I whirled around to face Dahlia, clutching the blankets. She looked up at me, eyes white with sorrow and shame.

"I'm so sorry, Jack, I never wanted to lie about this, but I—"

"NO!"

I couldn't look at her. I turned away, back towards the arched window. I buried my face into the blankets and screamed. A guttural, animal howl emerged from the root of my soul. I screamed again and again, into the empty blankets.

Somewhere outside of me, a voice was speaking.

"I'm sorry, Jack, I'm so sorry..."

"HOW COULD YOU?"

I spun back to look at her, only to see that she had shrunk back against the drawer set, cheeks lined with tears.

"I di—"

"HOW COULD YOU?" I repeated, vocal chords near-breaking.

"Because!" she shouted back. "I didn't know how else to get you to come!"

Dahlia's face had fractured with sadness. Her shaved black head quivered and shook as she stood on the other side of the room, hands buried into her dress.

"Why did you want me to come here, Dahlia?" I bellowed. There was terror underlying every word I said. "What do you want from me?"

"I want…I want…"

She was taking gulps of air in between sobs. She swept a hand across her face. Took a deep, final breath. Looked me straight in the eyes.

"I want to set us both free."

"What do you m—"

Dahlia lifted her left leg and kicked the mop bucket. It leaned towards me, mop handle suspended in air, then clattered to the floor. Out from under the stringy mop head flowed a tidal wave of solar-tinted water. It splashed out of the bucket and quickly covered the wood floor.

I took a step back out of surprise. My knees collided with the side of the bed, and I fell backwards, sitting down hard on the bed. In one hand, my cane. The other, blankets.

The floor was completely covered in a thin layer of water. Dahlia amongst it, long dress drinking up the liquid at the edges. She made a smooth crouching motion to her knees and unveiled something small and shiny from her hand.

Before I had time to protest, she had flicked it into being.

The lighter caught fire on the first try. The way a person grabs a snake, Dahlia dipped her hand downwards to kiss the water. Only it wasn't water she had encased the floor in.

It was gasoline.

The floor erupted into flames. I yelled and brought my feet off the floor, onto the single bed. An island in the lake of fire. Dahlia rose to stand, her dress quickly engulfed by hungry red jaws. She had stopped crying.

"What have you done, Dahlia?" I shrieked. "What have you done?"

A crackling noise had begun to fill the smoke-clogged air. Wood. Everything was made of wood. The house would be devoured.

"It's going to be okay!" she stammered, holding her hand out in assurance. Tongues of crimson and flickering orange nipped at the bottom of her dress, rising higher.

I jerked my head between her and the door. How could I cross a room on fire? I turned away, looking out the arched window. It had begun to snow: fat, lazy flakes of white falling to earth. I had to get out. I had to try.

I began to beat my cane against the window. The air was becoming unbreathable. It stunk of chemicals. Wood. Fabric. Mattress springs, as the bed beneath me caught flame. I hit the glass again and again, trying to break it. Not a crack.

"Don't, Jack!" she cautioned, her voice strung shrill. I'd begun to throw my body against the window, willing it to give way.

"What have you done?" I was yelling, smashing into the glass with my shoulder. I kept having to stop and cough, as the light became murky with heat. Smoke. Certainty.

I was going to die.

"What have you DONE?"

Raging, angry flames, leaping up the bed. My wife, entrenched in fire, swaying with an expression of excruciation. Why wasn't she screaming? Why didn't she scream, as she was burned alive?

"Jack, please!"

"What have you don—"

A rush of freezing air. And I was falling, unshackled by gravity, amongst the flakes. My hand still gripping the blankets. Cane. Then as suddenly as I realized what was happening, I smacked down hard on a snowdrift two stories below, a rain of broken glass and ash in my wake. I heard a shattered woman's scream.

"NO!"

Pain seared through my body, the force of impact catching up to me. Even with landing on snow, I felt like I'd hit cement. My vision turned grey. Black. Grey.

And then the world was white again.

Falling snow. All around me, virginal white. The colour of pearls, baby teeth, wedding gowns. I could see only white. Until I rolled my head over, across the heavens. To the house on fire.

Dahlia was at the window. She had both hands on the sill, as she looked down at me and wailed. I felt frozen. Plumes of black smoke and ash billowed out of the broken hole my body had made, desperate to stay alive after all.

"JACK!"

Her body was on fire. Her bald head was a matchstick, an inverse jack-o'-lantern. Over and over, voice enraptured by suffering, she screamed my name.

"JACK! JACK! JACK!"

It was too horrible to see. I couldn't bear to watch her die. I closed my eyes, brought my hands over my ears. Began to pray to whoever was listening.

"Please make it stop please ma—"

"JACK! JACK! JACK!"

"—ke it stop please—"

"JACK! JAC—"

"Stop it stop—"

A throaty coughing sound replaced my name. The roar of flames, as more of the cabin was feasted upon. Rushing wind. My babbling words for deliverance. Darkness.

The coughing worsened, reached a fever pitch, and then went quiet.

A whistling took its place, as hot air met cold.

I laid in the snow with my hands over my ears.

And prayed.

And prayed.

4.

It took a long time for the house to burn. I waited in the snow, not daring to move, until strips of fiery wood had begun to pelt the ground around me. Then I was forced to crawl on my hands and knees, across the snow. I could not let go of the baby blankets.

A torrent of black smoke stained the sky. The roof, after centuries of burning, collapsed with a fantastic crash. This blew shards of glass and puffs of ash out in all directions. The trees, wet with snow, laughed at the threat. Then went on creaking.

Nobody came. It seemed impossible that so much destruction could be belched into the heavens and no one would see. How was that possible? Where was everyone? Didn't they know that the world had ended? That Dahlia was dead?

I sat on the snow, clutching my cane and the blankets, rocking back and forth. Any feeling I had was gone. The snow had robbed me of sensation. My soul had broken for the last time.

With great reluctance, the fire had receded to a heap of embers. One of the walls still stood, while the rest had tumbled.

A wreckage. Blackened beams, glowing red. Astringent smoke curls. Somewhere in the ruins, my wife's body.

The weather had taken a turn for the worse. The falling snow had thickened, as a wind cantilevered off the tip of my nose. Biting. I could not bring myself to stand. But as the skies had turned shadowy, promising night, I'd had no choice but to rise and limp my way back to the car.

Where did mine go? I wondered absently. The convertible. *What had she done with it?*

The question knocked around my brain along with a hundred others, as I staggered to the Lincoln, hoping it was still where I left it. It wouldn't have surprised me to discover that it had been swallowed up by the ground. The world had taken everything from me.

So why not that, too?

Of course, the Lincoln was still there where I'd left it, dusted in fresh snow. The light was very low by the time I arrived, lifting my weary body onto the leather seat. I sat for a while, letting the heat run, listening to the car beep away for me to drive. The thought of going all the way home in the dark seemed unfathomable. So, after my bones were warm enough, I turned off the engine, laid the seat back. Closed my eyes and slept.

I had bad, confusing dreams. Images of black wings and jeering mouths. The plinking drip-drop of water in an abandoned cave. Twisted metal. Sun flares. A woman's sad song. Carrion. A ring that would not come off. And flames, the scent of smoke and stale fire.

When I awoke with a start, it was still dark. The car clock vowed 4:25 am. I reached for the ignition, awakening it with frozen fingers. With a groan, the engine came to life. Clouds of white air blew from my mouth as I shivered and shook, waiting to get warm. It was time to leave. With my right hand, I fingered the shape of my wedding ring through my left glove. It was still there. I felt a pang of relief at its presence. And a pang of grief.

~ ~ ~

I was home by mid-day. The drive took an extra 2 hours back, due to the snow. I'd gone blind staring at the falling speckles of white for so long, pirouetting in the headlights. When I shuffled up the steps and into my house of silence, I could still see imprints of white when I closed my eyes. I went upstairs, stripped, showered. Climbed into bed and slipped into medicated sleep.

For the next week, I spent life almost entirely unconscious. I couldn't bear to be awake. I'd come to and immediately be thrust into the reality of what had happened. So as soon as I was conscious, I'd pop another sleeping pill. Drag myself down the stairs to drink a meal supplement with vitamins, enough to prevent starvation. Then head back upstairs and go back to dreamworld.

Most of my dreams were upsetting. Some of them were tangible, clear mimicries of the things I'd seen in my life. My parents. The alley. Hospital rooms. Dahlia. Dahlia. Dahlia. I'd face all my old demons in sleep, often rendered with an exaggerated pen. Here comes the memory of the mugging, only the knife has grown to the size of a sword and I am 10 years old. There's the image of a burning cabin, only now the forest catches flames too. And the whole world burns down with her.

Then there were other dreams. Images and snatches of sounds that made no sense. As if imprinted from another's dreamscape. Ten thousand armed men, slashing each other's throats with crude weapons. Stray dogs, whining from hunger. Seasick slaves, vomiting upon each other below deck. Oil spills. Poverty. Rapes. Wars. Killing. All of history's worst moments, played out across a mental projection that changed so fast, it was difficult to fathom they had all happened. Humans who were vile and cruel and inconsiderate. Who hated. Who hurt. There seemed to be no end to the possibilities.

For the rest of winter, I dreamed about them constantly. I saw everything unspeakable in sleep. And when I woke, I felt nauseous, repulsed by the things I'd dreamed about. But equally nauseous by my own reality. There was no escape.

The end seemed inevitable. I had nothing left to live for. Even in sleep I wasn't safe. I was chained to a bombardment of suffering, and there was nothing I could do to be free. Except one thing.

A week from the first day of spring, I ordered a long, thick rope to the house. When it arrived, I taught myself—eyes bleary from crying and nightmares—how to knot a noose. It was a very simple thing to do. Any fool could learn. I made a promise that the next day, I would end it. I couldn't live anymore. I couldn't stand the pain a moment longer.

I threw the rope over the exposed roof beams of the bedroom. Then, I took a sleeping pill, my last, and fell asleep under the shadow it cast. Morning would bring peace. At last.

~ ~ ~

Except that night, I dreamed of something different. For the first time since I'd come back home, I didn't dream of blood, tears, and pain. I dreamed of love. I saw, played out across a hundred different stages, all the love that this world had seen.

Little girls, feeding baby birds with a water dropper. A painter, deep in the throes of creation. White-haired elders, holding each other's hands. Mothers with their newborns. Fathers singing bedtime songs to the daughters. Boys kissing tree-trunks. Dogs curled in warm beds. Weddings. Funerals: where the final stage of love, grief, begins. Nurses caring for the sick. A child, playing in the ocean. The sound of a promise being made, then kept. Forgiveness. Trust. Surrender.

And then the other images stopped. Something familiar took place instead. I saw, very clearly, my wife. And me. We were at a coffee shop. Then a beach. In a car. Lying in bed. In each picture, a ring of faint light encompassed us. I saw the truth to what we had shared. I saw the love.

When I awoke that morning, there was a dry, chalky taste in my mouth, as if I'd been travelling through a desert. My heart ached. I rolled onto my back and stared at the rope hanging in the sunlight across the room. Outside, I could hear the distant sound of birds, announcing the new season.

I laid and stared at the noose for a long time. I thought about all my wretched, broken body had been through. The suffering I'd endured. I thought about the moment Dahlia set the house on fire. How my first instinct, still, after everything, had been to survive. To jump.

What was the meaning behind it? What had I done to deserve so much pain? The noose hung still and silent. No answers spilled from its open mouth, caught in an eternal O.

With a groan, I pulled myself out of bed and stood. And I realized: my head came up above the noose. I'd slung it over the ceiling beams late at night, never noticing. But in the white light of day, it was painfully obvious. I was too tall to hang myself here.

A hard, rough laugh came out of my mouth. Then another. And another. Pretty soon I was tearing up with laugher at the cruel absurdity of the situation. Too tall to die. I laughed until my belly hurt, until I had to sit down on the bed again. Until I was crying. But still, the laughter rolled, bursting out of my chest like a weed through cement.

Eventually, the hilarity passed. I wiped my face dry, blew my nose clean of snot. I felt a bit lighter. A bit more empty inside. In a good way. I sighed.

She would've laughed too, I thought to myself, taking the noose down and coiling it in my hand. Just her brand of humour. Death foiled by height.

I opened the bottom drawer and stuffed the coiled noose under my sweaters. Maybe I'd need it again someday. But today wasn't that day.

~ ~ ~

Spring came early that year. I purged the house of everything my wife had owned. Her boxes of clothes, never unpacked. Furniture I'd inherited from her mom's house. A cracked Rolex watch. The suit she had bought me for our wedding, a shade lighter than black.

I threw it all away. Broke the furniture down in the yard with a sledgehammer, until all that remained were splinters in the dirt. The effort to do so nearly made me faint. Piece by box, I lugged the last remnants of Dahlia into the SUV's trunk and drove it to the dump. When I came home, the house felt like a blank canvas.

As the days warmed, I found myself sitting outside more. On the porch, reading a new book. Going for longer and longer walks down the road. The air smelled like nothing, but I could imagine the scents it held. Wet earth, after rain. Skunk weed. Bitter flower nectar. Manure, from the farms to the east.

I had the sudden idea, after staring out at my acres of scrubbed-over farmland for days, to grow something. It would be something to do. As time went on, the nothingness that had occupied my life for the past years seemed insane. How had I spent the hours doing almost nothing at all? A whole two years of my life, gone.

The reason, of course, was also gone. I'd been waiting for Dahlia. Waiting for my wife to come home so I could begin living again. Now life had resumed, and I had to do something, anything, to fill its passage. It was that or death. I chose, without even realizing it, the first.

~ ~ ~

In April, I drove down the road to my nearest neighbours. They lived in a much fancier house than I, with almost five times the amount of farmland than my measly acres. When I knocked on the door, a middle-aged woman with Velcro rollers answered. She regarded me with a dubious eye.

"Can I help you?"

I smiled, trying to look less intimidated.

"Hi, sorry to disturb you." I pointed north, up the road. "I'm your neighbour, just over the rise. My name's Jack."

She scratched her cheek, still frowning.

"Sara," she replied simply.

I nodded, folding both hands atop my cane.

"Nice to meet you," I said. "I was hoping to ask you for a favour. I've got a few acres I'd like to use, but they've been neglected for a while. Do you think you or your husband could go over my land sometime with your plower? I'd pay you, of course."

Sara let out a snicker at my obvious inexperience. Despite it, I felt no embarrassment.

"Plowing's done at the end of season, not spring."

"Yeah, I know."

Then: "I come from a farming background actually. In the prairies."

"Did you now?" she asked, raising a brow.

"I did."

"Could've fooled me."

She stared up at me, unbudging. I cleared my throat and tried again.

"That's why I know plowing in spring still gets the job done. In a pinch."

"Well. We're not really in the business of charity here."

"It's not charity," I reminded her. "I'd pay you."

"How much?"

I told her a figure that made her brown eyes pop. She laughed in disbelief.

"You'd pay that much to get a few acres plowed?"

When I didn't flinch at the question, she smiled. Broadly.

"Alright, Jack," she said, extending a hand. "You've got yourself a deal."

I took her coarse hand and shook it. Then turned to limp down the stairs.

Sara watched me go from her doorstep. As I reached for the car handle, she called out.

"Say, Jack!" I turned my head to look at her, hand shielding the sun. "Mind if I ask you a personal question?"

My stomach clenched up. I smiled weakly.

"Yeah, sure."

She pointed her finger down at me. At my cane.

"How's a young man like you already walking like a senior?"

I laughed, taken off-guard.

"Sorry," she said, holding up her hands. "Don't mean to be rude. Just wondering."

"No, it's fine," I replied. "I had an accident."

"What kind of accident?"

"Uh. Stairs. I fell down some stairs."

Sara nodded thoughtfully, savouring my answer. Her blatant nosiness was genuinely inspirational.

"Must've been some stairs," she said finally.

"They were. Stone."

"Ouch." She looked me up-and-down again from the top of her own stairs, as if seeing me for the first time.

"Well, I hope you get better soon, hey?"

"Yeah," I said. "Me too."

A gust of wind blew. Sara and I both shivered.

"Say," she said, glancing over her shoulder, then back at me. "It's not very neighbourly of me to not invite you in. I'm afraid it's just me right now 'til George gets home. He does most of the work with our son, Stephen. But you could come in for a cup of coffee if you like."

I looked up at her, standing in the doorframe with her hair rollers. I gave another smile.

"Thanks for the offer," I said. "But I can't today."

Sara pursed her lips and nodded.

"No worries. I'll get George or Steve to come by your place sometime. Get those acres of yours in order."

"That'd be great."

"Alright. Well, take care, Jack."

She held up a hand in thanks and closed the door, still in disbelief at her good fortune.

For a moment, I remained standing, taking in the cool spring day around me. Fortress-shaped clouds floated overhead, underbellies dark with shadow. Patches of keen blue sky peeked out from behind them. White sun. The outline of gulls, flying high.

I closed my eyes and breathed in the air that I could not smell. It felt cold, flowing into my nostrils. In a way, that was a kind of scent. Coldness.

I let myself feel everything my body was going through. The ache in my back. My sore arm. The empty pain in my chest where my love had been uprooted. My uncertainty. Fear. Loneliness. I breathed in cold air. Breathed out. Again. Then opened my eyes.

Unsteadily, I climbed back into the Lincoln and drove down Sara's dirt driveway, then turned left to head to town. I had some things I needed to buy for the house. Food. Books. Seeds.

And besides, it was still a beautiful day for a drive.

Part Four

Aria

0

The world ends with watching.

The feeling of vicious little flame mouths, biting into me. Jack's name, pealed over and over from my screaming lips. Vulgar, chemical smoke. A world of pain.

And then, without warning, I am finally *me* again.

The fire goes on raging. Paint drips off the wall like wax, as the whole wooden structure becomes a meal. Walls groaning at the threat of collapse. Mattress springs, uncoiling with a triumphant *zing*. Rushing air. Black smoke. Falling snow. A woman's corpse. And me.

I rise up through the roof, relishing the buoyancy of my old form. 30 godforsaken years in flesh. It feels so good to say goodbye to it.

Up and out, into the sky. Just high enough to hover, unseen, above the roof. Snowflakes spinning, wind blowing. I feel none of it. I can touch nothing, smell nothing. For better lack of a word, I *am* nothing. As I was, so I become again.

Only, there is a difference this time around. There is...sadness. I look down and see that I have, unmistakably, hands. Two legs. Hair, floating around me. Clear as water but there.

And when I move past the crest of the roof and see the man I had called husband, grief blooms within me. He is curled in the snow, fetal-shaped. I can tell that he is terrified. I can see that he's in pain.

Instinctually, I move down to comfort him. When I reach his whimpering body, I reach one vaporous hand out. It disintegrates upon impact. I cannot feel him. When I speak, my voice is still the woman's. Dahlia. It is not my voice. It is hers.

Panic starts to roil inside me. No. I cannot be stuck like this. Trapped in longing. All the old feelings of love are still there. The desire. The hurt. Raw as ever. I am still stuck.

I am still, impossibly, *her.*

~ ~ ~

Curiosity, for what it's worth, was all I had. For a long, long time, I was defined only by that one word. *Curious.* There was nothing else that came before.

A part of the whole. Watching without seeing: the seas brew, storms falter. Spews of volcanic misgivings into the atmosphere. Animal birth. Human birth. An unfolding of time, non-linear, circular. Past and future twisted and braided into a cross-stitch, breaching one to the other with all the effort of a second passing. In other words, watching the world, all the world, forever. It was all that I, *we,* knew.

The purpose of we, the conscious collective, is *to be.* That is all. Be present, flow, exist in the river that is. Ever-moving. Non-resistant. Void of identity. Pure energy soup, making up all that was, is, and will be. It's where everything comes from, where everything returns to. *The original form.*

Let me back up further. Picture this: the cosmos. No, no, too far. Let's stay local. Earth. Take in all that you can imagine and stretch wider. Much, much wider. 4.5 billion years of energetic death, rebirth. Destruction. Growth. Unfathomable pain. Beauty. *Love.*

It all has to come from somewhere. A life-giving rain of fire, endued with meaning. Everything infused with purpose, therefore rendering everything purposeless. Tomato, tomato. You get the gist.

What I mean to say is this. Everything that is here today has been here before. In some other energetic form. Stardust makes up the bones of each person, whether you were born in year 21 BCE or 2100 TE. *Everything* is an extension of the past, linked to the future. But, of course, most of us don't know that. And none of us remember being atoms of dirt, air, claw meat, bloodstone. Nor would you want to.

The original form is only present. It has no definition beyond *is.* Which, for as long as forever, I was. I did not really exist. I was part of *we.* We flowed through the world, never retaining, only releasing. Naturally becoming a part of the physical plane, piece by piece.

Drops of energy becoming solar heat, Kosmoceratops, corn crops, Cleopatra and each of her servants. A shard of consciousness infusing diamonds, canvas, every paint-stroke of Hokusai. At all points of time an exchange unfurling, between was, is, and will be. A river of conscious energy, existing just beyond the tangible. Transferring back and forth with the physical to become.

This is where *I* start. By the sea, to be specific. Or atop it.

There was a great waterspout. A twister of salt water and air, spiralling from ocean to heaven. The sound was explosive. Waves churned in fury. Blue, black, white. The spout was enormous, violent. It teetered on its one leg and stretched its neck to the sky. Above, the clouds were swirling. A monster of their own. But there was a moment, very briefly, where a tear occurred in the cloud cover. A glimmer of sun. A flash of light.

We, the collective, were just passing through. Flowing to no destination. Pieces of us split off, became the waterspout, the clouds, the sea, the air, the wind, the sky. Filled these impermanent things with energy, with presence. The waterspout wasn't a twist of atoms or an idea. It was a deafening sublime angel of spinning water and *being.* It existed. It was there, here, in the world. But only because of us, making it so. Giving it consciou*s* form.

We, the collective, have many names. Source. Father. Mother. Prana. Creator. Spirit. Qi. Names have no impact. The point is, we are everything and nothing. All things are a part of us. And we are a part of everything.

As the sun vanished from view again, the first sign of life ignited in me. *Curiosity.* Which is just another word for unquenched desire. One moment I was eternal energy, existing in a state of universal unity. And the next, I had a first thought.

The light.

Follow the light.

There was a sense of ripping. Which was equally new, since I had never felt a sensation before. And with it came the thought of I. Who was that? What was that?

No matter. I pushed on. *Follow the light.* I thought those words, or the approximation of those words, since I had no speech. And I was rising. Moving, independent. I rose up from the sea, past the stentorian spout. Through unfeeling wind. Through cloud.

Follow the light.

And I was there. Past the cloud cover, in empty sky. The light, which I would later learn its name as 'sun', was blinding. It enveloped me. All I could see was light. It filled my naked shape, invisible to the eye. Light. Light, light, light.

For some time, I remained like that, floating above the cloud-cover, bathed in sun. I had no other thoughts. My one wish, my first wish, had been fulfilled. I was content.

Like all things, the time came to an end. The globe I was on turned. The light moved on to the next. And the desire came back, again, inside me.

Light.

I want light.

I began chasing the light. Following the setting sun, which had moved without care on to the horizon. I moved as quickly as I could. But the setting sun was quicker. It coughed up one last burst of radiance, then vanished. The world changed. Darker. Emptier.

I kept rushing atop the clouds, determined to reach the light. The desire pulsed within me, growing stronger with each moment it was unfulfilled. *Light, light, light.* But I could not catch the sun. The air around me grew blacker. And new lights began to appear.

Pinpricks. Polkadots. Stars. Hundreds upon hundreds, burning above. I looked up and saw them all. But instead of relief, I felt confusion. Disappointment. They were nothing like the light I had just been submerged in. They weren't the light that I *wanted.*

I began to sink down below the cloud cover, feeling more confused by the second. For the first time, I was seeing the world through a lens. A lens of desire. Of meaning. I wasn't meant for that. I was meant *to be.* Not *to want.*

The world beneath the cloud cover was brooding. A storm was raging. I floated through the falling rain, howling wind, atop the thunderous, cruel waves. I wanted light. It was all I could think of. *Light, light, light.* The more I fixated on it, the worse the desire became. The worse *I* became.

All night, I drifted across the raging sea. Perhaps, if the world was a kinder place, a flash of lightning would have struck, satiating my desire. I might've been fulfilled, and—with the release of desire—sunk back into my original form as pure conscious energy.

But the lightning never came. I could not be satisfied. I floated through the world and *wanted.* Badly. The want grew inside me, made me *something.* I could've become anything. I could've blended with the rain and become water. I could've slipped into the sea to be a creature of the deep. Wind. I could've been wind, had I let go of desire and just *been.*

But I didn't know. All I knew, all I had to hold onto, was the wanting. I clung to it. I fed it. I made it me. By the time the light returned at dawn it was already too late. I had turned into a thing of desire. A rogue soul. I had become *me.* I watched the sunrise on the horizon. The storm had died away. It was beautiful. But I didn't feel full at all. I just wanted *more.*

~ ~ ~

And so began my first life. The Watcher. I watched the seasons change, out of order. The tides beat against the shore. Animals in infinite variation, devour each other. Breed. Travel. Fight. Run. Kill. Forests burn. Islands crumble. Snowstorms that buried the earth. Waves of water that drowned villages. Screaming babies. Laughing men. Public hangings. Women with their dresses lifted. Children facedown in mud. Broken donkey legs. Crude amputations. Rooms painted in gold. Temples. Huts. Mosques. Cathedrals. Tipis. Factories. Then back to jungles. Back to raucous, steaming rainforests. Desert storms. Wind-whipped tundra. Grasslands. Horned beasts. Flying things. Teeth. Torture. Summertime.

None of it made any sense. The world was happening non-linear, jumbled. I could hear sounds that meant nothing to me.

I spoke no language beyond surrender. I could only watch it all happening, never be a part of it. My confusion grew stronger. As did my desire. To know. To have.

Many of the sights excited me in ways I couldn't understand. I felt it like heat inside me. The spray of red from a tanned throat. Fuchsia flowers, opening. Bruise-purple clouds. The sound of sex. Metal, clashing. Whining animals. Procession bells. War drums. All the ways a person could cry.

This excitement started as one feeling. But the more I watched, it began to split down the middle. Two feelings were born. A fluttery, eager excitement, like when I would watch a ceremony of great joy. Such as sunsets. Such as weddings. Such as families, reaping their harvest for the season. Hordes of gazelles, leaping. Music. Fireworks. Geishas.

And then the other. A pulsing, clenching excitement. My first taste of anger. Watching a goat be kicked to death. Babies dashed to the ground. Roads of men, nailed to wood. The orange flash of a bomb, limbs flying. Women screaming. Begging. Houses burning. Cruelty. Gore. Sickness.

I grew more and more frustrated. Confused. I could not make sense of it. The world. It was filled with so much. Too much. The extremes were too acute. All I had to gauge it with was my three-pronged system of navigation. Curiosity. Good excitement. Bad excitement.

The oldest emotion won. *Curiosity.* I became enamoured with the beings of man. They were the most complex. One moment hundreds of them would be gathered in celebration, tossing handfuls of colour at each other. The next they were cutting each other's stomachs open. Tenderness followed by sadism. Laughter followed by laments. They made no sense.

I watched the humans closely. I felt my fluttery, clenched excitements. I learned nothing. I was, still, just a rogue soul. I'd been nothing and still very much was. I had nothing to relate to. Nothing to connect with. Unreachable. Untethered. Unseen.

Until one day. I have no way of knowing how long I had spent wandering. A few dozen years? 300? 10,000? Time was so infuriatingly fluid, moving forward and backwards and forward again. Past and present and future unfolding at once. It made everything seem so nonsensical. As if the world was nothing but a glorious nightmare. As if it were all fake. A cosmic joke.

Until one day. I found myself in a space with white light. There were beings, hustling on hind legs. Blue-skinned. Doctors, I would learn. All the names for things, I would learn. But for now, then, they were nameless. Only the three-prongs to guide me.

A woman was on the table. She was red-faced and wailing. The blue-skinned beings on all sides of her were shouting too. One was positioned between her legs. Juices. All three of my prongs lit up. *Curiosity. Excitement. Anger.*

Something was happening. I couldn't resist getting a better look, before being whisked off to some new, foreign scene. I drifted down through the light, close enough to the woman on the table, shrieking. Close to the bulge that was her middle.

All of a sudden, a trace of faint smoke fled the bulge. It was minuscule, much smaller than me. I watched it rise and vanish, without affair. *Poof.* I looked back at the bulge. And then I did a very stupid thing. I got close enough to touch it.

There was an intense collapsing sensation. The world went from light to dark. All of a sudden I could see nothing. Absolutely nothing. But I could *feel.* Pressure on all sides. Suffocation. I could hear hollering, commands. Voices beyond. But I could not see. I was in liquid. Hot. Everything was so hot.

My world was heaving, rising and falling. And then, it was slowing. Quieting. Thumping fading. Voices dimming. The pressure remained. *Breathe.* Without even knowing what that was, I knew I needed to. I needed to breathe right now.

Right above my head was a poking sensation. Which soon turned into a fissure of light. White light. Blue hands. A fantastic, heavy release. Beeping. Something tight, ropey pulled off my throat. *Finally.* Air. The blue-skinned doctors held me up, slick from birth. I opened my infant mouth. And began to scream.

~ ~ ~

Now, picture this. You come into a body that fits like a glove a hundred sizes too small. You feel constricted, smothered by your own skin. You try to move and fail to do so; at least with any of the lingering elegance of your past form. All the genial smoothness, the languid ease that came from being blown there to here, is gone.

Now you are operating a piece of machinery with all the grace of a bulldog. Your brain is filled with a million images and sounds without the context to understand them. Tight skin, too small. This body is too small. There is too much of you, *me,* to fit inside it.

So what do you do? You scream. I screamed and screamed. It was the only thing that I could do. The doctors cleaned me up, whisked me away from my sleeping mother. Stitched her belly back up again.

For the next few days, all I could do was keep screaming. It freaked everyone out. My mother shushed and swayed me, frowning. She spoke gibberish to a man, eyeing me with automatic distrust. More people came and went. Jabbed me with metal. Patted me. Wiped me. Swaddled me. Frowned and whispered. Shook their heads.

Eventually, I reached a point where the agony was too much. There was too much spirit inside me, now conjugated with a physical form. Too much knowledge. And the *tightness.* I was suffocating in that tiny body. Nothing could bring relief.

My overworked soul, so overwhelmed by stimuli, cracked. It disintegrated and sank to the depths of my budding infant mind. I went from screaming my head off until my throat gave out, to being completely silent. My body failed. I began to sleep.

For my parents this was a gift from god. Their baby girl, Dahlia, had finally stopped her tirade of screaming. Look at her, asleep in her crib. There was hope for her after all. It was just a phase. I was alright.

~ ~ ~

As I grew, the immensity of the past shrank. My brain had no choice. I was living inside a body that was severely underdeveloped. I couldn't even stand up. Let alone remember all of history. Not to mention, my soul had fused with a body. Which meant that it was now more a body than soul.

Here is something you need to understand. All soul energy comes from the river of the conscious collective. *All things* have this energy. In varying degrees, but still. There. A drop of rain is no different from an ocean. A person is infused with the same gift as grass. The question is: how much of that gift is given? How much to make something, *something?*

Regardless, when soul energy comes into physical form, it forgets what it was before. This is crucial. What would happen if everyone remembered being their original form? If they realized they were nothing but infinite energy, that they were as old as time itself? What if every slug, shark, and songbird remembered the same? Or even the stars?

Worse still, what happens to a soul if they have seen the world before living within it? All the glory and ghastliness. The visceral horror and awe of all that has been and is. How can anything possibly ever survive such weight, such baggage, without going insane?

This is what happened to me. That or death. Forget or die. Or at least, shove it far, far away, to the back of the mind. Seal it. Lock it. Bury it in concrete. Melt away the key.

Baby me, baby Dahlia. Sleeping in her crib. Shedding layers of self in order to survive. But no matter how much my brain tried to keep it hidden, tried to throw it all away, most remained. The scar stayed.

~ ~ ~

My father was the first to recognize something off about me.

"Her eyes, Sharon," he'd whisper, sitting at the dinner table. "There's something weird about her eyes."

I began to learn the ways of humans very fast. Frighteningly fast. By 3 years old, I could articulate better than some 7-year-olds. I potty-trained myself as soon as my legs were able to walk. My mother was ecstatic at this remarkable learning curve. Gone were the days of the nightmare baby. Her daughter was a *genius.*

"She can already string sentences together! And she never cries, never fusses. God, if I knew having a baby was going to be this easy, I would have started having them years ago!"

I'd watch her from my highchair, talking on the phone to her friends, a cosmo in her hand. If she caught me staring, she'd twinkle her manicured fingers my way. Smile.

"Oh, and Doreen. She's such a little *watcher.* Always checking things out. You can just see the cogs turning in that head of hers."

She called across the room to me, phone clutched to her chest.

"What are you thinking about, Dahlia? You thinking you love Mommy?"

I'd bob my head up and down in agreement. Yes.

"Ah! Doreen! She just *nodded!* Is that normal for her age? I mean, she just does things I can't even begin to understand..."

As I grew older, the past grew fainter. It was still there, like a choir just over the horizon. If I was left alone, unstimulated, I could hear the sound. Of the past. The world beyond. Where I came from. But it seemed so far away now. I had bigger things to worry about. Like eating Cheerios. And learning English.

Unlike my mom, my father was endlessly disturbed by my rapid development. In fact, my very presence alone seemed to rattle him.

"Does she have to sit with us for movie night?" he'd complain, staring at me from the end of the couch. I'd stare back from Mom's lap, unperturbed.

"Of course she does, honey," Mom would say. "She's being perfectly quiet. I don't see how that would change anything about movie night."

"But isn't she a little young for *Apocalypse Now*?"

"Oh, hush. She's only 2. It shouldn't make a difference."

We'd watched the movie, along with countless others over the years, that were often wildly inappropriate for a child. I'd watch the screen, enraptured. The three-prong guide came back. *Curiosity, excitement, anger. Ping ping ping.*

The world began to come into focus. I was able to put a name to things. Finally. People got married because they were in love. Animals were slaughtered for meat. Cruelty had no purpose. Rape could happen at any moment. If you were a woman. Or unlucky.

"Jesus, Sharon, cover her eyes!" my dad had shouted, during the butter scene in *Last Tango in Paris.* My mom, already drunk by the title card, had rolled her eyes. Squeezed me closer.

"It's fine," she'd slurred. "They're just acting."

My mom refused to part with me. For years I was her shadow, brought everywhere she went. It drove my father nuts. He couldn't stand how everyone fawned over me. Obsessed over the girl too smart for her own good.

"It's not fucking normal for a girl to talk like that," he'd snapped one afternoon, after a garden party my mom had thrown. At age 5, I'd answered on her behalf.

"Don't swear at Mom like that, David," I'd replied, standing up to my full height of three feet. My father's eyes had bugged out of his head like a galago.

"Don't call me David, you little demon! I am your *father!*"

"Dave, don't call your daughter a demon," Mom had said, horizontal on the TV couch, watching men's tennis. "Now both of you hush up. It's match point."

My father had raged and huffed and threatened. But in the end, he had gone out like most men do when they feel powerless. He'd started an affair. With his secretary. It was so fucking unoriginal. It was *so* Dad. I'd heard him whispering in his office one day, sexual stuff. I had already seen *Fatal Attraction* by then. I had also seen, in the recesses of my memory, multiple real affairs play out. I understood what they were now. Third ping. *Anger.*

"Mom, David's cheating on you," I'd told her, as she was suntanning on the balcony. She'd sat up with a start.

"Honey, I thought I told you not to use your dad's real name," she'd said, inviting me to sit at her feet. "Now why would you say a thing like that?"

I'd landed daintily on the lawn chair. Folded my 6-year-old fingers in my lap.

"Because, Mom," I'd said, "I heard him telling a woman on the phone that he couldn't wait to taste her pussy again."

Mom's mouth had dropped. There were many, many things in life that didn't faze her, such as movie violence and alcohol poisoning. But infidelity was where she drew the line. I told her what else I had heard. Made up a few more things. Then started to cry.

"I didn't want to make you sad, Mommy," I'd blubbered, sinking into her kaftan. She'd stroked my head and told me I'd done the right thing.

"It's okay, honey," she'd said. "Mommy's glad you told me."

David, the fucking coward, had denied everything. Called me a devious snitch who had seen too much scandalous TV.

"Why do you think she knows all that stuff anyways, Sharon? You've rotted her brain by letting her see that crap. Kids shouldn't be exposed to adult things."

"Dahlia is telling the *truth*," my mother had asserted, holding me in front of her like a human shield. "I believe her."

Nor had she needed to. Dad's secretary had come clean all on her own. Consumed with guilt for leading a married man astray, she'd called my mother in a fit of tears and vowed that she would never forgive herself. Mom had agreed and told her she was right. She shouldn't.

Dad'd crumpled out of existence like a bad bowel movement. Within a year, it was as if he had never existed. Gone out of the house, and eventually the country. The only thing to remind us of him were the exorbitant child support cheques that came each month. And that black obsidian globe, left to sit on my mother's dresser until my 13th birthday.

Those years were the happiest in hindsight, mostly because they were the simplest. I'd spend the days with Mom and her group. With Mango, my new dog and best friend. I kept learning about the world, while being sheltered from it. I started to enjoy being in a body. Being human. I thought that all I had to do to be happy was stay far away from all the bad stuff. Surely that couldn't be so hard. To stay out of trouble.

~ ~ ~

But that isn't how the world works. You cannot run from darkness forever. You can be a goddamn saint and the world will still find shit to sling at you. Coax you into the mud-pit. In my case, that came in the form of my uncle. Dahlia's uncle. Charlie.

He brought reality to my doorstep. Ugliness to light. All those horrible things I had seen before I was born or on TV. They didn't seem real, almost. I felt far enough away from them to pretend they hadn't really happened. Until it happened to me.

The anger I'd felt in that moment was like no other. It superseded all other forms of thought, of logic. Suddenly I became nothing but a seething vessel for rage. I could picture all the despicable things I had seen done to women, to girls. Things I hadn't had a name for before. But I did now. And I had more than just clenching anger to wield. I had a powerful, working body, capable of action. Of revenge.

So I'd hurt him. I hadn't felt bad. In fact, I wish I could've done worse. But what I *had* felt bad about was everything else. The way my mom had become frightened of me. Of how easily, I realized, it was to hurt something. It took almost nothing.

It also brought the wanting back. For 13 years, it had been appeased. Filled up with the constant buffet of stimuli and learning. But after the incident with Uncle Charlie, it reared its head within me. I wanted to feel better. I wanted the bad feelings to go away.

Because now, heaven help me, I was hitting puberty. Not only was I contending with all of history and an eternal mind. The aftermath from my uncle. My drunken, distant mother, afraid of me. But fucking hormones. Petty, mean girls who hissed things under their breath. Feelings of loneliness. Shame. Self-hatred. Periods. Horny teenage boys. The works.

And the more I grew into my body, the stronger I became. My magnetism exhausted me. There was no end to attention. Boys vying for dates. Men catcalling. Whistling. Old men grinning. Girls wanting to be my friend. Girls wishing I would drop dead. Teachers unsettled by my eerie knowledge of subjects. Except for math. I was always bad at that.

And then Mango. Then Mom. Then suddenly, I was in the thick of it, the awfulness of being alive. Of being a bad person. All I had *wanted* to do was give her a good death. Not somewhere with sterile overhead lights, that stank like the hospital room I'd been born in. Not for my Mango. She deserved grace.

But even with the best of intentions, I'd brought pain. I'd manufactured a tragedy. And I knew, in my heart of hearts, that that was why my mom had killed herself in the end. It was me. She couldn't live with the daughter I had become. I had killed her by my actions too.

~ ~ ~

So where does a girl go from there? Life, which had seemed relatively simple to wrangle a few years ago, now seemed impossible. Being a person was so *complicated.* I had so much to atone for now. I'd failed at the one thing I'd hoped to do, which was do it right. How was I just as terrible and bad as all the humans who had come before me?

Uncle. Dog. Mother. I moved on to friends next. I got into vicious, catty fights with girls and made their ears bleed. Obliterated men's hearts the moment I started dating. Because what else was there for me to do, except throw myself cunt-open into being an angry teenager? It was that or death, as the old ultimatum gonged again. Forget or die. Shove it deep, where it will fester. Unknowingly.

My body aged. I let myself be blown from person to person, place to place, not really caring where I ended up. No one meant very much to me. Everyone seemed replaceable.

During that time I learned—with a little practice—how to do some useful tricks. Such as expanding my energy beyond my physical body. It felt good to do that, like giving my soul breathing room. It was also an easy way for people to fixate on me if I wanted them to. To have power over them.

Like Jack.

He was the first one, however, to actually *see* anything. Most people just hooked their attention on me. Jack had been astonished, standing outside that doomed dorm party. His eyes had bulged as I'd moved closer.

"Holy shit, I can see your aura!" he'd exclaimed in shock.

I'd snapped back into my body immediately. Freaked. His friends had come over to say hi and apologize for him. I'd smiled and made myself as non-threatening as possible. Transformed my voice into sweet music. Another fun trick.

"Jesus, you're like…really pretty," the one girl, Li, had said when I'd given her back her gloves. I'd thanked her. Debated on flirting with her, but stopped. Turned.

The tall one. The one who had seen me. *Really* seen me. He was nervously grinning, a bashful giant. He'd said sorry for freaking out but:

"I could've sworn I saw something."

I'd laughed and told him maybe he had. *Maybe* he had second sight.

He'd gotten a weird look at that, as if I'd touched something deep.

"My mom used to say that about me," he'd replied earnestly.

His eyes had crinkled at the corners. As had mine.

We'd started chatting. At first, his two high friends had hung around, hoping to get in on the conversation. But once we had started talking, there seemed no stopping us. As if a dam had broken in both our throats. An immediacy of connection. Attraction. Bond.

He'd told me things that I'd have to wait months, even years to hear about again. Like his strained relationship with his dad. How he didn't want to be an electrical engineer. Or that his mother had died from a falling tree. We'd bonded over that, too, under the falling snow and streetlamp shine. Two dead mothers, two distant dads. Whoopee.

His friends were long gone by then. We'd galloped and traversed subjects, in-frenzied. Onto politics. The state of the city. Humankind. Mortality. Where do *you* think we go when we die?

It was the kind of conversation that you have, if you're lucky, only a few times in this life. Where you connect with a stranger on such a spectrum of thought, where both of you are so startled to encounter a mirror mind in the wild, that all either of you can do is talk *more.* What do you think about this, or this? Me too! Oh, I've never thought of it like that before. How interesting. Yes, so true. So true.

I'd left the party—despite its abrupt, chaotic ending—elated. I had finally met a good guy. Someone special. It seemed so silly in context, but it was true. I had never felt that feeling before, of being truly *into* someone. I'd been painting by numbers for a while by then, doing what I thought I should be doing. Blending in. But I had to give myself some credit, too. I'd become far more Dahlia than *me.* So maybe I was just acting like myself.

It was so hard to say where she ended and I began. The more time I spent in her body, the more I became like one. The wanting was worse than ever. Wanting attention. Wanting sex. Wanting love. And as things worsened, it amalgamated into an incessant wanting to feel better.

Whatever it took, whatever I deemed best in the moment, I'd do. Anything to get rid of the feeling of powerlessness, of loss. Of injustice. Of solitude. I cut and slashed and stabbed my way through the world, becoming more and more like the things I had always despised.

~ ~ ~

And now, there is no separation. The third life. Post-mortem. Watcher and Dahlia fused as one. I can remember both lives clearly now. I can feel the joy and pain of both. And now I have new pain, new longing. I see my husband lying in the snow and I want to make it all right for him. I want to be with him, still.

I try talking to him. My voice is feminine, Dahlia's. Not my original elastic timbre that replicated tremors and sirocco winds. Not my ancient tongue without language, that was all spiralling, mutable sound. Think tidal waves breaking. Think crackling storm heads. Think snakeskin smoothed against desert sand. Think hummingbird wingbeats. Think empty infinite space, stretching.

No. Now I just sound like myself. Like her. I float around him, watery-wispy, looking like I had long before burning alive. Before shaving my head. Before wasting away to a bone-skin girl in the woods. Before losing all hope in redemption. Before seeing death as the last solution.

I had wanted to go together. The two of us. Enough suffering on Earth. We deserved to be free. All I had wanted was to end his misery. And once again, good intentions had come to bite me in the ass. So now I was stuck because of unfinished business.

~ ~ ~

Jack. I watched him watch the house burn. Followed him, a limping wreck, back to the car. Watched him sleep. This was fascinating to see, because his spirit had detached mildly from his body. Hovered just beyond the perimeters of his skin. I got close enough to touch it, and when I had, I could see what he was dreaming about. Ugly things. Sad things. This gave me an idea.

I thought of my first life. Of the things I'd seen. The worst of it. I touched Jack's spirit as I did, willing him to see them too. Almost immediately, he had woken up with a start. I had smiled in the dark. Perhaps there was a way I could get him to die after all.

For weeks afterwards, I pummelled him with dreams. I made him see all the shit I had been forced to watch. Made him hear the screams of people crushed under horse hooves, of chained prisoners. Barbarity in a thousand shades. Blood in the same hue. Together, we relived the world. Baby porpoises torn to pieces. Mass graves. Dirty cops. Gunfire.

I let him see. I beat his spirit into submission. I whipped him with memory. It felt good to share the burden. And on some level, I knew that I was still angry at him. For giving me Iris. For bringing out the worst in me.

I was sure that was what I wanted. I wanted Jack to die, too. I wanted him to kill himself and set us both free. I wanted this whole bloody saga to end. But when I saw him tie up the noose, hanging for morning, something shifted inside me. I realized I was still doing what I had always done in life. Equating violence for answers.

Never, even in my purest acts of aggression, had I gotten what I wanted. Each time I'd paid the price. Not with killing Hale, or the night in the alley. With Uncle Charlie. Not with any of the violent things I'd done. Each time, I'd wanted relief. To feel better. To turn the tables of justice myself.

And each time I had suffered. I had blown up the world in attempts to save it.

Was this not any different? Was pushing my crippled husband to suicide not any worse? I let him fall into medicated sleep once more, waited for the tell-tale sign of his dreaming soul. Then I assumed my position above him. Touched his spirit. Then inflicted all the best things I could conceive of.

I was lucky that Jack was still a simple man. He'd risen in the morning, stood up out of bed, and then started to laugh. I was so confused. What was so funny about life's beauty? I didn't understand his reaction to what I had given him. Regardless, the result was what I had hoped for. He took the noose down. Went on with his day.

If I wanted to not repeat the past, I'd have to leave him alone. No more tampering with his dreams. No more fantasizing about him living or dying. I'd have to wait for his natural conclusion. It seemed fair. I would have to atone through time.

So I waited. I watched. In wonder, I saw him rebuild a life. Almost miraculously. It was slow at first. Small acts of healing. Spurts of anger towards me. I didn't blame him for them. I had, after all, tried to kill him twice. Put him through hell and back. Whether on purpose or not, it didn't matter. The effect was the same.

I began to think about my life, our life, more objectively. I thought of all the ways I, we, could've taken a different turn. Where would we be now, I wondered? Still in love, living in a beautiful house, with lots of friends and healthy bodies? It hurt to think about. I felt more to blame than ever.

Jack began gardening the land behind his new old house. I'd follow close behind him as he'd shake sunflower seeds into the dirt. Hobbling along with his cane, pausing only to stop and look at the sky. Stretch his back. I'd float right in his line of sight, unseen. Hope that he might see more than clouds and blue sky for once. Hope that he'd see me. That I wouldn't be alone anymore.

Never. My husband's gaze bored through me. And he'd carry on shaking seeds into the earth. I'd carry on too, floating behind him. I never knew a heart could break after death. Yet I could feel mine being torn, somewhere inside me where I used to have a chest.

~ ~ ~

Years passed. Jack lived his life alone, with me. Went to the neighbour's place for dinner or didn't eat at all. He became so thin, like a walking skeleton. The sunflowers grew tall in the field, turned their faces with the changing light. Summer blossomed and faded. Came again. And again.

In the second year, he began teaching at a school in the city. Only part-time, since he couldn't focus for long. I'd watch him in the classroom, reading to a room full of children.

"And so," my husband would say ominously, "the prince would climb up Rapunzel's golden hair to the top of the tower. But one day, when he got to the top, it wasn't Rapunzel waiting for him there. It was the *evil witch.*"

The first-graders would listen, enchanted. As would I. Jack was an excellent storyteller. He would've made an amazing father. I saw how patient and gentle he was with kids. How he would take time and really listen.

I couldn't recall seeing him so docile. So mellow. All his secrecy of self and resistance seemed to have dissipated. Again, I would mourn all those years where he had clung to his traumas. Where I had done the same. The two of us, unwilling to release, lugging the past around in bindles over our shoulders. What a waste of time.

Seeing him happy was hard. Seeing him crying and alone was hard too. Seeing him at all was hard, because the years had softened me too. All the layers of frustration and spite, of disappointment. It all fell away. I loved Jack, in all his brokenness. I loved him so much.

When it got to be too heavy, watching his life just out of sight, I would leave. I'd wander off into the world. Drift into empty air, up into the moonlit sky. Through the streets of the city, watching bodies shiver atop cardboard. Deep into the forest, where the only thing you could hear was serenity. Out to sea. My first, oldest memory. Of something like home.

I began to feel very sorry for myself. I missed having a body. I missed the sensation of water on my skin. I missed being able to eat, feel the sun's heat. I missed sleeping with Jack and the way he smelled. I missed my friends. I missed having friends. I missed being alive.

Once, sometime during the third winter, I tried to find Yvonne. I'd thought about trying before, but I'd been scared of what I might find. I floated into her apartment from the tenth-story window, only to find it empty. Empty of her, at least. Old pizza boxes and sneakers on the floor. Men's deodorant. Unmade bed. She was gone.

I tried searching for her, feeling an itch rise within me that I could not scratch. But no matter how long I looked, I couldn't find any trace of her. Genevieve had moved away too. As for Anita and Joanna, they looked hardly different since I'd last seen them. More mature, with crow's feet dawning from drinking. I watched their lives, waiting for Yvonne to show up and satiate that itch inside me. She never did.

Dejected, I'd returned to Jack. The world had nothing to offer me anymore. I had seen it many times over, for better or worse. He was my last thing I had to hold on to. And all I had to do, I hoped, was wait for him to die. Then I could dissolve. Into nothingness. Into my original form.

I hoped.

I waited.

I watched.

And watched.

And watched.

~ ~ ~

Autumn. 4th year. The lucky strike with a paring knife. Jack was cutting sunflower stems in the kitchen, talking on the phone. I kept my distance by the far ceiling, still hating the radiation waves of electronics all the same in death. Always a discomfort to be near them.

Jack was talking quite animatedly to Gabriel, still living in Paraguay. He was saying how he had an idea to start a charity. The blade sliced through flower flesh.

"...Could be something, right? I feel like I could make a big impact if I did it right. Seems like such a waste to be sitting on all this cash and not doing anyth—"

The knife slipped and cut through the meat of his palm. Jack swore, dropped the phone from his shoulder. Blood flowed onto the counter. I drew closer.

"Hold on, let me call you back. Yeah, I'm fine, I just cut myself. No, it's fine. I'll call you back."

Jack clicked off the phone, set it on the counter. Walked over to the sink and began to run water over his wound. Where he had been cutting stems, a small pool of fresh blood glistened. Something instinctually tugged me towards it.

Touch it.

I sunk down from the ceiling and extended a single finger to the blood. Upon contact, a prickling feeling occurred, as if I had touched a live wire. I kept my finger steady.

Jack turned from the sink and flushed white. All the colour dropped out of his cheeks like an elevator. He took a step back and almost fell. Grabbed the counter for balance.

"How...how..."

He could not get the words out. All he could do was gape, propped against the counter. I looked down at myself. And smiled.

My form had taken on a lovely pale tone. Not that the colour mattered. All I needed was to be seen. I had the look of water, spun from cotton. In the shape of a woman, of course. I still looked like Dahlia.

I tried to talk. I told him to relax, that everything was okay. But Jack only stumbled back further. He couldn't seem to hear me.

"Are you real? How are you here?"

I drifted nearer to him. He looked close enough to shit himself in terror. I tried to speak more, but nothing registered. His face remained frozen in fear.

So I made a move that was unmistakable. I cupped my eyes with my hands, bowed my head. I made it look like I was crying.

Jack stopped his empty questions. A hush fell over the kitchen, just a man and a ghost. Of course, I couldn't actually cry. But my sadness was not fake. My pain was steel-real.

I wiped what would have been my face. Looked up at him. Mouthed the words:

I'm sorry.

He didn't say anything back. But he began to spill tears for the two of us.

"I don't understand," he said finally. "Why are you here, Dahlia?"

I made a movement of struggling. Bound my wrists together. Tried and failed to pull them apart.

"You're…a prisoner?"

Head shake.

I beat against an invisible wall.

"Trapped? Stuck?"

Nod.

Jack, now with his back to the kitchen wall, slumped down to the floor. Pulled at his hair.

"Oh god, oh god, this can't be happening…"

I floated over to him, came down to his level. Tried to touch him, show him that I was nothing to be frightened of. But his eyes widened all the same.

"You're fading! Dahlia, don't go! Please!"

He was right. My hands, my swirling hair, they were dimming. Becoming less tangible. I made a motion across my hand. A cutting motion.

Jack just stared, cheeks wet.

"I don't…I don't understand what you're trying to say…"

I flew up from where he was on the floor. Pointed insistently to the paring knife. Made a move again, across my hand.

The small puddle I had touched had dried black on the counter. Used up. It was clear what Jack needed to do to see me.

Blood. Fresh blood.

He looked up at me with confusion. Then realized. Looked at his hand, still marred by lightning-ringed scars on his fourth and fifth fingers. The fourth still bearing a golden ring. And now: a coagulating gouge, from a paring knife.

With a grunt of discomfort, he pulled himself to standing. Hobbled to the other end of the counter, where the knife laid. Gave me another look, as I floated just above, watching.

Jack picked up the knife. Pressed it to the centre of his palm.

And cut.

~ ~ ~

I couldn't be completely honest with him, as much as I wanted to be. I didn't want to scare him further. Our conversations were mostly limited to one-way Yes/No questions. A steady supply of fresh blood. Patience.

Jack wanted to know how long I had been here, out of sight. The whole time?

No.

Only recently?

Yes.

Okay.

I could see the relief in his eyes. Who wouldn't? Nobody would want to be watched at all hours, especially when they thought they were alone. Humans were so gross in solitude. They did nasty things when nobody was looking. Jack, bless his heart, was no exception. So I let him think that I had only just come back. That I hadn't been watching him, at all hours of the day, for almost 4 years straight.

Was I in pain?

No.

Was I here because of him?

Yes.

What did he need to do to help me?

Shrug.

Die, I thought. You need to die.

"Hold on," Jack said, reaching for the knife. "I can't see you very well."

I put up my hands to stop him, to tell him to stop. I didn't want to see him hurt himself anymore.

Too late. Jack dragged the blade across his split palm. Winced.

"Fuck," he muttered, as he squeezed out some crimson drops onto a plate.

Reluctantly, I sank down and touched the blood. Soaked it up. Became as close to solid as I could be.

"I wish I could hear you," he said sadly. He drew the stained bandage over his cut hand. "I wish I could go back and change everything."

I nodded.

"Do you forgive me?" he asked, near-inaudible. "For the baby? What did you name her again? Iris?"

Yes.

"That must've been so horrible," he whispered. "Giving birth to something already dead."

His compassion startled me. As did his forgiveness. There was no hint of anger left in him, despite all the things I had done. All those years alone had mellowed his heart, made him soft.

I nodded again.

I forgive you.

"What was that?"

I repeated, over-accentuating my mouth shape.

I. Forgive. You.

"Do you really?" he asked again.

Yes.

"God," he said. "What did we ever do to deserve this?"

~ ~ ~

We talked every day afterwards. Or rather, Jack talked and I listened. He'd call out to the empty house, say he loved me. Go off to teach, for drinks with his work friends. Long drives to nowhere. I'd convinced him, through a series of charades, to stop cutting himself so often. Now he would do it only once a week. More often if he was feeling lonely.

"I just wanted to see your face," he mumbled one night, drunk off wine. He proceeded to sit on the couch and cry, telling me how hard it was to live without me.

"I keep having these dreams of when you were alive," he said, snot dripping from his nose. "They seem so real. And then I wake up, and I…I…"

He dissolved into more sobs after that. Poured himself some more wine. I made a note to pull back on sending him dreams for the next few days. Give him some breathing room.

I had tried to talk to his sleeping consciousness through dreams, but failed. All I could do was share things that had already happened. Memories. The past. I couldn't create any new thoughts, scenes to show him. I was limited to what had already been. What we had already seen.

Over the next months, I watched Jack live his life. Never more than a few feet away. He must have sensed that, too, because he stopped doing bachelor behaviour. Started acting a lot more civilized. He cleaned up after himself. Wore pants in the house and stopped watching porn. I felt proud.

He was still adamant about his charity idea. He wanted to start something that would fix the homeless crisis in the city.

"Just think about it, honey," he'd say to me while getting ready for bed. "I could start up something that would fix *everything.* All I have to do is find some more investors."

I couldn't respond. Nor would he have liked what I had to say.

He began to call around, looking for business partners. It was hard to watch. Jack had no idea what he was doing. He didn't even really have an idea. He had a desire, yes, a want to help. But no real plan of action. No skillset to navigate the monetary world.

"Listen," I heard him say on the phone, "I don't think you understand. I already have a large amount of…yes, no, I heard you. Right. But I don't want to just donate to an existing charity. I want to start something new. Something that will really fix the problem, not just a bandaid solution. How? Well, that's why I'm calling you, to see…"

He became obsessed. It was all he could talk about. The Sunflower Foundation. He was going to attract people to donate so much money, help so many people. Pretty soon there wouldn't be a single person sleeping on the streets.

"Just wait, honey," he said. "It's going to be big."

With no response but his own echo, a frown crossed his face.

"Dahlia? Where are you?"

I was right in front of his face. Growing more worried with each passing day.

He looked around, called some more. Then revelation dawned on him.

"Oh, right!" he laughed. He grabbed a knife off the coffee table. There were half a dozen scattered around the house, each beside a plate of dried black blood.

He undid the bandage on his hand. Cut along the centre of his palm, catching the blood on the plate. The wound never healed anymore. It remained a permanent scab, reopening.

"Dahlia! Are you here? I want to see you!"

He held the plate aloft, panning it through the air like a beacon. Beads of hail fell on the roof, celestial percussion.

The way a bad dog might come when they're called, I floated close enough to touch the plate of blood. Immediately, relief washed over Jack's face as I materialized.

"Ah," he said. "There you are."

~ ~ ~

One wet May morning, Jack crashed his car. My car, technically. It happened so quickly. One moment he was driving down the road from his house. Then the next, the vehicle had turned and driven right off the embankment. Slammed into the barbed wire fence and went still.

A car horn filled the rainy air. I floated down from where I'd been trailing behind him. I came up to the windshield in panic. Thick globs of water fell through me. Jack had his head leaned against the steering wheel. He wasn't moving.

I passed in and out of the car, pacing. I called his name, even though I was the only one who could hear it. Nothing was happening. The blaring horn carried on. Headlights lit up a field of grass.

Then, groggily, he sat up. The car horn stopped. No blood flowed from his head, but he looked stunned. Lost. He rubbed his face, took in his surroundings.

"Dahlia?" he called. There was nothing sharp in the car, so he got out. Almost fell to the wet earth. With his hand on the hood of the car, he eased himself to the barbed fence and grabbed hold. Squeezed. Then opened his palm to the heavens.

I lapped up the blood before the rain could wash it away. There wasn't much. But it was enough for me to be seen. For him to feel comforted.

I tried to point for him to get back in the car.

Hospital, I mouthed. *Doctor.*

"I can't hear you, honey," he said drowsily. He was wobbling on his feet. I pointed again to the car. He turned, head slick with rain. His eyes glowed in the glare of the headlights.

Like a lumbering giant, he hobbled over to the driver's seat. Climbed in. Shut the door. Then began to back out of the embankment, tires squealing in the mud.

I floated into the car once he was back on the road. When he saw me, he grinned.

"Hey, I'm fine," he slurred. "Don't look worry."

I shook my head savagely. Pointed. Mouthed:

Doctor. Doctor. Doctor.

Jack opened his mouth to argue. Furrowed his brow. The car ticked with anticipation.

"I don't think I need to," he said.

I kept shaking my head.

Doctor. Hospital. Help.

I was fading fast. He had to listen to me now. Before something worse happened.

Jack let out a sigh. Looked out at the illuminated road.

"Fine," he said. "I go."

He called the school to tell them he'd been in an accident. That he wouldn't be able to teach today. As he spoke on speakerphone, he drove towards the nearest hospital, weaving left and right on the road as he did.

~ ~ ~

The emergency room doctor confirmed what I'd suspected. He took one look at Jack's file and ushered him into the MRI room. Reluctantly, Jack laid down on the table. Allowed himself to be suctioned into the vortex of grinding, intrusive noise. I watched from above, helpless, as Jack's brain was reduced to splotches of colour on a screen.

After a few more tests, the doctor broke the news. Early on-set dementia. Not absolute, but highly likely. It was practically inevitable. After one brain injury, a person was living on borrowed time. After two, the loan sharks were already swimming your way.

"It's been about 6 years since your fall, yes?" the doctor asked, despite knowing.

Jack scrunched up his face to think. His tall, thin body looked grotesque in the gown.

"I think so," he replied. "Something like that."

"That's what it says on your file, Mr. Donner." The doctor let out a sigh. "Some people don't even see more than a year after such an injury. So you're one of the lucky ones. Just remember that."

Jack didn't say anything in return.

It was painfully clear this had been coming. I'd seen the signs for weeks. Months. The way Jack would forget what he was doing, mid-task. How students would snicker at their substitute teacher, struggling over his words. His obsessive delusions about creating the charity. Of forgetting that I was even dead sometimes.

I could not comfort him as I watched the doctors hand him brochures for care-aids. I could not hold his hand as he shuffled down the hospital hall with his cane. I could not tell him that it was going to be okay. Not as he cried in the car. I could only watch.

He seemed to have forgotten I was still right there, just beyond sight. Watching all of it unfold. Unable to speak. To explain. To help. It wasn't until he was already home, climbing up the front steps, that he suddenly lifted his head in remembrance.

"Dahlia?" he asked the air. "Are you still there?"

If I could've replied, I would've said that she had *never* really been there. There was no Dahlia. There was always just me inside her. Being her. But maybe that was the wrong way around.

I was so confused. I didn't know where I ended and she began. I'd lost that sense a long time ago. All I could feel was love turned pain. Watching Jack. Wanting to help but not being able to. Wanting to be a person again. Be a body. Wanting to go back and change it. Everything.

But I couldn't. I can't. I can't say anything, as Jack looks around the porch for me, for his dead wife to appear. I watch him turn around in confusion, forgetting what he must do to see me. I watch him enter the house with his head hung low. I watch him peel off his wet jacket, ascend the stairs. I watch him climb into bed with his shoes still on. I watch him cry.

And I wait for him to fall asleep.

~ ~ ~

That night, I send him dreams for the last time. I'd been prepared to send an onslaught over several nights, but in the end, it only takes one. I send two dreams, two memories: of us, and of a stranger. I marry the two images together. Intertwine them together to be a single message.

When Jack wakes in the morning, the fog in his eyes has receded. Clarity shines. If just for a day. Which is all that we need.

He sits statue-still in bed, emancipated ribs peeking out behind the sheets. Outside, it is still raining. Calling water. Singing for no one.

"Honey?" he asks. I am already there, floating at the foot of the bed. He leans over to the bedside table, grabs a plate and a knife. Lets flow with a wince. He ties the old bandage over and holds the plate aloft.

I drink it up. Fragments of him flow into me, as the blood turns black and I turn white. With a single, billowy movement, I sink down to his eye-line. He looks at me. Reaches out his hand and cups the air where my cheek would be.

"I think I'm ready," he rasps. Voice rough from sleep. "I'm ready to be with you, Dahlia."

I don't respond, nor can I. I let myself look sad. Because I am. I'm devastated. I nod and drift away. Lead him to the drawer-set on the far side of the room.

With a rickety step, Jack limps over to where I'm pointing.

"What is it? What are you trying to show me?"

He opens the top drawer and I point again, to the box near the top. I've seen him pull it out many a time before. To cradle it in his hands. To kiss.

Jack gives a weak smile. Lifts out the box and opens it. My wedding ring, his mother's, winks back at me. A solitary sparkle. Shard of rock-light.

Oregon.

"You know," Jack says, snapping the box shut and putting it back. "That's just what I was thinking.

I swish and turn in the air. I want him to see that I am happy about that. That we still are on the same page about things. That we think the same, even after death.

~ ~ ~

Jack makes the journey in one go. I watch nervously from above, trailing behind the car in fear that it will suddenly start zig-zagging. Veer into the wrong lane. Or that Jack will stop and forget why he's driving, why he's crossing the border with a near-expired passport and there is no luggage packed in the trunk. He doesn't.

The encroaching mental decline holds back. It waits on the fringes to see what happens next. Jack drives through the rain, through countryside and greening coastal forests. Spring leaves have debuted, have opened their mouths to receive the season and its gifts. I take in the beauty too: that which I have taken for granted all these many, many years.

As the car crosses state lines, the sky changes. It melts away from a ceiling of grey. Sun comes, in slivers. Churning teal-bone clouds stir up high like sea foam. Bursts of blue. Rain comes and goes, then comes again. The Lincoln races on.

He makes it all the way to the sea, to Cannon Beach. Then, much to my horror, the car quits on the road shoulder. To the right are crashing waves, beachside cottages. To the left, fields of farmland. Lazy mountains.

I descend from my position above the car. Come up to the driver's window. Cars drive past, blasting horns. Jack's barely pulled off the highway. He looks spooked.

He looks around the empty car, out the windows. Calls to me.

"Dahlia? Dahlia, are you there?"

For one, terrible moment, it is obvious that he has forgotten. He doesn't know where he is or how to reach me. I try something that I've never done before. I float towards him and cover his body with my spirit. Smother him. He is breathing in short, shallow breaths.

Then, he begins to calm. Slow. I hear whistling, as air passes in and out of his nostrils. I pull back from him, as he leans over to the glovebox. Grabs the boxcutter. He undoes his stained bandage, cracks open the car door, and spills blood on the rain-slick asphalt.

Immediately, I am there. I absorb what he has given, encourage him to share more. He does. His face doesn't even wince, as he digs the blade into his left palm, spilling red. I can feel myself growing stronger. Brighter.

"I don't know where to go," he says miserably. I gesture for him to start up again, then take my position at the hood of the car. The engine kicks into gear.

Like a ghostly figurehead, I lead the Lincoln further south down the highway. The road twists, rushes past electrical poles and tourists. It rises and dips, giving peek-a-boo views of the ocean. And then, with a confident turn of fate, it begins to climb.

The rain has cooled to a drizzle when we reach the turn-off that most would miss. Just as before, a wind-weary wooden sign swings, promising two words. Phaon Point. Jack kills the car, grabs his cane, and begins to stagger down the overgrown path.

I lead the way, past the brambles. Past salmonberry bushes, crowning pink flowers as their victors. Under a mixed canopy of trees, catching rain in their arms. The path curves downwards, draws narrower and narrower. Then opens.

~ ~ ~

Wind. I can't feel it. But the sound is ferocious, feral. Up so high, the air is whipped into hysteria, fresh off the ocean's scalp. The few trees that cling to the edge are shaking. Clouds change shape as fast as they can be named. Dolphin, castle, flapping linen sheets. Turned back to dolphin, a whole pod of them, leaping haphazardly through the sky. The ocean is crocodile-green, slate, tar-black. Blue stone. Crackling white, where the waves break. I hear them smashing into the cliffs below, detonating like falling angels. The sun is nowhere to be seen.

Jack struggles to keep his balance against the gale. I watch him: untouched by the wind, floating above him. I see a man in his mid 30s, nearing 60. His hair has thinned on top. His back is arched in a permanent, rising hump. The bones of his face jut. His clothes hang off his frame, as if he were only made of wire.

Trembling hand on cane, he eases towards the stone bench we had once laid upon. He sits down himself, catches his breath. Looks up at me.

I imagine what he must be thinking as he looks at me. Seeing what he thinks to be his wife, floating in a white gauze of energy. Dangling in empty space above him.

I know what he must be expecting. I have known since the first night I met him. When I asked what he thought happens when we die, and he answered:

"I think we go to heaven, no matter who you are."

No hesitation. He believes that life carries on after death, that we move into a new state of being, but just the same. That the person you were on Earth will be the same person you will always be. That you will always be just a person. A human. That another paradise awaits.

In all the years, I have never tried to convince him otherwise. How the world is a much older thing than such fairytales. That heaven and hell are found in life, not death.

That the universe operates by one simple rule: reuse. Rinse, repeat.

As he sits there, preparing to do what must be done, a new thought dawns in me. What if I've been wrong? What if Jack is not the reason I'm still stuck here, trapped? What if I am leading the last person who knows I exist to die, that when he dissolves into sinew and pure energy I will be left alone, forever? A wanderer until the end of time, if there even is one?

I cannot think of a worse fate. But it is too late to turn back. I must trust that love is all that I have left. That love is the last thing that binds me to this world. That when that dies, finally, *finally,* I can become part of the whole again. I can turn back into holy nothingness, become part of the wholeness I came from. I can forget everything I have seen and known. Release everything I have been. And become something new.

Jack rises to his feet. He limps towards the edge of the cliff, painted in moss. A spray of water, of rain, mists his face. His beautiful face. I am almost close enough to touch it. And I know, then, with every fibre of my being, that I am right. I love this man with all that I am. He is the last thing that binds me. He is what still makes me *me.*

With a heave, he throws his cane into the void. It falls like a spear as it descends into the waiting maw of water. Crashing, green-white waves. Howling wind. Jack looks up from the ocean, up to me. *Dahlia.*

I cannot hear him when he says I love you. Neither can he, when I say the same. And then he is a blur of body, falling. But right before he passes through me, into thin rushing air, I can see that he is smiling.

THE END

ACKNOWLEDGEMENTS

I would love to thank Michael Occhionero, my editor Julia Bifulco, and the entire team at AOS/Ace of Swords Publishing for believing in this story. You helped sharpen this book into a new weapon, and I wield it with pride thanks to you.

Thank you to my beloved family. While the process of writing *DAHLIA* was extremely solitary, the long-distance support of my mom, dad, and little sister/twin Malia, kept me going. Thank you for everything you have taught me. For the good and the ugly. We made it through in the end.

I would also love to thank Dr. Andrea Actis for being a beacon of light on my creative journey; Anne Tibbets and Lindsay Rose Nelson, for your legal advice (unsolicited and solicited); Meggie McDonough, for sharing that Tom Jones song at that party and sparking this novel into existence for me; my nana and Al Jamison, for both of your encouragement; Tyra V. Jones-Drysdale, for your many years of friendship and sticking through the dark times and into the better ones; Nataly Ramos, for your unwavering support and marketing assistance; Alexandra Zagas, for all the adventures and laughs; Ava Maria Safai, for your help with the cover design (and Miguel Carbonell Selva for painting it!); Luis Carbajal, for the kick-ass author photo; and Maddison Leroux-Pipe, for the incredible illustrated chapter markers.

Thank you to Mary Oliver, Gabriel García Márquez, Stephen King, Sappho, Allen Ginsberg, and Barbara Lewis/Van McCoy for allowing the inclusion of your words/lyrics/art; as well as each and every one of my other brilliant friends, teachers, colleagues, mentors, and role models, who have helped me on my path and provided joy/inspiration/wisdom along the way.

You are all loved immeasurably.

Thank you to the Divine, to this universe and all that it contains, for helping birth this story into being. Thank you to my dogs: Stanzie, Wolfie, Kiesa, Maestro, Oliver, Solomon, Symphony. And thank you to my older sister, Taryn. We never did meet, but I feel you with me. Don't you worry. I see the flickering.

AUTHOR'S NOTE

While *DAHLIA* is a work of fiction, three characters contained within it—Hale Donaldson, Uncle Charlie, Jack's great-grandfather—are all mirrored by real people. People who have personally left a stain on my own life, the lives of my closest loved ones, and/or of innocent strangers, through their cruelty, entitlement, and horrific actions. In some ways, *DAHLIA* offers a portal of catharsis that punishes those individuals—and others like them—in a world where they are often not.

If you, or someone you know is a victim of sexual violence, please know this: you are not to blame. You are not alone. Reclaim your title of innocence. And remember that stains can be washed clean. Always.

Let's keep imagining and building a world where such acts of evil do not exist.

I love you.

COPYRIGHT PERMISSIONS

Cover art:

Cover Art: Miguel Carbonell Selva, *Safo,* 1881, oil on canvas, 250 x 170 cm, (P006965). Madrid, Museo Nacional del Prado. © Photographic Archive Museo Nacional del Prado.

Epigraphs:

"One or Two Things" by Mary Oliver

Reprinted by the permission of The Charlotte Sheedy Literary Agency as agent for the author. Copyright © 1986 by Mary Oliver with permission of Bill Reichblum.

Quote from One Hundred Years of Solitude by Gabriel Garcia Marquez. Translated by Gregory Rabassa. English translation copyright (c) 1970 by Harper & Row Publishers, Inc. Used by permission of HarperCollins Publishers.

Excerpt(s) from CARRIE by Stephen King, copyright © 1974 and renewed 2002 by Stephen King. Used by permission of Doubleday, an imprint of the Knopf Doubleday Publishing Group, a division of Penguin Random House LLC. All rights reserved.

In-text:

From 'Song'', from Collected Poems 1947-1980 by Allen Ginsberg. Copyright (c) 1984 by Allen Ginsberg. Used by permission of HarperCollins Publishers.
From "Baby, I'm Yours" by Van McCoy. Copyright © 1965 Van McCoy Music, Inc. Used by permission of Van McCoy Music, Inc. All rights reserved. Performed by Barbara Lewis.

www.ingramcontent.com/pod-product-compliance
Lightning Source LLC
LaVergne TN
LVHW022112260326
834946LV00023B/345